# THE
# WALL

A HEAVENLY REALMS NOVEL – BOOK 1

## Rick Stockwell

Fervent Publishing

This is a work of fiction. Names, characters, places, and events are
the products of the author's imagination or are used fictitiously.

Scripture quotations are taken from the Holy Bible, New
International Version®. NIV®. Copyright © 1973, 1978,
1984, 2011 by the International Bible Society.

*Soli Deo Gloria*

*I dedicate this book to my wife, Donna,*
*who brightens every day of my life.*

# CHAPTER 1
# WAR

*July 2008, 12:32 p.m.*
*Helmand province, southern Afghanistan*

MARINE FIRST LIEUTENANT Jackson Trotman lay prone on a precipice overlooking a valley. His second-in-command, Gunnery Sergeant Cooke, lay by his side. The twelve marines in their patrol were already dispersed around the mountainside behind them.

The scraggly brown rocks dug into his chest, arms, and legs like porcupine quills. Dust covered him from head to toe, and only his shemagh kept him from breathing in the superheated air and fine dust. There wasn't a speck of green or a drop of water anywhere. The slight breeze gave little reprieve from the temperature of one hundred and fifteen degrees. The sun beat down without mercy, cooking him and his unit like bacon in a frying pan.

He stared through his desert binoculars at the dirt trail far below. Their mission was to interdict and neutralize Taliban forces in the area, and they had received an intelligence report that an insurgent patrol was on the move nearby.

Gunnery Sergeant Cooke turned to him. "Got a question for you, sir. How'd a nice college boy like you end up a jarhead in a hellhole like this?"

"Just serving my country, Gunny, with the finest fighting force in the world."

Cooke shook his head and rolled his eyes. "Uh-huh."

Jackson chuckled. "Not buying it?"

"Nope."

Jackson tilted his head. "The abundance of alcohol in Afghanistan?"

"It's a dry country in more ways than one, Lieutenant. Was it a girl?"

An image of McKenzie Baker sunbathing at State Beach on Block Island popped into his mind. He'd dated many women, but for some reason, the memory of her resonated more than the others. *Ridiculous. We only went on one date, and she blew me off. Why am I even wasting my time thinking about her?*

"Yeah, it was a girl, Gunny. I got a Dear John letter from my female dog, and that threw me over the edge."

Cooke snickered and didn't press the matter any further.

Finally, Jackson turned to face him. "Nothing much happening here. Let's move to Checkpoint Bravo. Are we good to go?"

"Looks clear to me, LT."

Jackson pointed down the mountain to his left. "Let's move out. It's down by that small hill over there."

"Roger that." Cooke addressed the rest of the patrol. "Okay, marines. Mount up!"

The group began their descent and reached the trail below about fifteen minutes later. Jackson had already divided his men into their three fire teams, each comprised of four marines. He then got down on one knee, listened for a few moments, and reconnoitered the area with his binoculars. Without much cover where they stood, he had to make sure his unit got to the checkpoint as safely as possible.

No sound or movement to signify trouble. Jackson kept a wary eye on the surrounding terrain. When they reached Checkpoint Bravo, he relaxed a little. The small hill had plenty of boulders for cover. He sat down against a large rock, tipped back his helmet, and retrieved his canteen. Right as he took a swig, rocks exploded and splintered all around him, followed by the *pat-pat-pat* of machine-gun fire from nearby.

Jackson jumped up and swiveled around the boulder to the opposite side. "Incoming! Incoming! Take cover!"

The distinctive *blam-blam-blam* of a DShK .50 caliber machine gun came next. The rounds pulverized the boulder that was supposedly protecting him, and he peered around the lower edge of it, hoping his head wouldn't get blown off. "Gunny, direct your fire to the top of that hill! I'm calling for artillery support."

"Roger that."

Jackson shouted into his headset, "Johnson!" Jackson pointed. "Call for artillery and lay it on that hill over there." He ducked as low to the ground as he could, cringing as bullets whizzed over his head.

His earpiece crackled. "Will do, sir."

"Make it quick!" Rounds fired by his marines impacted the hill while enemy bullets continued zipping through the air overhead. A cacophony of gunfire and smoke filled the air.

A few minutes later, high-explosive ordnance from the 155-mm howitzers zoomed through the air directly above Jackson's head, howling like a freight train, then impacted close to the target, causing a massive plume of rock, dirt, and dust to erupt into the air. The enemy gunfire ceased for a moment.

Then another shell exploded directly on the target.

Jackson breathed a sigh of relief. "Direct hit. Johnson, fire for effect."

"Roger that."

Multiple rounds pummeled the enemy position in succession, sending dirt and shrapnel flying all over the target area. Jackson and his men cheered. After a momentary lull in the barrage, some enemy survivors scrambled out of their holes and ran.

Jackson adjusted his helmet, then shouted to his marines. "Fire Team One, open fire, over."

The leader of Fire Team One responded, "Roger that, sir. Fire Team One opening fire."

Withering small arms fire cut down several Taliban soldiers, while others ran directly into the artillery barrage. The remaining stragglers scattered in various directions. Fire Team One picked off several more, but a few escaped.

Jackson pumped his fist. "Yeah! Cease fire. Great shooting, Sergeant Johnson. Good work, Fire Team One. Squad, prepare for a counterattack!"

The Fire Team One leader nodded. "Roger that, prepare for a counterattack,"

"Gunny Cooke!"

"Yes, sir!"

"Check their fields of fire. I want to make sure we're ready in case they come back at us."

"Aye, aye, sir!"

Jackson sighed. "And get a casualty report."

"Roger that."

Jackson stood and provided an incident report to his company commander over the radio, then headed for Gunnery Sergeant Cooke. Time to get the latest status.

Cooke gave a thumb-up. "No casualties, sir."

Jackson thrust his arms in the air. "Liberty's calling, Gunny. Nineteen days and a wake-up!"

"Don't rub it in, sir."

"Amsterdam, here I come. Woo-hoo!"

A .50-caliber rifle shot rang out from the same hill that the artillery had just pulverized. Gunny Cooke collapsed to the ground as the round lopped off his right leg just below the knee. He screamed, following it with a slew of profanities.

Jackson cursed as well. "Corpsman! Corpsman! The Gunny's hit!"

"Ahhh! Ahhh!"

"Blast it, Fire Team One!" Jackson yelled. "Take out that shooter and await further orders."

The navy corpsman attached to the marine unit ran over and dragged the gunny behind a large rock, fashioned a tourniquet around his right thigh, and gave him a shot of morphine. "We're going to need an evac, sir! He'll go into shock soon!"

Jackson shouted into his headset for helicopter support, "Hotel-Six, this is Charlie-One-Six, over."

The reply came about five seconds later. "Charlie-One-Six, this is Hotel-Six, out."

"Request medical evac at Checkpoint Bravo. Site is hot, over."

"Roger that. Medical evac at Checkpoint Bravo, the site is hot, out."

"We'll pop red smoke, over."

"Roger that. Red smoke. ETA ten minutes, out."

"Make it quick. A marine is in shock. Lost a leg, out."

Jackson ran over to Fire Team One's position. "Sergeant Taggert, you're the new platoon sergeant. What's the status?"

"Sir, the sniper's up in the machine gun nest at the top of the hill."

"I thought everyone was dead up there." Jackson adjusted his headset and yelled into it, "Fire Team One, remain in a support position! Take out the shooter if he sticks his head up. Fire Team Two, tag-team your way up to that gully and provide covering fire for Fire Team Three. Fire Team Three, get up that hill on the left. Envelope your way over to the machine gun nest straight ahead, then take them out! Let us know when you're in position."

Each fire team methodically moved into their assigned positions. A few moments later, the *wamp-wamp-wamp* of a helicopter echoed off the mountain faces in the distance. The bird curved around a nearby mountain and surged into view. Jackson popped a red smoke canister behind Checkpoint Bravo in the center of the makeshift landing zone. The smoke lazily drifted away from them toward the sun hovering just above the horizon.

The helicopter eviscerated the red smoke as it set down, replacing the smoke with a whirlwind of dust. The roar of the engines was deafening. The side door of the chopper sprung open, and a crewman hopped out with a collapsed stretcher tucked under his arm.

He ran over to where Gunny Cooke lay, unfolded the stretcher, and worked with the corpsman to lift him onto it. Another marine grabbed the battered, detached remains of Gunny's right leg and threw it onto the stretcher next to his good leg. The image didn't seem real; it was too horrible to process. Then, all he could think about was making them pay. Cooke grimaced as the corpsman strapped him onto the gurney and inserted an IV.

Jackson ran back to his unit. The fire teams were all in position. "Cover me, Fire Team Two. I'm going up with Fire Team Three."

Bullets pelted the dirt around the Taliban's position. Smoke and the smell of burned gunpowder filled the air all around them. He ran across open ground up to Fire Team Three's location as several .50-caliber bullets punched holes in the dirt around his feet. Once situated, he yelled into his headset, "Fire Team Two, continue covering fire!" They saturated the target area with small arms fire. "Lassiter, stay here and keep firing grenades on the target. Fire Team Three, let's move out."

Fire Team Three leapfrogged up the hill from rock to rock toward the enemy emplacement, covering each other along the way. The distinctive *blam-blam-blam* of the enemy's .50 caliber machine gun ripped through the air. Rock shards splintered all around them with each hit.

Jackson finally got close enough to throw a hand grenade at the position. The grenade landed right in the enemy fighting hole and exploded. After a moment, he instructed, "Cease fire, everyone." He waited for the smoke and dust to clear. "I'm going in."

Jackson rushed toward the enemy foxhole and leaped directly in front of it on his stomach. He then edged his way to the lip of the hole and peered over it. Two enemy soldiers lay in contorted positions on their sides. One appeared to be dead, while the other was only wounded. The wounded man eyed Jackson, flipped over on his back, lifted his AK-47, and tried to point it at him.

Jackson unloaded two rounds from his 9mm Beretta pistol, one into the man's chest and another into his head. He then slipped another magazine into his weapon. "Here's one gift wrapped for both of you from Gunny Cooke!" He aimed just below their knees and pulled the trigger several times, dismembering one leg from each.

As the sun disappeared behind the mountain, Jackson and his team donned their night-vision gear. He walked cautiously beside Staff Sergeant Tom Clark, his new next in command, just as he had several months earlier with Gunnery Sergeant Cooke. A minute later, a distinctive *thump* sounded in the distance.

Jackson cursed, then shouted, "Incoming! Mortars! Take cover!" He dove to the ground. They had walked right into a Taliban kill zone.

Seconds later, a mortar round landed only twenty or thirty feet away. The explosion knocked him back several feet. Jackson hacked dirt and dust out of his mouth while his ears rang and his head spun. His right side felt wet, with moisture creeping through his MCCUUs onto his skin. He flipped off his goggles to find dark blood all over his uniform.

He patted his side and legs but didn't feel any pain. "Clark!" He looked around but couldn't see anything through all the dust in the air. "Staff Sergeant Clark." He coughed, trying to clear his mouth and throat. "Clark! Where are you?"

The dust began to clear. Off to his right sat a pair of boots, standing up as if someone had just left them there. They were Clark's boots. Smoke drifted upward out of them. "Get off this ledge!" he yelled to his men. "The Taliban have it zeroed in!"

Jackson called for helicopter support and gave his perceived location of where the mortar fire originated. Within minutes, a UH-1N Huey attack helicopter with night-vision and heat-signature capability was dispatched to the scene. It took out the Taliban's mortar position with prolonged .50-caliber bursts.

They got justice, but it wouldn't bring Clark back. Sorrow rushed through him, but he pushed it down and locked it away... like he always did.

The next day, Jackson was in his hooch, lying on his rack, listening to Black Sabbath. Then, someone knocked on his door. "Come!"

"Lieutenant Jackson Trotman?" The man who entered had two silver bars on his uniform collar—a superior officer.

Jackson stood up. "Yes, sir." He always tensed when a senior officer approached him.

"Navy Lieutenant Jerry Thompson." Thompson smiled and held out his hand, which Jackson shook. "I'm one of the chaplains from Division. I heard you had a rough day out there yesterday. Would you like to talk about it?"

Jackson noticed the Bible tucked under his arm and chuckled. "Trying to save my soul, sir?"

"Well... ultimately, I guess, but I'm just here to help, to see if you need anything."

Jackson studied him. Thompson was soft-spoken, black, about six-foot-two, two-twenty, with a kind face. "No, sir. I'm fine. Just a little on edge, I guess."

"No problem. May I call you Jackson?"

"Yes, sir." Thompson's easygoing demeanor helped him relax.

Thompson read aloud from the hand-carved wooden plaque hanging from the foot of Jackson's rack, "The brave do not live forever, but the cautious do not live at all." He paused for a moment. "I like that. What's it from?"

"*The Princess Diaries* movie."

Thompson smirked and pointed to a footlocker across the room. "May I sit down?"

"Sure, sir." Jackson crossed the room and surreptitiously stuffed the contraband *Playboy* and *Penthouse* magazines on top of it into the footlocker. Then, after sliding the footlocker over for the chaplain, he shuffled a few steps and plopped down on his rack.

Thompson's grin returned for a moment, but then he sobered. "So, what happened out there last night?"

"Well, sir, an enemy mortar landed right next to me and blew my next-in-command to bits."

"What was his name?"

"Clark, sir. Staff Sergeant Tom Clark." Tears welled in Jackson's eyes. "He was a good marine, sir."

"I'm sure he was."

"It all seems so incredibly random and stupid, sir. He had a wife and two little girls. Why him instead of me?"

"That's a good question," Thompson said once he'd sat down. "It just wasn't your time yet, that's all. God's in control."

"Ha! That's a joke. How can you say that with all the random killing that goes on around here?"

Thompson leaned forward. "It's not random. God has a plan for your life, and my life, and for everyone's life."

"I don't believe that, sir. I make my own choices. I'm the captain of my destiny, if you know what I mean, sir."

"Sounds like you're paraphrasing 'Invictus.'"

"'Invictus'?"

"It's a poem by William Ernest Henley. It says, 'I am the master of my fate: / I am the captain of my soul.'"

"Sounds familiar. I like it. There's a lot of truth in it."

Thompson cocked his head. "Oh, really? Did you decide the year you were born, where you would be born, who your parents would be, what gender you would be, how tall you'd be, and what your mental capacity, health, and personality would be like?"

Jackson's chin tensed. "No, sir."

"We're all able to make choices, that's for sure. But a lot of the big stuff has already been decided for us."

He paused for a moment. This guy was a little weird, but Jackson couldn't refute his logic. "I hadn't thought about it that way before. How do you know God has a plan for our lives?"

"It says so in the Bible."

Jackson laughed. "The Bible? That's just a bunch of myths and fairy tales, sir. No offense."

Thompson sat up straight on the footlocker. "None taken. You're free to believe what you want. Here's a Bible. Take a look at Psalm 138, verse eight, and Jeremiah chapter twenty-nine, verse eleven. Those passages talk about God's plan for our lives." The chaplain wrote the references inside the front cover and handed the Bible to him.

Jackson shook his head. "Well, I doubt I'll ever read it."

"Maybe you will someday," Thompson said.

"Okay, sir. Thank you." Time to go, Chaplain. Jackson stood, put on his best fake smile, and shook the navy lieutenant's hand.

"Well, let me know if you need anything, Jackson. My office is a couple of buildings past the chow hall."

"Will do, sir. Thanks for stopping by."

With the man gone, Jackson lay down on his rack and shuffled through a few pages of the Bible. *What am I supposed to do with this thing?* What a waste of time. He opened his footlocker and shoved it down as far as he could under some clothes. It might be a little more interesting if it had some pictures. He chuckled, then put his headphones back on, reached into his footlocker, and picked up the *Playboy* magazine.

❧

Dust blew high in the air in front of his Humvee as they journeyed down the road back to base. About fifteen minutes into the trip, while traveling on a desolate dirt road, the rear of the deuce-and-a-half truck directly in front of him buckled upward in a ball of fire. The Humvee driver slammed on the brakes, swerved sideways, and came to a complete stop. The windshield on Jackson's Humvee was blown out, leaving shards all over his uniform.

The driver screamed profanities, then gasped for air and turned to Jackson. "Thank God I had my goggles on. Are you okay, sir? Sir? It looks like you're bleeding."

Jackson prodded his shoulder. "I'm okay." He winced when the pain stabbed at him. Maybe signing up for a second tour wasn't such a great idea. "I think I caught some shrapnel in my right shoulder. We need to check on the guys in front of us. C'mon. Let's go see if they're still alive." He got out.

The M35 truck lay on its right side with a sizeable concave gouge on the lower left side of the chassis. Diesel fuel leaked onto the road.

"Set up a defensive perimeter on the left side of the road near the truck," he said.

"Aye, aye, sir." The driver carried out his order.

"I'm going to run over to the truck and see if anyone is still alive in there."

Jackson climbed on top of the truck and struggled to open the cab door. He finally managed to heft it up and climb in. The driver was unconscious and lay on the opposite cab door against the ground.

Jackson took off his web belt, looped it around the front of the truck driver's web belt, and then made his way back up to the top of the cab. With the belt in one hand and grasping the marine's shirt collar in the other, Jackson pulled him upward and out of the cab.

Both of the driver's feet were gone. He was bleeding profusely, but Jackson kept going. He managed to get the marine out of the cab and drag the man about twenty yards to the right of the mangled truck. He got up and decoupled the web belts and tightly wrapped one around each thigh as a tourniquet.

A few seconds later, the truck exploded and caught on fire.

Just as Jackson stood up, an explosion in his left shoulder knocked him to the ground. He spun around to find two Taliban fighters running toward his position from the right. Jackson retrieved his M9 pistol from his holster and dove into the prone position. His training kicked in—take an extra half second to make sure the post was correctly lined up in the sight before firing. Bullets whizzed over his head. He slowly pulled the trigger as the silhouette of the first enemy soldier appeared behind his sight. *Pop.* One bad guy went down. *Pop, pop.* The other one went down.

Jackson flipped over on his back and looked down at his chest. Red stains traveled down the front of his uniform at both shoulders. He was getting dizzy, and his vision was becoming blurry.

The truck driver lying next to him regained consciousness and started screaming. A Navy corpsman arrived an began working on him.

Jackson looked around. Was someone else coming toward them? Even if there was, he was too weak to do anything. "God, if you're real, get me out of this mess."

Two shots rang out and someone dropped at his feet. The Humvee driver arrived. "Don't worry, sir. I've got your back." He threw a first aid kit on the ground next to Jackson's head.

He opened the lid, pulled out some gauze packages, ripped them open, and stuffed the gauze under Jackson's shirt, right over both shoulder wounds. "Nice shooting, Lieutenant. You got two of them at fifty yards with a pistol."

"Yeah, but it took two rounds to bring the second guy down. It would have only taken one round with a forty-five." Jackson's vision went in and out of focus. "Keep on the lookout for others."

"Roger that, sir. You're going to be fine."

Blackness overtook him.

✍

A month later, Jackson was recovering from his wounds at the National Naval Medical Center in Bethesda, Maryland. He got bored in his room, so he wandered the hallways.

As he came around a corner, a familiar voice echoed into the hallway from one of the patient rooms. "Well, ma'am, I know you outrank me, but why the hell should I care? What's the worst you can do—throw me out of the corps? Ha, ha. I'm already on my way out."

"No, but I can accidentally put something in your food so you won't get off the toilet for a few days," a woman responded.

Jackson paused, then strolled into the room. "Gunny!" He walked over to Cooke's hospital bed and held out his hand.

Cooke shook it. "Why, it's First Lieutenant Jackson Trotman, the Audie Murphy of Afghanistan! How the hell are you, sir? What are you in here for?"

"Got beat up a little after you left, but I'll be fine. It's great to see you."

The nurse's eyes narrowed. "I'll deal with you later, Gunnery Sergeant Cooke." With that, she left the room.

Jackson glanced at where Gunny's lower right leg should have been. "I'm glad you made it out okay. Too bad about your leg."

Cooke looked down. "It is what it is—nothing I can do about

it. I can't believe I won't be a marine anymore, though. I loved every minute of it."

Jackson walked over, placed his hand on Cooke's shoulder, and looked him in the eye. "Well, you know what they say. 'Once a Marine, always a Marine.' But I know what you mean. Not sure what's going to happen to me yet. I can't move either arm the way I used to. Physical therapy can only do so much. I may not be a marine much longer either."

"I never got a chance to tell you. Thanks for getting me out on that chopper."

He stepped back. "You're welcome, Gunny. I was just doing my job. You would have done the same for me. And we got the guys that did that to you."

Cooke gave him a thumbs-up. "Good. I've finished my surgeries, so I should be getting fitted for a prosthetic leg soon."

"That's great. Some of these guys are never going to get out of here."

"I know. At least my injury was below the knee. Somebody's always got it worse."

Jackson held out his hand to Cooke. "Yep. Well, I'm heading out, Gunny. Great seeing you. I'll check back with you later."

Cooke shook his hand. "Sounds good, sir."

Jackson went back to his room to search for some pictures of the old platoon. It might cheer Gunny up to look at them. As he rummaged through his duffle bag, he stumbled upon the Bible the chaplain had given him. He shoved it back to the bottom as soon as he saw it.

Still bending over the bag, he let out a sigh. He had nothing else to do, so maybe he ought to take a peek at it.

Two hours later, he lay on his bed, still reading and soaking up every word.

# CHAPTER 2
# THE OTHER SIDE

*June 2011, 10:00 a.m. (three years later)*
***Aetna Insurance Home Office, Hartford, Connecticut***

PAM SHUSTER SET the cup of coffee on her desk. The pain in her chest had become unbearable. Her arm hurt. Her jaw too. She stood and walked toward her office door. Lightheadedness made her sway. Not good.

"Jaime." Where was her administrative assistant? Sweat dribbled down her face. She swiped it away and wiped her palm on her dress. Her chest burned like acid was dissolving her lungs. She couldn't get enough air. "Jaime!"

Everything went fuzzy, then black.

She awoke to find herself floating above her physical body, which now lay faceup on the Oriental rug in front of her desk. *What's happening? What's going on?*

Two scraggly, emaciated creatures appeared, standing about seven feet tall, with oversized yellowish-brown teeth and skin. Their heads were bald on top with greasy, stringy hair on the sides. Death lingered in their eyes.

Each grabbed one of her arms with a vise-like grip, gritted its teeth, and roared at her. She screamed just as Jaime walked in, but Jaime paid no attention to her. Instead, Jaime just stared at her lifeless body on the floor.

The creatures launched directly upward, with her in tow between them, through ceilings and the slate roof, then high into the air. Downtown Hartford whizzed by hundreds of feet below. They followed I-84 East and then the Mass Pike toward Boston. Before long, they were over Cape Cod, then the Atlantic Ocean. She screamed until she was hoarse as the wind ripped violently through her hair.

Land soon appeared. A moment later, they dove into a cave at the top of a mountain, then through solid rock into a massive cavern. In the center of the cavern, a large circle opened to an Abyss that was emanating glowing red light. Overpowering heat enveloped her as they passed over the lava percolating at the bottom. The stench so overwhelmed her that she retched again and again sending vomit down her chest.

Thousands of people stood lined up below, all naked. One by one, a demon threw those at the front of the line into the Abyss.

Her transporters placed Pam at the end of the line. A man in front of her tried to flee, but one of the creatures grabbed him by the arm, twisted him around, and swiped his stomach with a clawed hand, disemboweling him. He dropped to the ground, writhing and screeching. She screamed—that poor man.

Better stay in line. Then she looked down and blinked in shock. She was naked too. *What is this place? Why am I here? Who are these horrible creatures?*

As she approached the front of the line, her legs went wobbly, and she collapsed like an accordion. One of her captors dug its claw into her back just beneath her rib cage, ripping through her skin like Jell-O. He then lifted her to her feet and released her. Searing pain throbbed throughout her back.

Hunched over, Pam now stood first in line. A man seated at a pitted wooden table looked up at her. A powerful spiritual presence like she'd never reckoned with before invaded her mind, searching her memories at incredible speed, at the same time evaluating every choice she'd ever made. It exposed her in every way—physically, spiritually, and morally—and stripped her of all privacy and pretension.

The man shouted something in a foreign language. Another creature wrote symbols on her forehead using some sort of charcoal marker, then he picked her up and threw her into the Abyss.

Down she went, flailing at ever-increasing speed, toward the glowing red blotch at the bottom. The heat blasted around her face like a meteor entering the earth's atmosphere. Hotter. Hotter.

Suddenly, a creature reached out from an opening in the wall of the Abyss and grabbed her, halting her descent. He pulled her into a cave. Deeper within the cave was an atrium full of naked people: some standing, some writhing in a pool of molten lava. Down many hallways, extending outward from the atrium, were thousands of prison cells. Moans, groans, and wails pierced the air. The heat was oppressive, and the stench putrid.

So thirsty. Drained of all energy, Pam labored to get a full breath.

A towering reptilian creature approached, grabbed her by the hair, and threw her into the lava pit beside several others. Excruciating pain assaulted her as hot irons seemed to sear every inch of her body. She screamed until her air ran out.

Jackson Trotman slouched in his red leather chair, casually flipping through the paper PowerPoint slides his boss, Fred Jorgensen, would be presenting to the Aetna Chief Information Officer the next day. Did God really want him to work at an insurance company for the rest of his life? At least as a marine, he'd been doing something for his country.

Suddenly, a woman's scream pierced the air.

Jackson bolted upright in his chair.

"Help! Quick! Someone, call nine-one-one!" The frantic voice belonged to Jaime Thurston, Pam Shuster's administrative assistant.

Jackson jumped out of the chair and ran to her cubicle, but she wasn't there. Crying came from the nearby office, so he hurried in. Pam lay faceup on the Oriental rug in front of her desk, her face ashen. Jaime stood beside Pam with a hand over her mouth, sobbing. Fred fluttered in a corner, staring at Pam.

Jackson dropped to his knees. "Pam! Pam, are you okay?"

She didn't reply.

He grabbed her shoulders and shook her from side to side. She didn't open her eyes, and her chest wasn't rising and falling. "She's not breathing. Jaime, call nine-one-one. Fred, call Aetna security." He began CPR, counting out thirty chest compressions to the beat of the Bee Gees' "Stayin' Alive" song, followed by two rescue breaths. He methodically repeated the process several times. No response.

Fred sputtered in the background. "This is Fred Jorgensen. We have a medical emergency on the third floor, room 3-0014... Pam Shuster... She's not breathing and has no pulse... We're giving CPR... Okay, hurry!"

Jackson continued the chest compressions. Sweat slid down his face, and he wiped it off with his shirtsleeve. His shoulders burned in the places he'd sustained war injuries. "Fred, I'm going to need help here pretty soon."

"No way, José."

Jackson craned his neck to eye Fred. "What?"

Fred stood against the office wall with his arms crossed tightly over his chest.

What was Fred's problem? Why won't he help? Maybe he's homophobic. "Is it because she's gay? What difference does that make? Are you going to let her die?"

"Not my job, man. We'll have to wait for the EMTs."

"She'll be dead by then!" Jackson bent down, blew two breaths into Pam's mouth, and then started compressions again. "What if I do the breathing and you do the compressions?"

"Sorry. I can't do it."

What a jerk! "You mean you won't do it." Jackson stopped, took a deep breath, shook and twisted his arms, and resumed CPR. When would those blasted EMTs get here? Then, it hit him. He hadn't prayed yet. He hoped it wasn't too late. *Father in heaven, please help Pam! In Jesus's name, I pray, amen.*

After three more rounds of CPR, Pam took a deep, wheezing breath and coughed several times.

Jackson placed a hand on her shoulder. "Pam?"

She arched upward, and her two-hundred-pound body convulsed. Jackson reared back against the wall. "She must be having a seizure."

"Oh God!" Pam screamed. "Get me out of here!"

Jackson looked at Fred. The man's eyes were wide, and his mouth hung open.

"The fire! Oh God, help me!"

What should he do? A baritone voice inside his head told him to pray. He fell forward onto his knees. "Father in heaven, please rescue Pam from wherever she is right now. Please save her. In Jesus's name, I pray, amen."

Pam's body relaxed onto the floor, motionless. She'd stopped breathing again. Jackson rocked forward into position and resumed CPR.

A moment later, Pam coughed and convulsed again. Then, finally, she opened her eyes.

"Oh, thank God!" Jackson shouted. "You're back, Pam. You're back!"

"Oh, no... Help me, Jackson! Oh God, help me! Get me out of here." After a few seconds, she lost consciousness and stopped breathing again.

Chills shook him. *Pam's life is in my hands.* What should he do next? More CPR? Then an old marine saying came to him: He who hesitates is lost. So, Jackson forced two quick breaths into Pam's mouth and resumed compressions.

After a few moments, she reopened her horror-filled eyes and gasped for air. "Jackson! Don't stop. For God's sake, don't stop. Save me, Jackson. Save me." She lost consciousness again, but this time she was breathing normally.

He eyed her closely, studying her chest movements to make sure she was still breathing.

Voices and metal clanging came from outside the office. An EMT, heavyset and in his midforties, walked into the office, then bent down and checked Pam's pulse. "What happened?"

"It's about time you guys got here. Her name is Pam Shuster. I found her lying faceup on the floor and not breathing. I've been giving her CPR. She just started breathing normally a minute ago. I had to revive her three times. She seems to be going in and out of consciousness."

A second EMT, a red-haired woman, arrived with a gurney. They lifted Pam onto the gurney and started checking her vital signs.

"Make sure you watch her every second," Jackson said. "She might stop breathing again."

The man nodded. "We'll take it from here."

Pam moaned, then exhaled as her hand flopped lifelessly onto the gurney.

# CHAPTER 3
## STRESS REDUCTION

JACKSON HELD THE glass doors open for the EMTs when they exited the rear of the Aetna Home Office building. Then, as they loaded Pam into the ambulance, he almost hopped in too. Somehow, he'd become responsible for her even though he didn't know her that well.

The air was humid, and dark clouds threatened in the distance. After the ambulance sped away with lights flashing and sirens blaring, Jackson faced the building. He couldn't go back in. His hands were trembling, and he had to punch his solar plexus a few times to relieve the acid reflux that had built up. *Man, I have to get out of here!*

He started walking in no specific direction. He turned onto Farmington Avenue, then broke into a light jog, even though he was still in his work clothes. He went down the hill, under the railroad bridge, and into downtown Hartford. He looked around, then turned into Bushnell Park. Walkways wound through wide-open lawns that were dotted with park benches and monuments. Children's shouts and laughter came from the playground, and carnival music emanated from the carousel building. He slowed to a walk. His mind began to clear.

Jackson sat down on a bench by the fishpond. The gold-domed state capitol building gleamed in the distance, and the reflections of trees played on the water in front of him.

He forced himself to reason. Yeah, what happened was traumatic, but it wasn't that bad. He'd seen a lot worse in Afghanistan. EMTs and ER workers dealt with this sort of stuff all the time. So why was he getting all stressed out about it?

Then it came to him—something he hadn't thought about in years. He'd been five years old at the time, sitting in the back seat of the family van with his older sister, Susan, on a cold January day. His father was driving while his mother sat in the front passenger's seat. As they approached an S curve in the road, their van slid sideways across the double yellow line toward oncoming traffic, then crashed head-on into a dump truck.

When he woke, he was in the back seat, still wearing his seat belt. His father was in the driver's seat with his head tilted in a strange way against the headrest and blood dripping from the corner of his mouth. Jackson saw his sister on a gurney through a hole in the windshield as ambulance workers applied chest compressions. His mother stood next to her, bloodied and wailing uncontrollably.

His father had suffered a severe concussion but later recovered. His sister didn't make it.

Jackson took a deep breath of fresh air and let out a long, trembling sigh. *I managed to keep Pam alive. Why couldn't the EMTs save my sister? How could a loving God allow that to happen?*

The carnival music didn't jibe with his thoughts. He fought back the tears for as long as he could, but as the image of his sister lying on the gurney resurfaced, the emotion welling within him became too much. He covered his face with his hands and sobbed. People were around, but so what? Let them stare if they wanted.

The wind picked up, and the temperature inched downward. A

drop of water darkened his dress shirt at first, then came dribbles, and finally, the sky exploded with rain.

He sat there on the bench, his head bowed, letting the rain soak him through and through, just like when he'd gotten drenched during his marine training at The Basic School. Only this time, he didn't have anything to prove to his instructors. There was a cleansing aspect to the rain. Somehow, it brought healing. Eventually, he took a deep breath and collected himself. As he walked back to the Aetna parking lot, he prayed that God was looking out for his big sister... wherever she was.

Jackson's alarm clock jarred him awake at five thirty the next morning. After using the bathroom and drinking a glass of water, he knelt beside his bed, prayed for his friends, family, and coworkers, and asked God to make him a blessing to others that day.

Even so, his heart wasn't in it. He retrieved his Bible and Bible reading plan from the nightstand. He'd already checked off many of the assignments on his way to reading through the Bible in a year.

He flipped through the well-worn pages, filled with underlined passages and circled cross-references, to the fifth chapter of John. Another glance at his nightstand ensured his journal was nearby for recording any thoughts or questions he might have for his friend Mike Tolbert, who had been discipling him for the past year.

His clothes for the day lay on the cranberry upholstered sitting chair near his bed. On one arm was his work clothes—a burgundy collared shirt, khaki pants, plaid boxers, beige socks, and Hush Puppies shoes. On the other was his exercise gear—a golden-yellow shirt, navy-blue shorts, black Under Armour stretch pants, and white socks. He put on his exercise clothes and neatly folded his work clothes in his gym bag.

By six thirty, Jackson was running on the treadmill at the New York Sports Club, just a short walk through an underground tunnel from his condo at Blue Back Square in West Hartford. With its white ceiling tiles, gray rubber flooring, and floor-to-ceiling mirrors on the left side, the exercise room looked much larger than it actually was. He glanced up from time to time during his run to see the twenty-something women strutting around in their tight Under Armour outfits. *I've got to stop staring at them. Father in heaven, please help me to focus on you instead of them.*

He set the treadmill at 7.0 mph with a zero percent incline. That meant he'd be running a mile in about eight and a half minutes—a far cry from his days as a baseball player at the University of Connecticut seven years earlier.

Most of the folks exercising around him wore headphones, but Jackson amused himself by imagining what might be entertaining them. The brunette forty-something lady struggling on an elliptical on his left was probably listening to Michael Bublé and pining about some lost love who got away. The slender, gray-haired professorial-looking gentleman on a stationary bike off to his right was probably playing Brahms or Beethoven or some other patrician piece that helped take his mind off the recent decline in his retirement account. The exercise machines hummed steadily, interrupted occasionally by the clinking of weights in the background. A breeze from a nearby rotating fan cooled the air slightly.

Jackson returned his focus to the Bible chapter he'd been trying to memorize. He set the printout from an online site on the treadmill display panel in front of him. Repetition was the key to Scripture memorization and stating short phrases from the passage repeatedly helped him. He usually whispered in public so the people around him wouldn't think he was weird. Although he was huffing and puffing a bit, stopping to take a breather was not an option.

*Praise be to the God and Father of our Lord Jesus Christ, who has blessed us in the heavenly realms with every spiritual blessing in Christ. For he chose us in him before the creation of the world to be holy and blameless in his sight. In love he predestined us for adoption to sonship through Jesus Christ, in accordance with his pleasure and will—to the praise of his glorious grace, which he has freely given us in the One he loves. (Ephesians 1:3–6)*

Questions bombarded him. *What does predestination mean? How can God know who I would be before the creation of the world? Don't I have free will, and can't I choose to follow him or not follow him? What really goes on in the "heavenly realms"?*

So many people have said we must wait until we get to heaven to know the answers. But would God leave us hanging like that? The answers had to be out there somewhere.

Jackson wiped his forehead with the front of his T-shirt. The air seemed to have gotten heavier. The words had power in them. His legs pounded on the insistent belt beneath him. He read a little further:

*I keep asking that the God of our Lord Jesus Christ, the glorious Father, may give you the Spirit of wisdom and revelation, so that you may know him better. I pray that the eyes of your heart may be enlightened in order that you may know the hope to which he has called you, the riches of his glorious inheritance in his holy people, and his incomparably great power for us who believe. (Ephesians 1:17–19)*

Jackson shook his head. He still didn't get it. After looking around to see if anyone was nearby, he said, "Father in heaven, please give me the spirit of wisdom and revelation, and enlighten my mind so I can understand what this means."

His attention drifted to the sports highlights displayed on the TV screen mounted on the wall above him. Then his mind shifted to all the work he had ahead of him at the office. The new website he was working on was going to be incredible.

He lifted the bottom of his T-shirt and wiped the sweat off his face. *Fred's been so nasty lately. It's not my fault the website is slow. I can't believe Kumar quit. Too many emails. I've got to get something done today.* He glanced at the display console. Four miles in less than thirty-five minutes. Not too bad for someone who would be thirty soon.

Jackson wouldn't have minded working out all day at the gym. Unfortunately, duty called. Those emails would sit in his inbox, festering like moldy mushrooms, until he answered them.

# CHAPTER 4
# THE OFFICE

IN THE OFFICE building, he stopped by the cafeteria, retrieved a large Styrofoam cup, and ladled some old-fashioned oatmeal into it, leaving a little room at the top for milk. After pouring in the milk, he securely fastened a plastic cover on top.

As he entered his cubicle, the red voicemail light on his desk telephone blinked at him. "Great. I haven't even sat down yet, and someone already wants a piece of me." He unlocked the overhead metal cabinet, retrieved his laptop, then played the message on speaker.

"Jackson, this is Fred. We've got another fire drill I need you to address. Give me a call as soon as you get in."

It was best to handle Fred's fire drill in person. Jackson walked down the hallway toward his boss's office, still seething over how Fred had refused to help him with CPR the day before. He shook his head, muttering, "What a jerk."

"Who's a jerk?" a voice asked from behind.

He cringed. It was Fred. Jackson turned and faced him. "I was just thinking about yesterday." He turned and kept walking.

Jaime looked up from her desk as he and Fred approached Fred's office. She took Jackson's hands in hers and looked him in the eye. "It was great what you did yesterday. Thank you so much for saving Pam's life."

He grinned. "You're welcome, Jaime."

He walked into Fred's office and dropped into his favorite chair without saying a word, then stared sternly at his boss. Dark circles hung under Fred's eyes as he stared at the computer screen.

Jackson broke the ice. "Sorry I left you hanging with the CIO presentation yesterday."

Fred yawned without looking away from his screen. "The CIO presentation doesn't mean squat in the grand scheme of things. I told Glenn what had happened with Pam. He was cool that we didn't get it done, given all the craziness yesterday. It turned out the big guy wouldn't have been able to make our meeting anyway. He had a Severity 1 outage to address. Glad I wasn't on that call. His executive assistant rescheduled our meeting to the day after tomorrow."

"Good." Jackson straightened. "I'm glad everything worked out."

"Glenn wants to see a draft of the presentation by noon tomorrow, so that means I want to see a draft by nine. Hope you didn't have any plans tonight."

Jackson smiled. "Remember this when you're figuring out my bonus, boss."

"Don't worry. I'll take care of you if you take care of me."

"Deal."

Fred swiveled away from his computer, centered himself behind his desk, and studied Jackson. Then he leaned forward. "So, how are you doing? That was something yesterday. You saved the day." Fred leaned across his desk, extending his hand to fist bump.

Jackson stood up and fist-pumped him back, then sat down and crossed his arms over his chest. Fred had been a real jerk, but Jackson needed to be gracious. "That was plenty of excitement for one day, thank you."

"I can imagine. You must have been exhausted."

"I was."

Fred's desk phone rang. He looked down at the phone display and sent the call to voicemail. Then he turned back to Jackson. "That was awesome what you did."

Jackson shrugged. "Thanks."

"It took a lot of guts." By the sincerity of his expression, he meant it.

"I appreciate that." How could he direct Fred to the spiritual implications of what had happened? He shifted in his chair. "That was pretty weird what Pam said after she regained consciousness."

Fred nodded. "I've been thinking about it ever since. It scared the you-know-what out of me. I hardly slept a wink last night. Thank God you had the guts to do CPR. I'm sorry, man. I was pretty lame yesterday."

"Well, at least you called in the emergency."

"Yeah, but I screwed up. Why do you think Pam cried out for you to save her? I mean, it sounded like she was in incredible pain."

Jackson paused for a second, weighing any possible fallout from an honest response. A twinge inside reminded him to be honest no matter the cost. "I think she was in hell."

Fred folded his arms across his chest. "My parents were Catholic, but I stopped going to church after I went to college. I don't know if there is a heaven or a hell, but I sure don't want to go to hell if there is one, and I hope I'm good enough to get into heaven."

Jackson opened his mouth but then paused, considering how to respond. He should probably quote some Bible verse about salvation by grace through faith instead of works, but his mind went blank. Would he get in trouble if he mixed religion and employment? His condo mortgage and car payments came to mind. Better to play it safe. "I know what you mean."

Fred put his hands on the desk and leaned forward. "You needed my help yesterday, and I refused. I couldn't bring myself to touch her. I'm sorry."

"Apology accepted. We all make mistakes, Fred. I know I've made my share. I still think about a guy I wouldn't pick up while driving during a blizzard. His car wasn't working, and he needed a ride, but I drove right past him. I still feel terrible about it, but there's nothing I can do about it now. All I can say is that I hope you'll learn from this experience and act differently next time."

Fred nodded. "Agreed."

❦

That evening, Jackson registered at the Hartford Gun Club's main clubhouse, then backed his car up to the outdoor rifle range. He retrieved a large duffle bag from his trunk and placed it on the range gun bench. One by one, he removed his weapons—an M1014 Benelli 12-gauge combat shotgun and an M4 carbine—and carefully laid them on the table, ensuring the barrels were both pointing down-range. He left his M1911 .45-caliber pistol in the bag but took out several shotgun and rifle ammunition packages.

A short time later, Mike Tolbert, his mentor from church, parked next to his red Mustang. Mike shook Jackson's hand firmly and spoke with a husky baritone voice. "Hey. Long time no see, buddy. How are you?" Mike's short black hair had gotten a little whiter, accentuated by his dark black skin.

Jackson sighed. "Oh, the usual. My boss is driving me crazy. He can be such a jerk sometimes."

"That's too bad. How's the Bible reading going?"

"Good, but memorizing it is tough."

Mike smacked him on the back. "You're doing great, Jackson. I've never seen anyone grow in the Lord as fast as you. Think about where you started a year ago and where you are now."

Jackson tilted his head. "You think so?"

"Sure. You used to drink like a fish, swear like a sailor, sleep around every chance you got, and dabble in pornography, right?"

He chuckled. "Yes, sir."

"And are you doing that stuff anymore?"

"No." *But I still think about it sometimes.*

Mike smiled. "That doesn't happen by the force of your will. That happens by God changing you on the inside."

Jackson folded his arms over his chest. "But there's still so much to learn."

"And there's always more to learn. We're all works in progress. It's called sanctification."

Jackson paused as he let the calming words seep into his spirit. "You're the only real friend I've got."

Mike put his arm around Jackson's shoulders. "Your time spent with God is more important than your time spent with me. You've been diligent in reading your Bible, but you need to be diligent in cultivating your relationship with God. Just hang in there. It'll come. It takes time to get your spiritual mind in shape, just as it takes time to get your physical body in shape. By the way, how's your prayer life?"

He shrugged. "I'm working on it. I'm having a tough time grasping this 'God's sovereignty versus man's responsibility' thing."

Mike nodded. "Yeah, that's a tough one. Theologians have been trying to figure it out for centuries. There are lots of Bible verses on either side. An old friend of mine, who's now with the Lord, once told me that it's like standing between two railroad tracks. The tracks seem far apart next to you, but when you look down the line, they seem to come together. Of course, the railroad tracks never converge, but in our lives, God's will and our efforts do unite when we seek him. God will make it clear to you one day when you're ready."

They donned their hearing protection and took turns firing the

M4 carbine at targets two hundred yards downrange, with Jackson scoring a little better that day.

Mike policed up the expended shells while Jackson secured his rifle in the duffle bag. They then moved to the skeet range and took turns firing the shotgun.

After they finished skeet shooting, Jackson asked, "Do you want to head over to the pistol range and fire the forty-five?"

"Not today. I need to get back to the family."

"No problem. Thanks for coming out on such short notice."

"My pleasure. I'm glad I was free. Thanks for inviting me."

Jackson laid his weapons on the gun table before inserting them in their respective gun cases. "You're welcome, Mike."

As he loaded the weapon cases in the trunk of his car, he exhaled. If only he had family waiting for him.

On his way home, Jackson stopped by Cracker Barrel Pub in Tariffville. He sat at a pedestal table in the barroom and ordered a blue-cheese-topped burger with fries. A sudden craving for a beer made him add that to his order. He only drank occasionally now, knowing how the Bible spoke against drunkenness, but tonight was one of those nights.

Two hours later, he'd downed five beers. A young woman walked in and sat alone at the bar with her back to him. She was a redhead and athletic looking, and on a whim, he got up and sat on the stool to her right.

"You're in my chair," a voice said from behind him.

Jackson bristled, gritted his teeth, and turned around. The man was big and burly, obviously used to getting his way, and a bully to boot. "And why is that?"

"She's my girlfriend."

He nodded at the empty bar stool on the left side of the woman. "Then sit over there."

"I like the right side better." The guy wanted to humiliate him to look like a big man in front of his girlfriend.

Jackson glanced at the woman. Chances were she was waiting for him to back down, just like all the other guys her boyfriend had confronted before him. But he wasn't about to do that. "Look, buddy, I don't want any trouble. Why don't you have a seat, and I'll buy you a drink."

"I think I'll take you up on that." He lifted Jackson off the stool by his armpits.

Rage swelled within him. Jackson twisted in midair and instinctively punched the man in the solar plexus, knocking him to the floor. When the guy tried to get up, Jackson snapped a roundhouse kick to the side of his head, knocking him out. He then reached into his wallet, threw three twenties on the bar, and made a beeline for the door.

He slammed the car door and drove off as fast as he could, hoping no one had gotten his car license number. *When am I going to learn? I can't handle alcohol. I've got to stop this. Oh God, please help me.*

When Jackson drifted off to sleep that evening, he was back in the marines, on leave in Amsterdam. He sat at a table outside a pub with four British Army officers from the Seventh Armored Brigade. Like the US Marines, the Desert Rats were also fighting in Afghanistan's Helmand province.

Their table sat on a cobblestone landing directly alongside a stagnant canal that navigated between rows of dimly lit three-story brick homes. With the temperature a comfortable seventy degrees, about forty degrees cooler than Afghanistan, they all wore shorts, casual shirts, and sandals. Jackson looked up whenever a young lady passed by, hoping to make eye contact.

An order of Wild Turkey shots and Guinness beers arrived. Each man picked up a shot glass in one hand and a beer mug in the other.

"Dang, you Brits sure can put 'em away." Jackson's words slurred as he spoke. "I don't think you've stopped drinking since we got on the plane."

"Have to make up for lost time," one of the officers said. "Haven't had a drink in a year. It looks like you're not doing too bad yourself there, mate." He lifted his Guinness, looking around. "Cheers."

The whole group raised their glasses in unison and clanged them together. "Cheers!"

Each man downed his shot in one gulp, then chugged his beer.

Jackson gasped for air as he finished. "I'm gonna have all the fun I can till I go back."

"Go back?" another of the British officers asked. "Did you sign up for another tour?"

"You betcha. I can't leave my men behind. They need me. Somebody's gotta ice those Taliban dirtbags."

"Blimey, mate! You're crazy!" the most junior of the four said. "I'm glad to be out of that dump and hope I never have to go back. Say, have you ever been to Amsterdam before?"

Jackson leaned back in his chair and clasped his hands behind his neck. "No. But I hear it's a pretty wild place."

"Right. Would you like to partake of some of its feminine delights?"

"Sign me up, mate."

The guys all chipped in and paid the bill. The senior British officers then stumbled down the cobblestone street to their hotel, and the junior officer and Jackson waited by the side of the road to flag down a taxi.

Moments later, shouting echoed from about thirty feet down the street. A group of four young hooligans had stopped the British officers. One of them shoved an officer to the ground and began striking him with some sort of wooden mallet. The other Brits fought back.

Jackson's adrenaline burned off the alcohol in his system. He sprinted toward the scene, grabbed the mallet-wielding wrist of the mugger, then wound his right leg up and blasted a karate kick to the man's left leg, breaking his kneecap. One down, three to go. At least the Brits had two of them occupied.

The next mugger Jackson faced brandished a knife. He instinctively pulled his Hawaiian shirt over his head, wrapped it around his left hand and forearm, and then crouched slightly. After moving side to side a few times, he lunged at the attacker, grabbing the man's knife hand with his wrapped hand. With his other hand, he punched the man in the larynx.

The knife-wielding man collapsed, gasping for air, as the other two assailants fled.

Jackson helped the fallen British officer to his feet. "Are you guys all right?"

They all nodded in affirmation.

"Thanks, mate," one said.

"Yeah. Where'd you learn to fight like that?" another one asked.

"The marines. I also happen to have a second-degree black belt in karate. Look, we'd better get out of here before the cops arrive. I don't want to spend my whole leave dealing with this."

They all fled the scene. As he ran behind the British officer, the man's form disappeared, and it was just Jackson running. And running. But he never seemed to get anywhere.

Jackson awoke in a cold sweat. Had he killed the guy in Amsterdam? He'd never bothered to find out. Snippets of Scripture popped into his mind. *Put off all these—anger, rage, malice.*

*Do not get drunk on wine, which leads to debauchery. Instead, be filled with the Spirit.*

He got out of bed and fell to his knees. *Oh God, please help me overcome my anger, take away my desire for alcohol, and give my life meaning and purpose. In Jesus's name, I pray, amen.*

# CHAPTER 5
# THE EIGHTH FLOOR

JACKSON VISITED PAM at St. Francis Hospital the following evening after work. He stopped by the admissions desk to get her room number, then got on the elevator. Hopefully, Pam was recovering well and would be happy to see him. He exited on the eighth floor and approached the acute care nurses' station. Two nurses in blue scrubs sat behind the counter, focused on paperwork.

One looked up. "May I help you, sir?"

"Can you direct me to Pam Shuster's room?"

"Are you a family member?"

"No, I'm a friend from work."

"She's with family. So, she may not want to have friends visit right now."

Jackson sighed. "Please tell her that Jackson Trotman is here. I'm sure she'll want to see me."

"I'm sorry, sir—"

"I saved her life a few days ago," he insisted. "I'm sure she'd want to see me."

The nurse shrugged her shoulders. "Okay, let me check. Wait here." She marched down the hallway, swung aside the yellow floor-to-ceiling curtain to one of the rooms, and walked in. A moment later, she reappeared and motioned for Jackson to come in.

The walls in Pam's room were light gray with dark gray trim. Bright fluorescent lights shone down from between the white ceiling tiles while machines hummed in the background. An untouched dinner tray sat on a nearby nightstand, and Pam was slightly propped up in the bed, wearing a green patient gown.

Jackson's breath caught as he drew closer. Her eyes were sunken and swollen with dark shadows underneath. Her short light brown hair looked greasy and disheveled, and her skin looked pale. "How are you, Pam?"

"Oh, been better, I guess." Her large frame filled the bed. "The doctors said I had a heart attack, but I'm doing much better now."

"I'm so happy you're doing better."

"Me too. It was good of you to come, Jackson. Have a seat." She watched as he pulled a chair over. "I heard what you did for me a few days ago. Thank you from the bottom of my heart." Tears filled her eyes. "How can I ever repay you?"

Jackson got a little teary himself. He took her hand, smiling. "You don't have to repay me. I was glad to help. I'm thrilled you're going to be okay. I can't take all the credit. I heard Jaime scream, and Fred called security to get the EMTs while I was with you."

"Jaime was in here earlier and told me about Fred. Some friend! What a piece of—"

"I know, I know. I wasn't too happy about that either." Jackson sighed.

"Aetna is incredibly supportive of LGBTs in the workplace. I'm going to talk to HR about him when I get back."

He didn't want his boss to get in trouble and have it traced back to him. Time to be a little more charitable. "Sometimes people freeze up under pressure. So maybe you should cut him some slack."

"That's kind of you, Jackson, but it's no excuse."

*Good. Fred deserves it.* "Well, if it means anything, he feels bad about it."

Pam shook her head. "What a disgusting human being. How can someone like that get into a managerial position?"

"He apologized to me today for not helping more. So, I don't blame you if you're angry with him. Quite frankly, I'm still a little angry too. But I think it's best to move on."

"I suppose you're right, but I can't just flip a switch and forgive him like that." Pam looked away, her lips trembling. "I'll try, but it may take me a little while… to be honest."

Jackson leaned toward her. "Do you remember what happened?"

Pam tilted her head. "What do you mean?"

"Well, right after I revived you, you started screaming like you were in agony. You said, 'Oh God, get me out of here.'"

Pam scowled. "Really? I said that?"

He nodded.

"Hmm."

"I'm sorry, Pam. I should have waited until you were feeling better before bringing this up. I hope I didn't upset you."

Pam shook her head. "Don't be silly. I'm a big girl. I want to know. You should never be afraid to tell the truth." She paused for a moment. "What else did I say?"

Just then, another woman walked in. Heavyset and fortyish, she had short dark hair.

"Jackson, this is my partner, Kate," Pam said.

He started to stand up. "Hey, Kate, how are you?"

"You don't have to get up, Jackson." She walked over and hugged him as he sank back into the chair. "Thank you for what you did for Pam."

"Jackson was just telling me about what happened after he revived me," Pam said.

He put his hands on his hips. "Maybe we should do this another time when you're feeling better."

Pam reached toward him and took his hand in hers. "No, please tell me. I can take it."

He hesitated a moment before responding. "You were crying out to God, asking him to get you out of the fire."

"What? Oh, that's a bunch of bull." Kate glared at him. "How dare you come in here and scare her like that."

He remained silent.

"Kate, he's just telling me what he heard. I believe him. I wouldn't be here right now if it weren't for him. Hear him out." Pam turned back to him.

He took a deep breath. "Well, I'm not sure, but I think you were in hell."

Kate huffed. "That's it. Thank you for what you did, but you need to leave. Now!"

Pam stared at him with wide eyes. "I couldn't have been in hell. I'm a good person."

"I'm sure you're a very good person, Pam, but I heard what I heard."

Pam studied him as he stood up, then looked down at her hands as she wrung them on her lap. Finally, she looked up. "I don't remember a thing. Are you sure about this?"

*Guess she doesn't believe me. I can't blame her.* "Fred was right there with me, and Jaime heard it too. It's strange you don't remember. Do you believe in heaven and hell?"

"Well, no, I never did. I've heard about this sort of thing on TV. Someone dies on the operating table, gets revived, and then wakes up screaming. What should I do?"

What should he say? The truth might make her angry. And then she might retaliate against him at work. *Better play it safe.* "Well, you're Jewish, and I'm a Christian, so I don't want to impose my beliefs on you."

"That's very considerate of you."

He hesitated, then said the first thing that popped into his mind. "Talk to your rabbi, read the Bible, and pray."

"Okay." Pam took a weary breath. "You know, I'm feeling kind of tired right now. I think I'd better get some rest."

"I think that's your cue to leave," Kate added.

Pam gave her a stern look, then turned back to him. "Sorry, Jackson. Thanks for visiting."

"It was my pleasure." He smiled at her. He glanced at Kate, but she was grimacing and looking the other way. After standing, he grasped both of Pam's hands. "Hang in there. I'll be praying for you to get better."

Pam nodded. "Thanks."

He left the room and headed to the parking garage.

As he got on the elevator, he shook his head. *That was a perfect opportunity to tell Pam about Jesus, and I blew it. I need to have a better answer ready next time.*

# CHAPTER 6
# THE SEVENTH FLOOR

IN A PRIVATE room on the seventh floor of St. Francis Hospital, Jeremy Brown sat next to his Aunt Lois. His mother lay on the bed in front of them, her eyes closed and her mouth wide open. Once vibrant, her skin was now gray, soggy, and sullen. Per her living will, she was on a comfort protocol—eight milligrams IV push of morphine sulfate per hour, accompanied by just enough saline to keep her veins open. She'd be passing shortly.

Jeremy, at her bedside for three days now, was exhausted. He shook his head and sighed, then got up and walked to the window. *What am I going to do now? I'm only seventeen.* He bumped his forehead on the glass as if trying to crush a fly against it. *Maybe I should join the army and ice some Ragheads.*

His mother coughed.

He turned and moved to the side of her bed. He bent down and studied her chest to see if she was still breathing. No movement.

Jeremy ran into the hallway and found an older nurse because she'd have the most experience. "My mother stopped breathing."

The nurse came into the room, checked for a pulse, then set his mother's hand back down on the bed.

"Why aren't you doing something?"

"Your mother's living will states that we should not resuscitate her," the nurse said.

She was right, but he couldn't accept it. He squared himself in front of her. "I don't care what she signed! Do something!"

The gray-haired woman calmly placed one hand on her hip and the other on his shoulder. "I'm very sorry for your loss. Your mother has left us, but she's gone to a better place."

Tears filled his eyes. "A better place? Ha. She's dead." He stormed out of the room, blasted through the nearby stairwell door, and sprinted down the stairs.

After dashing past the security guard, Jeremy jumped into his beat-up black Trans Am. With tears streaming down his face, he hollered at the top of his lungs and then slammed the steering wheel with his fists. "How could you take away my mother?" He guffawed. "Some loving God you are…" More tears blurred his vision. Maybe he shouldn't drive right now. But he needed to get as far away from this place as possible—now!

Jeremy revved the engine and raced down the hospital parking garage ramps as fast as he could, tires screeching at each bend. A man walked out the sliding doors just as he veered around the corner at the hospital entrance. He slammed on the brakes, but it was too late. There was no way he could stop in time. Shock widened the man's eyes as the car plowed right into him, sending him flying through the air like a rag doll.

The car jolted to a stop. Jeremy shifted the car into park and cursed. The thump of the man striking his car resonated in his mind. He stared for a moment at the unmoving body sprawled across the hood of a nearby parked car. Then, leaning forward in his seat, he gripped the steering wheel with both hands and smashed his forehead against it several times. What just happened? *Did I kill the guy?* He never should have been driving.

"Ma!" he shouted. "What should I do? Ma!" He looked all around.

A security guard jogged toward him.

He couldn't just sit there. He had to do something. He revved the engine again. If he stayed, they'd send him to jail. If he left… well, they'd just have to catch him.

He took a deep breath. "I'm out of here!" He took off, barreling down the garage ramp. Once he reached the bottom floor, he crashed through the exit gate and roared off down the street.

# CHAPTER 7
# THE PARKING GARAGE

JACKSON OPENED HIS eyes and rubbed his face. Above him was a concrete ceiling. Parked cars were all around. *Where am I? What am I doing here? How did I end up on top of this car?* People were shouting nearby. Two paramedics were transporting someone on a gurney toward the sliding glass hospital doors.

"No pulse!" The male paramedic straddling the gurney resumed chest compressions.

A hospital orderly rushed over to push the gurney.

The female paramedic adjusted the Ambu bag. "Hope they catch the guy that clocked him. Hey, isn't this the same guy who gave that lady CPR at Aetna a couple of days ago?"

The man looked down at the accident victim beneath him. "You know what, I think you're right. No good deed goes unpunished, huh?"

Jackson sat up straight on the hood of the car. They were talking about him? He stared until the gurney disappeared through the hospital doors, then slid off the car. After glancing around, he walked over to the security guard who stood outside the hospital entrance. "Hey, do you know what's going on?"

The security guard didn't respond.

He moved closer. "Hey, mister. I asked you a question."

Still no response.

Jackson tried to place his hand on the security guard's shoulder, but it passed right through. He reeled back, horrified. What was happening to him?

He gasped. He must be dead.

But he was only twenty-nine. And what would happen next? He should have taken the time to figure this out. Were angels going to come and whisk him up to heaven like Elijah? Or would an angel appear as the commander of the Lord's army did to Joshua? Would he see a bright light and walk into another dimension like in the TV shows? Or would black creepy things rise from the floor and drag him back down with them like in the movie *Ghost*? His hands shook uncontrollably.

Jackson frantically scanned the parking garage. Then he remembered a story his grandfather told him when he was a little boy. Pappi said angels came and took his grandmother away while he was sleeping beside her when he was five years old. The following day when he woke up, someone told him his grandmother had died in her sleep during the night. *That could be. Angels took Lazarus to be with Abraham. Maybe that is how it works.*

Suddenly, a bright light shone directly in front of Jackson. A massive being walked out of the light, dressed in a lightning-bright white linen robe with a golden sash over his chest. His eyes were like flaming torches, and his skin was the color of burnished bronze. About seven feet tall and muscular, he exuded explosive radiance.

Jackson cried out and fell prostrate on the floor, trembling.

The being spoke with a loud, commanding voice. "Do not fear, Jackson Trotman, mighty warrior. I have watched over you since before you were born. I saw you as you were being knitted together in your mother's womb. I am here to help you more fully understand the mystery of God's will and to develop in you the spirit of wisdom and revelation." The living being bent down and touched Jackson on the shoulder.

Instantly, the fear left him. "Why do you call me mighty warrior?"

"It is not who you are but who you will become."

"Who are you?" Jackson slowly stood up.

The being paused. "Think of me as the guardian of your soul."

Jackson gaped. "Guardian angel. Whoa. What's your name?"

"It is beyond understanding. But you may call me Mekoddishkem."

He squinted at the being's face. "May-cod-dish-kem?"

"Yes."

*This is incredible! I'm talking to an angel.* "Are we going to meet Jesus now?"

"No, but he has a mission for you. I will show you many things before you return to earth."

Jackson's insides squirmed. Not meeting Jesus was a huge let down. But then again, that meant he wasn't dead. "A mission? What mission? Why is God doing all this?"

"It is in response to your prayer."

Jackson tilted his head and put his hands on his hips. "What prayer?"

The guardian bent down to eye level. "The one you prayed while running on the treadmill a few days ago as you were memorizing the first chapter of Ephesians."

Jackson stepped back. "Wow! The God of the universe heard my prayer."

"Of course. Everything is in full view of the Lord."

Only God could know that. But what if this isn't an angel from God? What if this is a test? "I mean no disrespect, sir, but how do I know that this is real and not a dream? How do I know that you are who you say you are?"

Mekoddishkem just stood there in silence.

"It's written in the Bible that Satan can imitate an angel of light.

Please, sir, worship the God of Abraham, Isaac, and Jacob. Worship God the Father and his son, Jesus Christ." *Satan would never worship them.*

The heavenly being closed his eyes, lifted both his arms heavenward, and cried out with expressions of awe and adoration that Jackson had never witnessed before. He spoke in an unfamiliar language, but Jackson recognized some Hebrew words such as *Adonai* and *Jehovah*. Clearly, the being was not an angel of darkness. After a few moments, he lowered his arms and turned toward Jackson.

"What does Mekoddishkem mean?" he asked.

"It means to sanctify, dedicate, or set apart. It is God's will that all believers be sanctified—that they are made more like Jesus and are prepared to accomplish God's will."

"In the book of Revelation, it says that no one should add anything to God's Word," Jackson said. "Everything we need to know about God and his kingdom is in the Bible."

"Yes. That is true. But you know that when the apostle Paul was taken up to the third heaven, he saw things that he was not permitted to share with others."

"Is that where you will be taking me now?"

"Yes, but only a representation. It is not permitted for you to view such things or share them with others until the time appointed for you. Come now, I will show you. Touch my arm."

Jackson and Mekoddishkem passed seamlessly through the five upper floors of the parking garage and into the air above the hospital. They rocketed higher and higher, moving through the clouds as they went. Isaiah 40:22 came to mind: *He sits enthroned above the circle of the earth, and its people are like grasshoppers. He stretches out the heavens like a canopy, and spreads them out like a tent to live in.*

He looked back as they passed through the earth's atmosphere. The planets in the solar system appeared and disappeared in seconds. Nearby, stars and galaxies whizzed by as they pressed forward. "How are we able to travel so quickly? Even traveling at the speed of light, it would take thousands of years to get out of our galaxy."

"The laws of nature, as you understand them, do not limit us. You are limited to the dimensions of space and time. We are spiritual beings and travel in dimensions beyond your understanding. We will ourselves to go from this place to that place, and it occurs within the parameters set by God."

A blinding light enveloped them as they entered through a vertical fold in the heavenly canopy. The light emanated from a source on their right. God's throne, perhaps?

"Yes, that is heaven on the right," Mekoddishkem said.

Jackson looked at him. "I didn't say anything."

"I know. But I know everything about you, Jackson. I've been watching you your whole life. I know how you think."

He took Jackson by the arm and guided him to a plain white door that led back toward the edge of the canopy. The guardian turned a golden handle, pushed open the door, and walked through it onto a gray landing that stretched about twelve feet in front of them and about thirty yards to the left.

Jackson walked to the landing's edge. The brilliant light waned and then disappeared as Mekoddishkem closed the door behind them. Another light now governed. Ahead of them was nothing but space. He turned to his left, and directly in front of him was an immense shimmering white translucent structure abutting the edge of the canopy. Stars and galaxies were visible beyond it. A narrow slate gangplank extended out from the landing about fifty yards until it hit the edge of the wall. To the left and the right, upward and downward, the wall stretched before them as far as he could see. Every three feet, in every direction, were what looked like portholes on the side of a ship. About a foot in diameter, they had golden edging and clear centers.

"What is this place?" he asked.

The guardian looked down at him. "This is called The Wall."

Jackson stared all around. "What is its purpose?"

"To instruct you regarding the mystery of God's will and to develop in you the spirit of wisdom and revelation."

*Hmm.* The repetition of that line didn't clear anything up. "Why does God want me to learn these things? What's so special about me?"

"He loves you dearly, Jackson, and wants you to be sanctified."

*Unbelievable!* "God created this… for me?"

"Yes."

He bowed his head for a moment, then looked back at Mekoddishkem. "All this work… for me?"

"Yes." The guardian smiled.

"He must love me a great deal." Tears formed in his eyes.

"Yes, he does."

Taking a deep breath, Jackson shook his head. "This is amazing! How does The Wall function?"

"Come. Let me show you."

They walked to the end of the gangplank and stopped in front of a porthole. Mekoddishkem pointed. "Look through that portal. What do you see?"

He leaned forward and peered in. The clear circle became a frozen image. "Whoa. I can see my mother and father. How young they look. They're holding a baby. Is that me?"

"Yes. It is the day you were brought home from the hospital to your grandparents' house. Would you like to get closer?"

"Sure."

A mild stretching sensation blanketed his body, then they were pulled into the portal and immediately found themselves standing next to Jackson's mother and father. But instead of being frozen, the people now moved. His parents posed for a picture in front of his grandparents' house. His mother held him in her arms while a great aunt, whom Jackson could barely remember, instructed his parents to move a little closer together and smile. He couldn't remember that day, of course, but he'd seen a photograph of it. *Incredible.*

"Mom, Dad! It's me!" he yelled.

"They can't hear you."

He tried to hug his parents, but his arms passed right through their bodies. He quickly retreated, then wandered around the outside of his grandparents' house, surveying the hedges, the old front porch with the slider couch, and the gray crushed-stone driveway. The front yard seemed so much smaller than he remembered. The flinty hill in the back, where he used to play, had seemed like a mountain when he was younger but now looked more like a heap of rocks.

Jackson sucked in a breath. "This is so cool. I can feel the warm June air. I can hear the birds chirping and the cars passing in the distance. Every detail is so real."

His parents approached the front porch, beaming over their new baby. Two people and a two-year-old girl came out to greet them.

"There's Grandma and Grandpa… and Susan. They're alive."

"They are not," the angel said. "These are frozen slices of space and time that once was and cannot be altered."

Sadness washed through him. "Why did you bring me to this place and time?"

"To get you started on your journey, Jackson. What have you learned so far?"

"Well, all the daily activities of our lives have been recorded. As the Bible says, everything is in full view of the Lord. Does God use these portals to know what's going on in the world?"

"No. It is inherent within God's being to know all things at all times—past, present, and future. The Wall will help you understand more about God."

"Do we have to leave right away?"

"No. We can stay a little longer."

As Jackson entered the house, distant memories became sight. The beautiful cherry table with matching chairs sat in the dining room. The television in the living room was just ahead, past the fireplace. Opposite the fireplace and television was the old beige couch with a recliner next to it. The clock on the mantel above the fireplace gonged its long-forgotten melody.

He turned past the landing at the foot of the stairs and walked over it into the kitchen. The smell of freshly baked cookies filled the air. There, Junket pudding and Tollhouse cookies that his grandmother used to make were on the counter. She would store the cookies in a glossy white cookie tin with royal-blue edging along the cover.

He sat down on one of the breakfast nook benches. "This place holds my fondest memories. It's been about twenty years since I was last here. They sold the house to live closer to my parents." He swallowed. "I don't want to leave."

"I know you loved this place."

Mekoddishkem smiled. "I know you want to stay, but there is still so much for you to learn."

Jackson stood up. "How do we get out of here?"

"You can say or think whatever words you wish in order to leave. 'Exit portal' will work."

Jackson took one last look around. "Where do we go from here?"

"That is up to you."

He shrugged. "Okay. Exit portal."

# CHAPTER 8
# TOUGH QUESTIONS

JACKSON AND THE guardian returned to the gangplank adjacent to The Wall. He eyed the myriad of multi-colored galaxies in the background, then surveyed The Wall from side to side. "This is massive. What's in the other portals?"

"Each portal represents a human life. The portals on the left are windows into the lives of those who lived in the past. Those in the center are windows into the lives of those living in the present. Those on the right are windows into the lives of those not yet conceived."

Jackson leaned over to one side of the gangplank. "The Wall also extends upward and downward farther than I can see. What do the columns signify?"

"Every person represented in each column was or will be conceived during the same period."

"So, God knows all of the billions of people who ever lived, past, present, and future?"

"Yes. They all were created with a unique personality, unique gifts, and a unique life purpose."

Jackson considered that. "Can we see the past, present, and future of every person in every portal?"

Mekoddishkem nodded. "Yes. You cannot alter the past, as we saw in your portal. The present is. The future is ever-changing, ever-fluctuating because human beings have free will."

The image of his body lying on the gurney came to mind. Where was his body now? Was it on an operating table, on a hospital bed, or in the morgue?

"What exactly do you mean by free will?"

"Free will is the ability to choose what to do next, whether good or evil."

Jackson pursed his lips. "I've wondered about that. Why did God create human beings with free will?"

"He wants people to love him because they choose to, not because they have to. God created human beings in his image. Having the freedom to choose is part of God's character. He built that into people's makeup."

Jackson put his hand on his chin. "If mankind has free will, how can God know their future?"

"To use a medium you can understand, he can see it in their portal." Mekoddishkem gestured toward The Wall. "God is not locked into space and time. He can flow freely between past, present, and future by looking, in effect, into your portal. It's like God has you on DVR. He enjoys watching the game even though he already knows who won. From your perspective, you can change your future because you have free will. From God's perspective, he already knows your future."

"I hope you don't mind all my questions, Mekoddishkem."

"Not at all. That is one of the main reasons why I brought you here—for me to answer your questions."

Jackson looked around. *There's no noise here, no smells, no wind brushing against my skin. Just the nothingness of space. Incredible.*

"Once again, Jackson, God does not need The Wall to see all things. He can see and know all things because he is God. The Wall was created for your benefit so that you could understand these things more easily."

"I understand." Jackson paced around the gangplank. His biggest question was about his sister. For his entire life, he couldn't shake the image of his sister lying on a gurney dying. How should he ask about that? *I'll do what Abraham did when trying to convince the angels to save Lot.* "Since you don't mind, I have a few more questions. Why is there evil and suffering in the world?"

"Because sinful people choose to do evil. Can you tell me what God's will is for how people should live their lives on earth?"

That was an easy one. "Well, Jesus said there are two great commandments—to love God and to love your neighbor as yourself. So, I guess that's God's will for how humans should live their lives."

"You are much more to God than a mere human, Jackson. You are his adopted child, a prince in his kingdom, and greatly loved."

Jackson beamed.

"And how do you love God, Jackson?"

"By obeying his commandments and serving him with a joyful heart."

The guardian's eyes followed him as he walked around the gangplank. "And how do you love your neighbor?"

"By doing to others what you would have them do to you."

"Good. What else is God's will for people?"

"That they believe in Jesus Christ for the forgiveness of their sins." Jackson paced again. He needed to ask a few more questions—questions he'd always wondered about—before raising the subject of his sister's death. "Why does God allow evil to exist in the world?"

"Do you remember the parable of the wheat and the weeds?"

"The wheat represents the righteous people in the world, and the weeds represent the evil people in the world. They're allowed to grow in the field together."

"Yes. The roots of the wheat and the roots of the weeds are

intertwined. If God were to pull out the weeds, he'd pull out the wheat with it. Rather than do that, he allows the two to coexist until he accomplishes his will in each."

Jackson looked directly into his guardian's eyes. "Is that the only reason God allows evil in the world?"

"No, Jackson. If there were no evil in the world, circumstances would not force people to make moral choices. They would have no option but to do good. In other words, they would not have free will."

Jackson nodded. "Psalm 138:8 and Jeremiah 29:11 say that God has a plan for our lives. Does that mean he wants to take away our free will and direct our lives after all?"

"Those are the verses Chaplain Thompson gave you while you were in the marines, aren't they?"

He marveled at the guardian's ability to recall every minute detail of his life. "Yes. He wrote them on the inside cover of my Bible."

"God wants you to *choose* to do his will, so he can shower you with blessings and make you a partner with him in his work in a fallen world."

"How do we know what God's plan for our life is?"

"You have to go all in."

"What do you mean?"

"It is like in the game of poker when you bet all the chips you have. You must give your life to him fully. Then you will find out what his will is for your life. Then you will have great joy and hope for the future. What did Jesus say about this?"

"That we must lose our lives to find them," Jackson said.

"You are like a flower in God's garden. You exist to bring glory and pleasure to him, not to bring glory and pleasure to yourself. The gardener does not plant the flower so that it will self-actualize. This mindset should guide you if you wish to have a fulfilling life."

Mekoddishkem placed his hand on Jackson's shoulder. "Do what God calls you to do. Do not do what is safe or what your relatives, teachers, or friends tell you to do. Follow him. And don't be afraid to do something you don't feel gifted in if you believe God wants you to do it. Your life's work should come easily and be a joy, not a chore. Yet, even as you do God's will, you will have trouble in this world because people are sinful. The troubles you have in life shape you in areas that still need refining. Everything that happens in your life is ultimately for your good, from an eternal perspective, as you do God's will."

"Does God have a plan for evil people?" he asked.

The guardian angel removed his hand from Jackson's shoulder, then walked toward The Wall and pointed at it. "God is not willing that any should perish, but that all should come to repentance. He does not want anyone living apart from him. But for those who decide to turn and go their own way, their destiny will be eternal separation from God in hell. People make bad decisions, often without realizing it. Eventually, these bad decisions turn into bad habits, and these bad habits become so ingrained that they cause the person to turn away from God. You must consider every decision you make, no matter how big or small, to be sure you are making the right one."

"I thought no one could come to Jesus unless the Father draws them."

"That is correct. However, people can decide to ignore God's pleading and go their own way."

Jackson paused for a moment. "What is God's purpose for my life, Mekoddishkem?"

The guardian sighed. "Many professions are honorable. The apostle Peter was a fisherman, Paul was a tentmaker, and Luke was a doctor, but ultimately, God had other plans. You've made many choices that took you away from God's plan. To get back on track, you'll need to make many different choices."

What did that mean? He'd been striving to follow Jesus by reading his Bible, avoiding alcohol, and trying to stop staring at beautiful women. What else did God want him to do?

Mekoddishkem held his gaze. "What do you really want to ask me about, Jackson?"

"What do you mean?"

The personage came closer and looked deep into his eyes. "So far, you've asked me theology questions that you already know the answers to."

Jackson gulped. *He does know what I'm thinking.* "This will probably be my toughest question, and I mean no disrespect by it."

"Go ahead. I can handle your tough questions."

Jackson took a deep breath. "Why did God allow my sister to die in that car crash?"

Mekoddishkem stood, again towering over him. "Would you like to see her?"

Surprise overpowered him. Jackson went cross-eyed and fell backward.

# CHAPTER 9
# HER SPECIAL PLACE

WHEN JACKSON AWOKE, he was lying on his back on the gangplank. He looked around. *Where am I?* Mekoddishkem stood over him, mumbling what seemed like gibberish. *What is he saying?* "Your lips are moving, Mekoddishkem, but I can't process what you're saying."

His companion's lips pursed. "I will give you a moment. It must have been quite a shock to learn you could see your sister after all these years."

"Shock" was an understatement. There was some strange sizzling feeling on the top of his head. He couldn't think or focus.

The celestial being took him by the hand, pulled him up, and then placed his right hand atop Jackson's head.

Jackson involuntarily took in a deep breath. Warm, soothing energy penetrated his skull. "I feel much better now." He walked with his escort to the end of the gangplank, directly opposite The Wall. "So, can I observe the life of any person that ever lived, or ever will live?"

"Yes."

"How do I do that?"

"Just think of the portal you wish to access and then command The Wall to move it toward you."

He cocked his head. "Do you mean that I will move toward it or that it will move toward me?"

"It will move toward you."

He nodded. "It's interesting that The Wall moves toward me instead of the other way around. Does God come to us, or do we come to him?"

"Both. No one comes to Jesus unless God the Father reveals himself to that person. On the other hand, if you draw near to God, he will draw near to you. It is a relationship that God initiates."

Something came together in his head. "I can see now why God has to be holy and why he can only allow holy ones around him. Someone could use the knowledge gained through these portals for evil."

"That is true."

Turning to The Wall, he said, "Take me to the portal of my older sister, Susan Trotman."

The Wall whizzed by from left to right for a moment, then zipped straight upward for a few seconds and stopped. Jackson glanced at Mekoddishkem, then The Wall instantly snatched them into his sister's portal.

Jackson stood in a clearing in what appeared to be a lush ancient jungle. Mekoddishkem was by his side. Flowers of all different shapes, sizes, and colors abounded. Most of them were unfamiliar, but a white orchid caught his eye. Giant ferns and gangling vines hung off trees everywhere, both large and small, each displaying different hues of green.

He wiped his brow as he looked around, then smiled. The range and vividness of the colors were beyond anything he'd ever seen. Infinite varieties of insects hovered over the plants in the mist. There was no sun, only a bright light emanating from one side of the jungle.

He strolled along a worn dirt path toward a seven-foot-high

half-circle opening in the heavy brush. He stopped briefly, then followed his guide into a darkened hedge-enclosed tunnel, traveling down a slight decline. Jackson followed closely behind him, and his body tensed as they walked. Did creepy-crawly things live here, waiting to lunge out at them?

A soft blue light emanated from the end of the tunnel about twenty yards away, and a large pond gradually became visible. Jackson gasped as he exited the tunnel. An *Apatosaurus* grazed on the vegetation in the pond. He hesitated for a moment, but the guardian took him by the elbow and urged him to continue.

"What is this place? I thought I would see streets paved with gold, the twelve gates to the heavenly Jerusalem, and things like that. Not a jungle."

"Those things are all in heaven, Jackson, but we came to visit your sister. This jungle is her special place."

Jackson smiled. "God created this… for her?"

"Yes. Don't you remember how Susan loved dinosaurs?"

"That's right, she did. I'd forgotten." He inhaled deeply, then exhaled. "I guess that makes sense. She was only seven when she died, and this is what she would have wanted."

"Yes. Here comes Susan."

He swung around to find Susan coming out of the tunnel behind them. Her golden-brown hair, arranged in pigtails, shimmered in the light. She was in bare feet, wearing a white linen dress. He grinned as she walked toward them, but tears filled his eyes. He ran over and collapsed to his knees before her, opening his arms wide, but she walked straight through him.

"She does not know you are here."

Jackson wailed uncontrollably at the top of his lungs, then turned and watched through a flood of tears as she walked along the edge of the pond. "Why is she still a little girl? She died over twenty years ago. I thought she would be grown up by now."

"That will happen when God destroys the universe and creates a new heaven and a new earth, where he will dwell with men."

Jackson continued watching Susan as she walked away from them. Then, just ahead of her, a gigantic crocodile-like creature emerged from the pond. "Susan!"

She didn't respond.

He ran toward her. "Susan! Watch out!"

She walked right up to the crocodile, petted him on the snout, and then continued toward the *Apatosaurus*. She gave a loud whistle. The *Apatosaurus* turned in her direction, then came and bent down to her. They looked at each other face-to-face. Vegetation hung out of the dinosaur's mouth as he chewed. Susan reached out and placed both her hands around the animal's nose and hugged it.

He looked at the guardian and sighed. "I'm glad she's okay."

Mekoddishkem bent down, his eyes also filled with tears. "I remember that day, Jackson. I was right there with you. It was an accident. Your dad was driving too fast on that windy road, hit black ice, and slid into the oncoming dump truck. You can't blame God for everything bad that happens. Human beings are responsible too. Susan did not put her seat belt on like her parents told her to do, and she went flying head-on into the windshield. God does not stop every bad thing from happening.

"Yes, God could have intervened and somehow prevented her death, but it was not part of his plan to do so. It was part of his plan that you survive the accident so you could be here today. God knows that you have suffered greatly as a result of this loss. As you will see, God suffers greatly over the loss of his children as well. He is using this tragedy to refine you and test you. Ultimately, it is for your good. You can also use your experiences to comfort others with the same comfort you've received. She is fine and delighted to be here with her dinosaur friends."

"Does she stay here all the time?"

"No, there are people who take care of her when she is not here. Many children in heaven died before they were born or died at a young age, so they require guidance and education."

"I'm so glad you brought me here, Mekoddishkem, and I'm so glad she's okay. I'm ready to go now."

"Very well."

"Exit portal."

# CHAPTER 10

# 500 AD

JACKSON'S STOMACH FLIPPED like he was about to go on a roller coaster. "This is so exciting, Mekoddishkem. Can we visit other places now?"

"Of course."

"Can you show me... let's see... How about showing me my direct paternal ancestor in the year 500?"

"Of course, I can. But why did you choose that ancestor and that time?"

"Just a random thought, I guess. I want to test The Wall by making a request it could not have anticipated. I don't think it would make much difference if I said the year 500, 600, or 700."

"Are you sure it was a random thought?"

"Well, I think so." Jackson raised his eyebrows and looked up at his new friend. "Did God place that thought into my head, or did I think of it on my own?"

"It could be either, but it was your desire in this case. So, just give the command, and The Wall will move the correct portal to the end of the gangplank here."

Jackson faced The Wall. "Show me my ancestor, on my father's side, on an eventful day in the year 500."

The Wall shifted rapidly from left to right, whirling and humming as millions of portals zipped sideways in front of him. Then, The Wall veered rapidly downward, again making a whirring noise as the portals passed before him. Finally, The Wall stopped moving and presented a portal.

They stepped toward it and landed in a forest with substantial white oaks and maples towering over them. Chickadees chirped, and robins flicked up dead leaves nearby, looking for worms. The familiar *tat-tat-tat* of a woodpecker echoed in the distance. A bearded, toothless man with matted hair walked by in front of them. He was about five feet tall and hunched over slightly.

They followed him along a path to a shack made of crudely cut wood fastened together with wooden pegs and some twine, topped by a thatched roof of marsh grasses. The man approached a woman who was much younger and lovely in form but dirty and disheveled. With an infant strapped in a simple pouch on her back, she was hard at work threshing some grain she had just harvested. A boy of about fourteen walked toward them, carrying a sizeable skin-lined bowl filled with water.

"Where are we, Mekoddishkem?"

"We are near what in your time is called Aberdeen, Scotland. The boy is the man's son from a previous marriage. The woman is the man's second wife, and she's carrying their infant son. They are speaking Scots Gaelic."

The man placed his hand on his son's shoulder. "What took you so long, laddie?"

"Aye, 'twas the man from the other village, Papa," the boy answered.

"Mekoddishkem, I thought you said they were speaking Scots Gaelic? It sounds like they're speaking English."

"The Wall is enabling you to understand them, Jackson."

"The Wall has a built-in translator?"

"In a sense, yes."

The father's face clouded over. "What did he do, me boy?"

"He and his friends pushed me down and dumped out me water, Papa." The son then pantomimed how the man pushed him down.

The father scowled. "Aye, and why did they do that, laddie?"

"They like to hurt people. I think they are coming this way."

The father's eyes narrowed. He hurried into the shack and pulled out a sturdy metal-tipped spear. He gave the boy a crude hatchet and showed him how to use it. Finally, he handed his wife a hardwood stick with a pointed end and motioned how she should use it. The mother placed the sleeping baby in their home, then the three of them waited for the men to arrive. They stood side by side with their backs to the shack, the father standing in the middle.

A few moments later, a gang of three young men appeared at the edge of the woods. They moved forward and stopped about fifteen feet away, eyeing the family and their weapons.

The leader said, "Give us some food, old man." A few inches taller than the father, he had curly black hair down to his shoulders and pale white skin. "Aye, and after that, you can give us the woman."

The other men chuckled, then leered at her.

Without a word, the father hurled his spear at the leader. It passed right through the man's sternum and out his back. The ringleader toppled over on his side, dead. Snatching the hatchet from his son's hands, he rushed at the remaining men, but they turned and fled. The man placed his foot on the young man's chest, retrieved his spear, and then gathered his wife and son in his arms and led them back into the shack.

Jackson shook his head. "They lived in a rough world."

"Indeed."

Jackson paused for a moment. "What would have happened to me if that father had failed to defend his family?"

"That is an interesting question. Once again, you cannot change the past. The answer depends on the choices that the gang and the father would have made. The ancestor that was next in your line was the baby. If the father, son, and mother had been killed, the baby might have died unless it was taken in and raised by one of their neighbors. If the gang had been given food and left peacefully without attacking the mother, the baby would have lived, but the older son might not have learned how to survive and protect the family when the father died a few years later. Either way, it was God's will that the baby lived and that you be here today."

"There were so many choices made by so many generations over a fifteen-hundred-year period. How can it be that all these generations survived and led to my existence?"

"Consider the life of Moses. His Jewish ancestors had been slaves in Egypt for four hundred years. His mother nursed him and hid him, even though the Egyptians wanted all the Hebrew babies killed. She placed him in a basket on the Nile River, with only his sister to watch over him. A crocodile might have eaten him, or he might have starved to death or died from exposure, but God had his hand on him. Moses was raised in the pharaoh's household at just the right time so he could implement God's overarching plan for the Jewish people. Likewise, God has plans for every person. They may not be as grandiose as Moses's, but they are important, nonetheless. God takes the compilation of our choices into account yet accomplishes his will. God will bless you if you yield to his will rather than fight against it."

What had God's plan been for his life? Should he have gone to UConn and studied computer science? Should he have joined the Marines? Why hadn't he become a Christian earlier in life? Maybe God would have made him a pastor or a missionary if he hadn't made so many stupid choices.

Jackson was ready to leave. "Exit portal."

# CHAPTER 11
# 1755 AD

ONCE AGAIN, JACKSON and the guardian stood at the end of the gangplank, facing The Wall. Jackson didn't say anything for quite a while.

"Tell me what you are thinking," Mekoddishkem said.

He looked up at him. "Don't you already know what I'm thinking?"

"I want to hear you tell me. I want us to get to know each other better."

Jackson tried to put his thoughts into words. "It's mind-boggling to consider the number of variables involved in the accomplishment of God's will on earth when you allow for man's free will. It's an enormously complex intersection of events. How does he do it?"

"God's ways are not man's ways. You cannot fathom his understanding. He can do far more than you can imagine."

A tingling sensation flooded his body as the immensity of God's power humbled him. Jackson looked at The Wall. "Can we see another portal?"

"Of course. Which would you like to see?"

"Let's try visiting an ancestor on my mother's side. My mother said she had a forefather who fought with George Washington. Let's go see him."

"Very well. Would you like to see the ancestor who fought with him in the French and Indian War or the ancestor who fought with him in the American Revolutionary War?"

"I didn't know I had ancestors who fought in both wars with him. What do you suggest?"

"The French and Indian War. May I also suggest that you pick the date of July 9, 1755?"

"Why?"

"You will see."

Jackson addressed The Wall again, "Show me my maternal ancestor as he fought in the French and Indian War with George Washington on July 9, 1755."

Once again, The Wall whirled and hummed until the appropriate portal appeared, then it whisked them inside.

Jackson stood in the middle of a large grassy field facing a contingent of British soldiers. They were dressed in bright red uniforms and armed with muskets. Officers barked out orders, and men aligned themselves in formation. The sky was overcast, but the afternoon was quite warm. In the woods behind him, a large force of Native Americans was in position, maintaining good cover and concealment behind rocks and trees.

The opposing forces eyed each other. It had become eerily quiet as if the birds and animals knew something ominous was about to happen.

"Where are we, Mekoddishkem?" he whispered.

"In the woods near Fort Duquesne, which in your time is called Pittsburgh, Pennsylvania."

They were standing directly between thousands of British soldiers and Native American warriors who were about to fire at each other. "Shouldn't we move out of the way?"

Mekoddishkem pointed to the British formation. "George Washington is seated on the brown horse over there at the front, on the right. He was a twenty-three-year-old lieutenant colonel leading a contingent of Virginians attached to the British Army. There are fourteen hundred and fifty-nine British soldiers in the entire unit. Your ancestor is in the second row of troops behind George Washington."

How could he possibly know that? "Which one is he?"

"Let's walk over there."

They walked just to the left of George Washington, and Jackson gazed up at him. Young Washington sat atop his horse, his shoulders drawn back and hands steady at the reins. Even at his young age, he had a bearing that demanded respect. That strong countenance ensured the troops behind him would not lose heart. Who among them could have possibly known that this man would one day become the commander-in-chief of the Continental Army and the first president of the United States of America?

Mekoddishkem then led Jackson between the first and second rows of the formation and stopped directly in front of a young man of about twenty. The man stood at the order arms position, with the base of his musket resting on the ground by his right foot while he held the musket barrel with his right hand. The young man's hands were trembling, but his eyes were steady as he stood his post. The other soldiers in his row stood in the same position, although those in the front row knelt with their muskets at the ready, searching out targets in the woods. There, the Native Americans aimed at the British troops from their concealed positions.

"Where did the Native Americans get their guns?" he asked.

Mekoddishkem continued to watch the woods. "From the French."

"Why are the British standing in an open field while the Indians hide behind rocks and trees? That's hardly a good fighting tactic."

"The British were using European battle techniques they had learned from their ancestors. Those formations were better suited to an open battlefield—where the enemy employed a similar strategy—than to fighting an enemy in the woods. Look, the battle is about to begin."

Jackson and the guardian returned to the middle of the battlefield, directly between the two forces. Both sides stood there, looking at each other in silence, each waiting for the other to make the first move.

Gunfire erupted from the woods. Jackson gasped as two bullets ripped through his chest on their way to the British formation. Half a dozen British soldiers immediately collapsed after the barrage. Plumes of smoke enveloped the Native American's position. The British commander ordered the first row to return fire.

Deafening gunfire came from the British side, followed by a burst of smoke. Jackson winced as another bullet appeared to tear through his right thigh. The British rounds mostly hit the rocks and trees that the Native Americans hid behind. The first row of British soldiers calmly and methodically reloaded their weapons, as they must have done time and time again during training, while the second row fired into the woods. The second volley had little effect. The Native Americans fired at the British between volleys and remained hidden. Soon the entire battlefield was covered with a canopy of smoke. The pungent smell of gunpowder filled the air.

Jackson looked up at his fellow time traveler. "The British are being slaughtered. How many casualties were there?"

"After two hours, a thousand British infantrymen were killed or wounded while there were only thirty Native American casualties."

Jackson returned to his ancestor. The man had remained at his post. He didn't appear to be thinking about what he was doing, instead just firing and reloading, firing and reloading. "He's brave. Standing out in an open field while people are shooting at you takes guts. What's my ancestor thinking about right now?"

"Would you like to find out for yourself?"

"What do you mean?"

"You can enter the mind of the person and see what they see, feel what they feel, and think what they think. You see, God knows not only our actions but also our thoughts and motives. You cannot change anything, only observe."

"How do I initiate this?"

"Just overlap your body with his, and you will understand what he is sensing."

Jackson did as instructed. *Sweaty, dirty, and exhausted... so hot in his uniform. He's wincing, imagining what it would be like to have a round enter his left temple. He's trying to stay as low as he can while reloading. He can't wait until the officers give the order to retreat or charge. He doesn't care which. He only wants to get out of the middle of this stupid field. He's thirsty... He can't believe that Ian, one of the soldiers he went through training with, was killed. He thinks about being a boy again, playing at the beach in Virginia... He's wondering if he'll ever make it out of here. He keeps trying to hit a Native American who sticks his head out from behind a large rock on the left but keeps missing. Perhaps the sights on his musket are misaligned. He's going to try aiming a little higher and to the right next time. He wonders why the officers don't tell them to fix bayonets and charge; they're easy targets out in the open. He turns and sees... the corpse of one of his comrades with his brain matter exposed... a wounded soldier lying on his side in the fetal position, rocking back and forth, wailing for his mother.*

Jackson moved away from his ancestor's body and returned to his angelic guide. "That was intense. There's nothing scarier on earth than combat." He surveyed the field in front of him. "Look at all the carnage! This battle is ten times worse than what I saw in Afghanistan."

"Yes."

Jackson shivered, then looked away from the bodies. "So, God knows exactly how we feel and what we're going through in life?"

"God knows everything. He uses your life on earth as a training camp to test you and prepare you for your eternal life. But he also desires to work through you to accomplish his purposes on earth for others. The momentary suffering you experience on earth is nothing compared to the joy that awaits you."

Jackson examined the leader of the Virginians. "Look at George Washington. He's still sitting on that horse directing the battle. Where are all the other officers?"

"They've all been killed or wounded."

"But Washington doesn't have a scratch on him. How is that?"

"Let's go over to the Native American side of the battle and listen to what their chief has to say."

Jackson and Mekoddishkem walked across the field and into the woods. Bullets whizzed through the air, bark exploded, and branches fell from the trees all around them. They walked straight to a particular Native American.

"Men!" the chief shouted, probably in his native tongue. "Direct your fire at the man on the horse." He pointed at Washington.

The Native Americans all aimed their weapons at George Washington and fired, but none of their rounds hit the mark. Washington's horse was shot out from under him twice, and each time he mounted a fellow officer's horse and continued the battle. His enemies fired twelve or thirteen rounds each at him.

"Stop firing at him!" the chief finally ordered. "This one is under the protection of the Great Spirit."

Jackson looked at the guardian. "Did George Washington have a guardian angel protecting him?"

"Yes."

"Can I see him?"

"Yes."

Jackson's eyes widened as Washington's guardian angel was revealed, hovering in the air in front of him. Pearly white robes billowed out like a protective shield. As the firing subsided, Washington led the retreat of the remaining troops.

"Let's walk back with them to their camp," Mekoddishkem suggested.

The British camp was subdued. Washington, however, bustled about making sure the wounded were cared for and the able-bodied were fed. Then he retired to his tent. Washington took off his coat and draped it on a camp chair. Four ragged circles marred the front of his uniform jacket. The bullets had passed through his uniform but not reached his body.

Mekoddishkem pointed. "God intervened and divinely protected George Washington."

"Why does God directly intervene in the lives of some people, but not in the lives of others? Why were a thousand British infantrymen killed or wounded that day, but George Washington was able to leave the battlefield without a scratch?"

"Psalm 91:7 says, 'A thousand may fall at your side, ten thousand at your right hand, but it will not come near you.' God can have mercy on whomever he decides. Ultimately, he is sovereign. God had a special purpose for George Washington later in life, like Moses. He intervened to ensure he accomplished his purposes through the future president."

"Amazing! What should we do if we aren't special like George Washington?"

"George Washington was never taken to The Wall, Jackson."

He bit his lip. "I guess the safest place to be is following God's plan for your life, even if it is on a battlefield."

"Absolutely. God protected you while you were on the battle-field too."

Jackson gulped. "He did?"

"Yes. Let me show you."

# Chapter 12
# Semper Fi

JACKSON ENTERED HIS portal with Mekoddishkem. The guardian said, "Here you are in Helmand province, southern Afghanistan, out on patrol during the summer of 2008. You were a marine first lieutenant then stationed at Camp Dwyer."

Jackson stumbled backward. "Whoa! It sure is weird to see yourself walking around in 3D. Hey, there's Gunny Cooke! He's walking. I guess this was before he got shot. Can we get closer?"

"We will go up to the Taliban's position."

Jackson balked. "The Taliban's position?"

"Yes."

"I thought this terrain looked familiar. That's right, the machine gun nest is right up there on the hill, isn't it?"

"Yes."

They instantly moved to the nearby hill, standing directly in the middle of the Taliban's machine gun emplacement. The terrain was dry, dusty, and rocky, just as he had remembered. Three machine-gun teams and one .50-caliber team were in position, each stationed about ten yards apart.

His gut wrenched as he watched his team, some two hundred

yards in the distance, walking straight into the kill zone. "Isn't there anything we can do to stop this?"

"No, Jackson, there's nothing we can do. We cannot change the past."

"That can't be! We've got to stop this! My gunny is about to get his leg shot off."

The Taliban commander shouted, "Kill their commander first!"

"They were aiming at me?"

"Yes."

The .50-caliber team fired first. The round impacted the boulder beside Jackson.

"Did you block that bullet?"

"No, but I was right there with you. The fifty-caliber operator was just a bad shot."

"Why did I have a guardian angel if I wasn't a believer yet?"

"Because God knew you would become a believer."

Jackson shook his head. "I'll have to think about that. Why was Gunny Cooke later shot?"

"God had a different plan for him."

"I thought you said you blocked bullets for me."

"I did. That happens a little later. Here come the 155 howitzer rounds you ordered."

The ground beneath Jackson shook as the first round struck some fifty meters to his right. A moment later, multiple rounds came straight at him. The rounds impacted and exploded precisely where he was standing, sounding like a dumpster had been dropped from fifty feet in the air next to his head.

He yelled and jumped as each round pulverized the ground beneath him, sending dirt, dust, rocks, sticks, and body parts spewing in all directions, including right through him. It was as if he were standing in the middle of a tornado.

As the dust cleared, Jackson turned to his guide. "That was intense."

Many of the Taliban soldiers got up and began running out of their holes. One man, who had lost an arm, toppled over. Jackson's patrol cut down several fleeing soldiers with small arms fire. Jackson and the guardian positioned themselves directly behind the one Taliban team that had remained at their post. Blood dripped from the ear of the soldier operating the .50 caliber.

"Those were some tough fighters, staying at their post after a fusillade like that." A few moments later, someone ran across the open terrain directly in front of them. "Was that me?"

"Yes."

He looked over the shoulder of the Taliban fighter as the man fired. "Looks like he had a perfect bead on me. Is this where you were protecting me?"

"Yes."

"Show me, please."

"Of course."

Jackson zoomed right next to a 2008 version of himself. Mekoddishkem floated between him and the machine gun emplacement in slow motion. Round after round fell harmlessly to the ground next to the younger Jackson as he ran, while others impacted the ground nearby.

"I had no idea, Mekoddishkem. Thank you."

"It wasn't your appointed time."

Jackson took a deep breath and looked around. "Don't we each have a set number of days to live here on earth?"

"Yes."

"But what if someone murders us? Or what if we do something stupid like walk in front of a bus, overdose on drugs, smoke two packs of unfiltered cigarettes a day for thirty years, become an alcoholic, or something else like that? Can't we cut our lives short by our own bad choices?"

"Yes."

"I don't get it. How can both be true?"

"There is a complex intersection between God's will for your life and your will for your life. God does not force his will on you. You must choose to yield to it."

Jackson sighed. "This is astonishing, Mekoddishkem. Where does prayer fit into this equation? Do prayers protect people on the battlefield?"

"Absolutely."

Jackson looked down and shook his head. "Was someone praying for me?"

"Yes."

Jackson perked up. "Who?"

"Your mother."

Jackson fought through a lump in his throat. "Wow. I'll have to thank her someday."

"Someone else was praying for you too—that you would become a believer."

Jackson smiled. "I bet it was that navy chaplain, right? Oh, wait, I didn't meet him until later."

"Correct. There was one other."

"Who?"

Mekoddishkem crossed his arms over his chest. "Let us go to Amsterdam, right after your first tour."

His stomach sank. Not Amsterdam. That was the last place he wanted to go with his guardian angel.

༄

When they arrived, Jackson slumped to his knees. A 2008 version of himself stood outside a brothel in Amsterdam, gawking at a prostitute seated in the window display. She was wearing pink lingerie and was urging him to come in. His younger self walked down the dank alley to the entrance. Across the alley, he read a sign above a door that said *Christian Missionary Center*. Displayed in the bay window, to the right of the door, was another sign: *Do you not know that your bodies are members of Christ himself? Shall I then take the members of Christ and unite them with a prostitute? Never!*

Jackson shook his head. "I can't believe I did that. What can I say?"

"There's not much you can say, Jackson."

"There are no secret sins, are there?"

"No. Everything is in full view of the Lord."

"God was trying to reach me even then, wasn't he?"

"The Holy Spirit was using this passage to reach you, and someone was praying for you."

"Who?"

They passed seamlessly through the front façade of the Christian Missionary Center. Inside, a gray-haired gentleman straightened some papers on an old wooden desk with a dark lacquer finish. He turned off the desk lamp, looked up, and saw the young Jackson reading the 1 Corinthians passage in the window. "Father in heaven, please rescue this young man from his sinful, youthful lusts and draw him to yourself. In Jesus's name, I pray, amen."

"What a godly man. He didn't even know me. Did it make any difference?"

"Yes. The prayer of a righteous person is powerful and effective."

Jackson pursed his lips. "What led me to do this in the first place?"

"You chose to. Although you were drunk and had been overseas for a year, your lust drove you, and you didn't care about the consequences. Your only desire was to follow the thoughts and cravings of your sinful nature. Let's go back to when you were a boy to see how you got to this point."

❦

The Wall transported them to a boy's bedroom. His friend Gary and a twelve-year-old version of himself were searching for something under a bed. Gary retrieved a magazine, put it on the bed, and showed Jackson the pictures of naked women.

Gary smiled while the young Jackson gaped in wonder as they turned the pages.

A moment later, Gary's older brother, Eddie, walked in. "Hey, that's mine. Give it to me." He grabbed the magazine and pushed Gary to the floor. "Leave my stuff alone!"

Jackson snarled at him. "St-st-st-stop."

"N-n-nooo," Eddie said and shoved Jackson to the floor. "What are you, stupid or something? How come you talk like a dummy?"

The younger Jackson began to cry.

Eddie laughed. "Oh, the poor little Jacky. Need to go home to your mommy?" He kicked Jackson in the side and stormed out of the room.

Mekoddishkem paused, then said, "Eddie and some of the other kids in school were very cruel to you because of your stuttering."

Tears formed in Jackson's eyes.

"But you overcame it and are stronger now for it."

He bit his lip and nodded his head, then took in a deep breath. "Yes, I had to go to a lot of speech therapy classes when I was younger. They helped a lot. I feel bad for the people who aren't able to overcome it."

"They're in good company. Moses was slow of speech and tongue too." Mekoddishkem swept his hand at the magazine that now lay on the dresser. "You should not urge or awaken love before its time."

He frowned. "Agreed. I'd forgotten about that." He had seen enough. "Exit portal."

# CHAPTER 13
# HIDDEN MOTIVES

BACK AT THE Wall, Jackson faced Mekoddishkem. "Did you protect me when the enemy mortar killed Staff Sergeant Clark and when the IED exploded right in front of my Humvee?"

"Yes. And many other times."

"Thank you. God allowed me to be wounded on the battlefield so I could be here today?"

"Yes."

"I was responsible for killing a lot of people while I was in the marines. I didn't overthink it at the time. It's different now after watching them die during that artillery barrage. They weren't just targets in a video game. They were someone's son, or brother, or father."

Mekoddishkem put his hands on Jackson's shoulders and looked into his eyes. "You were defending your country and protecting the men in your patrol. Suppose you hadn't ordered that artillery attack, many other marines in your patrol would have been killed or injured. God has ordained the state with the right to protect its citizens, and individuals with the right to protect themselves, which is what you were doing."

"But one of the Ten Commandments is not to kill."

"The sixth commandment is that you shall not murder."

"What's the difference?"

"What you did was kill armed enemy combatants on the battlefield during a time of war. You were trying to kill them, and they were trying to kill you. You have the right to defend yourself, your comrades, friends, family, and country when under attack. Your service was honorable. I will show you what murder is. Ask to be taken to the portal of Jaime Thurston."

What? "You mean, Pam Shuster's administrative assistant?"

"Yes. On the day you were instrumental in saving Pam's life."

He swallowed hard. What was Mekoddishkem implying? "Take me to the portal of Jaime Thurston on the day I helped save Pam's life."

He and the guardian arrived at the office as Pam spoke to Jaime. "There's no way I'm going to make it to the cafeteria again today. I've just got too many meetings. Do me a favor and get me a cup of coffee."

"Will do," Jaime said.

They followed Jaime as she walked to the cafeteria. She flipped mink-colored bangs from her face and mumbled, "It would be my pleasure to get her ladyship's coffee again. I'm so sick of this. She treats me like garbage all the time. I can't believe the word she used at my annual review last week—adequate. Adequate? I work my tail off for her but no raise or bonus this year. Really? What a wench. I'm sure I'm the only AA at Aetna who has to get her boss coffee. Well, I won't have to put up with her much longer."

Jackson looked up at his counselor. "I had no idea she was that angry."

They followed Jaime through the coffee line and to the condiments counter to add cream. While she was there, she crushed some pills into Pam's coffee cup.

"What are those pills?"

"Midodrine. They help people who experience low blood pressure while standing. Jaime stole them from her aunt's medicine cabinet."

"Why?"

"Pam has heart disease and high blood pressure. Jaime is hoping they'll kill her."

"Kill her? How could she do such a thing?"

They followed Jaime back to Pam's office where Jaime placed the coffee on her desk. Pam didn't acknowledge the action or even say thank you. Jaime smiled, turned, and then gritted her teeth as she walked back to her desk.

An hour later, Jaime came back into the office. Pam was lying on the couch and looked up. "Do you have any Tums or ibuprofen?"

By the time Jaime returned with a bottle of ibuprofen, Pam had collapsed in front of her desk. Jaime set the timer on her pink phone for four minutes and returned to her cubicle.

Jackson shuddered. "Why four minutes?"

"She read in a magazine that four minutes is the maximum time the brain can survive without oxygen."

"I can't believe she's just letting her die."

Jaime's phone vibrated. She walked into Pam's office, managed to conjure up some tears, and screamed, "Help! Quick! Someone, call nine-one-one."

Jackson jumped as a pre-accident version of himself ran into the room and began performing CPR on Pam. Jaime moved slowly to Pam's desk, looked around, and then took the empty coffee cup and slipped out of the office.

Jackson shook his head. "I had no idea."

"Things are not always as they appear, Jackson."

With a heavy heart, he said, "Exit portal."

Jackson and Mekoddishkem returned to the gangplank. Jackson ran a hand through his hair. "Are there any other little secrets I should know about?"

"Well, since you asked, there is another. It involves your earthly father."

Why had he asked? He couldn't take many more shocking revelations. "Well, what is it?"

"Ask The Wall to take you to your father's portal five days ago at two in the afternoon."

Jackson did as advised. The Wall took them to the front of a twelve-story building with a white facade. "I know this place. We're in Toledo, my hometown. That's the Grand Plaza Hotel over there."

"Correct," the guardian said. "Let us go inside."

They entered the hotel and stood in the lobby. Jackson's father soon strolled in the front door and walked straight into the elevator.

Mekoddishkem nodded at him. "Let's follow him."

Jackson snarled. "I don't think I'm going to like this."

He stood next to his father on the elevator. His gut wrenched as he looked at him. Fifty-seven years old, about five feet eight inches and one hundred and seventy pounds, salt-and-pepper hair parted in the middle. He wore a white shirt, red bowtie, light blue seersucker suit, and his trademark Spiaggia white wingtips with burnt-red rubber soles. His dad's hands were in his pockets as he chewed gum feverishly.

Jackson clenched his fists. "Dad! What are you doing?"

His father didn't flinch.

They got off the elevator and followed him down the hallway to room 517. His father knocked on the door, and an attractive young woman answered. She wore a lacey white translucent negligé.

Jackson gasped as his hands flew to his head. "Traitor! How could you do such a thing?" He turned away and shook his head. "I've seen enough. Exit portal."

They returned to the gangplank.

"I can't believe he could do this to my mother and our family."

"Adultery is a horrible thing," Mekoddishkem said.

Jackson hung his head. "How long has this been going on?"

"Since your mother was diagnosed with breast cancer two years ago."

"Some father." Jackson sighed. "Well, I'll deal with him when I get back. Does my mother know?"

"Yes. A friend of hers told her."

Jackson folded his arms. "I'm wondering if I shouldn't know about all this private stuff."

The holy being held his gaze. "You should never be afraid of the truth. One other thing, Jackson. Your boss, Fred, is also engaging in adultery."

Jackson cringed. "He is? I've met his wife. Who with?"

"Jaime Thurston."

He arched upward. "What?"

"Yes. Pam threatened to expose them."

"That must have been another reason Jaime tried to kill Pam. Maybe ignorance is bliss." Jackson scratched his head. "What should we do now?"

"That is up to you."

# CHAPTER 14
# THE PRESENT

JACKSON TOOK A deep breath. "Well, we've been focusing on the past so far. How about seeing something in the present?"

"Very well."

"Is entering a portal during the present pretty much the same as entering a portal during the past?"

"No. It is very different. I think you will find it to be quite frightening."

Jackson cocked his head. "Why?"

"We will be entering another dimension. You will be able to see things you were not able to see before."

"Like what?"

"You will find out."

Jackson placed his hands on his hips. "Is there anything I need to do to prepare?"

"No. Just stay next to me."

So, where did he want to go? An idea came to him. "What about the person who hit me with the car? Let's see what he's up to."

The guardian walked toward The Wall. "Very well. His name is

Jeremy Brown of Farmington, Connecticut. Just specify 'present day' when making your command."

He turned to The Wall, then stopped and looked back. "Mekoddishkem, what is the present?"

"That is an insightful question. From your perspective, the present is that time in your universe that is right now. From God's perspective, the past, present, and future are all right now."

"How can that be?"

"Consider The Wall. At any time, you can enter a portal and be in the past, in the present, or the future. The Wall is a representation of God's incredible ability to see and know all things, past, present, and future."

Jackson returned to facing The Wall. "I wish to see Jeremy Brown of Farmington, Connecticut, in the present."

Once again, The Wall whizzed to a portal, then swept them in. They sat in the back seat of a car. Jeremy was driving frantically through West Hartford, racing through the Bishops Corner section of town on Route 44. Then he began climbing Avon Mountain.

As they passed the entrance to Reservoir 6, a West Hartford Police cruiser sat parked by the side of the road. Soon, a siren was blaring behind them. Jackson glanced at the dashboard: seventy miles per hour in a forty-mile-per-hour zone. He then turned and looked out the back window. The cruiser was in pursuit with its lights flashing.

The car engine roared as Jeremy increased speed. They reached the crest of the mountain, then began descending its backside into Avon. The grade was steep, between ten and fifteen percent, and the police cruiser was now directly behind Jeremy's car.

Jeremy trembled and hyperventilated as he drove. He took his hands off the wheel, one at a time, and wiped his face with the front of his shirt, then cursed.

"He is distraught because his mother just died in the hospital where you were visiting Pam," Mekoddishkem explained. "He hit you while racing out of the parking garage. He doesn't want to take responsibility for what he did."

"What time is it? Has time normally passed since we left the hospital parking garage?"

"Of course. Time stops for no one in this world. It's about six thirty in the evening."

"I saw a *Star Trek* television episode where time moved very slowly in one dimension but very quickly in another. Is that the case here?"

"Such things are not for you to know, Jackson."

He glanced back at the police cruiser chasing them again. "What's going to happen next?"

"You will see."

"He hit me with a car and left me to die. That's a terrible thing to do to another person."

"It is. How does that make you feel?"

"Angry, I guess. But I've done terrible things too."

"You have."

"And if I want God to forgive the things that I've done wrong, I need to forgive those who've done wrong to me. Correct?"

"Correct."

"Well, it was an accident. I don't wish Jeremy any ill will. So, I forgive him."

"It is good that you have forgiven him."

"I wouldn't be here right now, with you, if he hadn't hit me, so God used this awful accident for my good."

"Yes, he did."

Jeremy weaved around several cars traveling in front of him. The cruiser followed close behind. The traffic light at the foot of the mountain was red.

Jeremy cursed. "What do I do now?" He looked in his rear-view mirror.

Each entrance to the four-way intersection had three lanes, with the left-most lane reserved for cars turning left. Jeremy maneuvered at high speed around the three lanes of traffic backed up in front of him. As he turned to get back onto the westbound lane, his tires screeched, and the car began to fishtail, becoming perpendicular to the traffic he'd just passed. A tractor trailer approached from the right and honked. Jeremy screamed as he spun the wheel, but it was too late.

Jeremy's scream was cut short. The car's front end collapsed as if it were in a vise, enveloping Jeremy and crushing him, sending blood everywhere. The car's rear end became airborne and rolled over sideways again and again toward the oncoming traffic that had stopped for the red light. Jackson and Mekoddishkem got out of the car once it stopped rolling, passing seamlessly through the mangled mass of metal. Jackson rushed back to the car but there was nothing he could do. Jeremy's body was disfigured beyond recognition.

Traffic halted in all directions. The police cruiser came to a stop in the middle of the intersection. The officer got out and ran over to Jeremy's car. The officer picked up his shoulder-mounted handset. "Dispatch, this is Unit Twenty-three, over."

A response crackled over the officer's handset. "Unit Twenty-three, this is Dispatch, over."

"Dispatch, we need an ambulance and an extrication at the intersection of Route 44 and Route 10 at the foot of Avon Mountain."

"Roger that, Unit Twenty-three. An ambulance and the fire department will be en route shortly."

"Better send out the supervisor too. Out." The officer walked over to the wreckage and shook his head. "What a waste."

# CHAPTER 15

# CONSEQUENCES

JACKSON SURVEYED THE wreckage of Jeremy's car. Skid marks lined the nearby pavement, and the smell of burned rubber and gasoline filled the air as sirens blared in the distance.

The ambulance arrived first, followed by the police and fire department units. The police directed traffic while the firemen applied the Jaws of Life to extricate Jeremy's body from the vehicle. After they pried the steel apart, one of the policemen standing nearby walked away and vomited.

Jackson stared at the heaving man. "Mekoddishkem, I know that police officer. It's Mike Tolbert. He's a good friend who's been discipling me for the past year. He goes to my church."

"I know. Tell Mike that his wife is pregnant with twin girls."

"Really?"

The heavenly being gave Jackson a curious look.

"Cool."

The police supervisor arrived and shouted orders to his team.

"What happens now to the spirit of Jeremy?"

"You will see in just a moment."

Two creatures flew in from the east and descended upon the

wreckage as Mekoddishkem spoke. They were about seven feet tall, emaciated, and clothed in filthy, tattered black rags—a sharp contrast to the lightning-white linen Mekoddishkem wore.

Jackson grasped the guardian's arm tightly. "What are they? Can they see us?"

"They are demons. They serve their father, Satan. They cannot see us. You do not have to be afraid of them, as long as you stay close to me."

One of the demons bent down, placed his hand on Jeremy's battered head, and retrieved his spirit from his corpse. A look of horror came over Jeremy's spirit face as each demon grabbed one of his arms. "Help! Someone, help me!" he screamed. "Get your hands off me, you freak!"

But no one was there to help. He twisted and turned, trying to free himself from their grip, but the demons held fast. One on each side of him, they rose and flew eastward.

"The poor kid."

"Did Jeremy ever accept Jesus as his Savior?"

"No, he did not."

"Since Jesus said that no man comes to the Father except by him, does that mean he will be going to hell?"

"Yes."

"But I forgive him for what he did to me. It was an accident. Is there anything we can do to stop it?"

"No, Jackson. It is too late."

Jackson stared at the wreck in front of him. "Did God preordain that Jeremy goes to hell?"

"God is not willing that any should perish, but that all should come to repentance. People have free will to choose their destiny. They can choose to follow God's way or their own way. Many people will be shocked when they come to the end of their lives and find that God will not accept them into heaven."

Jackson gestured with his head.

"Would you like to follow them?"

Jackson recoiled. "To hell? Oh, I don't know."

"You're afraid—and you should be. Touch my robe."

The guardian whisked Jackson several hundred feet into the air. They followed the demons and Jeremy, staying about twenty yards behind them. Jeremy continued to struggle, flailing his body back and forth like a fish in the talons of an eagle.

As the sun set behind them, they quickly traversed eastern Connecticut, then flew over Rhode Island. Soon, they could see Cape Cod. A moment later, they were over the open Atlantic Ocean. The air whipped through Jackson's hair and flapped his clothes at a furious rate, but for some reason, he didn't feel cold. He must have been insulated from the temperature while traveling. After all, space would be a lot colder than this. The sky darkened as they rapidly crossed the time zones.

Fortunately, the night sky was clear, illuminated by a plethora of stars and a full moon. Still, he had to strain to see Jeremy and the demons ahead of him. The night lights sparkled innocently off the rippling ocean waters below, oblivious to the dreadful mission unfolding above them.

"Where exactly is the entrance to hell, Mekoddishkem?" he asked.

"It is not for you to know the exact location. However, you will see for yourself soon enough."

They passed over a large landmass, then over another large body of water. Finally, Jackson and Mekoddishkem came to a mountain in the middle of the high desert somewhere in the Middle East, and at the top of it was a cave opening that was only accessible by air.

As they approached, many other pairs of demons arrived from all different directions, clutching wide-eyed souls between them. Mekoddishkem and Jackson entered the cave with the rest of the spirits. Jackson looked around at the demonic horde. Did they know he was watching them?

"They can't see you, Jackson."

He let out a huge sigh. The cave was dry and dark at first, gradually becoming damper. After about a hundred yards, they came to a solid rock wall. They passed through the rock for about ten yards and came out into an enormous cavern. It was brutally hot and filled with smoke, and pitch black except for a red, glowing Abyss, the opening to which was about fifty yards in diameter.

Thousands of naked people stood nearby in lines. Many were wailing and screaming. At the edge of the Abyss, other demons periodically cast departed souls from the head of the line into it.

"Mekoddishkem, the stench in this place is horrible. It smells like rotting garbage."

"It is rotting flesh."

His stomach turned, and he looked away. "There isn't much air in here either. I feel so weak. I can hardly breathe."

The guardian then said, "Let us go down into the Abyss."

Jackson stared at him. He couldn't be serious. "I'm not going down there!"

"I understand your fear, but I must urge you to go. You must see and understand these things."

Jackson shook his head.

"Touch my hand." His companion held out a brightly shining hand. When Jackson touched it, the fear left him. "Now, will you go?"

Jackson shuffled slowly to the side of the Abyss and peered over the edge. It seemed to go down forever. His stomach dipped as he looked down. Far below them sat a red glowing lake of lava at the bottom.

Mekoddishkem jumped, with Jackson in tow, as if they were leaping out of an airplane on a parachute jump. The deeper they went, the hotter it became. Cavernous openings dotted the sides of the Abyss all the way down. Most of them were about nine feet high and six feet wide, and each had a demon standing in the entrance. Spiritual bodies of the damned fell past the demons, who seemed to examine each one as they went by. Periodically, a demon would reach out, grab a soul, and pull them into its cave.

The guardian stopped their descent, and both of them remained suspended in the air. The cacophony of moaning and groaning was deafening. Jackson had to shout to be heard. "Where are these souls going?"

"To a place of torment, to be held for the great white throne judgment."

"How is it determined where each soul will reside in hell?"

"The greater the sins they committed in life, the lower they will go into the Abyss, and the greater their suffering will be."

Jackson looked around. "Has Jeremy fallen into the Abyss yet?"

"Not yet. The authorities need to decide which level to put Jeremy on. Then they will place a mark on his forehead and throw him down."

"Why did God make hell?"

"He had to make a place for those who refuse to repent of their sins and want nothing to do with him."

"Why must they suffer the penalty of their sins? Why can't God just forgive them all?"

"Because God is just. God must punish sin because it is an affront to him, a holy God."

"Did the people here believe there was a hell when they were living?"

"Some did, and some did not. They all do now."

Jackson whirled around, gawking with horror at all the different openings in the Abyss and the demons guarding them.

"Here comes Jeremy," Mekoddishkem said.

Jackson looked up. Jeremy was falling toward them, screaming. He passed them, sinking deeper and deeper into the Abyss.

Jackson felt sick. "I think I'm going to throw up." He turned to one side, overwhelmed by gut-wrenching dry heaves. When they stopped, he said, "It feels like someone poured acid into my stomach." He wiped his mouth with his forearm. "Where will he end up?"

"Let us go see."

They shoved off downward, trailing Jeremy as he continued his free fall farther and farther into the Abyss. "Is there anything we can do to help him?" Jackson asked.

"No. It is too late."

Jackson felt the superheated air deflecting off them as if he was driving through the Afghan desert with the top down when it was one hundred and twenty degrees outside. "I was hoping he would have stopped falling by now." He grabbed the guardian's arm. "This just doesn't seem fair. He was only a kid."

"Jeremy had several opportunities to accept God's forgiveness, but he refused. He knew what he was doing."

It still didn't seem right. "What about infants and small children or the mentally disabled who are not able to understand the gospel? Are they still considered sinful?"

"What does it say in 2 Samuel 12 when King David's first child with Bathsheba died?"

"I don't recall."

"King David said he would go to him one day."

"So, David thought that he would be with his son in heaven one day. At what age does a human being become accountable?"

"What does the Bible say about that?"

"I can't think of anything. According to Jewish custom, the age of accountability is thirteen."

"Correct. The Bible does not specify an age of accountability. It is different for everyone. God is just. He will judge each person fairly, regardless of their age. In the case of Jeremy, he is accountable."

"What about people who've never heard the gospel? How can they be held accountable?"

"What do the first and second chapters of Romans say?"

"That the existence of God is obvious from the creation."

"He will judge people fairly based on their faith in him and their obedience to their consciences."

A demon grabbed Jeremy and pulled him into an opening in the wall far below them.

Mekoddishkem stopped their descent. "Let us go in after him."

"No!"

"Did I not tell you that they cannot see you? There is nothing for you to fear as long as you stay close to me."

Jackson squared his shoulders and took a deep breath. Then he went with Mekoddishkem and followed the demon and Jeremy into the hole in the wall. Inside, he struggled to breathe. "This heat is unbearable. It's much worse than Afghanistan."

Jackson and his guide stopped just in time to see another demon take Jeremy and throw him into an antechamber that contained a pond of molten lava. Thousands upon thousands of souls were already in the pond, weeping and gnashing their teeth. Another enormous demon picked Jeremy up from the chamber floor and threw him into the pond. He screamed in horror as his spiritual flesh burned but was not consumed.

Jackson turned away, sickened once more. He leaned against the entrance to a hallway carved into the rock until his stomach calmed down. Then, curiosity got the better of him. He stepped inside. The hallway was lined with individual prison cells as far as he could see. Jackson glanced over his shoulder. Mekoddishkem was standing next to him. "Who is being kept in these dungeons?"

"Former angels who sinned. They're in chains, held for judgment."

Jackson leaned over and peered through the ancient bars of one of the cells. A huge angel was seated on the floor, leaning against the back wall. His arms and legs were shackled, and his head slumped downward. Long, stringy, dirty hair covered his face. Jackson stared at him for a moment. Suddenly, the fallen angel's head lurched upward, and he let out a piercing wail.

Jackson shuddered and staggered backward. "Let's get out of here."

"Very well, Jackson."

"Is the suffering this bad for everyone in hell?"

"Some are punished less severely. Many are left alone in cells to think about what they did in life and what might have been. Others, like Jeremy, are tortured for a time, then put in cells."

"Like the parable of the rich man and Lazarus?"

"Tell me more."

"In life, Lazarus, impoverished and covered with sores, was laid by the entrance to the rich man's house, but the rich man did not pity or help him. When they died, the rich man went to hell, but Lazarus went to be with Father Abraham in paradise. The rich man asked Father Abraham to let Lazarus dip the tip of his finger in water and touch his tongue because he was in agony in the fire."

"Precisely."

They left the antechamber and went back out into the center shaft of the Abyss. A slow, unending stream of spiritual bodies fell down from above. Tears dribbled down his face. "Why? Why would God allow a place like this to exist?"

Mekoddishkem looked around. "Hell is a place devoid of his protection and character. There is no mercy, no love, no justice, and no compassion in hell. Nothing good exists here. It is the consequence of people choosing to reject God's offer of forgiveness and to follow their own way."

"I can understand Hitler or Stalin or Jeffrey Dahmer being here, but not Jeremy. He's just a kid who had a tough life."

"God is just," said the guardian. "He gave Jeremy many opportunities to repent and turn to him, but Jeremy allowed bitterness in his life to overtake him. Most people have a full life span to repent and turn to God, but you never know when your time on earth will be up. So, you must be sure you are right with God before it is too late. By the way, Hitler and Stalin are here, but Jeffrey Dahmer is not."

"What? He murdered, mutilated, and cannibalized many young men and boys."

"Seventeen to be exact. But while in prison, he recognized that he was a sinner, asked God for forgiveness, accepted Jesus Christ as his Savior, and was baptized."

"Are you kidding me? Was it genuine, or was he just trying to con everyone, as he had done so many times before?"

"Only God knows a person's heart, Jackson. Some people can fool everyone on earth about conversion, but no one can fool God. Regardless of what people do in life, God is willing and waiting to forgive. They may still suffer the natural consequences of their sins, such as spending the rest of their life in prison for crimes committed while on earth, but God wipes away the eternal penalty of their sin."

Jackson nodded slowly. "Moses and David were murderers, and the apostle Paul was an accessory to the murder of Stephen. They didn't end up in hell. So, I guess God can forgive anyone, regardless of what they've done."

"That is correct."

"Thank you for showing me this, Mekoddishkem. I've read about hell in the Bible. I knew it was bad, but I didn't realize it was this bad." He took one last look around. "Did I learn everything I was supposed to?"

"Yes. We can leave now."

"Good. Let's get out of here. Exit portal."

# CHAPTER 16
# SOUL MATE

JACKSON STARED AT the endless expanse of The Wall and the universe displayed behind it, his mind reeling. His body must be lying somewhere in the hospital, lifeless. "Mekoddishkem, why does God allow people to die?"

"It was not God's original plan that people should die. He designed Adam and Eve to live forever, but they sinned by eating from the Tree of the Knowledge of Good and Evil. God warned them that they would die if they ate from it, but they ate anyway. Their descendants all suffer death because of that choice.

"But you are not merely a product of your ancestors, Jackson. God placed you in a certain time, in a certain place, with certain parents and certain physical, mental, and emotional characteristics and gifts so that you might seek him. The training camp you are in, called life, is specifically designed for you, and God has given you an important role to play in it if you choose to do so. Therefore, you are accountable for all of your choices and actions."

Jackson nodded at his guardian's statement. "And we, in turn, can affect our offspring by our actions."

"Absolutely. The evil you do may pass down three or four

generations. On the other hand, the good you do can pass down to a thousand generations."

"I remember reading a study comparing the accomplishments and character of fourteen hundred descendants of Jonathan Edwards, the eighteenth-century pastor and theologian, with twelve hundred descendants of a notorious prisoner named Max Jukes of the same era. The study found that the prisoner left a legacy of about three hundred paupers, fifty women of ill repute, seven murderers, sixty thieves, and one hundred and thirty other convicted criminals. The Edwards legacy produced thirteen college presidents, sixty-five professors, numerous clergymen, and many other people of distinguished character and accomplishment." He laughed. "How in the world did I remember all that?"

"Your mind is unencumbered by sinful thoughts right now, Jackson."

"Nice. You know, in a way, the concept of original sin is irrelevant because we've all added on to the original sin by our own free will."

"Yes. All have sinned and fallen short of the glory of God."

But since God had forgiven him, he could look forward to his future. "Mekoddishkem, will I ever get married?"

He smiled. "I was wondering when you were going to ask about the future. Yes, you will get married."

"Will I have children?"

"Yes, but the number depends on many choices."

"What choices—and made by whom?"

"Let me show you." The angel walked to the end of the gangplank. There, he swiveled to face Jackson. "Ask to see your wife on the last day of her life."

Jackson bristled. "What? You've got to be kidding me."

"No."

Was the guardian seriously asking him to peer in at someone whom he probably hadn't met yet—but would fall in love with and marry—and then watch her die right before his eyes? "Why would you ask me to do such a thing?"

"You will see, Jackson. Remember that God loves you, and he loves your wife, and he wants what is best for both of you."

He shook his head as he walked toward the edge of the gangplank. "Show me my future wife on the day of her death." Then, out of the side of his mouth, he muttered, "I can't believe I'm doing this."

Once again, The Wall zoomed to the appropriate position and pulled Jackson and Mekoddishkem into the portal of his future wife.

He stood amid a wedding reception at a hotel. He surveyed the scene, taking in the golden chandeliers, shining mirrors, Oriental rugs, and lavish ice sculptures. A long table covered with crisp white table linens held an enormous shrimp plate piled high over crushed ice. A middle-aged man wearing a white coat and chef's hat carved roast beef for the guests standing in line.

Jackson strolled around the room with his guide, invisible to the wedding guests. He focused on the stunning bride. Midtwenties, five feet six inches, athletic, pale complexion with brunette hair swept upward into a Hepburnesque bun. Her laughing brown eyes surveyed the audience, relishing the attention rendered her. Warmth flooded in. Of course it would be her.

"McKenzie Baker? I've loved her ever since the day I met her. But I haven't seen her in years. She looks even more beautiful than I remember her."

They'd met seven years ago on a comfortable summer evening at the Spring House Hotel on Block Island. McKenzie had stood at the entrance to the lobby with menus in hand, ready to escort patrons to a table for dinner or to one of the bars for cocktails. Thursday night was Martini Night at the Spring House, so people came from all over the island to mingle at the fully stocked outdoor bar melded into the side of the wraparound porch.

Jackson had caught McKenzie staring at him. She then abruptly shifted her concentration to the reservation book. *Interesting*. He approached on her right and stopped beside her.

She looked up. "Welcome to the Spring House, sir. Are you here for dinner or drinks?"

"I'm here to meet nice girls. Know any?"

She blushed but didn't miss a beat. "I'm sure you won't have any trouble finding a young lady to socialize with, sir. Are you here for the week?"

Jackson chuckled. She was a bit on the formal side, but that was okay. "No, I'm here for the summer. I'm a lifeguard down at State Beach."

"Oh. I've been there a few times this year, but I didn't notice you."

*More interesting.* He turned on his bluster. "I certainly would have noticed you. You'll have to say hello the next time you're down there."

She escorted him to the bar, then got busy helping other customers, so he decided to strike up a conversation with some older ladies to pass the time.

A half hour later, McKenzie approached him as he left the washroom. "Aren't they a bit old for you?"

*Wow! I like this girl.* Jackson reached out his hand. "We haven't been properly introduced. I'm Jackson Trotman."

Beaming, she shook his hand. "McKenzie Baker."

He moved closer, clasped her hand with both of his, smiled, and gazed into her eyes. "Maybe I'll see you down at the beach this weekend."

McKenzie removed her hand and stepped back, then shrugged her shoulders. "Perhaps."

She'd come to the beach that Friday, and they'd had fun on a date that Sunday, but he screwed it up by getting drunk. The beautiful bride before him didn't seem to have any regrets. She glowed with the promise of a happy future.

By the bar, groomsmen stood, nursing drinks and flirting with the bridesmaids. The groom was absent. Wait, maybe he was the man dressed in tails that was just coming in.

The sound of a single spoon tapping a wine glass cut through the air. More guests began tapping their glasses in response.

The groom swung around, and Jackson's breath caught as the future version of himself walked to McKenzie and kissed her on the lips. He glanced down at her stomach. She had a baby bump. "Wait a minute." He faced the guardian. "She's pregnant. How did that happen?"

Mekoddishkem eyed him solemnly. "How do you think?"

"Oh. Not good." Then a realization hit him. "Are you telling me McKenzie is going to die on our wedding day?"

"Yes."

Jackson instinctively started toward the bride and groom, then stopped. He was in a spirit state. "This can't be. We've got to stop it. What can we do?"

"Jackson, we cannot intervene directly in the events we're witnessing."

"Didn't you say we can alter the future by making different choices in the present?"

"Yes."

"Maybe this isn't my wedding day. If it were, some of my friends and relatives would be here. I don't see anyone I know."

"Take another look, Jackson."

He glanced around again. His mother and father stood nearby, all dressed up, along with other friends and relatives. "This can't be happening."

A man wearing a business suit and a vinyl Richard Nixon mask entered the reception room from a side door. No one else saw him except the maid of honor. She drew back against a wall and slipped into a crouch. The man took long, purposeful strides toward her.

He removed a 9mm pistol from a holster hidden in his suit coat and aimed it at her. The bride attacked and tried to wrestle his gun away. He pushed her back and fired three rounds into her chest. Circles of blood formed on her pristine white dress. She fell backward into the arms of the maid of honor, who was still cowering behind her.

Screams and crying erupted in the hall.

A man in a brown suit rushed in from the hallway—his friend, Mike Tolbert. "Stop! Police!"

The gunman turned and raced out the side door. Mike ran after him.

Jackson's future self yanked several napkins off a nearby table and used them to apply pressure to his bride's wounds. He then began giving CPR. One of the groomsmen was on his phone, pleading with a 911 dispatcher.

Two angels soon came and retrieved the unborn baby's spirit from McKenzie's body. A few seconds later, two demons arrived for McKenzie.

"No!" Jackson ran full speed and leaped through the air to tackle one of the demons, but he passed right through its spiritual body and landed on the floor directly behind them. He screamed as they extracted McKenzie's spirit.

She seemed to stare right at him as the demons carried her off to hell.

He fell to his knees, crying. "Not McKenzie. Not her."

The guardian knelt next to Jackson, put his arm around him, and wept with him. Finally, Mekoddishkem said, "Exit portal."

# CHAPTER 17
# A LITTLE SURPRISE

JACKSON LAY ON his back on the gangplank, staring up into the darkness of space above him. He drew in a deep breath and exhaled, then closed his eyes. Once he'd gathered himself, he stood and turned his back to The Wall. "I'm beginning to think I'm better off not knowing all this. I'm not sure how much more I can take."

Mekoddishkem held his gaze. "I have not fully answered your other question yet."

"Which other question?"

"Whether you'll have any children or not, and how many."

Jackson placed both hands on his hips. "I never got past the wedding day with our unborn child. How could I have any other children?" He paused for a few seconds, thinking. "Did I marry someone else later in life?"

"No."

"Was any child of mine ever born out of wedlock?"

"No."

Jackson frowned. "I give up. How could I have any children if I never got married again and never had any children born out of wedlock?"

"What does Jeremiah 1:5 say?" the guardian asked. "You know this. You memorized it a year ago."

"God was speaking to the prophet Jeremiah." Jackson repeated the verse by rote. "'Before I formed you in the womb I knew you, before you were born I set you apart.'"

"Correct. What does that verse mean?"

"That God knows us before we were born." His mind was spinning. "What exactly are you saying?"

"You had another child that was conceived but never born."

Jackson froze. Not again. "How can that be?"

"Let us go and see."

Jackson put his hand on his forehead and sighed. He ordered his feet to move to the end of the gangplank, but they wouldn't obey. There was another child he had never known. Why did his guardian angel have to show him all his failings in one day? Then Mekoddishkem's words came back to him. *Never be afraid of the truth.* He forced one foot in front of the other until he came to the end of the gangplank and stopped next to Mekoddishkem. This time without any command, The Wall whirled, and a portal appeared before them. Apparently, Mekoddishkem didn't have to speak to control The Wall.

"Whose portal is this?" he asked. "Where are we going?"

"It is your portal, Jackson." At once, The Wall plucked them into it.

They were standing in a bar. The lights were low, and loud music was playing. Waitresses wearing white aprons bustled around tending to their customers.

"Do you know where we are, Jackson?"

It looked familiar. "This is a bar that I used to go to when I was in college." His gaze rested on a table. "There I am sitting in that booth over there with some of my baseball buddies." He chuckled. "Everyone looks so young... and I look wasted."

"You were drunk."

They walked to the table where Jackson and his friends were seated. One of his buddies called the waitress over. "Do you know what the girls at that table over there are drinking?"

The waitress said, "They're drinking martinis, sir."

"The hard stuff, eh? Send them over another round on me."

"Very well, sir."

Jackson grinned at him. "What do you think they'll do?"

"I don't know." Jerry shrugged. "Worst case, we'll need to switch to martinis."

He chuckled. "And the best case?"

"Do I need to explain that to you?"

The younger Jackson watched in anticipation when the waitress delivered the drinks to the young ladies a few moments later. The women looked at the waitress with puzzled expressions, then shifted their gazes to the guys. The first to catch his eye was a Hispanic girl with thick black hair, tawny skin, and deep brown eyes. Gorgeous. She huddled with the others, then led the way as they picked up their newly delivered drinks and walked over to the guys' table.

Jackson gulped. He and his friends stood as they neared. The men grabbed a few nearby chairs, and everyone scrunched around the table.

The Hispanic girl stumbled, then sat on Jackson's lap. She gazed at him and smiled. "You have beautiful blue eyes." She reached over and touched his hair. "And beautiful black hair. It's so thick. What's your name?"

He grinned back. "Jackson." The music blared in the background, so he had to speak directly in her ear. "What's your name?"

"Cassandra Alvarez."

He placed his hand on her shoulder. "That's a pretty name."

Jerry clapped Jackson on the back and raised his mug with the other hand. "Here's the hero of today's UConn baseball game. He hit a home run in the bottom of the ninth inning to win the game."

Cassandra high-fived Jackson. "Nice!"

They continued chatting. Cassandra was a UConn sociology student and had a parttime job at a local storage unit facility. She cracked him up with her stories about crazy things found in abandoned storage units including a live hand grenade, a dog skeleton, and a breast enlargement machine.

About an hour later, the waitress stopped by. "Last call, guys."

Jerry waved her off. "Why don't we continue the party at my apartment? There's plenty of room for all of us, and I've got beer in the fridge."

The younger version of himself met Cassandra's gaze and arched his eyebrows in question.

She smiled. "Sure."

Jackson turned to the guardian with his head down. "We don't need to stay any longer, Mekoddishkem. I know what happened next. Let's exit the portal."

"Very well."

Standing on the gangplank again, Jackson shuddered. "Once we got to the house, the guys and girls all paired off."

"That is correct."

He put his hand over his face. "And Cassandra conceived?"

"Yes."

"And what happened after that?"

"She took a morning-after pill to ensure the baby would not come to term."

He fell to his knees. "I've sinned."

"Yes."

Jackson bit his lip. "I'm so sorry."

"Being sorry is good, but it isn't enough. You need to ask God to forgive you. You know he will."

Jackson bowed his head. "Father in heaven, I'm so sorry for

committing this terrible sin. Please forgive me and cleanse me. In Jesus's name, I pray, amen."

Mekoddishkem smiled. "As far as the east is from the west, so far has he removed that sin from you, Jackson."

He breathed deeply. "So, this is why the Bible says drunkenness leads to debauchery?"

"Exactly."

"What happened to my child?"

"You will be able to see her one day in heaven."

*Her.* He'd had a little girl. "But she was never born."

"She's still a person in God's sight. She was made clean, and angels took her directly to heaven. She has a portal, too, just like everyone else."

"Can I see her?"

"You'll see her soon enough."

*What does that mean?* "What form will she take in heaven?"

"That of a young child. You will be with her forever."

He stared at the guardian. "So, I will spend eternity with someone I was responsible for creating and then indirectly responsible for killing."

"Yes."

"Will my daughter even know what happened?"

"She will so fully forgive you that it won't matter. If you love someone, you won't dwell on how they've hurt you in the past."

"But I still feel terrible."

"If God chooses not to remember your sin, why should you?" Mekoddishkem spoke gently.

"And like my sister, she will one day become an adult when God creates the new heaven and the new earth."

"Correct."

"Why didn't God stop it?" he asked.

"Do not blame God for your bad choices," Mekoddishkem spoke

sternly. "God allows people to make choices, even terrible choices. Otherwise, they would not have free will."

Jackson sighed. "What did God plan for my daughter to be like?"

"He had gifted her with leadership."

"She might have become a great leader?"

"Yes."

Jackson choked up. "What should I do with this information?"

"Move on. There is nothing you can do about it. God has forgiven you and wants you to press on to perform the good works that he has prepared in advance for you to do."

What incredible love and forgiveness God had given him. And yet, the consequences remained. "The consequences of some sins are manifested before we die, while others manifest themselves after we die."

The angel nodded. "Correct. 'The sins of some are obvious, reaching the place of judgment ahead of them; the sins of others trail behind them.'"

# Chapter 18
# Who's to Blame?

AS JACKSON WALKED back along the gangplank toward the landing with Mekoddishkem, he shook his head. "This is way too much information for me to process in a lifetime, let alone a day."

"Indeed. It has been heart-wrenching for you. And this is only a taste of what judgment day will be like for many."

Most people wouldn't have a clue what was coming. "God must see thousands of these crises every day."

"Yes."

"And he feels the pain of everyone who goes through them?"

"Yes."

He whistled softly. "That's quite a burden to bear."

"It grieves him deeply, Jackson. But he is God. He can bear it."

"What should I do with what I have learned?"

"That is up to you."

Jackson paced back and forth. "I want to save McKenzie and our child from the horrible death that awaits them, and I want to save McKenzie from hell."

"That is a worthy pursuit."

"I also want to find out who killed her so I can prevent it from happening."

Suddenly, Mekoddishkem turned away from Jackson.

Jackson moved toward him. "What is it?"

"I am being called away."

"Oh." Jackson stared. "Why?"

"I am not permitted to say."

"You're not going to leave me here, are you? When will you be coming back?"

"Do not be troubled, Jackson. I will be back soon."

"Can I use The Wall while you are gone?"

"I would not recommend it."

"Why?"

"It could become perilous for you. Without me, you would be in the same dimension as the other spiritual forces in the portal."

"Oh. The demons would be able to see me?"

"Yes."

Jackson shook his head. "But I can't just wait here and let her die. I've got to do something. I need to find out who is going to kill her and why."

"You must do what you think is right, Jackson." The guardian moved toward the door.

"Wait!" he called after him. "Are there any weapons I can use to battle the forces of evil I might encounter?"

Mekoddishkem stopped. "You have three options. You can put on the full armor of God at any time, you can call out to God for help at any time and he will send me, or you can exit the portal at any time. Do not hesitate to use these weapons. If you do not use them, the demons of Satan will overpower you. May God be with you, Jackson."

"And may he also be with you, Mekoddishkem. Oh, wait. Where is she right now, and where does she live?"

"McKenzie is at the beach and lives in Marblehead, Massachusetts." Mekoddishkem strode quickly out of the massive chamber.

After he left, Jackson stood on the landing, praying silently. *Father in heaven, what should I do next?* He paused for a moment, waiting for an answer—no time to wait. *Please give me wisdom and protection as I go forward on this journey. In Jesus's name, I pray, amen.*

He jogged down the gangplank to The Wall and issued his command. "Take me to the portal of McKenzie Baker of Marblehead, Massachusetts, in the present." The Wall whirled into position, and he took a deep breath.

Jackson stood in a parking lot by the ocean. A nearby sign read Devereux Beach, Marblehead, Massachusetts. Not a cloud in the sky, and by the sun's location, it was about one o'clock in the afternoon. The air felt like a steam bath.

He stepped onto the crowded beach and walked toward the water, scanning the beachgoers as he walked, but no one resembled McKenzie. Strange, blurry splotches hovered over many people. He rubbed his eyes, but the splotches remained.

Jackson squatted and dipped his hand in the water. Chilly but strangely refreshing. He surveyed the beach again. Covered picnic tables, a snack bar, a set of barbeque grills, and a playground area surrounded him. The terrain was rocky in some areas. Similar to the Mohegan Bluffs Beach on Block Island where he'd had his first date with McKenzie.

On that day, seven years before, the chalkboard sign at the Mohegan Bluffs Beach entrance had displayed Warning—Rip Tide Today. The waves had been huge along the seaweed-strewn rocky shoreline below, the biggest he'd seen all that summer. Too big to swim much, though several people were doing so.

After exploring other parts of the beach, he and McKenzie had packed up and made their way to the stairs for the long climb to the top of the bluffs. Jackson took McKenzie's hand, helping her up the steep incline to the first step. The warmth of her touch resonated deeply, nearly taking his breath away.

As they were about to grab the rope railing, a scream cut through the air. Jackson turned toward the shoreline. A mother was shouting.

His lifeguard instincts triggered him to scan the ocean for the little girl he'd seen earlier, the one in the purple bathing suit. He couldn't locate her anywhere. He jumped down from the steps and ran to the mother. "Which way did she go?"

She pointed toward the ocean, slightly to her left.

"Call nine-one-one."

He sprinted into the sea. After taking a deep breath, he dove under the water and surveyed the ocean bottom. Nothing. He had to move quickly. He surfaced for a breath and then submerged again, this time going farther out. Still nothing. The undertow was strong and pulling him to his left. He surfaced again for another breath and went with the current.

When he swam back down, the little girl's body was visible, suspended vertically underwater about thirty feet away and five feet beneath the surface. He dared not take his eyes off her. The current was strong, drawing her farther out. A seven-foot blue shark approached the girl's motionless body.

Jackson quickly took another breath, then swam on the surface toward the girl. His whole body tensed. Would the shark attack him? It seemed like it took an eternity to get there. He took a quick breath, then submerged directly above where he estimated the girl and the shark would be. The shark appeared to be sniffing her back. Jackson grabbed her and pulled her away. The shark advanced, so he punched its snout and retreated toward the shoreline with the girl in tow.

The shark moved closer, and he punched it again. He struggled against the current and desperately needed another breath but refused to take his eyes off the shark. Tucking the girl under his left arm, he continued swimming backward until he felt the sand and rocks beneath his feet. He needed air. The shark still hovered about five feet away, staring into his eyes.

Jackson finally surfaced and gasped for air, then trudged out of the water with the girl hanging limply from his arms. A crowd had gathered. As he lowered her to her back on the sand, the mother screamed and knelt beside them, placing her hand under the little girl's neck. Jackson nudged her away and forced two quick breaths into the girl's mouth.

She didn't respond.

He checked for a pulse and found one, so he tried a few more breaths.

The little girl suddenly coughed, spewing out seawater. She gasped, opened her eyes, and reached for the woman. "Mommy!"

The woman swept her daughter into her arms and held her tight. Then, after a few seconds, she handed the girl to her husband, turned to Jackson with tears in her eyes, and hugged him. "Oh, thank you. Thank you so much. How can I ever repay you?"

He'd been heroic at that moment. Too bad the look of admiration in McKenzie's eyes hadn't lasted past that day.

He shook himself and scanned Devereux Beach again. There she was, about twenty feet away. She wore a yellow two-piece bathing suit with an ivory crocheted straw hat and oversized sunglasses. She lay on her back on a large dark red cotton blanket with her head propped up on a beach bag. She was fair-skinned and trim, yet curvaceous and beautiful, with straight long dark brown hair. Another woman lay on her belly on the blanket, propped up on her elbows, looking at McKenzie. The companion was buxom, blond—with brilliant blue, turquoise, and purple highlights—blue-eyed and beautiful with a flushed complexion and a tattoo on the small of her back. Her bright chartreuse bikini barely covered her. A blurry area hung above them.

Jackson sat cross-legged on the sand a few feet away from their blanket, trying to focus on their faces. He scooted closer to McKenzie.

Listening in on private conversations was a little sleazy but it had to be done.

McKenzie looked over at the other woman. "Monica, was that sunblock SPF 30? I hope it gives me enough protection. You know how easily I burn."

"You should be fine, babe," Monica said, with a thick Boston accent.

"It's so good to spend time with you again. What's it been, six months?"

"About that. It was at Christmas." Monica sat up. "Tell me about your new gig."

"I'll be in the marketing department at the Aetna Insurance Company in Hartford."

*Aetna? So that is how we're going to meet again.*

"I'll mostly be creating content for their websites. One project I'll be working on will give producers access to Aetna's marketing materials."

*That's my project!*

"Sounds like a great fit for you," Monica said. "You always did like that kind of thing. So, when do you start?"

McKenzie adjusted her sunglasses. "A week from Monday."

"That soon?"

"I gave my old company two weeks' notice. I told Aetna I needed to find an apartment in Hartford and have some time to relax before starting the new job. It's been almost a month since I accepted their job offer. I just need to finish packing up my apartment in New York City. The movers will arrive in a few days. I plan to attend a Brown alumni event that afternoon before driving to Hartford."

Monica shifted onto her right side. She had a faded white cloth bracelet on her left ankle and a blue amulet attached to a gold chain hanging around her neck. Her fire-engine red nails and lipstick matched perfectly. "Well, good for you, big sister. Glad you got some time to chill."

*So, Monica is her younger sister.*

"Thanks. How's Starbucks?"

"It's a job. My boss is the bomb. I like the people I work with, and I like my customers. I'm not sure it's something I want to do for the rest of my life, but it's fine for now. So, anything happening on the man front?"

"Not really. I dated this guy from Harvard Business School for a while. He was rich and intelligent but too arrogant. He became tiresome, talking about himself, his toys, and his career accomplishments ad nauseam."

"Was he a good lover, at least?"

McKenzie shook her head. "He was extremely deficient in that area."

Monica chuckled. "Extremely deficient? Why don't you just say he was a dud in the sack or something like that?" Monica sighed and rested her chin on her hand. "Maybe you'll find Mr. Right in Hartford."

"Maybe. I'm delighted about the job but concerned there won't be enough cultural activities available. I adore the theaters and museums in New York. I guess I'll just have to see what happens. What about you? Any special guy?"

Monica gave a sly smile. "How do you like my nails?"

"Beautiful! Did you do them yourself?"

"Nah, I got them done. My sugar daddy takes care of me."

"Sugar daddy? Talk to me."

"We've been going out for about three weeks."

"What's his name?"

"Ronaldo."

"How did you meet him?"

"He's a regular customer. One day he asked me out, and that was that. He gave me a credit card and lets me buy little things whenever I want."

"That's unusual. Is Ronaldo older?"

"A little. Thirty-eight."

McKenzie frowned. "And you're twenty-three."

"Yup. He's got his own business and has plenty of money."

"Does he make you joyful?"

"Well, sure, but it's not forever."

"I see. What does Ronaldo do?"

"He has an interior decorating and home construction business, takes care of the rich people in Marblehead. Oh, and he went to the Rhode Island School of Design, right next to Brown."

"Remarkable. I took a class at RISD one semester. I loved it."

Monica turned on her side, facing McKenzie. "Well, that's the upside. The downside is that he's a bit of a control freak. He wants to know my every move. I can't do anything without checking with him first. It's like he thinks I work for him or something. I'm probably going to cut the cord soon. Just haven't found the right replacement model yet."

"That's too bad. Sorry things haven't worked out better. Are you intimate with Ronaldo?"

Monica gaped at her. "You think I'd go out with a guy for three weeks and not sleep with him?"

McKenzie laughed. "Sorry, an ignorant question on my part."

"But one time, when I didn't do what he wanted, he grabbed me by the throat. Don't tell Mom. She'd freak."

McKenzie sat up and took off her glasses. "Then you need to break it off right away."

"Well, he said he was sorry." Monica shrugged. "And he says he loves me."

"Men always say that to get what they want." McKenzie pointed her right index finger at Monica. "Next time might be worse. Men like that usually hit again. Get out now. I saw this kind of thing when I volunteered at the Women's Center in Providence."

"Easy, sis. Don't you think characterizing this as domestic violence is a bit over the top?"

"No. Anyone who would do that to you is a reprehensible jerk. You should drop Ronaldo immediately."

Monica sighed. "Maybe you're right. But I don't want to leave him unless I find someone better. I don't like riding solo if you know what I mean."

McKenzie shook her head. "What's wrong with you? He's vile and a creep."

"No worries, girlfriend. I know how to take care of myself. But, hey, speaking of creeps, whatever happened to that guy at Brown who was stalking you?"

Jackson leaned forward, focusing.

"I got a restraining order on him. He called me on the phone a few months ago. I was terrified. I have no idea how he got my number. It was unlisted. Maybe he found it online. Or perhaps he somehow hacked into my work or home computer. Who knows? That's the main reason I'm moving."

"What was his name again?"

"Dexter Lancaster."

Monica's eyes widened as she stared at something over McKenzie's shoulder. Jackson glanced back. About twenty feet away, a man stomped through the sand. Jackson returned his gaze to Monica. After putting on a happy face, she got up and walked over to the man and kissed him on the cheek. She gestured from McKenzie to the man. "This is Ronaldo Espinosa, my boyfriend."

McKenzie glared at him.

Ronaldo looked fit. He stood about five feet ten inches, brandished a narrow black mustache, and had his jelled black hair combed neatly back. The starched aqua-blue button-down shirt he wore was open at the top, complimented by pressed khaki shorts and shiny cordovan penny loafers with no socks.

"Monica," he said with a slight Spanish accent. "You were supposed to be home an hour ago."

"Sorry. I didn't think it would be a big deal to stay out with McKenzie a little longer."

Ronaldo gritted his teeth. "This is unacceptable. We're supposed to be over at Chip and Alice's house in half an hour for cocktails, and you still haven't taken your shower or gotten dressed yet. You know how I hate to be late. This client is important. I have to maintain a good relationship with them."

"Sorry, I forgot. Can you go ahead without me? I'd rather spend time with McKenzie than go to another one of those dreadful cocktail parties."

Ronaldo leaned forward, getting right in Monica's face. "Without you? I can't go there alone. I do business with them." He grabbed Monica by the elbow. "We need to go now."

"I'm not going now." Monica yanked her arm back. "Where do you get off grabbing me like that? You don't own me. Now go without me. Just tell them I'm not feeling well or whatever you want. I don't care. I'm staying right here with McKenzie."

"Why, you—"

"Whatever."

Ronaldo scowled, then turned and stormed off to the parking lot. The women watched as he got into his black BMW sedan, slammed the door, and screeched toward the main road.

"That went well," McKenzie said.

Monica chuckled.

McKenzie held her gaze. "It's not funny. He's a loser. I know this isn't easy for you, but let the boy-man go."

"He did have a point. I forgot about the cocktail party, which wasn't right."

"Stop making excuses for him. Things happen. It's not like you're married to him." McKenzie stood and looked Monica directly in the eye. "I don't like the way he got physically aggressive with you, grabbing your arm like that. It concerns me."

Movement made Jackson look up. The blurry images now came into focus. Creatures hovered above the people on the beach, leaning toward them and whispering things in their ears. They were similar in appearance to the demons that had retrieved Jeremy Brown's soul at the car accident, only much smaller in size—perhaps four feet tall. Same filthy, tattered robes and bald heads with greasy, stringy hair hanging from the sides. Yellowish-brown oversized teeth and deadly cold eyes disfigured their faces.

Jackson leaned in to listen.

One of the demons whispered in Monica's ear, "He loves me. I know he does."

Another demon whispered in McKenzie's ear, "Yeah, like I've got a chance of finding a nice, handsome guy in Connecticut. Hey, look at that guy over there. Maybe I should hook up with him."

The demons were speaking thoughts into their minds.

Jackson got up and headed down the beach. Other demons were speaking thoughts into other people's minds. But near the water, a powerful-looking angel holding a sword stood guard over a family. The demons stayed away from them. Other angels watched over the children playing in the water.

He returned to the women to listen. They were now lying on their towels facing each other.

"Look at that little girl over there," the demon whispered into McKenzie's ear. "That's about how old my baby would have been by now. She has straight brown hair, just like me... But, no, I had to do it. I wasn't ready to have a kid back then. I was only nineteen. I had my whole life ahead of me. There was no way I was ready to be a single mom. But how could I have been so cold and stupid?"

McKenzie had gotten an abortion? How awful for her. This demon sure was laying a guilt trip on her.

The demon hovering above her suddenly looked directly at Jackson.

He froze. Was it staring at him or just in his direction?

The demon grabbed another demon and pointed at Jackson. In unison, they both cried out, "Notzrim!"

They could see him. Every demon on the beach glared at him. Within a few seconds, they had formed a semicircle around him, forcing him back toward the water.

Jackson's mind raced. He remembered Mekoddishkem's instructions: call for the armor, call for him, or exit the portal.

"Armor!" he cried out.

Instantly, he was wearing the armor of God—a shining gold belt, breastplate, boots, shield, helmet, and sword. Then, the semicircle of demons began closing in. Grinning and leering, they produced daggers from underneath their robes. McKenzie's demon was in the rear.

What should he do? Of course! He was in spirit form, not limited by space and matter. So, he dove straight down into the sand and came up directly behind the demons, then he rushed at McKenzie's demon with his upraised sword. Jackson brought his sword down hard on the demon's right shoulder, nearly severing his torso in half. He then slashed at the other monsters, severing hands and feet.

The demons pummeled Jackson with darts and daggers. At first, his armor served him well, but there were too many of them.

"Mekoddishkem! Help me!"

With a loud crash, Mekoddishkem fell from the sky and landed on several demons, crushing them. Then he raised himself from his crouched position, unsheathed his sword, and decapitated five or six of them, forcing the entire group to flee.

Hunched over and gasping for air, Jackson looked up at his protector. "Thank you." He straightened. Amazingly, the humans still lay on the beach, oblivious to what had just happened. "The battle is not against flesh and blood, but against the powers of this dark world and the forces of evil in the heavenly realms."

"That is correct," the guardian said. "Come. Let us leave this place. We've defeated them for now, but they'll be coming back soon and in greater numbers."

Suddenly, an enormous black reptilian creature with huge wings emerged from the ground directly in front of them.

"Exit portal!" Jackson yelled.

The creature jumped forward, grabbed Jackson by the ankle, and landed on the gangplank of The Wall with them. It looked up at The Wall, momentarily stunned, and Mekoddishkem severed the creature's arm. It reeled backward, screaming in agony. The guardian then vigorously slashed at its torso with his sword, eventually subduing him.

Mekoddishkem paused for a moment to look into Jackson's eyes, then grabbed the creature by the tail and returned with him into Jackson's portal, leaving Jackson standing alone on the gangplank.

# CHAPTER 19
# ONE DESTINATION

MEKODDISHKEM RETURNED TO the gangplank about ten minutes later.

Jackson ran a hand through his hair. "Man, that was close. What was that thing?"

"A powerful and dangerous fallen angel. Millennia of practicing evil have warped him so much that he no longer looks like an angel."

"Where did you take him?"

"A prison cell in the Abyss."

Jackson sat down on the gangplank. "Those were some nasty creatures we saw on the beach."

"God expelled Satan from heaven, along with one-third of the angels who had followed him. These fallen angels, also known as demons, have served him ever since. As a result, Satan is in control of the physical world and the social, political, and sometimes religious affairs of humanity. The demons exist to do his bidding. Their goal is to steer people toward hell."

"Why do they want to do that?"

Mekoddishkem shrugged. "Satan hates God. God made people in his image, so Satan hates people. He cannot hurt God, but he can hurt God's children."

Jackson crossed his legs and rested his arms on his knees. "Why does Satan hate God?"

The guardian paced around the gangplank. "Pride. Satan, also known as Lucifer or the devil, was second only to God in beauty and power. He eventually became discontented and wanted to become like God, so he rebelled. He can't stand the fact that human beings will one day assume his former lofty position as having authority over the angels and creation."

"I noticed there was an angel on the beach. Was it a guardian angel?"

"Yes. Every Christian is assigned a guardian angel, who watches over them."

Jackson stood up. "Why did that one family have an angel standing over them with a drawn sword?"

"They are believers who have dedicated themselves to doing the work of God on earth. They are prime targets for the Evil One and require protection. They are not to be touched."

"What about everyone else?"

"God's angels protect his children. God does not allow anything to happen to his children without it first being filtered through his will."

Jackson paused, then looked deep into the guardian's eyes. "Even bad things?"

"God may allow bad things to happen if it is part of his plan for them. Consider what happened to Job. Satan could not kill Job's children without first getting God's permission."

"What about the angels who were watching over the little children playing in the water?"

"The children are innocents. They are under the special protection of God."

Jackson crossed his arms over his chest. "What about young and older adults who are not currently his children? Do they have guardian angels?"

"Some may, per God's plan for their lives, but most do not."

Jackson sighed. *I guess that means McKenzie doesn't have one.* "You said the demons would be back soon. What about the ones you crushed and decapitated? Will they be back too? Can you kill a demon?"

"Not in your understanding of the word kill, Jackson. Demons are immortal spiritual creatures, just like angels. You cannot kill them. However, the angels will throw them into the lake of fire one day, which will be their spiritual death."

"I've read about the lake of fire in the book of Revelation, but what is it?"

"A gigantic pit of burning sulfur where anyone whose name is not found written in the Book of Life will be sent after waiting in hell to be judged. Would you like to see it?"

Jackson exhaled. "Seriously?"

"Yes."

He shook his head. "I don't know if I can take any more of this. It sounds even worse than hell."

"It is. The lake of fire is a horrible place, but I think you should see it. You should never be afraid of the truth."

"Maybe so, but to be honest, I'm not sure I want to go."

"I understand. Once again, you will be safe as long as you stay with me."

*I don't think I'm going to like this.* "All right. Let's go. I'll keep a tight grip on your robe this time. What command should I give?"

"Command The Wall to show you the lake of fire as it will be on the day of the great white throne judgment," the guardian said.

Facing The Wall, Jackson issued the command. The Wall immediately moved from right to left and continued for several moments. "Why is it taking so long?" he asked.

"It is moving to the end of time as you know it."

"How can you say it is the end of time as I know it? Won't time continue after the great white throne judgment?"

"God will put a new paradigm into effect. The righteous will live forever with him in the eternal kingdom."

The Wall stopped at a portal on its extreme right side. The straight white edge of The Wall extended upward and downward as far as they could see. Stars were visible to the right of it.

Jackson and Mekoddishkem entered the portal and found themselves suspended in the air. Miles below them and ahead of them was an enormous white cubed megalith. On top of the structure was a throne, and seated upon it was someone from whom lightning-bright light emanated. Off to the left of the throne was the lake of fire.

"Is that Jesus sitting on the throne?" Jackson asked.

"Yes."

"Incredible. Look at how Jesus's glory overpowers everyone else's, like a lighthouse shining out into the darkness. Can I meet him?"

"It is not the appointed time for you to meet him face-to-face. We are here only to observe."

"The great white throne will occur after Jesus has defeated all his enemies, including Satan. He has just commanded that all the unrighteous be summoned from hell to appear before him. Let us go watch their exodus."

Jackson and Mekoddishkem flew down from the sky into the cave opening in the mountain, through the solid rock wall, and into the Abyss's large cavern. Just after they arrived, the top of the mountain exploded, leaving the cavern open to the sky. Huge plumes of smoke gushed forth from the Abyss. Slowly, the ground beneath them began to tremble as billions of souls from the side caves were swept into the central shaft and then burst upward into the sky like water spouting from a massive geyser. As they left the opening, legions of angels guided them to the sacred assembly. The souls continued pouring upward out of the chasm in a seemingly unending stream. Demons also exited the shaft and were taken to the place of judgment.

Mekoddishkem and Jackson returned to the great white throne.

Then came a rushing sound like a strong wind, and a swirling tornado cloud traveled directly toward them. As the cloud drew closer, it turned out to be the massive migration of souls from hell. The unrighteous souls approached, and the angels before the throne guided them to their places.

All the unsaved human beings, angels, and demons now stood before their Creator and Judge. The time for mercy had ended.

An enormous angel stepped forward. His robe shone so brightly that Jackson could hardly look at him.

"That is the angel Michael," Mekoddishkem said.

Michael commanded the assembly to bow to their knees before the righteous Judge and confess that Jesus is Lord, to the glory of God the Father. Like a wave crashing against the seashore, the great assembly fell forward in unison before Jesus and acknowledged that he was the Lord of all. The few who refused to bow were decapitated, and their remains tossed into the lake of fire.

At the head of the crowd, angels opened huge books. Jesus would be judging each person according to what they had done in life. The unrighteous—those whose names were not written in the Book of Life—wailed with dread over their impending fate.

Demons shrieked as angels cast them alive into the lake of fire.

Jackson and Mekoddishkem flew down closer to the lake of fire, hovering about a hundred yards above it. Waves of horror flooded Jackson's spine as the angels carried condemned souls away from the throne and hurled them into a vast lake of burning sulfur, their bodies flailing in the air as they fell. The lake was already teeming with billions of demons and people, all wailing in agony.

"Enough, Mekoddishkem! Let's get out of here!"

"Very well."

Jackson then reconsidered. "No, wait... Who do I know down there?"

"Are you sure you want to see them?"

"Yes. I should never be afraid of the truth."

He held on to the guardian as they glided over the surface of the lake of fire about twenty feet above it. It stretched in all directions as far as he could see. It looked like slow-moving lava. The heat blasted up into his face as if he were in a superheated sauna.

He cupped his free hand over his nose and mouth so he could breathe. The stench of burning flesh and smoldering sulfur wrenched his stomach, while the cacophony of shrieks and cries from the condemned filled the air and crushed his soul. Billions upon billions were writhing and flailing in the burning sulfur. All were naked.

Mekoddishkem stopped and pointed downward. Jeremy tried to push his way through others to get to the edge of the lake, getting struck mercilessly in the process. Tears formed in Jackson's eyes. The poor kid.

With Jackson still clinging to Mekoddishkem's robe, they moved on and stopped over Fred Jorgensen, who had his arms raised and was screaming at God. Pam shuddered as the sulfur splashed up and down her body like waves at the beach. Jaime jumped up and down like a pogo stick, trying to get a split second of relief.

Next, Mekoddishkem hovered directly above Monica, who was hyperventilating as she screamed. Finally, he stopped above McKenzie. She looked up, silent, with tears streaming down her face.

Jackson erupted with a primordial scream. "That's my wife down there! That's my wife!" He let go of Mekoddishkem's robe and dove in after her. The pain was excruciating, as if someone had poured acid over every inch of his body. He jumped as high as he could and feverishly wiped the slop off his face and arms as quickly as possible. He shrieked in agony as he landed next to her. "It's burning! It's burning the skin off my legs!"

He tried to grab McKenzie, but his arms passed right through her body.

Mekoddishkem swept down and pulled Jackson out of the lake, leaving McKenzie and his coworkers behind.

As they flew into the sky, Jackson shook uncontrollably. Mekoddishkem held him tightly, but he refused to be comforted. "The worst part about this, Jackson, is not just the suffering they will be enduring," he said. "The worst part is that they will be there for all eternity with no hope of escaping their fate."

Jackson screamed, "Get me out of here! Exit portal!"

# CHAPTER 20
## STALKER

JACKSON STOOD ON the gangplank and stared into space, not saying a word. The images from the lake of fire assaulted his mind—continuously. His entire body trembled. He folded his arms over his chest and rocked himself back and forth.

He kept rocking for what seemed like hours, and from time to time, he'd hack up some phlegm, striving to expel the nasty crud he'd vicariously ingested at the lake of fire. Finally, he looked up at Mekoddishkem, who stood next to him. "All those people in the lake of fire... is their destiny set, or can it change?"

"For Jeremy Brown, it is too late. But it is not too late for the others. There is always hope for people as long as they are alive."

He stood and paced. "We need to give them time to choose a different destiny."

"Jackson, there is something else you should know about McKenzie."

His stomach burned. What more could there be to deal with? He swallowed hard before asking, "What's that?"

"Ask to go into her portal while she was attending college."

"Which day?"

"The day she got pregnant."

Jackson gritted his teeth, brooded for a few seconds, and then exploded. "No! I'm not doing it. That's private information. Look, whatever she's done, I forgive her. It's the past. There's nothing she or I can do about it. And besides, I'm no better than she is. I've probably done worse things. So, let's drop it. I don't want those images put into my head because I know they'll never get out."

The guardian held his gaze. "Trust me."

*What he's asking me to do is cruel. I don't want to see McKenzie with another man.* "I may be heading to a PTSD psych ward after all this. Now you want to pile more on? Not happening. I can't take anymore. I've had it, I tell you. I've had it." His body and voice shook. "Combat was a piece of cake compared to this."

"Trust me."

"I can't."

"Trust me."

He couldn't watch some guy taking her into a dorm room and having his way with her. Jackson shook his head, then yelled as loud as he could. Tears poured from his eyes and dripped down his face. He collapsed to his knees and stretched his arms upward, remaining in that position for some time.

Jackson finally sighed and calmed himself. *Mekoddishkem has shown me some hard things but hasn't steered me wrong yet.* He stood on shaky legs. "I should never be afraid of the truth. Take me to the portal of McKenzie Baker, the day she got pregnant in college."

McKenzie stood on a sidewalk beside a young man, waiting to cross a city street. Behind them was a building with a sign above the entrance that read Brown University Philosophy Department.

The young man spoke first. "I'd be careful around Dexter. I've heard stories about how he treats women."

She shrugged. "Don't worry, Mason. Dexter's brilliant but harmless. Most loudmouths are trying to overcompensate for some hidden deficiency. And if you're right and he does mistreat women, he's a loser."

McKenzie and Mason stared at each other, eyes bulging, as a man walked down the steps directly behind them. When the man had moved on, Mason leaned over and whispered, "Oops. What if Dexter heard you?"

She scoffed. "So what if he did."

Jackson fought the urge to reach out and touch her as she walked by him. She hummed Prince's "1999" song as she strode up North Main Street toward the Women's Center of Rhode Island. Located just off the Brown campus, vines entangled the shelter's entire three-story redbrick façade except for the windows. She unlatched the beige wooden gate and crossed the enclosed courtyard to the front entrance. After opening the mahogany door, she wiped her feet on the mat, walked in, and closed the door behind her.

Jackson and Mekoddishkem passed through the wall to follow her.

McKenzie greeted the receptionist as she signed the volunteer sheet, then she headed down the hallway to the left and entered a children's playroom. Decorated with cobalt-blue walls above tan wainscoting and sky-blue wall-to-wall carpet, it contained various red plastic slides, seesaws, and tunnels neatly lining the sides of the room.

She flung her barn coat over the hook on the pine coat rack. A young black girl and an even younger black boy lay on the floor. They were scribbling on coloring books with a plethora of crayons on the floor. McKenzie plopped down cross-legged between them after picking up a dog-eared copy of *Goodnight Moon* from the bookshelf against the wall. "Hi. My name's McKenzie. What are your names?"

The little girl, dressed in blue jeans with a pink Barbie shirt, flipped over on her back but didn't make eye contact. "Why are you here?"

"I'm a volunteer. I come here every Wednesday afternoon after class."

"Do you go to school?"

McKenzie turned over on her belly and propped up her head with her hands. "Yes. I go to the school right up the hill from here."

"Why are you here?"

"I want to help families who are having problems."

"Why?"

"Because I grew up in a family that has problems. My dad drinks a lot."

"Oh… My dad does drugs."

Tears dribbled down McKenzie's face. "I'm so sorry." She wiped them away and shook her head. "What's your name?"

"Shanya." She looked up at McKenzie with droopy eyes.

"How old are you, Shanya?"

"Five. How old are you?"

McKenzie laughed. "Nineteen. Are you in kindergarten?"

"Yes, but I'm not going to school right now. We had to move because my mom's boyfriend got mad. I'll be going to a new school soon."

"I'm so sorry you had to move, Shanya. I hope you like your new school. Who's your little friend next to you?"

Shanya frowned. "He's not my friend. He's my brother. His name is Terrence. He's four."

McKenzie reached over and took the little boy's hand in hers. "Hi, Terrence. My name's McKenzie."

He pulled his hand back without looking at her.

McKenzie glanced back at Shanya. "Would you like me to read you a story?"

"Sure."

As McKenzie picked up the book, the scene shifted. Jackson held on to Mekoddiskem's robe as The Wall apparently transitioned them to later that evening.

Mekoddishkem pointed at McKenzie. "She's walking across the Wriston Quadrangle to meet some friends at the Sigma Chi fraternity. It's located in that four-story redbrick building over there, which is connected to Olney House, where Angela lived."

"Angela?"

"Yes. The high school friend you slept with while you were in town for the UConn baseball game against Brown."

"Oh." Now another bad choice was out in the open.

Mekoddishkem and Jackson followed McKenzie as she flipped her ID over the card reader to get inside. She descended the gray stone stairs to the basement, and the smell of stale beer increased with every step, as did the heat and cacophony of voices.

McKenzie stashed her coat on one of the couches and weaved through wall-to-wall people to where they were playing beer pong.

Within a minute, Dexter tapped her shoulder from behind. His dirty-blond shoulder-length hair hung loose, and his scraggly beard needed a trim. About six foot five and all muscle, he towered over her. "Want a beverage?"

She hesitated, eyeing the beer. "Sure."

Dexter handed her the plastic cup.

She nursed her drink as they watched a beer pong game that was underway. "Do you want to play the winner?"

"How do you play?"

McKenzie laughed. "You don't know how to play beer pong? You need to get out more, Dexter." She pointed to one of the tables in the dimly lit room. "Ten of those plastic cups are filled halfway with beer and arranged in a triangle so that they're like pins in a bowling alley, but you're not trying to knock them down. Each team of two tosses a Ping-Pong ball into the cups at the opposite end of the table.

Whenever a Ping-Pong ball lands directly in a cup, the defending team has to chug the beer in the cup."

Dexter rubbed his beard for a second. "What the hell. I'll play."

Five minutes later, Dexter had landed seven Ping-Pong balls in the opposing team's cups. McKenzie hooted as each of the tossed balls found its mark. "Are you sure you've never played this game before?"

"Nope. First time."

McKenzie lost her balance. She grasped the edge of the table to steady herself but couldn't. She stumbled, and Dexter caught her by the arm before she fell.

She cursed. "I think I'd better get home." Her words came out slurred. "Not feeling too good."

He pulled her closer. "I'll help you."

McKenzie stared at Dexter with glazed eyes. "Okay."

Jackson grabbed Mekoddishkem's arm. "What's happening to her?"

"Dexter laced her beer with Rohypnol."

"What's that?"

"It's a date rape drug."

He snarled at Dexter. "Monster!"

Jackson tightened his grip on Mekoddishkem as The Wall again transitioned them, this time to a dorm room.

A younger version of himself was getting dressed as a woman lay asleep in a bed nearby. The clock on the nightstand displayed 1:04 a.m.

Mekoddishkem said, "This is after you slept with your high school friend, Angela."

Jackson sighed. "I should have gone back to UConn after the baseball game with Brown instead of staying with her. She talked me into it."

"You went with her of your own free will."

"You're right. I did."

135

The younger Jackson left a note for Angela, then walked into the hallway and closed the door. Downstairs in the lobby, a groan came from the Sigma Chi lounge. He stopped for a moment. Another groan sounded in the darkness. He entered the lounge and turned the lights on.

It had to be McKenzie lying faceup on the leather couch, although younger Jackson wouldn't have known her name. Her hair was matted and strewn across her face.

After his attempts to rouse her failed, Jackson picked her up, put her over his shoulder, and walked outside.

In the quadrangle, he found a passing student. "Where's the infirmary?"

"Andrews House. Just go out that archway, turn left on Brown Street, and it's about one hundred yards on your left."

"Thanks."

He'd just turned onto Brown Street when footsteps came up behind him. "Put her down," a man's voice said.

Jackson spun around. It was Dexter, but his younger self had no idea what he was up against. "Do you know her? I've got to get her to the infirmary. She's totally wasted."

"Give her to me. I'll take care of her. She's mine."

Jackson hesitated. "I'm not leaving her with you."

A blow hit Jackson in the face, knocking him to the ground. McKenzie fell full force on top of him. He pushed her off and got up. Blood dripped from his nose. He stuck his left hand straight up in the air and began waving it. When Dexter looked up, Jackson kicked him in the groin.

Dexter groaned and lurched forward.

Jackson punched him as hard as he could in the left temple.

Dexter counterpunched, knocking Jackson to the ground. Dexter straddled him and punched him in the head again and again.

Jackson tried to block the blows with his forearms, but Dexter was too strong.

A siren blared, and flashing lights lit up the night. Dexter jumped up and sprinted back through the Wriston Quadrangle arch.

Two campus police officers ran over and helped Jackson to his feet.

"Are you okay? What happened here?" one asked.

Jackson pointed to the woman lying on the pavement. "I found her in the Sigma Chi lounge on a couch. She was out cold. I was taking her to the infirmary, then this big guy came up from behind and started attacking me."

The officer looked at Jackson's face. "Looks like we need to get you to the infirmary too."

The two officers draped her arms over their shoulders and dragged her to the infirmary. Jackson tagged along behind.

As soon as the girl was safely inside, he slipped away to his car and sped off.

"I remember not wanting to get involved in some long, drawn-out police investigation," Jackson whispered to Mekoddishkem.

When they returned to The Wall, Mekoddishkem said, "That's all I wanted to show you, Jackson. I didn't want to make this any more painful than necessary."

"Evil. Pure evil. How can someone do that to another person?"

The merciless beating he'd taken came to mind in a fresh new way. He'd spent years hating the guy and training five days a week in a karate dojo to make sure it never happened again. Now he wanted to beat Dexter to a pulp more than ever.

Jackson took several deep breaths. He needed to play it cool and get more information about Dexter. "Where does he live?"

"New York City, at the Olympic Tower on Fifth Avenue in Midtown East."

The angel had answered. What a surprise. After all, Mekoddishkem knew his thoughts. His heavenly companion must have known he intended to kill Dexter.

The guardian put his hand on Jackson's shoulder. "I know you are angry, and you want to punish Dexter, but first, allow me to answer your other question."

"What question?"

"How could Dexter rape McKenzie?"

"Oh, yes. Why would Dexter do something like that to McKenzie or any woman?"

"Power and malice."

"What do you mean?"

"Dexter was raped as a boy."

Jackson's eyes widened. "Oh."

"As he matured, he desired to have power over others so he would feel secure, not only sexually but in all areas of his life. He specifically targeted McKenzie that night because she had maligned him after philosophy class earlier in the day."

"I feel bad that Dexter had such a traumatic upbringing, but he's still responsible for his actions, isn't he?"

"Absolutely. Just like you're responsible for your actions, Jackson."

He shrunk back.

"You know what you need to do now, don't you?"

"What?"

Mekoddishkem paused.

Jackson set his jaw. *I'll forgive him after I kill him.*

He walked up to The Wall and issued a command without first consulting Mekoddishkem. "Take me to Dexter Lancaster of New York City in the present."

The Wall did not move. Was Mekoddishkem blocking it?

"Wait, Jackson."

"Why? Look at what he's done! He's a monster."

"Let God avenge. He will repay Dexter for what he's done to you, to McKenzie, and others."

"I know he will someday, at the judgment, but I need to help McKenzie now—and protect her from Dexter now."

"Since you are choosing to go back," the guardian told him, "you won't be able to access The Wall anymore. I will see you again soon."

Jackson hesitated. "Wait. What do I do next?"

"That is up to you."

"But there's still so much for me to learn. How do I help McKenzie?"

"You have five months, Jackson."

"What do you mean? Five months for what?"

The guardian disappeared.

*He must mean I have five months to save her. I've got to hurry.* Everything suddenly went black.

Dexter awoke at seven o'clock on a Tuesday morning in June. Beside him lay a woman. What was her name again? It didn't matter. She'd looked a lot better with clothes on.

He drew back the blinds and gazed down Fifth Avenue. He'd done well, very well. He was on track toward opening his own hedge fund soon. Deutsche Bank had been good to him but not good enough. He'd made $100 million for them in 2008, but they only gave him a paltry $10 million as compensation—what a rip-off. *I'll show them.*

He rummaged through his walk-in closet. He'd wear the gray pin-striped Brioni suit today, along with the Di Bianco bluchers he got at Barney's last week. *I never thought I'd pay $500 for a shirt, but what the hell.*

His driver would be arriving at eight o'clock, so he needed to hurry. He didn't want to be late for his eight-thirty breakfast with Blackstone at the Loews Regency.

After he showered and dressed, he woke up his one-night stand and told her to leave. No, he wasn't going to call her.

At eight o'clock, he stepped into the elevator and reviewed the appointment calendar on his phone. *I've got that Brown mixer tonight. I need to stay focused to get out of work on time.*

Eight hours later, he left work triumphant. The meeting with Blackstone had gone well. They planned to give him $100 million to manage, along with office space and administrative support. He'd get a hefty bonus if he delivered strong results.

Dexter arrived late for the Brown alumni event at Cipriani's that evening. Hopefully, McKenzie would show. Dexter had made sure she was on the invite list. He mingled around, glancing at name tags and engaging in small talk, but didn't see her. He was about to leave when she came out of the ladies' room.

Her eyes widened when she saw him. She immediately made for the exit. He followed and touched her arm.

She glared up at him. "Hello, Dexter. Raped anyone lately?"

He sighed. "McKenzie, we've been through this before. I swear it was consensual. I'm so sorry you think otherwise."

McKenzie cursed. "I'll never forgive you for what you did to me. I don't ever want to see you again. Do you understand me?"

*Don't get flustered. No always precedes yes.* "Wait! I organized this party to see you again. I've done extremely well." He stood tall. "I'm about to open a hedge fund of my own."

McKenzie put her hands on her hips. "What's a hedge fund?"

"It's a vehicle for investing other people's money."

"Isn't that for the ultrarich?"

Dexter leaned in and whispered, "Yes. I made ten million dollars at Deutsche Bank last year and could make into the billions if my fund takes off."

McKenzie smirked. "Good for you, Dexter. I hope you have a nice life counting all your money." She turned to leave.

He grabbed her by the elbow. She couldn't leave without giving him a chance. He stared deep into her eyes and choked up. "I've worked so hard all these years to prove to myself—and you—that I'm a success. I'm not a loser."

"What's that got to do with me?"

"You called me a loser. I heard you talking about me in front of the Philosophy building back at Brown."

McKenzie paused for a moment. "That was years ago. I do recall saying you'd be a loser if you didn't treat women right. Well, my opinion hasn't changed." She wrenched her arm away. "Seriously, Dexter, you need to get on with your life and forget about me. I'm not interested in you. Do you understand me? I'll never, ever want to go out with you, no matter how much money you make or how famous or 'successful' you become. Is that clear?"

He didn't answer. This wasn't going the way he'd planned. Where was her compassion? Everyone deserves a second chance, don't they?

She turned and stormed out.

Stunned, he went to the event organizer and asked for the bill, then said he needed to leave. After paying, he walked out the door and tried to flag down a cab.

Giving up wasn't in his nature. He would hire a private detective to track her down and keep tabs on her. In the meantime, he needed to get drunk.

# CHAPTER 21
# BACK IN THE SADDLE

JACKSON AWOKE TO a beeping noise. He lay on a bed with his upper torso slightly elevated. The bed had metal bars on the sides. He didn't have metal bars on his bed at home. *Where am I?* He looked down at his arms. Wires and tubes were hooked up to them.

The fog gradually lifted from his mind. He was in a hospital. Then amazement filled him. God must have brought him back.

Jackson lifted his head, then groaned and placed his hands gingerly on his chest. "Man, that hurts. That kid whacked me pretty good." He dropped his head back to the bed.

His mother and father walked in the door. "Nurse!" his mother cried out. "He's awake! Oh, thank God. Jackson, how do you feel?"

"Been better, Ma." His words sounded slurred, so he spoke more slowly. "But I'll be okay. How long have I been here?"

"Three days." Tears rolled down her cheeks as she clasped his hands.

*Three days?* Jackson stared around in wonder. "That's a long time to be unconscious."

His mother sobbed. "The doctors didn't think you were going to make it. They said you died on the operating table twice. We were so worried about you, but we prayed and prayed."

"Glad to see you're okay, son," his father said. "You had us worried for a while, but your mother and I are glad you pulled through."

*Your mother and I?* Like his dad hadn't betrayed the meaning of that phrase. He wanted to yell at his dad right now, but he'd wait until they were alone. "Thank you for praying for me."

His father bit his lip and turned away.

A nurse came into the room and checked Jackson's vital signs. "Glad to have you back, Mr. Trotman."

"How long have you been here?" he asked his parents.

"Two days." When the nurse moved away, his mother took her place. "We got a call from your boss saying you'd been in an accident."

"Fred?"

"Yes. You were still wearing your Aetna badge at the time of the accident. We flew in from Ohio and have been here most of the time since. We're staying at a hotel in downtown Hartford."

A doctor walked in a few moments later. "Welcome back to planet earth, Mr. Trotman."

Jackson mused at the irony of the doctor's salutation, then looked at his nametag. *Ervin Matheson.* "Thanks, Doc."

"I'm the attending physician for the ICU. I read over your chart, and I must say, it was touch and go for a while there. We lost you a couple of times and had to perform CPR to get you back. You sustained a severe concussion, a ruptured spleen, bruised ribs, and a nasty gash on your left thigh. You lost a tremendous amount of blood, so we had to perform several blood transfusions. You were in the emergency and operating rooms for a day and then in the ICU for two days."

Jackson sighed. "That's quite a list of injuries." He shifted a bit in his bed to get more comfortable. Everything hurt, especially his chest and thigh. "How long will I be here?"

"Probably another five days or so. It depends on how quickly you recover. Then you'll need to rest at home a couple of days before returning to work."

Jackson shook his hand. "Thanks for everything."

"You're welcome."

"I guess I should thank the Red Cross too."

"Yes." Dr. Matheson turned to leave but then stopped. "They found the man who hit you."

"Yeah, I know. That man was just a kid. He died at the foot of Avon Mountain."

The doctor looked at the nurse. "I thought you said he just woke up."

The nurse's eyes widened. "He did."

Dr. Matheson returned his gaze to Jackson. "How did you know that?"

*That's right. These people don't know about The Wall yet.* "I was there with my guardian angel. We saw the whole thing, sitting in the back seat of his car when the tractor trailer killed him."

The doctor grinned. "Right. You must have heard your parents or one of the staff talking about it when you were semiconscious."

Jackson's father exchanged a glance with his mother. "We didn't know who hit our son. We never talked about it."

"No. I was there." He looked at his parents. "You believe me, don't you?"

His mom smiled, although it didn't seem genuine. "Well, I don't know, Jackson. That's a pretty incredible story."

"You've had a severe accident, son," his dad added, "so maybe it was just your imagination, or maybe you did hear one of the nurses talking about it."

"There have been studies that show that comatose patients can hear what people say even though they aren't responsive," Dr. Matheson said.

Jackson rolled his eyes. *They don't believe me.* "But I didn't just hear it. I saw it. I can tell you every detail of the accident because I was there. I can also tell you about all kinds of other things I experienced. I saw Dad's ancestor in the year 500, and Mom's ancestor fighting in the French and Indian War with George Washington. Oh, and I saw hell too, and the great white throne judgment and the lake of fire. It was horrible. You've all got to make sure you're right with God, so you don't end up there."

His mom moved closer. "There, there, Jackson. You need to get some rest."

"No. Mom, Dad, you've got to believe me!"

She patted his shoulder. "We do believe you, dear. Now please calm down. You've had a rough couple of days."

"I'll have the nurse give you something to help you rest," Dr. Matheson said. "We'll start you with physical therapy tomorrow. I'm also going to order a psychological evaluation to make sure there hasn't been any injury to your brain." He scratched his head. "I have to admit, though. It's weird you knew how the hit-and-run driver died."

"His name was Jeremy," he told them. "Jeremy Brown."

The doctor motioned for his parents to follow him into the hallway.

*I've got to make them believe me.* "Dad, can I talk to you before you leave?"

He moved closer. "Sure, son."

After the doctor, nurse, and his mother left, Jackson drilled his father with a stare. "I saw you at the Grand Plaza Hotel a week ago, entering room 517. I know what you were doing."

His father's face turned as white as a ghost.

"Mom already knows. You need to stop, Dad, and ask Mom and God for forgiveness, or you'll end up in hell. Trust me. Hell is a horrible place." Jackson leaned over, picked up the Gideon Bible on the nightstand, and handed it to him.

His father pressed his lips together and walked out the door.

*Father in heaven, please help my earthly father repent of his sin and turn to you for forgiveness and restoration. In Jesus's name, I pray, amen.* Jackson thanked God for how wonderful Mekoddishkem had been to show him so many things. Then, a Bible verse popped into his head: *From everyone who has been given much, much will be demanded.*

He had a responsibility to do something with what he'd learned. But what if he'd imagined it? What if the journey to The Wall was all just a dream? Perhaps he did have a traumatic brain injury and was hallucinating the whole time.

"Where did that thought come from?" he asked aloud. "Of course, it was real. How could I even consider such a thing?" Then he remembered how the demons whispered things in people's ears, trying to get them off track from their actual purpose in life. There was only one way to deal with that. "Shut up in the name of Jesus. The Lord rebuke you, you foul spirit."

Other verses came to mind: *Resist the devil, and he will flee from you... Come near to God and he will come near to you.*

The lies must have been spoken into his ear by a demon, followed by an angel or the Holy Spirit conveying scriptural truth. He lay back on the bed. There was a war going on in the heavenly realms over him—and every living person. Satan and his minions were trying to get him off track while the Spirit of God sought to keep him on track. He wasn't worried about going to hell because Jesus promised he would never forsake those who trusted in him. But Satan and his servants could make a Christian unfruitful in life. How could he keep that from happening to him? Mekoddishkem's comments about free will came to mind. He had to choose to follow God.

His dad was another story. He didn't appear sorry for cheating on his wife or have any desire to stop. He also didn't appear to have any fruit in his life from abiding with Christ. Therefore, even if he had prayed to receive Christ, his conversion could not have been genuine, and he would be condemned to hell. His father would be one of the people to whom Jesus says, "I never knew you. Away from me, you evildoers!" *Father in heaven, please rescue my earthly father before it's too late.*

The nurse returned and injected something into his IV. Seconds later, there was nothingness, as if someone had just flipped off a light switch.

∽

Jackson slowly opened his eyes. Turning his head to his right, he found his mentor from church sitting next to his bed. He blinked a few times and then smiled. "Mike." His voice slurred a bit. "Sorry, I'm feeling a little dizzy. What time is it?"

"About ten in the morning." Mike Tolbert spoke forcefully with a deep, rich baritone. "How are you?"

"I've been better. I'm a little spacey at the moment. The nurse gave me something to knock me out last night, and I'm not quite with it yet."

"I understand. How are you feeling otherwise?"

"Well, I hurt all over actually, especially my chest and my left leg." He shifted a little. "Thanks for taking the time to visit."

"My pleasure. We were all worried about you. The whole church was praying for you, and God Almighty answered our prayers."

"He sure did. Please tell everyone that I appreciate their prayers."

"I'll be sure to pass that along."

"Thank you, sir." He leaned over and lowered his voice. "Could you close the door? I have something I'd like to talk about."

"Sure." Mike got up and closed the door, then returned to his chair. "What did you want to discuss?"

"They told me I died several times while I was on the operating table."

"Really? I wasn't aware of that."

"I had an out-of-body experience while I was unconscious."

Mike stared at him, eyebrows raised.

"I told my parents and the doctor about it, but they didn't believe me. They think I got hit a little too hard on the head, if you know what I mean. You'll believe me, won't you?"

"Well, I know you to be an honorable and trustworthy young man, Jackson, so I have no reason not to believe you. What did you see?"

"After the car struck me in the hospital parking garage, I woke up and watched the EMTs carrying my body away on a gurney."

Mike gasped. "Really?"

"Then an angel came and took me into the heavenly realms. Only we didn't go into heaven but to a chamber next to heaven." Then, with his mind becoming more coherent, he spoke about what he'd experienced at The Wall.

"Whoa. Hold your horses there, Jackson." Mike leaned over, put his left hand on Jackson's arm, and looked intently into his eyes. "That's quite a whopper you're telling me right now. Are you pulling my leg?"

Jackson's face tensed. "No, sir."

"You swear you're telling me the truth?"

"Yes, sir."

"That doesn't make any sense."

"I know."

"I need time to think. For starters, you need to slow down. You're going way too fast for me."

"Sorry. I know I'm throwing a lot of information at you all at once."

Mike stood and paced around the room. "What do you mean, you saw the kid who hit you taken to hell?"

"My guardian angel, Mekoddishkem, took me with him to hell,

and we saw Jeremy Brown thrown into the Abyss by demons. There were demons all around us, but we were invisible to them."

"How did you know the kid's name?"

"Mekoddishkem told me."

"Maybe you just heard someone talking about all this in your room while you were unconscious."

"That's what the doctor said. I guess you don't believe me either."

Mike put his hands on his hips and faced Jackson. "Well, you've got to give me a little time to process this, Jackson. After all, it's quite an incredible story."

Jackson sat up slightly. "It's not a story, Mike. It's the truth. I saw it with my own eyes."

"Okay, okay. I'm sorry. But there is nothing in the Bible about a wall."

"I know. Mekoddishkem said it was just a representation, a way to help me understand the mystery of God's will and to develop in me the spirit of wisdom and revelation."

Mike cocked his head. "You're referring to the first chapter of Ephesians?"

"Yes, sir. I had been memorizing it before the accident. Later on, I saw lots of people in the lake of fire, including my future wife."

"You saw all that in the few days you were unconscious?"

Jackson nodded. "Yes."

"Did you see Jesus?"

He smiled. "Yes, but only from a distance. Mekoddishkem told me it wasn't the appointed time for me to see him face-to-face."

"What did he look like?"

"I saw him at the great white throne judgment. The lightning-bright light of his glory far outshined all the other beings at that assembly. He was seated on a giant platform amid a vast stadium that stretched for miles and miles to his left and right."

Mike sat down again. "Do you know what Mekoddishkem means?"

"It's a Hebrew word that means to sanctify."

"Right. Have you studied Hebrew?"

"No."

"How did you know what it means?"

"Mekoddishkem told me."

Mike leaned back in his chair and studied Jackson. "What else did you learn?"

"That everything in the Bible is true and that the terrible events prophesied millennia ago will happen one day. I'm sure of it because I saw them with my own eyes."

"Why do you think God allowed you to experience these things?"

"Well, I've been memorizing the first chapter of Ephesians, and I asked God to show me the mystery of his will. He answered that prayer. I think he also wants me to help save my future wife and coworkers from hell and the lake of fire."

"Jackson, we already have the Bible, so we don't need you to tell us what's coming."

Stung by this rebuke, he remained silent.

"Do you remember the parable about the poor man Lazarus?" Mike went on.

"Yes. Father Abraham said that even if someone came back from the dead to warn the rich man's five brothers about hell, they still wouldn't believe. He also said that the Scriptures were sufficient for everyone to believe."

Mike nodded. "Exactly. Do you recall what's written in Revelation about not adding to the Word of God?"

"Yes. God will curse that person. But I'm not adding to anything in the Bible. I'm just confirming what it says, bearing witness to it."

"That's good. I'm glad you understand that difference. You must be extremely cautious that this isn't the kind of puffed-up, idle notions Paul warns us about in the second chapter of Colossians."

"I couldn't agree more."

"Are you sure you aren't violating any of those principles?"

*He still doesn't believe me. I can't blame him.* "I don't think so. I sure hope not. I'm just reporting what I saw."

"Did you know that the mystery of God's will that's referred to in the first chapter of Ephesians is revealed later in the book of Ephesians? It speaks about the inclusion of both Jewish and gentile believers in the New Testament church."

"I didn't realize that. So, it's like the example in the eleventh chapter of Romans of the wild olive branches, or the gentiles, being grafted in with the cultivated branches, the Jews, and both becoming part of the same tree with a single root, which is Jesus."

"Exactly," Mike said.

"You know, one of my coworkers, Pam Shuster, is Jewish. I saw her in the lake of fire. How could I help her?"

"There are a lot of prophecies about the coming Messiah in the Tanakh, otherwise known as the biblical Old Testament." Mike opened the inside front cover of his Bible. "I've got a chart around here somewhere that lists them." He finally pulled out a piece of paper and handed it to Jackson. "Here. Check this out."

| Old Testament Messianic Prophecy | Old Testament Reference | New Testament Fulfillment |
|---|---|---|
| He will be of the seed of Abraham | Genesis 12:1–3 | Matthew 1:1, Galatians 3:16 |
| He will come from the tribe of Judah | Genesis 49:10 | Matthew 1:2 |
| He will come from the line of David | 2 Samuel 7:16 | Matthew 1:1 |
| He will be born of a virgin | Isaiah 7:14 | Matthew 1:23 |
| He will rule the world one day | Isaiah 9:6 | Matthew 28:18 |
| He will suffer for our transgressions | Isaiah 53, Psalm 22:1-18 | John 19:1–30 |
| He will enter Jerusalem on 04/06/0032 | Daniel 9:20–27 | Matthew 21:1–11 |
| He will be born in Bethlehem | Micah 5:2 | Matthew 2:4-6 |
| He will enter Jerusalem on a donkey | Zechariah 9:9 | Matthew 21:1-11 |
| He will be betrayed for 30 pieces of silver | Zechariah 11:12–13 | Matthew 26:14–15 |
| His garments will be divided | Psalm 22:18 | John 19:24 |
| He will be pierced | Zechariah 12:10 | John 19:34, 37 |
| His bones will not be broken | Psalm 34:20 | John 19:36 |

Mike gave him time to read the list before speaking. "The most compelling to me is the one found in the ninth chapter of Daniel. It predicts the Messiah will come 483 years after King Artaxerxes decreed the rebuilding of Jerusalem, as described in the second chapter of Nehemiah."

"Really? I wasn't aware of that."

"I read a commentary on this topic by John MacArthur. Let's see if we can find it on the internet." He began typing on his smartphone screen. "Here it is. MacArthur's commentary on Daniel 9:20–27."

*And so, all we need to do is calculate it a little bit. If Daniel is correct, [from] March 14, 445 BC to April 6, 32 AD is gonna be 173,880 days. Well, let's think about it. From March 14, 445 BC to April 6, 32 AD is only 477 years and 24 days. So we're a few years short. We have to deduct a year because 1 BC and 1 AD is the same year. So we really have 476 years and 24 days. Now, we have to convert to our calendar of 365 days, so we multiply that all out, plus 24 days, and we get 173,764; and we're still short. But we have Leap Year every four years. So 476 divided by 4, gives us 119 Leap Years, so we add 119 more days to 173,[7]64, and we get 173,883 days, 3 days too many.*

*You say, "Close is good enough for me." Close is not good enough for God. Sir Robert Anderson went to the Royal Observatory in England and he found out that according to their solar calculations, a year is 1/128 of a day longer on the calendar than a solar year. So every 128 years, we have to lose a day. And if you're dealing with 483 years, that'll be 3 of those. So you drop those out and you have 173,880 days. Just exactly as the Word of God said.*

The staggering accuracy of God's Word blew Jackson's mind. "I've never heard that before."

"April 6, 32 AD is the day that Jesus made his triumphal entry into Jerusalem riding on a donkey, otherwise known as the first Palm

Sunday. Just point your Jewish friend to God's Word, and the Holy Spirit will do the rest. Now, what's all this talk about your future wife?"

Jackson looked into his eyes. "While I was at The Wall, I asked Mekoddishkem if I would ever get married. He said I would. Then he took me into the future, to our wedding reception. A masked man walked in and shot her. I'm pretty sure I know who did it. I'm on a mission to prevent it from happening."

"That's a terrible thing to see, Jackson." Mike leaned forward. "Are you sure you weren't having a nightmare or something?"

He glanced at the Monet print on the otherwise bland beige wall, sighed, and then turned back to him. "I'm sure." He shifted in his bed again. I want to do everything in my power to keep her from going to hell, even if we don't end up getting married." Realization struck him. "Hey, maybe that's an idea. If we don't get married, she won't get shot."

Mike shrugged. "Maybe not, but she would probably end up in the same place unless you do something about it. Either way, you need to help her. And you need to help your coworkers too. I suggest you pray for them every day."

"Will do."

"Are you dating her now?"

"Well, no. I haven't seen McKenzie in seven years."

He gaped. "You haven't seen her in seven years, and you're gonna marry her?"

"Yes."

He leaned back and stared at Jackson for a moment. Finally, he chuckled. "That's the craziest thing I've ever heard."

"I agree. But I'll be meeting McKenzie at work as soon as I get out of here."

Mike's eyes widened. "Well, I'm going back to the station now. I need to think about what you've said."

Jackson nodded. "Okay. Thanks again for stopping by, Mike."

*He thinks I'm crazy.* There was one more thing Jackson could tell him that also might make him believe—Sally's pregnancy—but that might push him over the edge. What if he was wrong? What if it had just been a dream?

# CHAPTER 22
## FREEDOM

FOUR DAYS HAD passed since Jackson woke up in the hospital. He received physical therapy twice a day and could now walk down the hallway and back, but that was about it. He hadn't shaved or showered yet that morning and felt dirty. A half-eaten sandwich sat on one nightstand, while the Bible and a dog-eared magazine sat on the other. The TV was on, but he wasn't paying attention.

Michael Jackson's "Thriller" video began on MTV. He watched as Michael and his date walked past a graveyard. The dead in the cemetery rose from their graves, followed the two of them to a city street, surrounded them, and then began dancing. Michael's date was shocked to see him leading the ghouls in a dance.

What would it look like when the dead rose from the grave at the rapture? Too bad Mekoddishkem hadn't shown him that portal.

Mike Tolbert poked his head through the doorway. "Hey, Jackson."

*Oh boy, here we go.* "Hey. Come on in." Jackson stood up from sitting in his wheelchair and shook his friend's hand.

"How are you doing?"

Jackson lowered himself again while Mike sat in a nearby chair. "I'm feeling better, but it sure is getting old sitting here all day."

"Did your parents head back to Ohio?"

"Yes. My mom and dad were here for a week. I thought that was enough. I convinced them I would be fine if they left. They call once or twice a day to make sure I'm okay."

"That's nice. Not much your parents can do at this point."

"Right."

Mike wrapped his hands around a canvas bag he held on his lap. "I came here for a couple of reasons. Obviously, I wanted to see how you were doing. But I've also been thinking about the out-of-body experience you described. I went over to the Christian bookstore to look for any books on this topic, and I found two that I thought you might be interested in."

He dug in the bag and handed Jackson two books. "The first is called *90 Minutes in Heaven* by John Piper. It's a story about a Baptist minister involved in a serious car accident who is declared legally dead at the scene. He's taken up to heaven for ninety minutes, and then he comes back to life to tell about it. The second book is called *23 Minutes in Hell* by Bill Wiese. It's a story about a Christian man who was abruptly ripped from his house, thrust into hell, and then rescued after being there for twenty-three minutes. Both are short reads."

Mike reached into his bag and pulled out two more books. "I got this next one from my library called *Beyond Death's Door* by Maurice Rawlings. He was a cardiologist who documented various out-of-body experiences. All three authors are sincere, and I believe they are telling the truth. I'd like you to read the books and see if your experiences line up with theirs. Oh, and here's one other book I love, *More Than Meets the Eye* by Dr. Richard Swenson. It talks about the possibility of there being multiple dimensions in the universe, among other things."

Jackson smiled. "And I didn't think you believed me."

"Well, to be honest, I'm still not sure that I do, but after reading the first two books, I now think it's possible what you said is true."

Someone knocked on the doorframe, and Dr. Matheson walked into the room. After introductions, he said, "I have good news for you, Mr. Trotman. You can leave the hospital tomorrow morning."

*Yes!* "Great. I'm ready to get out of here."

The doctor smiled. "I've heard good reports from the physical therapists. You've been working hard, and I think you're good to go. You'll need to take it easy for a few days at home; then, you can start back at work on Monday."

Jackson stood and shook the doctor's hand. "Thanks for all that you and the entire staff have done for me."

The doctor nodded and left.

Mike stood up. "I guess I should be going too. Let me know what you think of the books."

"Yes, sir. Thanks for picking them up for me. How much do I owe you?"

Mike waved his hand. "Nothing. Don't worry about it."

"Really?"

He grinned. "Just put something in the offering plate."

Jackson waited for him to leave, then closed his eyes. Father in heaven, please rescue McKenzie, Monica, Pam, Fred, Jaime, and even Dexter from the lake of fire. Please help them to recognize their need for your forgiveness. In Jesus's name, I pray, amen.

## CHAPTER 23
# WORKING AGAIN

AFTER A WEEKEND at home eating pizza and watching movies, Monday morning came quickly. Jackson wasn't physically ready to start running on the treadmill yet, so he went directly to work. There, he said a quick prayer while parking his car. *Father in heaven, please help me to meet McKenzie, and please give me the right words to say to her. In Jesus's name, I pray, amen.*

He hobbled into the Aetna cafeteria, then ladled oatmeal into a Styrofoam cup while leaning on his crutches. He added a little milk, then fastened a plastic cover tightly over the cup. But how would he carry the oatmeal while using crutches? He should have brought a backpack or something with him. How stupid.

A soft, beautiful voice came from behind him as he was about to ask someone for assistance. "May I help you?"

Jackson turned. McKenzie stood right there. The cup slipped out of his hands and fell onto the floor. Fortunately, it didn't spill. McKenzie bent down, picked it up, and handed it to him.

*Boy, God works fast. She's so lovely, and so willing to help a stranger.* "McKenzie? Is that you?"

Recognition flickered in her eyes, and she smiled. "Jackson?" She carefully hugged him.

Tears welled in his eyes. He lost his composure for a few seconds and had to look away. He then took a deep breath and deftly wiped his eyes. "It's so good to see you. How are you? What's it been, seven years? You look great."

"Thanks. You look great, too, except for the crutches. What happened?"

"I was struck by a hit-and-run driver a few weeks ago. This is my first day back at work. So, what have you been up to for the past few years?"

McKenzie put a hand on his shoulder. "I'm so sorry. Are you alright?"

"I was in the hospital for over a week, and I'm still sore, but I'll be fine."

McKenzie shifted her weight and put her hands on her hips. "Glad to hear it. I graduated from Brown and worked for Fidelity in New York up until a few months ago. What have you been doing?"

"Graduated from UConn with an IT degree, joined the marines, earned an MBA at UConn, and then joined Aetna after working as a summer intern here between my first and second year of business school."

"The marines? Wow! What took you in that direction?"

Jackson bit his lip. What could he say? That he was depressed after losing her? No, that would scare her away. He would have to give her the pat answer and let her probe further if she wanted to. "To serve my country."

"That's really honorable."

She looked deeply into his eyes, the same way she'd seemed to when she was being dragged away to hell by the demons. Chills went through his spine. *Only five months to save her. Stay focused.*

"Thank you for your service. My brother's a marine. So how can I help you?"

*Her brother's a marine.* Jackson grinned. "It would be great if you could take this to the cash register for me. I can wait there until a coworker comes along to take it the rest of the way."

"I've got a few minutes. I don't mind taking it to your desk for you."

"You don't have to do that."

"It's no problem at all."

"Thanks. That's very kind of you." Jackson handed her the oatmeal, then placed his weight on his left crutch while keeping the other crutch tucked under his right arm. They started toward the cash registers. "How long have you worked here, and how do you like it?"

"I like it a lot. The people are nice, and I'm enjoying my work."

Jackson greeted the cashier, clumsily took out his wallet, and paid for the oatmeal. Of course, he couldn't let on that he knew anything about her, so he asked, "What department do you work in?"

"Marketing."

They left the cafeteria and started walking to the elevators.

"Which line of business?"

"All lines."

He chuckled. "Oh, you must be a bigwig."

McKenzie shrugged. "Not really. I'm developing content for a new website that will provide the producers with information about Aetna's various product lines."

Jackson faced her. "I'm working on that project too."

She cocked her head slightly to one side. "What's your position?"

"IT project manager. My team is building the website that will host the content you're developing."

"Nice. I guess we will be working together, then."

He grinned. "I guess we will."

They boarded the elevator. "What floor do you work on?" McKenzie asked.

"Third."

McKenzie pushed the button for the third floor. "What an amazing coincidence that we'll be working together after all these years."

Jackson shifted his weight on his crutches. "I don't believe in coincidences. I think things happen for a reason." Hopefully, he wasn't coming on too strong.

"And how do you like working here, Jackson?"

"I like it most of the time. I have a great team. My boss is pretty good, but he can be a pain in the you-know-what sometimes. I guess that's true of any job."

"Yeah. No job is perfect."

"What did you do at Fidelity?"

"I worked in their marketing department, doing similar communications work."

He decided against asking why she left. She would tell him when she was ready.

When they reached Jackson's floor, McKenzie stepped forward and held the elevator door for him. They approached his cubicle. Someone had filled it with yellow balloons and a big yellow sign that read WELCOME BACK JACKSON! in red letters.

He paused at its entrance. "That was so nice of my team to think of me." Then, after leaning his crutches against the inside wall of his cubicle, he hopped over to his chair and sat down.

She set the cup of oatmeal on his desk.

He looked up at her. "Thank you so much, McKenzie. I appreciate it." His mind raced, trying to think of an excuse to see her again soon. "Listen, why don't I take a look at our calendars and set up some time to talk about your requirements for the new website?"

"That sounds good. Just let me know." She smiled. "It's nice to see you again."

"Nice to see you too." Maybe she didn't remember how things were the last time they were together.

Several coworkers came over to his desk to greet him, but his gaze stayed on her. McKenzie glanced back over her shoulder as she walked toward the elevators.

After the commotion died down, Jackson swiveled his chair toward his desk and tried to start working but couldn't concentrate. His heart was pounding. He stared into space, thinking about her.

He shook his head, fighting to focus. He had over five hundred emails to go through, and he'd need to clear them out as soon as possible so he could send McKenzie the meeting invitation. Then he had to find out how the project was going. After all, that was why Aetna was paying him.

It took a few minutes to retrieve all the emails. As Jackson waited, he glanced at *The Princess Diaries* sign he had hanging on his cubicle wall: "The brave do not live forever, but the cautious do not live at all."

"No time for caution, Jackson." He reviewed his online calendar to see which meetings he needed to attend that day.

He spent three hours listening to conference calls on his headset while sifting through the emails to determine which ones he could delete, which he had to file, and which he had to read. Toward the end of the day, his inbox was getting somewhat under control. After copying as many emails as possible to his hard drive, he finally got out of email jail.

He reviewed McKenzie's electronic calendar and saw an opening at eleven on Wednesday morning. He emailed her an invitation with the subject Producer Content Requirements. About thirty seconds later, he received her acceptance.

For the rest of the day, he couldn't stop smiling.

❧

When her work slowed down that afternoon, McKenzie let her mind wander to Jackson. Their first and only date on Block Island had been a bust. The day had started out memorable with his courageous rescue of a little girl. After the beach, they agreed to each return home to freshen up and then they would meet at a local restaurant.

By the way he slurred his greeting, he'd drunk several beers before she arrived. He consumed four more beers with dinner. In the end, she had to help him stagger back to his place behind the Surf Hotel on Dodge Street.

She took his keys out of his pocket, unlocked the outside door with the house key. Inside, she helped him onto his bed, took off his shoes, pulled the blanket over him, and made sure she locked the door behind her as she left. How many times had she done the same thing for her father?

As she walked back to Ballard's to get her bike, anger simmered inside her. She should have been on a date, enjoying the company, the stars, and the cool night air, but she'd been on a date all alone. Jackson might have had a tough day saving that little girl and fending off a shark, but that was no excuse.

When they'd met today in the cafeteria, the jolt of attraction had shocked her. Seven years hadn't changed their chemistry. But if Jackson's behavior hadn't changed, it would make no difference. She refused to date a drunk like her dad.

# CHAPTER 24
# BUSINESS BEFORE PLEASURE

TWO DAYS HAD passed since Jackson's oatmeal rendezvous with McKenzie. He spent his entire Wednesday morning planning for their meeting at eleven, anxious to spend more time with her—alone.

Typically, the project manager would invite the business analysts to the first system development meeting with the customer. After all, they would be gathering and documenting the requirements. Hopefully, she would overlook this slight breach of protocol in not inviting them.

At five minutes before eleven, he made his way to the conference room. His underarms were sore from leaning on the crutches, making him wince a little as he walked. In conference room 3-EC, he propped the crutches against the wall, put his notebook and pen on the conference room table, and made sure that everything was aligned perfectly.

The glass outer doors gave him a perfect view of anyone who approached. At precisely eleven, McKenzie walked down the hall with a confident smile, entered the conference room, and closed the door behind her. Wearing a black dress with black stockings and black heels, she had her neck adorned with white pearls and her ears with matching earrings. She had reconfigured her shiny dark hair into a bun. Her stunning display of femininity was a little dressy for the business-casual environment at Aetna, but it made an impression on him.

He decided to be a little bold. "You look maavalass, daaling," he said, mimicking Billy Crystal's impersonation of Fernando Lamas.

Her smile returned. "Why, thank you, sir."

His phone vibrated. He pulled it from its carrying case and looked at the display window. "My boss." He allowed the phone to continue buzzing.

"Aren't you going to answer it?"

"Nah. I'm in a crucial meeting with a client."

Her grin widened.

"So, where were we? Oh, yes. How are you?"

"Doing well." She sat down across the conference table from him, opened her laptop, and placed her spiral notebook next to it. "I'm still trying to find my way around the building and the city, but I'm getting there."

"Where do you live?"

"I've got a short-term lease at Hartford Twenty-one, at least until I can figure out where I want to live."

"That's a pretty swanky place."

McKenzie shrugged.

His phone buzzed again, but this time it was a text message. He opened the phone and looked at it: *Answer your phone NOW!*

"Your boss again?"

"Yes."

"Maybe you should answer it."

"I remember when they were building Hartford Twenty-one, while I was at UConn. It looks nice from the outside."

"It's nice on the inside too." She then eyed him. "Jackson, it's your boss. You'd better answer it."

He sighed. "Yeah."

Instead, he texted Fred back: *Tied up with customer right now. Can I get back to you in a few?* He leaned forward and focused his attention on her again.

He received another text message from Fred: *Don't give a RIP if UR busy. Glenn needs proj info for mtg with CIO at NOON!*

"Perhaps I could show you around sometime," he said as nonchalantly as he could.

"I like visiting new places."

"I've been living in Connecticut for a while now and know my way around. I could give you a tour of the area. Would you like to get together Saturday? I know where all the best spots are."

She hesitated. "Well… I don't know."

He tried to smile. "Why worry? I'm on crutches. You can always run away or kick me in the leg if I don't behave myself."

"True."

"Maybe it would be more exciting to stay home and wash your cat or vacuum your apartment?"

She grinned back. "What were you thinking of doing?"

He sat up straighter. "I wanted it to be a surprise, but—" His phone buzzed again. "One second. My boss is freaking out. Let me call him."

"Sure."

He listened as Fred screamed at him for not calling back right away. At one point, he had to move the phone away from his ear because the yelling was so loud. He looked at McKenzie, shook his head, and rolled his eyes. "Okay, Fred. What would you like me to do?" In short angry bursts, Fred explained what he needed. "Right. I'll get it to Glenn before noon, and I'll cc you."

Fred hung up the phone without even saying goodbye or thank you.

"Sorry about that. We have these blasted fire drills all the time.

I have to get something to my boss's boss by noon. Now, where were we?"

"You were going to tell me what you planned to have us do on Saturday."

"Right. I was thinking about going for a train ride on a real steam locomotive, for starters. The countryside is gorgeous in Essex, south of Hartford. I have to do something where I don't move around a lot because of my leg. There's a lot of other fun stuff to do in that part of the state too."

McKenzie nodded. "Okay."

"So… is that a yes?"

"Yes."

"Great. Why don't you give me your cell number, and I'll pick you up at around eleven on Saturday morning? I'll plan out the whole day for us. That's what project managers do, you know—plan."

She beamed. "Sounds great."

McKenzie gave him her number, and he entered it into his contacts list.

"Okay, so why were we meeting here again?" he asked. "Oh, yeah, to determine your requirements. I've got to run, but I'll schedule another meeting to do that. Okay?"

They both stood.

"Thanks." She picked up her laptop and notebook, then turned to leave.

Jackson loaded his materials in his laptop bag. "I'll see you on Saturday."

She smiled at him as she left the room. "I'm looking forward to it."

He couldn't have been happier. *Thank you, Father.* He was already planning the rest of the details in his mind and would spare no expense to make sure that she had a great time with him.

❦

At eight thirty on Thursday evening, McKenzie called her sister. Her workout in the apartment building's exercise center had been great, but she needed to talk to someone.

"Hey!" Monica greeted her when she answered.

"How are you?" She switched the phone to her other ear as she crossed the kitchen. "Let me put you on speaker while I get my dinner ready." She placed her phone on the granite countertop and walked to the refrigerator.

"Good. How about you?"

"I met this guy at work."

Monica gasped. "Tell me. Is he cute?"

"More like... ruggedly handsome."

"Ruggedly handsome? Ooh! Sounds delicious. What's he like?"

McKenzie pulled out a head of romaine lettuce, a red pepper, and a tomato, then placed them on a cutting board next to the phone. "Late twenties, single, very nice, and very funny. I met him about seven years ago while working on Block Island."

"What's his name?"

"Jackson."

"What's he look like?"

She started chopping. "About six-foot-one, maybe one-eighty. Very fit and muscular with deep blue eyes and black hair."

Monica squealed. "Sounds dreamy. You think he has potential?"

"Oh, I don't know. We haven't been on a date in seven years." She slid the chopped vegetables into a large bowl. "He used to have a drinking problem. Not sure if he still does. We'll see. He's taking me around the Hartford area on Saturday, and I think he likes me."

"Why?"

"Because he couldn't stop staring at me."

"You're beautiful, so it doesn't surprise me."

McKenzie chuckled. "You're too kind."

"So, what are you going to be doing in the Hartford area?"

"I don't know." McKenzie gazed out the window and over the river. "We're going to ride on an old-fashioned steam locomotive, but he didn't tell me the rest."

"That sounds... well... boring."

"Oh, I forgot. Jackson is on crutches right now, so he can't move around much. I'm looking forward to going out with him again. I liked him before—a lot, actually—but was turned off by his drinking." She poured some olive oil and balsamic vinegar over the vegetables and sat down on a stool at the kitchen island to eat. "What's happening with you? How's the control-freak boyfriend doing?"

"About the same." She lowered her voice. "There's an assistant principal at a nearby school who kind of likes me, but I haven't gone out with him yet. He seems nice but probably doesn't have as much money as Ronaldo."

"Maybe you should give him a try anyway. Money isn't everything. Smile and talk to him the next time you see him. Invite him out to lunch or something and see what happens."

"We'll see."

"Well, I'd better go. I don't want to get you in trouble with Cro-Magnon man. I've got to take a shower and check email before I go to bed."

"Let me know how your date goes."

"Will do." *I can't wait.*

✧

Jackson smiled as he sat down at his desk Friday morning. He couldn't wait to pick McKenzie up at her apartment the following day and get to know her again. Suddenly, his mind flashed back to the lake of fire, zeroing in on Fred instead of McKenzie. He hadn't talked to Fred about his experiences at The Wall since he'd returned to work. Jackson pulled a Bible tract from his top drawer, put it in his pocket, grabbed his crutches, and shuffled to Fred's office.

Fred snapped his computer closed as Jackson entered. "Jackson! What can I do for you?"

He plopped into his favorite chair. "Well, I just realized that I haven't really talked to you since my accident."

"No problem. We're all pretty busy right now. I know how it is."

Jackson tapped his good leg. "Have you thought any more about Pam's screams after I helped revive her?"

"Not lately."

*Father in heaven, please give me the right words to say without losing my job.* "I think it was a warning from God. We all need to take it very seriously. There is a real heaven and a real hell. And if you're not sure where you're going, you're not going to like where you end up."

Fred leaned forward in his chair. "Whoa. Where is that coming from?"

"Did you know I technically died twice on the operating table?"

"No."

"I had some extraordinary out-of-body experiences while I was unconscious in the hospital, and I can tell you that if you don't get right with God, you'll end up in hell."

Fred smirked. "Okay, Jackson. Whatever you say."

"I know I'm coming on strong, but it's because I'm concerned about you. Here. Take a look at this." He placed the Bible tract on Fred's desk. "It will tell you how to get right with God. I can review it with you now if you like."

Fred glanced at the tract but didn't touch it. "Look, Jackson. I'm sure you mean well, and I know you've been through a lot, but don't ever talk to me like that again. If I want spiritual help or advice, I'll ask for it."

"Okay, Fred."

Jackson shuffled back to his desk, shaking his head. *That did not go well. What did I do wrong?* He sighed. *Mike and the Bible are right. Some people won't listen, even if someone comes back from the dead and warns them about hell.*

## CHAPTER 25
# FIRST DATE... ROUND TWO

JACKSON SLOWLY LEFT his condo Saturday morning. Although he was now off the crutches, he had to move carefully. Another beautiful day awaited him, about seventy-five degrees with a bit of humidity. He glanced down at his polo shirt and shorts, then adjusted his dark blue Red Sox cap. *Lord, I pray all goes well on my date with McKenzie. Please keep us safe and help us to have a great time today. In Jesus's name, I pray, amen.*

He arrived in front of McKenzie's building a few minutes early. They had agreed she would meet him at his car so he didn't have to take the elevator up to her apartment. Then, at one minute after eleven, he called her.

"Hey, Jackson," she said. "I'll be down in a few minutes."

"I'm on Trumbull Street in the car. I'll see you in a few."

He got out, walked around the car's front, and leaned against the front passenger's door. He surveyed the thirty-six-story Hartford 21 structure, admiring the sea-green windows that traversed the entire left corner of the postmodern building, offsetting an otherwise white façade.

A few moments later, McKenzie appeared. Everything about her was enchanting—the way she smiled, her thick brown hair, and how she carried herself. She looked beautiful in her purple linen shirt, white capris, and Birkenstock sandals, but one thing caught his attention most. She wore a pink Red Sox hat. "You're a Red Sox fan?"

McKenzie grinned. "You betcha."

"Awesome. How'd Boston do last night? I missed the game."

"Beat Baltimore three to two."

"They're still in first place, then?"

"Yep. A half a game ahead of the Yankees."

Impressive. "Sounds like you know your stuff."

She shrugged. "My dad is a huge Red Sox fan. I guess it rubbed off on me."

He pushed away from the car and stood up straight with his shoulders back. "Did you notice something different about me?"

"Hey, no crutches! Let me see you walk."

Jackson took a few turns back and forth on the sidewalk.

She applauded. "Wonderful. Enough walking for now, though. I can see that you're still struggling a bit. But it's great that you're off the crutches."

"Anyway, I've planned our day around my little handicap. There won't be a lot of walking, but there will be a lot of sightseeing. First, we'll go down Interstate 91 to Route 9 to ride on the Essex Steam Train, which will end at the Connecticut River. Then we'll take a riverboat ride up the river. We can have lunch on the train or the boat, whenever we get hungry. After that, we'll have dinner at the Gelston House Inn in East Haddam, which has beautiful views of the river. And after dinner, we're going to see a show at the Goodspeed Opera House next door."

"Sounds fantastic." She glanced at his car. "Nice ride. I love Mustangs, especially convertibles.

He opened the door for her. After she was seated, he closed it, then got in on the driver's side. "My dad's a Ford dealer, so I got it at a ridiculous discount."

"Nice. Can we put the top down?"

"Sure." Jackson started the car, put the top down, and pulled away from the curb. "Where did you grow up again?"

"Marblehead, Massachusetts."

"That's on the shore, isn't it?" Instantly, he recalled the demons hovering over the beachgoers' heads.

"It's a charming resort town. Many wealthy people who work in Boston live there, but my dad is an electrician, and my mom is a schoolteacher. It was a great place to grow up."

Jackson had to talk louder as they got on the interstate. "Sounds like it. You don't have much of a Boston accent. Why is that?"

"I don't know. I guess it disappeared when I went to Brown."

"You said something about having a brother in the marines?"

"My younger brother, Duncan. He's in Afghanistan right now, serving with the Third Battalion, Eleventh Marines."

*Good unit. Three-eleven saved my bacon a few times.* "That's an artillery battalion."

McKenzie brushed her hair to one side, but it was no use with the wind whipping it around. "Yes."

"What's his job there?"

"Lance corporal. He helps fire the big guns."

Jackson glanced over at her for a second. "When was the last time you saw him?"

McKenzie looked away. "He was home on leave last year."

Jackson touched her hand, then quickly pulled back. "When's he coming home again?"

"November, I think."

Jackson turned on the radio and selected a classical music station for background music. He adjusted the volume so it wouldn't interfere with their conversation. "It's quite a sacrifice he's making, being away from home so much. I know. You must be very proud of him."

"I am. I wish we weren't over there, but I support Duncan and all our troops one hundred percent."

"Do you ever pray for him?" The question came out of Jackson's mouth before he could filter it.

McKenzie looked straight at him. "What good would that do?"

*I should have waited to bring up the spiritual stuff until later.* He laughed, not knowing what else to do. "How about them Red Sox?"

McKenzie folded her arms across her chest. "Very funny. But I don't believe in God."

"Are you saying there is no God or that you're not sure if there is a God?"

"I'm not sure. I think there may be a God. If he or she were to come up to me and shake my hand, then I'd believe. But since I can't see him or touch him or listen to him or use any of my other senses to experience him, then I'd have to say he probably doesn't exist. My parents raised me Catholic, but I guess I'm an agnostic. Do you believe in God, Jackson?"

"Yes."

"Why?"

*Please give me the right words to say, Lord.* "Well, for starters, it's evident from the creation."

"What do you mean?"

Jackson thought for a moment. "Well, take the human eye, for example."

She scoffed. "I read somewhere that some scientists think the eye has a stupid design."

"The eye is a pretty amazing thing. First, light enters through the cornea, which is the primary focusing mechanism, and then moves through the iris, which controls the amount of light that enters. After that, the light passes through the lens for further focusing and then on through the retina. The retina contains light-sensitive photoreceptor cells. They convert the image into electrical signals that the brain can interpret. The eye takes pictures continuously and develops them instantly. The retina contains one hundred and twenty million rods used for dim vision, night vision, and peripheral vision, and seven million cones used for color vision and fine detail. Each eye contains one million nerve fibers that connect the photoreceptors in the retina to the brain's visual cortex, where it reconstructs images in such a way that we can see them. Not only can the human eye allow me to see to avoid other cars on the road, but it can perceive millions of shades of color in the scenery around us."

She stared. "How can you just rattle all that stuff off like that?"

"I did an internship for one semester with a startup that was trying to build an artificial eye. I also read about it in a book called *More Than Meets the Eye*. My friend, Mike Tolbert, gave it to me, and I thought it was fascinating. The author, Richard Swenson, is an MD and has a degree in physics. But actually, I hadn't told you the best part. There is more processing power in the human retina than in the laptop you use at work."

McKenzie shook her head. "I don't believe that."

"It's true. If you do the math, a single nerve cell can process five million instructions per second. If you then calculate a million of these nerve cells processing images simultaneously, the number goes up to five trillion calculations per second for each eye. That's way above the processing speed of any computer in 2011."

She nodded a few times. "But these processes you described, while impressive, were inherited through evolution."

"Have you ever read Darwin's *On the Origin of Species*?"

McKenzie coughed. "Well... no."

"Darwin seems like a reasonable and honest guy to me. Do you know what he said about the human eye?"

"No."

"He said that for the human eye to have been created through natural selection seems 'absurd in the highest possible degree.' And later, in a letter to a friend, he said that 'the eye to this day gives me a cold shudder.'"

"Darwin said that?" McKenzie looked at him thoughtfully.

"Yes. It takes a lot of faith to believe that all the complex, inter-dependent processes within the eye occurred by chance."

"Well, most, if not all, of my professors at Brown believed in evolution."

He grinned. "With all due respect, I disagree with your professors."

She glared at him. "Man, are you arrogant... and small-minded."

He shifted in his seat. *Be careful, or this will be a short date.* "I'm sorry you feel that way, but I'm compelled to disagree. They believe that something came from nothing. Where did that something originate? Dr. Swenson said that 'The something then became a prebiotic soup with hydrogen, carbon, nitrogen, and water vapor... The soup bubbles into compounds like methane and ammonia.' Lightning—wherever that came from—strikes the soup several times, resulting in an amino acid, followed by the spontaneous creation of other amino acids. Then it strikes again, resulting in a protein, then somehow more complex proteins are produced. After a while, you have a living cell with thousands of proteins created by a DNA strand with three billion base pairs. This was all the result of 'random beneficent mutations.' But you're not done yet. Somehow, you must get from that single cell to millions of different organisms, each containing trillions of cells, all conveniently organized in such a way as to support the various functions required for life."

McKenzie considered that for a few moments before speaking. "Well, as unlikely as it seems, it's still possible."

"But is it probable? I think evolution, as an explanation of our origins, is more a matter of faith than fact. Anyway, I'm sorry if I've been boring you with all this stuff. Instead of me droning on and on, let me get you a copy of Dr. Swenson's book. I think you'd find it interesting reading."

"To be honest, I'm not sure I'd read it. Creationism is for Bible-thumping simpletons who haven't taken the time to understand the scientific proof behind evolution. They just say, 'God did it.' But evolution is a fact." She put a hand over her mouth as if she couldn't believe she'd called him a simpleton.

Jackson sighed. *She didn't hear a word I said.* "Mutations at the cellular level are a fact because this can be proven over and over again in the laboratory using the scientific method. Species-to-species evolution, like a fish evolving into an ostrich, is just a theory. Scientists have not proven it in the laboratory, through the fossil record, or by any other method you can come up with."

"That's a bunch of bull… manure, Jackson. No respectable member of the scientific community believes that."

He laughed. "You've got some fire in those bones, McKenzie. I like that."

McKenzie fumed. "Don't patronize me, Trotman. Chimpanzees share ninety-eight percent of the same DNA as humans, don't they?"

"Creation scientists disagree on the exact percentage, but it's very high."

"There's your species-to-species evolution proof right there."

"Whatever genetic similarity there is, it points to a common designer rather than evolution. When I programmed in college, I would reuse subroutines all the time. Why reinvent the elbow, so to speak."

McKenzie grimaced. "Well, there's plenty of evidence that fossils are millions of years old."

"Oh? Have you heard of the fossilized miner's helmet?"

"The what?"

"Google 'fossilized hats.'"

McKenzie took her phone out of her pocketbook and typed in the search criteria. "It says there's a miner's helmet on display in a Tasmanian museum that's been completely fossilized."

"Correct. How long does it say it took for it to become fossilized?"

"About fifty years. How come I've never heard of that?"

"I'm not sure."

McKenzie took a deep breath. "I didn't expect to have an intellectual discussion like this on a first date."

*Technically, it's our second date, but I won't bring that up.* "Me either. Maybe we'd better change the subject."

"I think you're right. I'd still like to know how you remember all that stuff."

Jackson smoothed his hair with his hand. "I'm fascinated by it, mostly."

He smiled at her. Once again, he'd better lighten things up, or she'd want him to turn the car around. "Did you play any sports in high school or college?"

"Soccer in high school. I started on the varsity team my senior year but wasn't good enough to play in college. I just took up running instead."

"You look like you're in pretty good shape. I used to run at the health club a lot, but I've had to take a break since the accident. Maybe we could go running sometime."

"Sure. What sports did you play in high school?"

"My favorite sport was baseball. I played it in high school and college."

"That's right; you played for UConn."

"Yep. I also played soccer in the spring and hockey in the winter during high school. I have a funny hockey story. I was out on the ice when an opponent took a shot and hit me with the puck in the groin area."

McKenzie laughed, but quickly stopped. "Oh, I'm sorry, that must have hurt."

"Not at all. Fortunately, I was wearing a cup. Unfortunately, it made a loud, distinctive ping sound so that everyone in the rink knew exactly where I was hit."

McKenzie covered her mouth, giggling.

"I was pretty embarrassed. I can still remember people in the stands and some of the players laughing at me."

McKenzie's giggling turned to guffawing. Jackson couldn't help but join in.

Twenty minutes later, they arrived at the Essex Steam Train parking lot. Young families milled around, the children bursting with excitement at seeing Thomas the Tank Engine and a real old-fashioned caboose. Jackson and McKenzie smiled at each other as they walked to the yellow and red clapboard train station. He bought their tickets, and they boarded the restored train soon after.

Within minutes, the train glided effortlessly through the bucolic countryside. The hiss of the steam, the periodic whistle blasts, and the clickety-clack of the tracks took him back to an earlier, simpler era.

"Isn't it beautiful out here?" he asked.

"Yeah. I had no idea there was this kind of attraction in Connecticut."

"There are lots of beautiful places here."

McKenzie leaned back and stared out the window. Several minutes later, she spoke again. "Jackson, did you ever serve overseas?"

"Yes."

"Where?"

"Afghanistan."

"My brother has told me a little about it, but not much. What's it like over there?"

"Well, I was in the southern part. It was sweltering. The soil is brown and rocky, and there's dust everywhere. The camps smell horrible from open-pit garbage burning. There isn't a whole lot to do when you're not out on patrol."

"Did you see any action while you were there?"

"Yes." He didn't want to talk about it and turned his attention to the small white clapboard church ahead of them. "That's a beautiful old church, isn't it?"

"Yeah."

Time to steer the conversation back to God, but gently. "Did your parents take you to church when you were growing up?"

"We went to mass regularly when I was little. My mom was really into it, but it never stuck with me. It just seemed like everyone was pretending. I stopped going when I got to college."

He glanced at her. "Did you have any Christian friends in college?"

"No. I was more interested in partying than religion. How about you?"

"I was a real partier in college too. I drank like a fish and did all the bad stuff."

McKenzie furrowed her brow and took a deep breath. "Do you still drink a lot?"

"Nope. I don't drink at all now."

Her jaw dropped. She gaped at him.

"Alcohol was wrecking my life. I'm sure you haven't forgotten our last date on Block Island. I couldn't stop drinking on my own, so I asked Jesus to take away my desire for alcohol, and he did. I'm a new person now."

She continued to stare. "Jesus? You're one of those born-again Christians now?"

"Yes."

"Wow." McKenzie sniffed and stared out the window. Eventually, she faced him again. "How in the world did you go from being a college playboy to a jarhead to a Christian?"

"I had some experiences during the war that scared me. I almost died several times, but God spared me for some reason. A navy chaplain gave me a Bible, and I began reading it. I soon realized I was a sinner and needed God's forgiveness. I accepted Jesus as my Savior, and he forgave me. God is now helping me become more like Jesus every day."

"Whoa. You *have* changed."

He smiled. "I've found a great church here, Valley Community Baptist in Avon."

"Baptists are a bit extreme, aren't they?"

"I guess that depends on your point of view. I don't think so." He looked out the window again. "They're Bible-believing. They don't force anything on you. You should check it out for yourself sometime. By the way, don't let other people tell you what to think about a particular denomination. Every church is different, and none are perfect, but some are better than others."

McKenzie crossed her legs. "That's fair. How's your leg feeling?"

"It's still a little sore, but at least the stitches are out. It gets better every day." The train began slowing down. "Looks like we're coming to the end of the line here."

"That went by quick."

The train engine came to a stop and exhaled mightily. Jackson struggled to get up from the wooden bench. McKenzie reached out to help. The warmth of her hand flowed into his. He didn't want to let go. It was too much like touching her hand for the first time on Block Island. He held her hand as she helped him walk down the steep steps to the stone landing below.

Finally, she tilted her head toward him. "Can I have my hand back now?"

"No." He smiled. "You wouldn't turn a cold shoulder on a disabled veteran, would you?"

She smirked. "Disabled veteran, my foot. You're milking this phantom disability for all you can get, Jackson."

"Smart lady."

They boarded the riverboat next and ignored the tour guide speaking over the boat's intercom as they sat on a wooden bench on the top deck, baking in the sun. An abundance of green trees and white clapboard homes dotted the shoreline. He identified the medieval-looking Gillette Castle atop a hill overlooking the river, while the humming of the diesel engine brought a calm steadiness to their excursion.

"Jackson, you still haven't answered my question. What was it like over there?"

He sighed. "It depends on the job you're doing. Some people hardly ever leave the bases, which are generally safe, while others are out on the front lines all the time. Being in an artillery battalion, your brother deals with explosives all day, which can be dangerous. On the other hand, he isn't usually right on the front lines like the infantry, so he's probably not being shot at much. However, attacks do happen on bases, and some IEDs explode on the roads between bases, so you have to keep your guard up at all times."

"Were you ever shot at?"

"Yes. Many times."

"Can you tell me about it?"

He fidgeted. How could he expect her to open up to him if he wasn't willing to go first? "Are you sure you want to hear this?"

"Yes. Tell me."

"Okay. I was on patrol once, and we came under heavy machine gun fire. We returned fire, killing some of the Taliban enemies. I then told artillery to blanket the enemy position, and that killed most of the rest of them. We thought they were all dead, but two survived the barrage and shot my next-in-command's leg off. After getting the gunnery sergeant on the helicopter, I ran up that hill and killed both of them."

"That sounds extremely dangerous, and it sounds like you were incredibly brave."

"Thanks. There are other stories I can tell, but I'll save them for another time."

"Could you tell me one more now?"

"I guess. While on patrol, we came under mortar attack. My second-in-command was blown to bits right next to me and…" He tried to finish, but his voice broke.

"Tell me," she said quietly.

He pressed his eyes closed to get through the rest. "I thought I was hit, but it was his blood spattered all over my uniform. He had a wife and two little girls."

"I'm so sorry. I can't imagine how you would feel after that happened."

"Horrible. I wish I had done a better job protecting my marines, but I did the best I could. I can't imagine what the staff sergeant's family must have gone through when they heard the news and what they're still going through today. I feel a little guilty on both accounts. Why were they maimed or killed instead of me?"

Rather than "correct" his feelings of guilt, as many well-meaning people would, she merely nodded. "What else?"

"Why do you want to know all these details?"

"I want to get to know you better, Jackson. The marines were an important part of your life."

"Yes, they were. Although I didn't think about it at the time, I feel bad for the families of the men I killed. They were someone's son, uncle, father, or brother too. Just so you know, I've never told anyone about this before."

McKenzie inhaled deeply. "Thank you so much for sharing."

"You're welcome."

Her eyes rounded into a sad expression. "Should I be worried about my brother?"

"The one thing I've learned from my experience over there is that no matter how crazy things get, God is ultimately in control. I suggest you send your brother lots of emails and letters and care packages to show he's not forgotten."

She reached over and squeezed his hand. He laced their fingers together and let the quiet settle over them.

Eventually, they both got hungry, so McKenzie went down to the main deck and bought them each a salad to tide them over until dinner. Then they sat and talked, but with periods of comfortable silence.

After the boat ride, they reboarded the train for the trip back to the parking lot. Jackson placed his arm on the bench behind McKenzie. She nodded off soon after they started, using his arm as a headrest. She was still asleep when they arrived at the parking lot, and he gently woke her when the conductor started walking through the car.

She yawned. "Oh, I needed that little catnap. How long was I out?"

"About twenty minutes." He flexed and wiggled his right arm a few times. "My arm fell asleep. I have to get the blood flowing again."

"Sorry. Guess I must be a pretty exciting date."

"No worries," he said. They moved toward the exit, where McKenzie helped Jackson off the train.

"It was probably my stimulating conversation that caused you to conk out."

"No, it's not you. To be honest, I've been having nightmares lately."

"Oh. What about, if you don't mind me asking?"

"There's a guy from college that I ran into at a Brown party in New York City recently. He's been stalking me. He's the main reason I left New York. I'm scared he's going to find me and hurt me."

"That's terrible. I'm so sorry you're going through this. He sounds like a crazy person. Don't you worry. If he comes around, I'll take care of him."

"I believe you would. That's why I slept."

As they walked to his car, he looked at his watch. "Now it's time for the next leg of our journey. Off to the Gelston House Inn for dinner. We'll be a little early, so we can walk along the river for a while or tour the theater next door. They also have Adirondack chairs to sit in and watch the river flow by, just like at the Spring House on Block Island. The show starts at eight. I have a six-thirty dinner reservation, but we can go to dinner earlier if you wish. Whatever you'd like to do is fine with me."

She grinned. "You don't have to manage every detail so carefully, Jackson. Let's just play it by ear and head in for dinner whenever we get hungry, but no later than six thirty."

"Sounds like a plan."

About fifteen minutes later, they approached a bridge that crossed the Connecticut River. The lights at the bridge entrance flashed, and a traffic gate descended in front of them.

"I've never seen a bridge like this before," she said.

"They had an article about it in the paper a while ago. It's a moveable steel swing-truss bridge, meaning that a major section of it swings sideways ninety degrees to allow large vessels to pass through." Moments later, a yacht passed through the bridge opening as the car traffic backed up behind them.

After a few minutes, the bridge rotated back to its original position. As they crossed it, the six-story Goodspeed Opera House jutted upward from the shoreline on the other side. Just past the theater was the Gelston House Inn. Its Victorian architecture complemented that of the theater.

As they walked along the wooden bridge from the parking lot to the inn grounds, Jackson pointed out the little inlets below and some of the wildlife that lived there. They sat on the Adirondack chairs for a while, then walked up onto the front porch and into the Gelston House lobby.

The hostess escorted them through the formal dining room to the patio off the rear of the building, where she seated them at a table for two beneath the white-and-green-striped awning. The waiter soon came and took their food and drink orders.

Jackson leaned back in his chair and smiled at McKenzie. "This is fun," he said with a mischievous smile. "What other controversial topic would you like to discuss? Gay marriage? Politics?"

"Something safe. How about the Red Sox?"

"Okay. Who was the last Red Sox player to win the Triple Crown, and what year did he do it in?"

"Easy. Carl Yastrzemski, 1967."

Impressive. "Okay, smarty-pants. How many home runs and RBIs did he have that year, and what was his batting average?"

"Forty-four home runs, one hundred and twenty-one RBIs, and his average was .326."

Jackson was stunned. "How could you possibly know that?"

"Yaz was my dad's favorite player. He knew everything about him."

They discussed their own favorite players and game moments, and her knowledge of Sox trivia continued to astound him. She was an even bigger fan than he was.

McKenzie looked up. "Did you ever wonder why I didn't want to go out with you again while we were working at Block Island?"

"I figured it was my drinking."

"Yes. My dad gets blasted most nights after work and every weekend."

"I'm sorry to hear that."

"I don't want to go out with a drunk."

"I understand. But as you know, that's not an issue for me anymore."

"I know. Good for you, Jackson."

"Yes. Thank God. I'm glad you took the job at Aetna."

"I'm happy we reconnected too."

The waiter brought their food—gluten-free seared salmon with asparagus and risotto for her and pan-seared rib-eye steak with mashed potatoes and vegetables for him. She offered him a taste of her fish, which he enjoyed, and he offered her a bite of steak.

She shook her head. "No, thanks. I try to avoid red meat. Studies show it feeds cancer cells. Did you know that it takes your body several days longer to digest meat than it does other foods?"

"I didn't, but I guess that makes sense. Meat is much denser than other foods, so it must be harder to digest."

"The meat may also have extra hormones in it that aren't healthy. The bigger the animal, the more money the rancher makes. If you're going to eat meat, at least get it at a health-food place like Whole Foods or Trader Joe's, so you know it doesn't contain any harmful chemicals. It's still healthier to avoid red meat."

"There are two Whole Foods stores right in West Hartford. One's within walking distance of my condo."

"Nice. Do you shop there?"

"Once in a while, but I'm not as health-conscious as you are. May I ask you a personal question?"

She shrugged. "Sure."

"What's it like to eat gluten-free all the time?"

"It's not too bad anymore. There are so many gluten-free products out there now. I can get gluten-free pancakes, cookies, brownies, and all kinds of stuff like that."

They continued talking, alternating between Red Sox trivia and health-food tips.

Finally, Jackson looked at his watch. "We better go. We've got to pick up the tickets." He paid the check, and they walked to the Goodspeed Opera House. "How did you like the restaurant?"

"It has a wonderful ambiance." She smiled. "The food was delicious, and I enjoyed the company."

He grinned back. "I'm glad you liked it. I enjoyed the company too."

McKenzie's eyes widened as they stepped into the opera house. *Good. She's captivated by it.* Unlike modern theaters, the foyer was small, cramped, and filled with many people. But the details were exquisite. A steep hourglass-shaped magenta-carpeted staircase led to second-floor gold colonnades and an ornate gold ceiling. Polished green granite trim complemented the wooden railings, and the cream-colored walls reflected light coming from a brass chandelier hanging in the center of the lobby.

They found their seats in the orchestra section and sat down. He opened the program and began reading from it with Shakespearean bravado. "Experience one brief shining moment that was Camelot. Relive the enduring legend of King Arthur, Guinevere, Lancelot, and the Knights of the Round Table in an enchanting fable of chivalry, honor, and brotherhood. Dazzling and spellbinding with sweeping romance and historic grandeur, this classic musical speaks to our time and for all time."

McKenzie chuckled. "Sounds exciting."

As the show started, Jackson placed his hand on hers. She looked at him and smiled. He kept it there throughout most of the first act until they began to clap. At intermission, they browsed through a memorabilia store, then meandered to a bar where he ordered a seltzer with lemon for both of them. From there, they stepped out onto a tiny open-air patio overlooking the river.

Suddenly, an image of McKenzie writhing in the lake of fire popped into his mind. He shuddered and glanced over at her to see if she'd noticed. Fortunately, she was looking out over the river.

They went back into the theater for the next act. The singing was great and the pageantry of King Arthur's court impressive for such a small theater.

Afterward, Jackson and McKenzie slowly sashayed along their row to the aisle, then merged with the crowd into the lobby. He kept his hand on her elbow the whole time, only dropping it when they were outside.

On the wooden bridge by the side of the river, she stopped and faced him. "I've had a wonderful time with you today, Jackson."

"Even though I'm a Bible-thumping simpleton?"

McKenzie appeared a little flustered. "Oh… ah… sorry about that."

"No worries. I've had a great time too." She leaned a little closer. His heart beat faster. She wanted him to kiss her. As he was about to oblige, raindrops trickled down on him, followed by a pattering rain. "Oh no. The top's down."

A torrential downpour soon engulfed them. Jackson hobbled as fast as he could beside McKenzie toward his car, but they got soaked along the path to the parking lot. He fumbled with his keys, trying to open the car door for her. They laughed hysterically as they sat in the bucket seats, getting drenched while he frantically tried to get the convertible top back up, and continued laughing even after the roof was securely in place.

They didn't say much on the way home, shivering even though the heat was on. They held hands until he pulled up to her apartment building. He got out and walked her to the door.

She rummaged through her purse, trying to find her keys. "Thank you for a wonderful day."

"I'm so glad you enjoyed it. I'll give you a call, and we'll plan to do something again soon, okay?"

"That would be fantastic."

He took both her hands in his, but a bunch of college kids showed up just as he was about to kiss her good night. They weren't leaving, so he shrugged and released her hands. "Have a good night."

"You too." She unlocked the front door and went inside.

She walked through the glass exterior doors and to the elevators. She entered the elevator, turned, and waved to him as the door closed.

Although the date had started off a bit rocky, he'd gotten a glimpse of the real McKenzie, a woman who loved her brother and the Red Sox but hated drinking and red meat, a woman he was falling in love with. "Best day of my life."

# CHAPTER 26
# ANTICIPATION

MCKENZIE AWOKE AT ten thirty the following morning. She threw on some sweats, took the elevator down to the ground level, and began the two-block journey to Starbucks to pick up coffee and a newspaper. What was Jackson doing right now? Just the thought of him made her happy.

Back in her apartment, she opened the *Hartford Courant* and searched for a review of the show. She couldn't find one. Then she went online and retrieved a review on the *Courant's* website. The reviewer had liked it as well.

It had been a wonderful evening. Her lips pursed. What would it have been like to kiss Jackson? Soft and sweet? Or needy and passionate? Monica would have an opinion. She should be up by now. So, McKenzie grabbed her phone and texted her: *You up yet?*

The response came within seconds: *Yep.*

McKenzie called her and set her phone on speaker. "Hey."

"So how'd it go last night? Inquiring minds want to know."

She leaned on the countertop and gazed out over Downtown Hartford, smiling. "He's so nice. It was the best date I've ever had."

"Nice? Did you invite him up to your apartment?"

"Of course not. It was only a first date." McKenzie rolled her eyes. "Besides, he's a Baptist, so he probably isn't into that sort of thing right away."

"Baptist? Maybe you'd better lose him then, babe. Not your type."

McKenzie sat on one of the barstools at the island. "Normally, he wouldn't be. But there's something different about him. In a way, I wish I wasn't so attracted to him."

"Why?"

"It was so much easier to dump him before because of his drinking, but he's changed. He's got all these off-the-wall ideas about God and evolution and that kind of stuff, and it bugs me. It's against everything I ever learned in school. On the other hand, he's so nice and respectful that I love being around him." She sighed. "I think he's the nicest man I've ever met."

"That's something coming from you, Miss Picky. I'm happy for you."

"Well, let's see what happens."

"Has he ever been married?" Monica asked.

"I don't know. I don't think so, but I didn't get around to asking Jackson about past loves yet."

"Do you think he's Mr. Right?"

McKenzie sniffed. "You're unbelievable."

"Come on. You can tell me. I'm waiting."

"I don't know. Maybe."

"Did he say he would call you?"

"He said he'd give me a call to do something again soon."

"Sounds promising. When do I get to meet him?"

"What's the hurry?"

"We've been waiting a long time for you to meet a guy like this. I'm so excited for you."

❧

The Sunday morning service had just ended when Jackson spotted Mike Tolbert among the crowd in the lobby. He'd just learned that Mike's mom had died from a heart attack a week ago. "Hey, Mike. I'm so sorry to hear about your mom." They shook hands. "How are you doing?"

"All right. It was a shock, her passing so suddenly. I had just talked with her a few days earlier. I guess you never know when your time is up. She was a Christian, though, so she had things all squared away spiritually."

"I'm sure it's a relief to know she's with the Lord. How's your dad doing?"

"He's pretty broken up, trying to figure out why God allowed it to happen. So am I."

"I know it sounds trite, Mike, but God has a plan for each of us. It was simply her time to go. You can trust that she's in good hands now."

"Yeah, I know, but she was only seventy. They were planning to enjoy another fifteen or twenty years together. I guess that will just have to wait until they get to heaven." Mike looked him over. "Enough about me. How are you?"

"Well, I know this may not be the best time, but are you free for lunch today? I have something important to talk with you about."

"I think we're free." Mike glanced around. "Let me check with Sally."

Jackson chuckled. "Wise man. I don't want to cause trouble in paradise. Tell her that she and the kids can come along. I know Sunday afternoon is family time for you guys, so I'm buying."

Mike grinned. "Sounds good to me."

"Great! Oh, I meant to call you about those books you gave me. I read them all. The book *23 Minutes in Hell* was spot on with what I'd observed, especially some of the descriptions of the Abyss. And *90 Minutes in Heaven* confirmed that what I experienced was possible.

And finally, *Beyond Death's Door* included a true story about a guy crying out that he was in hell while the doctor tried to revive him. That's what happened when I tried to revive Pam, the Jewish coworker I mentioned. Thanks so much for sharing these books with me."

"I'm glad the books were helpful. It's great to see you up and around again."

"Oh, and I met the woman I told you about—the one from work that I'm going to marry. I went on a date with her yesterday. Her name is McKenzie, and she's fantastic."

Mike gaped at him, then shook his head and smiled.

With a wave, Jackson headed to his Sunday school class.

❧

Jackson arrived for lunch at Cosi's first. As he was reviewing the menus hanging on the wall, the Tolbert family arrived.

Jackson greeted Mike and Sally, then looked to the kids. "Hey, Joshua, Sarah, and Benjamin? How are you doing? Boy, you're all getting big!"

"Yes," Sally said.

They stood in line together and placed their orders at the register. Jackson paid the bill, and after getting their drinks, they found a large table. Sally took scrap paper and crayons from her tote bag so the kids could draw while they waited for their lunch to be delivered.

"How are things at work, Mike?" Jackson asked.

"Not too bad."

Sally beamed. "He just got promoted to lieutenant."

"Lieutenant Tolbert! Congratulations, sir." Jackson stood, locked his body at attention, and saluted.

Mike chuckled. "At ease, Trotman."

"No, seriously. That's a great accomplishment."

Mike nodded. "How are things in the insurance business?"

"Not too bad."

"That's good. I hear a lot of people are getting pink slips these days."

"I've been fortunate. Haven't gotten one yet."

The server arrived with their orders. Sally cut up the food for her youngest, and everyone ate in relative silence.

When the kids finished their lunches, Sally got out some coloring books, walked the kids to the comfy chair section of the restaurant, and then returned, seating herself so she could keep a watchful eye on the kids.

Mike continued eating. "So, what's this important matter you wanted to discuss with me?" he asked with his mouth full.

"There are two important things." Jackson chewed his sandwich thoughtfully. What was the best way to say this?

"I think God not only wants to instruct me, but he also wants me to help save my wife. And I think he wants me to warn my coworkers about what's coming."

"Why do you think he wants you to warn people? We have the Bible. It's still the number one bestseller in the world, you know."

"Society has changed. Most people don't read the Bible anymore. They don't know about this stuff."

"True."

One of the kids started whining, so Sally left to investigate.

Jackson continued. "You were at the accident at the foot of Avon Mountain a few weeks ago. It involved the kid who hit me in the St. Francis parking garage."

Mike stopped chewing. "How did you know that?"

"Because I was there too. I saw you. The accident was one of the places I traveled to with my guardian angel."

"Really?"

"I was sitting in the back seat of the kid's car, invisible and in another dimension, when it all happened."

Mike leaned back in his chair. "Right."

"I'm telling the truth." He then explained precisely how the accident happened.

Mike slowly nodded. "It did happen like that, but maybe you heard about it in the news accounts or inadvertently saw the accident reports online and just forgot."

"When the fireman pulled him out with the Jaws of Life, you turned aside and threw up. Was that in the accident report?"

He shook his head. "But someone could have told you about it."

"Yeah, or maybe I'm just telling the truth! Let me tell you something else." Jackson put both hands flat on the table. "This could come as a surprise. Did you know Sally is pregnant with twin girls?"

"What?" He called Sally over. "You're not pregnant, are you?"

She scowled. "Not that I know of."

He turned back to Jackson. "There. Do you see? You're wrong, and this is getting a little weird and way too personal for me. I don't like it. What makes you think she's pregnant anyway?"

"The angel told me. He specifically mentioned twin girls."

Mike pursed his lips. "We need to end this once and for all. Honey, we're going to CVS to get a pregnancy test."

Sally brightened. "This is exciting. I'd love to have more children."

Mike glared at them. "Both of you, stop it—right now! I deal in facts. Hard facts. Evidence." He shifted his gaze back to Jackson. "Time to talk about something else. What else is going on in your life?"

He grinned and then told them about meeting McKenzie and their date the day before.

"Is she a Christian?" Sally asked.

He knew a lecture was coming. "No."

"You'd better be careful, Jackson." She glanced at her husband. "God is such a central part of your life now that there will always be conflict in your household if you two aren't on the same page about that. The Bible says we shouldn't be unevenly yoked."

"I agree. But I know that McKenzie will end up in hell if I don't help her. We've got to pray for her. I'm planning to invite her to church next week. Would you pray that I'll set a good example for her and that the church service will have a positive impact on her?"

"Of course. You should be praying for McKenzie too."

"I have been. Maybe I'll see you guys next week and can introduce you." He caught Mike's eye. "Can I ask a favor?"

"Of course."

"Can we step outside?"

"Sure. I'll be right back, honey."

Sally smiled at him. "Thanks for lunch."

"My pleasure. It was great seeing you." He waved to their children as he walked past them to the door. "Bye, kids!"

"Bye, Mr. Trotman," Joshua and Sarah said in unison. Sarah jumped up, ran over to Jackson, and hugged him. Jackson smiled and smoothed Sarah's black curly hair. She grinned and ran back to her brothers.

Mike and Jackson walked outside onto the hot, sunny patio. The Route 44 traffic hummed steadily by as they sat down at a table under an umbrella.

"I'd like you to check out someone for me," Jackson said.

Mike pulled a pen and a small notepad from his shirt pocket. "Who? And what's this about?"

"His name is Dexter Lancaster, and he lives at Olympic Tower, Fifth Avenue, New York, New York. He's been stalking McKenzie for years. She has a restraining order out against him, but I think he's going to try to kill her one day."

"Whoa." Mike looked up. "What makes you think that?"

"I believe he was the masked man who killed her while I was in her portal."

Mike blew out his breath. "Here we go with the portal thing again."

"Mike, you've got to do this for me. Even if you don't believe me, can you at least check him out? I would appreciate it."

"Can you tell me anything about him?"

Jackson shook his head. "Not a lot. He's a hedge fund trader who's been obsessed with her ever since college. I'm pretty sure he's single. He's a loner."

"I know the profile."

Mike raised his voice as a tractor-trailer roared by. "I'll see what I can do."

"Thanks, Mike. Don't let McKenzie know we're doing this, okay?"

"Got it. We'll keep it between us. Don't you go telling anyone about this either. I could get into trouble."

"I certainly don't want that, but I think her life depends on it."

Mike gave a slow, skeptical nod.

# CHAPTER 27
# MANDATORY MEETING

MCKENZIE TURNED ON her laptop Monday morning and opened her email. A meeting invitation from Jackson with the subject Mandatory Meeting with Project Manager awaited her. She smiled as she opened it. He had scheduled their meeting from noon until twelve thirty in the Aetna cafeteria. *Man, this guy moves fast. I guess he did have a good time on Saturday.*

She had trouble concentrating that morning but got through her meetings and emails. At five minutes to twelve, she took the elevator down to the cafeteria level. The door opened, and Jackson stood there smiling. He stepped closer, glancing briefly at her lips, and then gazed into her eyes.

Of course, he'd never kiss her there, so she squeezed his hand.

"I had a great time on Saturday," he said as they walked toward the cafeteria. "Did you do anything fun yesterday?"

"Slept in late, went to Starbucks, read the paper. It was a pretty quiet day. Did you do anything?"

"I went to church in the morning. Would you like to come with me next week?"

McKenzie winced. Church was the last place she wanted to go.

Why couldn't they just go out and have a good time? "I don't know. I haven't been to church since I was a kid."

"I understand."

She stopped, facing him. On the other hand, he had totally changed for the better. This church stuff definitely worked for him. Maybe she could go. She just didn't want him pushing his religion on her. McKenzie sighed. "I don't want anyone to try to convert me."

"Understood. We'll try to keep everything low key, okay?"

"Agreed."

"Great. We can work out the details later in the week. I think you'll enjoy the service and the people."

She laughed. "I can't believe I'm going out with a right-wing fundamentalist Christian."

"Don't forget narrow-minded and intolerant too."

She chuckled. "Of course."

They went to the stir-fry area in the cafeteria, got their food, and then sat down in a booth.

"How's your day been so far?" she asked.

"Not too bad. I wish I didn't get so many emails."

"I know what you mean." She took another bite and swallowed. "What did you do after church yesterday?"

He grinned. "Oh, I had a hot date with a supermodel, but I blew her off because I got tired of her. She just wasn't up to my standards. I like my women beautiful *and* smart."

McKenzie smiled back.

"Actually, I went out to lunch with a friend and his family. His mother had just passed away, so he had a lot on his mind."

"Oh, that's a shame."

"Yeah, she was only seventy." Jackson stirred his rice. "But she was a Christian, so he knows she went to heaven."

"I try not to think about dying."

"I know what you mean. It's not a pleasant topic, but it's something we all have to go through someday."

McKenzie coughed. "I was despondent when my grandfather died. He was so nice. He always listened to me and was very interested in whatever I was doing. He told me I could do anything I wanted in life. His advice was to work hard, play hard, obey your parents, love God, and love others. I'd forgotten about that."

"Sounds like he was a very wise man."

"He was."

"I loved my grandfather too. We did a lot together, like fishing at the lake by his house. Those were some of the best times of my life. I really miss him."

"I miss my grandfather too." She tapped Jackson's arm. "You would have liked him. He always had a Bible handy."

"Do you have a Bible at home?"

"No."

"May I pick one up for you?"

"I guess, but I'm not sure I'd ever read it. It's just a bunch of ancient legends and fables."

He nodded. "I used to think the same thing back when I was in the marines. Can you give me an example of why you think that?"

"The Genesis account. It says that God created the earth in six days. Pretty much everyone in academia believes that's preposterous. All the scientific disciplines agree that the earth is billions of years old."

Jackson tapped his fork on his plate. "Well, there are a bunch of different interpretations about the Genesis account. Even Christians disagree about it. The Young Earth camp argues that the days of creation were six solar days, primarily because each day section in the first chapter of Genesis ends with, 'And there was evening, and there was morning.'"

He set his fork down. "Then the Day-Age folks maintain that

the Genesis days were long periods of time. They argue that the Hebrew word for day is *yom*, which can mean a twelve-hour day, a twenty-four-hour day, or an indefinite period. They cite Psalm 90, which says that a thousand years are like a day to God. They also note that the land produced vegetation on Day Three, but how could that have been done in a single solar day?"

She nodded.

"Then the Gap Theory states that the shell of the earth had already been there for a long period of time before God began the creation process over six literal twenty-four-hour days. Others view the Genesis days as a metaphor."

He paused to catch his breath. "Still, others view the days as theological rather than chronological. They point out that time corresponds to the earth's rotation around the sun. However, God did not create the sun and stars until Day Four, so how could there be solar days before that? There are several other views on this subject, but those are the major ones."

She'd never heard any of these arguments before. Why did it all have to be so complicated? "And what do you think the answer is?"

"Theologians have been arguing over this topic for centuries. I don't want to be dogmatic about it because there are persuasive arguments for and against each view."

"What's your best guess?"

"I think God must have created the universe with the appearance of age in six solar days."

"You mean he created everything old?"

"Yes. God created Adam and Eve as adults, not babies. Jesus changed water to fine wine at the wedding feast in Cana, which presumably means he changed it into aged wine instead of grape juice. These examples illustrate how God may have created the observable universe with the appearance of age while allowing it to occur in six literal solar days, as the Bible says." He cleared his throat. "The bottom line is, did we get here by accident, or did God design us? That's the fundamental question."

It was a fair question. "Thanks for the explanation."

"Any other questions?"

"That's it for now."

Someone dropped a tray in the kitchen, creating a huge crashing sound. Jackson chuckled, and a few people nearby clapped.

Jackson dug his fork in his food, lifted some noodles, then held the bottom of the fork with one hand, arched the top of the fork back with the index finger of his other hand, and aimed it at McKenzie, pretending to catapult the food at her. "Food fight."

She lifted her hands in a defensive position. "Don't you dare!"

Jackson returned his fork to his plate. "Party pooper."

They both laughed.

They continued talking and eating. When they finished, he slid out of the booth. "Unfortunately, I've got a one o'clock meeting I have to prepare for, so I need to take off." He smiled down at her as he picked up his tray.

This lunch had gone by way too fast. She reluctantly followed suit. They returned their trays, walked together toward the elevators, then got into the first one that arrived. It was empty except for them.

"Would you like to go to the Hartford Stage this weekend?" he asked as the doors closed. "Horton Foote's *Dividing the Estate* is playing. It's supposed to be good."

"I'd love to, but I'll have to take a rain check."

Jackson's jaw dropped. "How come?"

"My great aunt is taking me on a guided tour of Italy for ten days. We planned it a long time ago. We're leaving Friday morning."

Jackson frowned. "Oh."

At least he was sad to see her go. "Don't look so down in the dumps, Jackson. It's only ten days."

"That's a long time."

"I'll be back before you know it."

"Why didn't you tell me earlier?"

McKenzie smiled and touched his hand. "I didn't want to spoil the fun we were having."

"Where will you be going in Italy?"

"We'll be staying overnight in Rome, Sorrento, and Florence. We'll also be visiting Naples, Pompeii, Capri, and Venice."

Jackson grinned. "That sounds fantastic."

"I'm sure it will be."

"I take it she's pretty wealthy."

McKenzie nodded. "She is—and I just happen to be her favorite niece."

"Obviously. Well, I hope you have a great time." As they approached her floor, he eyed the ceiling. "Do you think they have security cameras in these elevators?"

"I don't know. Why?"

"I don't want to get into trouble." He leaned toward her, but the doors opened when he was inches from her lips. He drew back quickly just before several people walked in.

Foiled again. But she had to give him credit for trying. Would they ever get a first kiss? Hopefully, it would be worth the wait. "Give me a call in a few weeks, and we'll work out another day and time to go out."

"Sounds good." Jackson squeezed her hand as she exited the elevator.

She waved as the door slowly closed between them. She hated to leave, but maybe the time away would be good for her and give her a chance to get her head on straight. On paper, Jackson was all wrong for her, but the pull of him was getting harder and harder to resist.

❦

After a few hours at work, Jackson needed a little zip to keep going. So, he headed downstairs to the cafeteria to get something—anything. Maybe fruit, a smoothie, or a cookie.

As he approached the cash register, Jaime stood at the condiment bar stirring something into a cup of coffee. A chill went up his spine as he recalled her crushing the heart medicine pills into Pam's coffee. He paid his bill and approached her. "Hey, Jaime."

"Jackson. How are you?"

"Fine. Hey, can I talk to you for a minute?"

"Sure."

"Let's sit at one of the tables over there."

Jaime's eyes lit up, confirming his suspicions that she had a crush on him. Did she fall for every guy that smiled at her? They sat opposite each other near the window, and Jaime grinned brightly.

"This is going to sound weird, but when I was in the hospital, I had an out-of-body experience and saw a lot of things—strange things that are difficult for most people to believe."

Jaime shifted in her chair. "Try me."

"One of the strangest things I saw was you and Pam together in her office when she had her heart attack. She was lying on the floor, and you were standing over her."

Jaime swallowed. "That's weird."

"And the odd thing was that you stood there looking at your phone for four minutes before you cried out for help."

Her eyes widened. "That's ridiculous. Why would I do such a thing?"

"Because you wanted to be sure that the pills you crushed and put in her coffee would render her brain-dead before anyone came to her aid."

Jaime clenched her teeth and leaned forward. "You're insane."

"I'm telling the truth. And you know it. Why did you take the coffee cup out of the office after I started CPR?"

She shook her head. "I don't have to answer that because I didn't do it."

"You need to ask God and Pam for forgiveness, Jaime."

"Screw that. There's nothing to forgive, so why should I ask for forgiveness?"

"I want you to go to heaven, not hell."

"Oh, I see. Are you into all that born-again stuff now?"

"Yes, but it's really about you trying to murder Pam. God saw the whole thing and showed it to me. You need to get right with God before it's too late."

Jaimie stood up, pointing at him. "You listen to me very carefully. If you ever come near me again, I'll call HR and have you fired for harassment." She stormed off in a huff.

# CHAPTER 28
## REVISITING THE STALKER

TWO WEEKS HAD passed since Jackson's lunch with McKenzie. He was sitting at home on a Tuesday night when he heard a knock at the door. He got up to answer. "Who is it?"

"It's me, Mike," came the muffled answer from the other side.

Jackson opened the door. "Hey, this is a surprise. Come on in. Do you want something to drink?"

"Nah, I'm good." He sat down on the couch. "I got some information for you about that stalker." He pulled a piece of paper from his pocket. "He lives in Olympic Tower on Fifth Avenue, just like you said. By the way, how did you know that?"

"The angel told me."

Mike snorted. "Figures. He works as a hedge fund trader for Deutsche Bank in Manhattan. He's worth millions and is in the process of establishing his own hedge fund. It turns out the FBI has been investigating him for months."

"For what?"

"Insider trading."

"Whoa. That's not good—for Dexter, I mean." Jackson nudged Mike's elbow. "I take it you believe me now."

"Yes, but not just because of that."

"Then what?"

"Sally's pregnant. The drugstore test came back positive. We went to the doctor today, and he confirmed that there are two babies baking. It's too soon to tell if they're girls, but I wouldn't be surprised if they were."

Jackson laughed. "Congratulations. Do you think you can handle twins?"

"Well, God doesn't give us more than we can handle, with his help, so I guess so." Mike shrugged and then grinned. "Anyway, it looks like your stalker may soon be going away for a very long time."

Jackson clapped his hands once. "That's great news. Thank you so much, Mike."

"Remember that you can never, ever say a word of this to anyone. We could both get into a lot of trouble."

"My lips are sealed. Hey, do you want to walk across the street for ice cream?"

"Thanks, but I need to get back to the family." Mike got up and stretched. "Oh, I almost forgot to ask. Sally is dying to know how things are going with you and McKenzie."

"Great."

"What do you guys talk about since you're so different?"

"A bunch of things. We talk about the Red Sox a lot. We've had several intellectual discussions too, like creationism versus evolution, stuff like that."

He nodded. "Well, remember you don't change people's minds about God through intellectual arguments. They're changed through reading and hearing the Word of God, through prayer, and through seeing our faith lived out by loving one another."

"I know. I'm getting McKenzie a Bible."

"That's a good start. Keep praying for McKenzie—and try not to act like a jerk."

Jackson chuckled. "Thanks for the vote of confidence, buddy." He walked him to the door. "Thanks again for everything, and congratulations."

Jackson closed the door behind him and sat down with a sigh of relief. The sooner Dexter was behind bars, the better. He had to make sure McKenzie had a chance to change her destiny before the five months were up.

He called the Hartford Stage, purchased two tickets for the Friday night performance, and then made early dinner reservations at Hot Tomato's for that night. He glanced at his watch. She had to be home by now.

He texted McKenzie: *Are you back home yet?*

McKenzie responded about two minutes later: *Yep.*

Jackson called her, his pulse speeding up when she answered. "Hey! How was your trip?"

"It was phenomenal. The art and architecture were just breathtaking."

"Hope you didn't meet any Italian bozos while you were over there."

"Nope, there's plenty of bozos right here in the United States."

Jackson chuckled. "Ouch. Hey, I made some reservations for this Friday night at Hot Tomato's for dinner and then at the Hartford Stage. Does that sound okay?"

"Absolutely. What time would you like me to be ready?"

"Why don't I swing by around six fifteen? Hot Tomato's is only about four blocks from your apartment, so we can walk from there. Then we can stroll to the Hartford Stage and eventually, back to your apartment. Sound good, or would you prefer I drive?"

"Walking is fine."

"If it's raining or if we change our minds, I can drive." He paused and grinned. "I've missed you. I'm glad you're back."

"Me too."

❧

Jackson picked up his phone Wednesday night to call McKenzie but then put it down again. Questions plagued him. Should he call her every day? Should he have lunch with her every day? Would she think he didn't like her if he didn't call? He didn't want to suffocate her and have her think he was a creep like Dexter.

His stomach felt tight and acidy. *If only I could get a good night's sleep.* But she filled his dreams. Not to mention most of his waking moments—at the gym, at the office, and even when he got home.

The phone rang, and he jumped up. It must be McKenzie. But the phone display read *Dad.* Jackson's stomach tightened further. "Hey, Dad."

"Hey, son. How are things going?"

"Fantastic. I'm feeling good, and I met this great girl—I mean, woman. We just started going out a few weeks ago."

"That's great. Listen, I wanted to talk to you about that matter you mentioned in the hospital."

Jackson gulped. "The other woman?"

"Yes. I don't know how you knew, but you were right. I broke off the relationship and have spent the past month trying to patch things up with your mother."

"I'm so glad, Dad. That's the right thing to do. And make sure you patch things up with God too."

"With God?"

"Yes. You need to ask God for forgiveness so you and Mom can put this behind you and get on with your lives."

"Funny, you sound just like *my* father." He paused. "Well, okay, son. That was all I wanted to say."

Jackson beamed. "Is everything else going all right?"

"Yup."

"Great. Take care."

Jackson clicked off his phone and looked heavenward. "Thank you, Father, for helping my dad."

♾

On Thursday morning, Jackson heard that Pam Shuster was back at work. He hadn't seen her since the hospital, so he swung by her office to see how she was doing. Someone was walking out of her office as he approached. He glanced down at the Oriental rug. Memories of giving her CPR flooded back. *Lord, please give me the right words to say.*

"Hey, Pam. How are you?"

Pam rose from her chair and rushed over to hug him. "Jackson. It's great to see you. I was so sorry to hear about your accident. Please, have a seat."

He sat down on a chair in front of her desk. "Thanks. I heard you were back, so I thought I'd pop by for a quick visit. You sure look better."

She grinned. "You're not supposed to tell a lady that."

"Oh, sorry. You know what I mean."

"I know. I feel a lot better." She sat down, leaned forward, and placed her forearms on her desk. "I can't help feeling partially responsible for your accident. If you hadn't come to visit me in the hospital, you never would have been hit by that car."

"Oh, please, Pam. If you hadn't been in the hospital, you wouldn't be here right now. God is in control of these sorts of things. He works out everything for our good and his purposes."

She scowled. "How can you say that? Someone almost killed you."

"I know. But it's not just about what's best for me, Pam." He paused for a moment. "It's about what's best for everyone, including you."

"That's so sweet."

"Do you remember what I told you happened after I revived you?"

"Of course."

"Have you thought any more about what I said about getting right with God?"

"Yes. I've been reading my Bible—the Tanakh—when I get a chance."

"Great." He hesitated. *What passage should I mention?* "Take a look at the twelfth chapter of Daniel tonight."

"What's it about?"

"The resurrection of the dead."

"I plan to work late tonight, so I probably won't get to it until this weekend."

He sat forward. "Pam, you need to get serious about this."

She stared at him. "Why?"

"You never know when your time on earth will be up. This will sound crazy, but when I was unconscious, I had an out-of-body experience. An angel came and took me to a place near heaven where I was able to travel to the past, present, or future of anyone who ever has lived, or ever will live."

Pam chuckled nervously. "Do you think you might have been hallucinating?"

"I wasn't. I traveled into the future and saw you after you had died."

Pam clenched her teeth. "I don't think I'm going to like this."

"No. But you said at the hospital you should never be afraid of the truth, right?"

"Yes."

*How do I phrase this nicely?* Jackson paused, then shook his head. "I'm sorry to have to tell you this, Pam, but I saw you in agony in a place called the lake of fire, which is where people who don't accept Jesus as their Savior go. It's where they go after hell and after the great white throne judgment."

She stood up, leaned forward, placed her hands on her desk, and glared at him. "You think you're so smart, don't you—quoting all these Bible verses all the time. I have a tough question for you, and I doubt you'll be able to answer it."

"Ask your tough question."

"All right. How can a loving God allow AIDS to exist? It's killed millions, particularly members of the gay community. Does God hate gays?"

"God originally intended for people to live forever, but death and disease entered the scene because of sin. AIDS strikes both gays and straight people. God's model is for a man and a woman to be married and live together in a monogamous sexual relationship. Suppose someone steps outside of that relationship, either with the same sex or opposite sex. In that case, they leave themselves open to contracting various diseases, such as AIDS, herpes, gonorrhea, syphilis, or other STDs. If everyone stayed in monogamous relationships, many of society's ills, including AIDS, would disappear."

"What do you mean?"

"If everyone stayed in monogamous sexual relationships their entire lives, AIDS and other STDs would disappear within a generation."

"Who gave you the right to tell me what I can do with my body or who I do it with?"

"I'm just telling you what God's Word says, Pam."

"I think you need to go."

"But I thought you always wanted to know the truth?"

"Get out!" She walked around her desk, grabbed him firmly by the arm, and pulled him toward the door. "The only reason I'm not going to call HR or security right now is that you saved my life. I'm eternally grateful for what you did, but this conversation is over for good. Do you understand me?"

*If she only knew. Lord, please open her eyes.* "I understand. I'm sorry you feel that way."

He stepped out into the hallway and began walking away but then looked back at her again. "Oh, make sure you get your own coffee from now on."

"What's that supposed to mean?"

"Bye, Pam."

Some of the people outside Pam's office stood up in their cubicles and gawked at him as he walked away.

He hung his head. *Lord, what am I doing wrong? I told her the truth.*

∽

Friday finally rolled around. Jackson was back to exercising on the treadmill in the morning, albeit at a much slower pace. He trudged through the day, left work at four to get a haircut, then went home and ironed a shirt and pants to make sure he was looking good for his date.

He called McKenzie at exactly six fifteen. "Hey, I'm down at the Trumbull Street entrance to your apartment. You ready?"

"I'll need another five minutes or so. Why don't you come up?"

"Okay. It'll be great to see your apartment. What floor?"

"Tenth. Turn right out of the elevator, and my door is the last on the right."

He walked through the ground-floor door after McKenzie buzzed him in, but he had to slam it a few times to get it to relock. She should call maintenance and have it fixed. After taking the elevator to the tenth floor, he found her apartment and rang the doorbell.

The door unlocked on the other side. "Come on in, Jackson!"

The hair dryer started as he opened the door. He walked into the open living room. The entire back wall was glass, with the Downtown Hartford skyline and Connecticut River as a backdrop. Modern furniture surrounded him, and the pictures on the taupe walls were of a corresponding contemporary variety. He didn't recognize the artists, except one of the prints appeared to be a Picasso.

Jackson picked up a photograph of four people from one of the glass end tables. Probably McKenzie's mother, father, and brother. McKenzie and her sister were in the picture too. Familiar music played, but he couldn't quite place it. When the hair dryer turned off, he called, "Is that Bach?"

"Yes. I see you know your masters."

"A little."

"It's the Concerto for Two Violins in D Minor. One of my favorites. If you're thirsty, grab a glass of water."

The kitchen sat off to the right side of the living room. It had the requisite stainless steel appliances, mahogany hardwood cabinetry, and speckled granite countertops. But he wasn't thirsty. The bedroom entrance was on the left side of the living room; the door was halfway open. A soft off-white reflection from a lamp glowed inside.

A violin rested on one of the bookshelves. "Do you play the violin?"

"A little."

"You'll have to play for me sometime."

He sat on the couch. A hardcover book about Italy, a Red Sox 2004 World Series Victory memorabilia book, and a copy of the latest *People* magazine lay on the coffee table. Hmm. It was not the reading material he'd expect of a Brown graduate, but perhaps that was part of what made her so intriguing.

"I'll just be another minute!" she called.

"No problem." Jackson stood and began pacing. Hopefully, she didn't take too long. If she did, they'd have to rush through dinner and dash over to the Hartford Stage.

McKenzie made her entrance. She wore a yellow sundress with matching espadrilles. A polished brown stone attached to a thin gold chain adorned her neck. Her hair looked shorter and sassier, and he discerned a hint of perfume. His gaze swept her from top to bottom and then from bottom to top. Her hair was flawless, and her face was perfectly made up. "You look great."

"Why, thank you, sir." She smiled. "You look pretty dashing yourself."

"Thanks." Jackson glanced around. "You have a beautiful apartment."

"Thanks. I like it."

He walked over to one of the paintings. "I didn't take you for a modern art type of person. I figured you'd be more interested in impressionistic art."

She shrugged. "I took an art class at RISD."

"RISD?"

"Rhode Island School of Design. It's right next to Brown. I think it influenced my taste quite a bit."

"Oh." He raised his eyebrows. "We'd better get going." He took her elbow and moved toward the door. "We should drive, just to make sure we get there on time. It would probably be easier for you too, given the shoes you're wearing."

When they walked outside a few minutes later, a man leaned against a black BMW sedan, staring at McKenzie. Jackson took a closer look at him. Dexter? "What is he doing here?" he whispered.

McKenzie looked at him. "What did you say?"

"Oh, nothing." After a few steps, he nodded toward Dexter. "Do you know that guy?"

"What guy?"

"Over there, leaning against the BMW. He's staring at you."

McKenzie screeched. "Not him again! He's the guy from college who's been stalking me for years. I've taken out restraining orders on him in two states, but it never did any good."

"I'll take care of it." Jackson walked toward him. It was Dexter— but how? His teeth clenched as he moved closer. He was not going to let that slime ruin her life any longer. He got right in his face, even though Dexter was significantly taller than him. "I don't know what your problem is, but stay away from her!"

Dexter snickered. "Oh, yeah? And what if I don't?" He reached out and grabbed Jackson by the front of his shirt.

Jackson instinctively pressed both his thumbnails into the back of Dexter's right palm, flexed Dexter's wrist downward and inward sharply, and forced him to his knees.

He cried out in agony. "Stop! You're breaking my hand!"

Jackson got eyeball-to-eyeball with him and snarled. "This is nothing compared to what I'll do to you if you ever come near her again, you monster." He increased the pressure and forced Dexter lower. "Do you understand me?"

Dexter mumbled something under his breath.

Jackson tightened his grip even further. "Do you understand me?"

Dexter gulped. "Yes! Yes! I understand. Now let go of me!"

Jackson released him, backed away, and then walked back to McKenzie. He gently escorted her to his car and then let out a sigh once they were inside. His heart pounded. "How did he find you?"

"I don't know. Dexter's the main reason I left New York City. I needed to get away from him."

"He must have been tracking you. Somehow, he got your personal information, maybe off the internet. You should change your cell phone, email address, Facebook account, and anything else you can think of that might lead him to you. We'd better report this to the police too."

"Will do. Thanks for doing that. I think you frightened him."

"That was the general idea. I hope you're right."

It only took a few minutes to drive to Hot Tomato's and park the car. "Would you like to eat inside or outside?" he asked.

"Well, I don't know."

"Don't worry about him. Let's not allow that little incident to ruin our evening, okay?"

"Jackson, that wasn't a little incident."

"It was to me. Don't worry; I'll keep you safe."

McKenzie looked around. "Well, it's a nice night. Let's eat out on the patio."

"Patio it is."

They were escorted outside to a metal table with matching mesh chairs. From that spot, they could see the Soldiers and Sailors Memorial Arch, the Connecticut State Capitol building, and Bushnell Park on the other side of Asylum Avenue. Soon the noise of traffic faded into the background. After silently looking over the menus, McKenzie ordered the sea bass while Jackson ordered the ravioli.

"Can you tell me a little more about this guy?" he asked after the waitress left.

She frowned. "I'd rather not, but I guess you should know. Dexter was an economics major at Brown. We took a philosophy class together. He's now a millionaire financier on Wall Street. I unexpectedly ran into him at a Brown Alumni event in New York a few months ago and told him never to go near me again. Obviously, he didn't listen." McKenzie choked up, and Jackson placed his hand on top of hers. "I'm trying to move on with my life and not think about it. Let's talk about something else. Are you okay with talking more about what happened during your accident?"

Jackson took a moment to organize his thoughts. After telling her about reviving Pam and the accident in the parking garage, he swallowed. "There's something else about the accident that you should know."

"What's that?"

He paused as the waitress brought over their salads. When she walked away, he continued. "I had an out-of-body experience. I saw myself being carried away on a gurney as they were giving me CPR."

McKenzie cocked her head. "Really?"

"Yeah. I've told several people, and most of them don't believe me."

She gazed into his eyes. "I believe you."

He grinned. Of all people, he'd thought she wouldn't. "You do?"

McKenzie smiled. "Yes."

To keep from freaking her out like he'd done with Fred and Pam, he moved on to a different subject. "Getting into Brown was quite an accomplishment."

She shrugged. "I saw how hard my parents worked, and it just seemed natural that I should work hard too. I got good grades and SAT scores and managed to get in. In high school, I also organized a group of students to raise money to fight human trafficking. Girls worldwide are forced into prostitution and spend the rest of their lives in misery, even in Connecticut and Massachusetts. We later started a national human trafficking organization chapter in my town to continue the fight. The chapter is still in existence today. The Brown admissions people must have liked that."

*Impressive.* "That's incredible. It must have made you feel good to help those girls."

"I guess. But I did it because these girls and young women needed food, shelter, and the tools to start a new life, not because I wanted to feel good. I wanted to fight against the pond scum that lies to these girls and traps them in a life of slavery—and the losers who use these girls to fulfill their sexual fantasies."

Jackson gulped. Amsterdam came to mind. "Understood."

"There are so many needy people out there." She looked away and drew a long breath, then returned her gaze to him. "How can you believe in a God who allows so much suffering in the world? How can you believe in a God who allows women to be beaten, abused, sexually assaulted, and stalked? How can you believe in a God who allows children to get cancer?"

He leaned back in his chair. "Those are all fair questions, and there's no simple answer. Every situation is different, but there are some general principles about this outlined in the Bible. First of all, people have free will. They can choose to do good or choose to do evil. In the case of women being beaten and abused, it isn't God's fault that their husbands or boyfriends or rapists or pimps do such terrible things. It's the perpetrators' fault, either because they are intrinsically evil and malicious, or because they're under the influence of drugs or alcohol, or because they were abused as children and are just passing it on. Regardless of the reason, the perpetrator is responsible. And I believe there will be consequences for their actions, either in this life or when they stand before God at the final judgment."

He sat up, folded his arms, and put his elbows on the table. "Regarding children with cancer, once again, it's difficult to say because God's plan in each situation may be different. No one wants to see another person suffer, especially a child, but suffering is part of life. Some people have to suffer more than others or in different ways. Suffering allows people to learn and grow in ways they wouldn't have otherwise. It stretches us and those near us. The Bible talks about God using suffering to refine people and test their faith—will the person who is suffering seek God or shake their fist at him and curse him?"

He shifted forward in his chair. "The Bible also talks about suffering producing perseverance; and perseverance, character; and character, hope. So, suffering, though difficult, especially for children, may have a purpose. Jesus can relate to our sufferings and comfort us because he suffered more than any of us will ever suffer."

She eyed him solemnly. "It's easy for you to sit there and say that, but what do you know about children suffering?"

Jackson teared up and took a moment to regain his composure. "My older sister was killed in a car crash when I was five. I was in the car with her." He cleared his throat. "The image of the EMTs giving her CPR is forever etched in my mind. I'm beginning to understand that, subconsciously, it was part of the reason why I used to drink so much."

McKenzie covered her mouth with her hand. "Oh, I'm so sorry."

He looked away for a moment. "It's okay. It happened a long time ago."

She frowned. "I have some other tough questions, but they can wait. I don't want to upset you."

Someone briskly approached their table. Jackson turned and the person immediately threw a drink in his face. Jackson instinctively stood up, ready to fight. He looked at the person and backed down instantly. "Angela, is that you?" He picked up a napkin and wiped the liquid off his face.

"Yeah, it's me, you son of a—"

"What did you do that for?"

"Is that all you have to say? Wham, bam, thank you, ma'am, and I never hear from you again? Some nerve!"

"What are you talking about?"

"You don't remember? You took off without even saying goodbye."

The events of their one-night stand at Brown came back to him. Great. McKenzie was sitting there, listening to all this. "That was seven years ago, Angela."

"So?"

Jackson exhaled. "I'm sorry, but I told you I had to get back to UConn for an eight o'clock class. I left you a note. I didn't mean to disrespect you."

"You sicko. I heard you picked up some passed-out girl in the Sigma Chi lounge right after sleeping with me."

He shook his head. "Look, it's obvious I hurt you. I'm sorry about that." She was the one who'd put the moves on him, not the other way around, but that didn't really matter. "Let's put this behind us and move on."

"Go to hell!"

He cringed at her words, realizing afresh how terrible it was to wish that on someone.

Angela then threw her glass down on the brownstone pavers at his feet and stormed off.

He sat down and picked the shards off his pants and shoes. He reluctantly peeked up at McKenzie. She had a smirk on her face, then she burst into laughter.

She shook her head. "Wham, bam, thank you, ma'am?" She slapped the table and laughed so hard that tears formed in her eyes.

He shook his head, chuckling at first, then laughing right along with her. "In my defense, that happened in college before I became a Christian."

"I know, Jackson. I'm just busting your chops."

৵

In the Hartford Stage parking garage, Jackson and McKenzie climbed the series of concrete stairs to the ground level and then strolled arm in arm through an alleyway to the front door. Jackson retrieved their tickets, and they found their seats, about ten rows up in the center section.

The play—about a dysfunctional family fighting over the matriarch's estate before she had died—had many funny moments. During intermission, they ran into some people Jackson knew from church. He introduced McKenzie, and they all talked as they sipped seltzers with lemon.

"They seemed like pretty normal people," she said as she and Jackson walked back to their seats.

Obviously, she still felt a little uncomfortable about going to church. He asked God how he could put her at ease. Moments later, a thought came to mind. "Why don't we go to church on Saturday night at five instead of Sunday morning? That way, you can kind of ease your way into this church thing."

"Sure, if you like."

"Good. I'll pick you up at four thirty tomorrow. Maybe we can get dinner and go to a movie afterward."

"Sounds good."

After the play, they left his car in the parking garage, rather than try to find another space near McKenzie's apartment. So, they strolled the two blocks along Trumbull Street, enjoying the evening and chatting about the play.

"Would you like to come up for coffee?" McKenzie stopped. "Oh, that's right, you don't drink coffee. I might have some herbal tea."

"Sure."

They took the elevator up to her apartment, and she put the kettle on. Jackson tossed his keys and wallet on the counter, then went to the window. People walked along the thoroughfare ten stories below, and streetlights off in the distance marked the path of I-84 and I-91. The reflection of the moon glistened off the Connecticut River in the distance. "It's a great view from here at night. It's a lot nicer than the view from my condo." He glanced at her. "You'll have to come over and see it sometime. Hey, there's a movie theater right in Blue Back Square. We could go to a movie there tomorrow, and then I could show you my condo."

"Great. The tea should be ready in just a minute. Go ahead and sit down if you'd like."

Jackson moved to one of the love seats.

A few moments later, McKenzie brought two mugs of hot water and placed them on coasters on the coffee table, along with a small basket containing an assortment of herbal teas. She sat down next to him, and they each selected a tea bag and placed it in their mug to steep.

"Jackson, what did that woman mean tonight when she said you had another woman after her?"

He shifted his weight on the love seat. "Do you really want to talk about this? I mean, it's personal, and it happened a long time ago."

"Yes, I do. I believe in transparency in relationships."

He sighed. "Okay. I went to high school with her. She was my girlfriend for a while, but we parted after graduation as friends. I texted her that I'd be up at Brown for a baseball game and thought we could have dinner as friends. After dinner and some drinks, I walked her back to her dorm room. I planned to leave right away because I had an eight o'clock class the next morning, but she threw herself at me, and I'll spare you the rest."

He stood up. "A few hours later, still hungover, I got up and walked out through the Sigma Chi entrance but heard moaning coming from inside their lounge. I walked in and found a woman lying on the couch. She was sloshed and nonresponsive. I was worried she might die of alcohol poisoning, so I picked her up and planned to bring her to the infirmary. I later realized someone had given her a date rape drug. On the way to the infirmary, a huge guy attacked me and tried to take the woman away from me. He beat the snot out of me, but fortunately, the campus police arrived and rescued me." He gave McKenzie a meaningful stare. "Recently, I recognized the guy who I fought with on Brown Street."

"Who was it?"

"Dexter."

McKenzie blanched. "What? Dexter?"

He peered at her. She was putting it all together.

"What night did this all happen?"

"It was a long time ago. I remember it was during the week. Maybe we can look it up online." It took a moment for him to google the Brown vs. UConn baseball game during the 2004 season. He perused some of the links, then confirmed the date. "It was April 28, 2004."

McKenzie turned as white as a ghost.

What should he do next? Could she handle him telling her an angel had shown him everything?

She put her hand on her chin, obviously deep in thought, and didn't say a word.

*It looks like transparency in relationships only works one way with Miss McKenzie.*

Jackson stood, took her hands in his, pulled her off the couch, and slipped his arms around her. When she rested her head on his shoulder, he breathed in the scent of her hair, then kissed the top of her head. He could feel her heart beating through her thin sundress. Then she looked up into his eyes.

All he could think about was getting her into the bedroom. His body burned inside, craving her. What would it be like to touch her? To make love to her? He quickly stopped himself. *Shut up in the name of Jesus!* He exhaled. *What am I doing? I must have gone through with it the first time. That's why McKenzie ended up with a baby bump at their wedding.* He was a total hypocrite.

He blew out another breath. *Must get out of here. Run!*

He removed her hands from his waist and pulled away. "I'd better go."

She stepped back. "Why? What's wrong?"

"Nothing. I've had an incredible evening with you. I need to go."

*I can't control myself much longer. I'm two seconds away from blowing it. God, help me.*

"Um… okay." She looked puzzled. "Here, have some tea before you leave." She handed him his mug.

"Thanks." He took a sip, then walked to the kitchen and placed the cup in the sink. He moved quickly to the door, but as he put his hand on the door handle, she took it, pulled him toward her, and stood up on her toes to kiss him good night on the cheek. Jackson hugged her again, more tightly this time, then slipped out the door and closed it behind him.

In the elevator, he hunched over, trembling. The walk back to the parking garage would do him some good.

⌖

McKenzie locked the door behind Jackson and sat down on one of the love seats. How was it possible that Jackson was the one who'd saved her? And yet, he hadn't seemed to recognize her when they'd met later on Block Island. When should she tell him? He must suspect it was her since he recognized Dexter. Was that why he'd gotten up and left like that? She couldn't figure him out.

Moments later, she heard a knock at the door.

She got up, smiling. Guess Jackson changed his mind. She hurried across the room and flung open the door.

Disbelief froze her in place. It wasn't Jackson standing in the hallway.

Dexter rushed inside, grabbed her arm, and pushed the door closed behind him. She shook involuntarily as he dragged her toward one of the love seats. She couldn't breathe. It was all happening again.

Except this time, she'd have the strength to put up a fight. Summoning her deepest ferocity, she clawed at his face and neck with all her might, digging deep scratches in his skin. He reciprocated with a hard slap to her face that knocked her to the floor.

She looked up at him, tasting blood. "Dexter, get out!"

"Shut up! You belong to me! You've always belonged to me!"

She shook her head. "Never."

"I'm going to show you what you've been missing all these years." He dropped to his knees.

She spat in his face. "Get away from me, you creep!"

Dexter slapped her again and grabbed her clothes as she punched his face and chest. He threw her back onto the love seat. "Remember that night in college after the Sigma Chi party? You seemed to like me then." He laughed and moved closer to her.

"Liar! You drugged and raped me on the couch."

Dexter's eyes widened, then he chuckled. "You're delusional."

She looked around for a weapon as she continued to challenge him. "No, I have a witness. My friend picked me up off the couch and was taking me to the infirmary when you attacked him and beat him up."

"Prove it."

"I will." Maybe she could pick up the lamp. She inched toward the end table while she glared at him. "There's no statute of limitations in Rhode Island for rape. I'm going to make sure you get put away for a very long time."

Dexter gritted his teeth and pulled her close. "I'll just have to make sure you don't tell anyone."

She screamed and kicked at him as hard as she could. "Help! Somebody, help me!"

❧

Once Jackson reached his car, he patted his pockets for his keys. Ugh. His keys and wallet were back in McKenzie's apartment. So, he turned and jogged back.

Odd. The front door to her building was slightly ajar. Not great for security, but at least she didn't have to buzz him in again. He stepped off the elevator to the sound of muffled screaming. McKenzie's apartment door was closed, but the sound came from inside.

He shoved the door open. A man was struggling with McKenzie on the love seat. The man turned and glared at Jackson. *Dexter.*

Dexter threw McKenzie down on the love seat and squared off, facing Jackson. White hot fury flashed through Jackson's blood. How dare this man put his hands on McKenzie again. He'd been warned. Now Jackson would hit him where he wouldn't expect it.

Jackson brought his leg back and kicked Dexter in the groin. Dexter growled in pain but stayed on his feet.

Jackson punched him in the temple with one fist and in the stomach with the other. Dexter buckled over. If the man wouldn't go down, it was time to force him down. Jackson grabbed him by the throat and ran him across the room, finally throwing him on top of the glass desk, which collapsed under his weight. Shards of glass flew everywhere.

Jackson got on top of him, ignoring the stab of glass in his knees, and punched him in the face with all his might. But Dexter wasn't done. He landed a punch to Jackson's solar plexus that took the wind out of him.

While capturing one of Dexter's arms under his knee, Jackson clamped his hands around Dexter's throat and began choking him. Dexter flailed his loose arm and his legs wildly as he gasped for air.

"Jackson! Stop!" McKenzie pulled on his shoulders. "You're killing him!"

Jackson released his grip, then punched Dexter in the face one more time, as hard as he could, knocking him unconscious. The rage he'd felt as he'd stood over the Taliban soldier who'd shot Gunny Cooke had come back to him. If he'd had a gun, he would have blown Dexter's head off.

Jackson switched his attention to McKenzie. He held her face in his hands, inspecting her bloody lip. Maybe some stiches, but nothing serious. He went to the kitchen, grabbed an ice pack from the freezer, then wrapped it in a cloth towel. Back on the couch, he held her close as she sobbed and iced her lip.

His heart pounded. *I can't believe I'm still capable of such violence. I thought that would go away when I became a Christian, but it's still there, buried deep. I had to protect McKenzie.*

Jackson pulled his cell phone from his pocket and dialed 911, then let her take it from him.

"Hartford nine-one-one. What is the nature of your emergency?" the dispatcher asked.

"A man just tried to rape me." McKenzie's voice trembled.

"Where are you?"

"Hartford Twenty-one. Tenth floor."

The dispatcher took more information and said officers should be there shortly. Jackson pulled her toward him, gently cupping her chin and tilting her head so that she looked into his eyes. "I'm so sorry this happened. Did he hurt you otherwise?"

"No. Dexter didn't get far. Thank God you came back." She shook her head. "I should never have opened the door without checking to see who it was. I just assumed it was you. I hope they lock him up and throw away the key."

Bits of shattered desk glass toppled off Dexter onto the hardwood floor. He'd regained consciousness and was moving. Jackson reached over to grab him by the collar but suddenly, a sharp pain sliced through his lower abdomen. His body began to shake uncontrollably, and he screamed in agony. Electrical wires protruded from just above his belt buckle. He fell backward. Dexter had fired a Taser at him.

Dexter stood over him, grinning and laughing.

Something hit Dexter in the shoulder and made him wince. McKenzie had thrown some object at him. He transferred the Taser gun to his left hand and crept toward her, keeping an eye on Jackson as he moved.

McKenzie screamed. Jackson tried to get up but couldn't. Paralyzed, he could only lay there and imagine what was going on. *Oh God! Help!*

Dexter kept the electrical current flowing into him without mercy.

Sirens blared in the distance.

*Please let that be the police.* Jackson's teeth clenched together so tightly they might break. *Help me, Jesus. I can't take this anymore.* The sirens abruptly stopped on the street below.

From the corner of his eye, Jackson caught a glimpse of Dexter edging toward the door, while still keeping the Taser on. The wires extended farther and farther from the gunstock.

Finally, he let go of the Taser and ran out the door.

Jackson gasped for air. The front of his stomach burned from the pincers that had delivered the shock. McKenzie jumped up and locked the door. He managed to get to his feet and move to the apartment door sluggishly. He opened it and glanced down the hallway toward the elevator, then opened the fire door and peered down the stairwell. "No sign of him," he said.

Back in her apartment, they looked out the window. A police cruiser had parked below on Trumbull Street. Soon, two police officers were on the tenth floor, and Jackson let them into the apartment. As he held McKenzie's hand, she answered all their questions, wiping away tears as she spoke.

When they left, he patted the love seat. "Can I have a blanket? I'll be sleeping on your couch tonight."

# CHAPTER 29
# RUNNING

JACKSON AWOKE TO the sounds and smells of vegetables sauté-ing. He sat up and ran a hand down his face. McKenzie was in the kitchen with her back to him, cracking eggs into a bowl next to the sink. "Good morning," he said without getting out from under his blanket.

She smiled over her shoulder. "Good morning."

She was safe. They were together. What more could he ask for? "What time is it?"

"About ten."

Jackson stood. "No way. I never sleep that late."

"Well, we both had a rough night."

True. "What are you making?"

"A nice, healthy omelet with tomatoes, peppers, onions, and feta."

"No bacon or sausage?" He grinned, waiting for a reaction.

"Not on your life."

He walked to her and took her in his arms. "How are you feeling?"

"Sore and a little shaken up." She sighed. "I'd be a lot better if I knew Dexter was behind bars rather than out on the loose somewhere. Thanks for staying. I feel much safer when you're around."

"Thank God I left my keys here. Just let me know if you need anything. I can even swing by and pick you up for work on Monday if you'd like. It wouldn't be any trouble."

She smiled. "That's sweet of you to offer. I'll think about it."

Jackson released her and went to the window. "Looks like a nice day. I know you've just been through a lot, but would you like to go running? It would be a good stress-buster."

"Do you think it's safe?"

"I'll be there if anything happens."

McKenzie flipped the omelet. "I'm not going to let Dexter ruin my life. Let's go for it, then. Do you feel up to it?"

"My leg is much better now."

"Where's your favorite place to run around here?"

"West Hartford Reservoir Number Six on Avon Mountain is great. There's a 3.6-mile dirt trail around it. The views are spectacular. It feels like you're walking in Switzerland."

After breakfast, McKenzie placed the dishes in the dishwasher and dressed in her running clothes. They walked to Jackson's car, and he discreetly looked around for Dexter while holding her hand.

At his condo, he parked along the curb. "Fair warning, my condo is a mess."

"Understood. I won't judge."

He opened the door to his home and scanned the living room. He quickly removed newspapers and dirty clothes from the couch. "You can sit here while I get dressed."

Jackson put on his running clothes, then walked with McKenzie to the car. Hopefully, she wouldn't notice the Smith & Wesson Bodyguard .380 pistol in a wallet holster tucked in the pocket of his running shorts.

They drove west up Avon Mountain on Route 44. Although a little humid, the day was clear and sunny. It had been a few weeks since he sat with Mekoddishkem in the back seat of Jeremy's car as he sped up that same road. Jackson turned right at the reservoir entrance, where the police officer who later chased Jeremy had been parked. They followed a paved road for about a mile to the rear of the watershed area and parked in the lot near the water treatment plant.

As they got out of the car, McKenzie looked east. "It's gorgeous up here." She surveyed the Hartford skyline below. "I can see my apartment building."

He grabbed his water bottle. "Wait till you see the running trails."

They started at a leisurely pace on a dirt trail through the woods, passing pine trees and the reservoir on their left. "Is this pace good, or would you like to run a little faster?" he asked.

"A little faster is fine with me."

After running for about half a mile, they came to a fork in the trail. "Do you want to run to the top of the mountain or go around the reservoir? There's a beautiful view from the top, but it's a very steep climb."

She slowed to a jog. "How far is it to the top?"

"About two miles."

"I'm still a little sore, but my legs and cardio are fine. Let's go for it."

About halfway up the mountain, Jackson was breathing hard and struggling. The run was brutal. *Me and my big mouth! I should have given myself more time to get back in shape.* He strained just to put one foot in front of the other as he trudged up the steep trail. McKenzie ran about ten yards ahead of him, and it didn't look like she was breathing hard. *I'm sure she's impressed with me now.*

She glanced back over her shoulder. "This is a great workout, Jackson. I'm glad I did a lot of hill training on the treadmill, but there's no substitute for a real mountain trail."

"Yeah," was all Jackson could muster as he continued pounding his way up the mountain. *Guess I'd better add hill training to my treadmill repertoire from now on.*

A few minutes later, Jackson heard twigs and brush crackling. A black bear was up ahead on his left, meandering with her two cubs around some bushes. McKenzie screamed and ran away. The mother bear pursued.

Jackson instinctively started yelling and ran uphill toward the bear, trying to distract her. The bear turned and charged him. Jackson waved his arms and tried to make himself look bigger, then pulled out his pistol and pointed it at the bear. She halted about fifteen feet from him, paused briefly, then returned to her cubs and trotted away.

Jackson blew out a heavy breath. Good thing she kept her distance. This little pistol wouldn't have stopped her.

Jackson tucked the gun in his shorts, ran to McKenzie, and took her hand. "Are you okay?"

"Yes, I'm fine, but that was scary. Thank you, once again, for saving me."

"You're welcome. The key thing with black bears is to let them know you're here. They usually shy away from humans, but we must have surprised her. If you do encounter one, you're supposed to walk away quietly. If you can't do that, make yourself look bigger, make noise, and as a last resort, fight back by throwing rocks or sticks at them."

McKenzie wiped her brow with her shirtsleeve. "Hope we don't see them on the way back."

They resumed their trek up Avon Mountain. The mountain path alternated between worn trails and dry streambeds. They crossed under power lines and sometimes had to leap from one rock to another to stay on the route. Splotches of aqua-blue paint on trees along the way marked the trail. They turned right onto an asphalt road when they reached the summit, ran past a cell phone tower, then stopped at the Heublein Tower.

Jackson bent at the waist to catch his breath. When he looked up at McKenzie, she appeared to have barely broken a sweat. He handed her the water bottle and nodded at the tower. "It looks like a castle, doesn't it?"

"Yeah."

The six-story tower—with a stone façade on the first floor and white stucco on the remaining—sat atop a cliff overlooking the other side of Avon Mountain. Jackson pointed to the scenery. "That's the Farmington Valley in front of us. Farmington is way over on the left, Avon is directly in front of us, and Simsbury is on the right. Canton is way off in the distance behind Avon."

McKenzie walked toward the edge of the cliff. "What a view!"

"Don't get too close to the edge. It's a long way down."

"Can we go inside the tower?"

He looked back at it. "Probably. It should be open by now."

They walked up the six flights of stairs. Their reward was a three-hundred-and-sixty-degree view of the countryside below.

"It was worth all the hard work it took to get up here," she said.

Yes, it was. But he would have to train pretty hard to keep up with Miss McKenzie.

He gazed out the window, enjoying the view, then held her hand. He glanced over at her and discovered she'd been staring at him. He moved closer. She peered into his eyes for an uncomfortably long time, not saying a word. Slowly, he leaned toward her. She bit her bottom lip, sparking a fire inside him. He cupped her cheek and pulled her closer. When their lips were only inches apart, he ran his thumb along her lower lip and spoke with pure honesty. "McKenzie, you are the most beautiful woman I've ever met."

She bridged the distance between them. Her lips were warm and soft. He pulled her against his chest and lifted her up. As he took the kiss deeper, she raked her fingers along his back. Good thing they were in public.

❦

Dexter needed a cheap and secluded place to hide while contemplating his next move. After all, he was now on the run from the law for multiple offenses.

The Peoples State Forest campground in Barkhamsted seemed like a good option. He drove to the Torrington Walmart to purchase a tent and some ammunition for his Marlin Model 60 rifle. He later purchased food and other supplies at the Riverton General Store, paying cash for everything so as not to alert the authorities to his whereabouts. As a precaution, he parked his car at the opposite end of the campground from his campsite.

He'd been on top of the world, making tens of millions and living in a posh Manhattan condo on Fifth Avenue. Now he was living in a tent and running from the law. The cops would never catch him, though. He was too smart for them.

His life, everything he'd worked so hard for, was ruined, all because of McKenzie. He'd offered her everything—money, prestige, and perhaps someday, fame, but she'd turned him down. She'd pay dearly for her disrespect.

He'd figure out a way to kill her and her boyfriend and never get caught.

# CHAPTER 30
# CHURCH TOGETHER

JACKSON PARKED HIS car along Trumbull Street at four fifteen that Saturday afternoon, near McKenzie's apartment building entrance. He had dropped her off a few hours earlier after their run so she could take a shower and relax before he picked her up for church.

As Jackson walked toward the building, he encountered a homeless man sleeping on the sidewalk. The man's legs shook violently. He had to be an addict. Jackson couldn't slip him any money because he'd just use it to buy more drugs.

Seven years ago, he'd had another encounter with a homeless person, during that time he'd been in Providence for the baseball game against Brown. He'd been standing on Thayer Street outside a CVS pharmacy, waiting for his high school friend, Angela, to come out. A disheveled woman got out of an old car and approached him. "Excuse me, sir, but could you spare some money so I can buy diapers for my baby?"

"You'd just use it to buy booze or drugs."

"No, sir. I do have a baby, and I do need diapers for her."

Angela walked out the pharmacy door. Jackson turned to the woman and said, "I'm sorry, but I can't help you," then left. A moment later, he heard a baby crying. The regret had chased him ever since.

Jackson checked his watch. There was a McDonald's a few blocks away. There was still time for him to get there and back before McKenzie would come downstairs.

McKenzie stood in the lobby when he returned, beaming as she waited for him. She looked beautiful in her cobalt sleeveless sundress and brown leather wedge sandals.

He opened the lobby door for her, took her hand, and pulled her close. "You look beautiful."

"Thanks." She teared up before looking away.

"Hasn't anyone ever told you you're beautiful?"

She tried to smile. "No one that mattered."

Jackson gave her a hug. "Did they ever fix the front door to your building? That must be how Dexter got in."

"Yes."

"Good." He led her to the car. Once she was seated, he took a gospel tract from the glove compartment, then jogged over to the homeless man and stuck it in his pocket, along with the McDonald's gift certificate.

McKenzie stared at him as he hustled back into the car. "What was that all about?"

"Oh, just paying off an old debt." He retrieved a gift-wrapped package from the back seat and then handed it to her.

"Oh, I love presents!"

Jackson smiled. "Open it."

Inside was a brown leather New International Version Study Bible. He'd had her name embossed on the front cover in gold lettering.

"Wow. What a nice Bible, Jackson."

"Well, you can't go to a Baptist church without a Bible, so I thought I'd make you look official."

McKenzie hugged him. "Thank you so much."

"You're welcome."

Jackson could have taken several routes to the church, but he went by way of Route 44 over Avon Mountain to give them more time to talk. He rolled down the windows to get a bit of fresh air flowing. "There's more I'd like to tell you about my accident."

"Uh-oh. Sounds ominous."

"No, I'm serious. Did you hear about the kid who died at the bottom of Avon Mountain last month?"

"The one who got hit by a tractor trailer?"

"Yeah. We're going to be driving right by the spot where he died."

"That's creepy." She nudged her hair to the side as the wind blew it.

"He's the kid who hit me in the parking garage at the hospital." She looked at him. "Really?"

"Remember how I said I saw myself being carried away on a gurney? After that, a heavenly being appeared to me and showed me many things. One of them was the kid's accident as it was happening."

After some silence, she shook her head. "I don't see how that's possible."

"I agree, but it happened. I'm telling you the truth."

"I hope so. Because if you're not, I'll never trust you again. Do you understand that?"

He could hear the tension in her tone. "Yes."

"Then I believe you."

Shocking—but she'd surprised him before. Plus, they had been through so much in such a short time. He chuckled nervously. "I didn't think you would believe me, so I had prepared a physics argument."

She arched her eyebrows at him. "Sorry to disappoint you, Einstein."

"No. I'm thrilled that you believe me. I know it's quite a bit to grasp. There are some other places I went to and learned about with the angel, but let's talk about that later."

They soon reached the church, and Jackson led her up the back stairs to the balcony. They sat down as the worship team began leading the congregation in a contemporary Christian song, with the words of the song projected on screens above and to the right and left side of the pulpit so everyone could sing along.

After the ushers took the offering, the pastor spoke about the parable of the prodigal son, who had left home and squandered his inheritance but eventually returned to his father, realizing he would be better off as a servant in his father's house than living in squalor. The pastor argued that everyone is like the prodigal son because everyone has done wrong. Still, they will receive forgiveness and a warm welcome if they return to our heavenly Father, just like the prodigal son received a warm welcome when he returned to his earthly father.

McKenzie quietly listened. Jackson couldn't read how she was reacting to the message.

After the service, Jackson and McKenzie stood in line to meet the senior pastor. Jackson introduced them, and then he and McKenzie walked into the lobby.

"He seems like a normal guy," she said.

"He is." He glanced around, looking for Mike or Sally. "Would you like to have dinner here and meet some people, or would you prefer to go somewhere else?"

"Jackson!" Mike's voice echoed across the room, and he, Sally, and their children approached. "Who's your friend?"

Jackson gestured toward his date. "McKenzie, this is Mike and Sally Tolbert, along with their three children."

McKenzie shook hands with Mike and Sally, then knelt to meet the kids. "Hello, my name is McKenzie. What are your names?"

Joshua stepped forward first. "I'm Joshua."

"And how old are you?"

"I'm eight."

"What grade are you in?"

He put up two fingers. "I'm going into second grade."

McKenzie chuckled. "That's good. Do you know who your teacher will be next year?"

Joshua nodded. "Miss Crowley."

"Is she nice?"

"Yes."

Then, turning to Sarah, she said, "And what is your name, young lady?"

"I'm Sarah. I'm six, and I'm going into first grade."

"Wow, that's great. Did you like kindergarten?"

Sarah nodded. "Yes, I did."

"Who was your teacher?"

"Mrs. Gademan."

"Was she a good teacher?"

Sarah nodded again. "Yes."

Then McKenzie addressed the youngest Tolbert. "What's your name, little guy?"

Benjamin ran to his mother and hid behind her, wrapping both arms around her left thigh. Sally said, "This is Benjamin, and he is three years old. He will be going to preschool in the fall."

"Oh, that's exciting. I hope you have fun in preschool, Benjamin."

Benjamin remained standing behind his mother, keeping a stiff upper lip.

"Hey, why don't you guys join us for dinner here at church?" Mike suggested.

Jackson looked to McKenzie.

She shrugged. "Sure, why not."

᠕

After selecting her food from the buffet, McKenzie sat beside Sally at a circular table in the dining hall while Mike and Jackson helped the kids get their food. The hall contained approximately twenty tables. People gradually filled the room, talking as they gathered their meals or sat at tables.

Sally had short black hair, smooth black skin, and an infectious smile. She buttered her roll then looked up. "What did you think of the service, McKenzie?"

*She's direct. That's okay, as long as she doesn't try to convert me.* "I enjoyed it. I loved the music, and the message was interesting."

"What did you like about the message?"

"I guess how the father welcomed the wayward son back even though he'd squandered all the inheritance money on prostitutes and lascivious living."

"How do you think that applies to us?"

McKenzie considered that. "I'm not sure."

Sally pulled her chair closer to the table. "It means that we have all sinned against God, just as the wayward son sinned against his father. Our heavenly Father is ready to welcome us back to him with open arms no matter what we've done."

*She is trying to convert me.* "Well, I've certainly made my share of mistakes, but I'm not that bad."

"Have you ever told a white lie?"

McKenzie crossed her arms. "Of course. Haven't you? Haven't we all?"

She nodded.

"Have you ever gotten drunk?"

McKenzie shifted in her chair. "Yes."

Jackson arrived at the table with Mike and the kids. *Finally, he's back.*

Benjamin hopped onto his mother's lap, and Sally picked up his plate and placed it in front of her. Jackson joked with the other two kids while they ate.

McKenzie looked to Mike. "What do you do for work, Mike?"

He swallowed the bite already in his mouth. "I'm a police officer. I lock up bad guys like the one you brought with you to church."

She smiled. "Oh, and does Jackson have a record?"

"A mile long. I think you caught Jackson between life sentences."

Jackson snorted. "Thanks for the character reference, buddy."

Mike gave Jackson a playful shove. "Anything I can do to help."

McKenzie laughed. At least they'd found a safer discussion topic.

❧

After finishing his dinner, Jackson pushed his plate away. "Mike, can I talk to you for a second?"

"Sure."

They got up from the table, walked to the church's back door near the kitchen, then stepped outside.

"What's on your mind?" Mike asked when they faced each other. "McKenzie seems like a great girl."

"Thanks. We got a visit from our friend Dexter Lancaster last night."

He scowled. "I thought they were going to lock him up."

"Me too. Dexter tried to rape McKenzie. Fortunately, I'd forgotten my keys at her apartment and came back just in time." He continued describing what had happened that night after leaving McKenzie's apartment to walk to his car.

"Man. That's terrible. I'll be sure to check it out in the morning." He shook his head. "How's McKenzie handling it?"

"She seems okay."

"Keep close tabs on her. Sometimes traumatic experiences creep up on people a day or two after they've had time to process it fully."

Hopefully, that wouldn't happen. "I'll keep that in mind."

"Well, we'd better get back inside. I'll stop by in a day or two and give you an update."

"Please do. I'm afraid of what I might do if Dexter comes near McKenzie again."

They returned to the table and said their goodbyes. As Jackson drove them out of the church parking lot, McKenzie asked, "What were you and Mike talking about?"

"The attack last night. I didn't want to say anything in front of the kids."

She wrung her hands. "I still can't believe it happened. Thank God you came back."

Jackson grinned at her words. He reached in the back seat, retrieved a copy of the *Hartford Courant*, and handed it to her. "Any movies look interesting?"

"Well, let's see… there's *Ice Age: Dawn of the Dinosaurs*, but that's a kid's movie. Then there's *Public Enemies*, but that's too violent. There's *My Sister's Keeper*, but that's too sad. *Transformers: Revenge of the Fallen*, but that's a guy movie. Oh, then there's *The Proposal* with Sandra Bullock. That looks good."

Jackson cringed. "Sounds like a chick flick tearjerker to me. I might have to take out some Arnold Schwarzenegger DVDs and show you what a real movie looks like."

"Well, you've chosen everything we've done so far," she said. "Now it's my turn."

He couldn't deny that. "You have a point there. I guess I got a little carried away being the tour guide. Okay, chick flick it is."

After a few minutes of silence, she looked over at him. "Can I ask you a personal question?"

*Uh-oh.* "Sure."

"Did you sleep around before you became a Christian? I mean, besides Angela?"

"Yes," Jackson said it without hesitation. "I was like the prodigal son in the pastor's sermon tonight."

McKenzie paused. "Did you ever sleep with a prostitute?"

He pictured Amsterdam's red-light district, Polish section. The young woman behind the glass. The Christian Missionary Center with the Scripture taped to the inside of the window.

His mouth went dry. "Why do you ask?"

"Because in the parable, the prodigal son slept with prostitutes."

*Why did I say that?* He had no good answer. "Well, would it make a difference if I did?"

"Just answer the question."

*God, help.* He couldn't lie to her and say no. But what would she think of him if he said yes? He'd never told anyone else about this before. Still, he had to be truthful. "Yes."

She exhaled. "That's terrible."

*Oh God, I hope I didn't just blow it.* "I'm a sinner like everyone else. Haven't you ever done anything when you were drunk that you're now ashamed of?"

McKenzie squirmed. "Well… yes."

"Then isn't it hypocritical to hold me to a higher standard than you hold yourself to?"

McKenzie looked out the side window, seeming to consider that. "I suppose so. But what you did was still wrong."

"Agreed. And whatever you did was still wrong too. You've done bad things in the past, and I've done bad things in the past, so let's call it even."

McKenzie took a deep breath. "Fine. Deal."

"Just remember that in the parable, the father took the son back *despite* what he'd done."

"Right."

# CHAPTER 31
# BLUE BACK SQUARE

AFTER THE MOVIE, Jackson and McKenzie got ice cream at a store across the street. Then they walked hand in hand through Blue Back Square to his condo. Sweat dripped down his underarms as he opened the door. The wedding scene with McKenzie's baby bump came to mind, then the shooting and the demons taking her to hell. She had to decide to follow Christ on her own. He couldn't force her, but the five-month deadline was drawing closer, and he was running out of time. *Father in heaven, please draw McKenzie to yourself and help me behave around her. Please also help me to relax and have fun. In Jesus's name, I pray, amen.*

McKenzie walked through the living room and stood in the kitchen. "I love this. Nice white cabinetry, stainless steel appliances, and hardwood floors." She then turned back into the living room. "Definitely a bachelor pad. It's nice but needs some TLC." She grinned. "But that's okay. I love you just the way you are, Jackson."

How should he respond? Had McKenzie just said she loved him, or was it just an expression? Finally, he smiled. "I love you just the way you are too, McKenzie."

She turned away. "So where are the Monets, Manets, Renoirs, Van Goghs, and so forth, Monsieur L'Impressionniste?"

"This way, Mademoiselle, s'il vous plaît."

She glanced out the window. "The location is great. You have a nice view of the stores."

He chuckled. "It's not quite the Taj Mahal you live in, but it works for me."

As he led her on a tour of his condo, she stopped to look over the cherry gun cabinet in the hallway near the master bedroom. His rifle, shotgun, and pistol were visible through the tempered glass front. "I guess you like guns."

"It's an old hobby. I go to the range once in a while to fire them. I don't use them as much as I used to."

"Why not?"

He shrugged. "I'm not sure. I don't have the desire anymore, for some reason."

They returned to the living room. He pointed to the sliding glass door. "Next to the entrance to the grand patio, you'll find *On the Terrace* by Pierre-Auguste Renoir."

McKenzie sized it up. "The real name is *Two Sisters (On the Terrace)*."

"Hmm. Learn something every day, I guess. Okay, know-it-all, the gloves are coming off. In what year did the Red Sox first start playing at Fenway?"

She laughed. "Oh, been doing a few Google searches lately?" Then, faking a yawn, she answered, "In 1912. Got any others?"

"In what year did Cy Young win the Pitching Triple Crown, and how many wins did he have that year?"

"In 1901, and thirty-three wins."

"What was Ted Williams's batting average during the 1946 World Series?"

McKenzie hesitated for a moment. "I'm not sure I know the answer to that one. I guess you got me."

Jackson brandished a broad smile and was about to give McKenzie the answer, but she interrupted.

"But if I had to guess, I'd say his average was two hundred—five for twenty-five."

"Twerp!" He rushed toward her. She shrieked and dodged him. He went one way around the couch while she went the other. Eventually, he caught up to her and pushed her backward over the arm of the sofa. She sprawled on her back, and he knelt on the floor next to her as they stared into each other's eyes, laughing and breathing hard. He kissed her, and she slid her arms around his neck.

She was a fantastic kisser. He came up for air. "Are you doing anything tomorrow?"

"Nope." McKenzie was still smiling. "Are you?"

"Nope. Would you like to go tubing down the Farmington River?"

"That sounds like fun." Then she pulled him back down to continue where they had left off.

A few moments later, he drew back. "I'd better take you home. It's almost one in the morning. I could stay up like this in college without a problem, but not anymore."

"I guess you're right."

He helped her off the couch and stood staring into her eyes. "I'm finding I want to be with you all the time now."

"I'm starting to feel that way too," she whispered.

"Do you want me to sleep on your couch again tonight?"

"I'll be fine. I'll be sure to keep the door locked and bolted."

He eventually nodded. "Promise me you'll call me if you need me."

"I will."

He took her hand. "We'd better go now, or we'll never get out of here."

On the way home, McKenzie asked, "Where should I start reading in the Bible?"

A warm feeling flooded his chest. She was willing to be open to his beliefs. That meant more that he could say. He cleared his throat. "There are a lot of opinions on that. My suggestion is to start with the book of Matthew and work your way through the entire New Testament. Pray before reading and ask God to guide you."

After parking the car, Jackson escorted McKenzie to her apartment, checked every room and closet, and then kissed her good night. "Are you sure you don't want me to sleep on the couch again? I don't mind."

"I'll be fine. But thanks for offering."

As he drove home minutes later, McKenzie filled his mind and his heart. She was beautiful, kind, and a great kisser. If only he could spend every moment with her.

# Chapter 32
# Tubing

JACKSON ARRIVED AT McKenzie's apartment at one o'clock the next afternoon. When she opened the door, he hugged her.

He yawned when he stepped back. "I was pretty tired this morning. I slept in until ten again. That's two days in a row."

She winked at him. "I stayed up late reading the Bible. I'm fascinated by it. I went to sleep after about three hours of reading and woke up a little while ago."

*The Lord must be drawing her to himself. Praise God.* "Fantastic. Do you have any questions?"

"I wrote some down, but let's talk about them later."

"Sure. You ready to go?"

A few minutes into the forty-minute drive to the tubing area, she asked, "Where exactly are we going?"

The air was hot and humid, so he put the top down. "Farmington River Tubing. It's in Satan's Kingdom State Recreation Area in New Hartford."

Her eyes widened. "Did you say Satan's Kingdom?"

"Yep. That's its real name."

"Weird."

"You're telling me. I always feel kind of funny going there. But the Bible does say that the world system is under Satan's control, so the name isn't that far off base."

"If God is God, why isn't he in control of the world? Why is Satan in control?"

*She's finally interested.* "Ultimately, God controls Satan because God created him. He kicked Satan and the angels who followed him out of heaven because Satan wanted to be like God. If you look at the story of Job in the Old Testament, Satan had to ask God for permission to afflict Job in all the terrible ways he did—destroying his property, killing his children and slaves, and afflicting his body with sores. God had to approve the events, and he put a limit on them—Satan couldn't kill Job." He glanced at her. She seemed to be tracking his explanation. "The entire world is fallen due to sin. The most powerful of all fallen, sinful creatures is Satan, so he controls the world, but only within the parameters set by God."

They rode in silence for a few minutes. McKenzie seemed to be considering what he had said.

Jackson finally glanced over and smiled at how the breeze buffeted her hair.

She drew a breath. "So, tell me about this tubing ride we're going on."

"It's about two and a half miles long and has three sets of rapids. They'll give us something like a truck inner tube to ride on and a life preserver. A school bus will pick us up at the end of the trip and take us back to the parking lot."

"Are there any lifeguards?"

"Yes, but only at one of the rapids."

"Is it scary?"

"Not at all. But you can follow me if you like."

He stopped at a traffic light at the intersection with Route 202. The light turned green, and he proceeded through. Suddenly, a pickup truck full of high school kids sped through a red light at the intersection, heading straight for the passenger's side of their car. Bracing for impact, he cried out, "Jesus!"

McKenzie turned and screamed. The screech of brakes filled the air. The truck lurched to a stop a few inches from her car door. Jackson jumped out of the car to confront them, but the kid backed up and took off.

He went to her side of the car. "Are you all right?"

She stared at him. "Yeah."

He rounded the car and got back in. "The driver had a cell phone up to his ear. Thank God their truck stopped in time."

A car horn honked behind them, and he shifted into gear and started driving again.

"We were lucky," she said.

He turned on the hazard lights, pulled the car off to the side of the road, and then turned to her. "I don't believe in luck. It wasn't our time yet. God protected us."

They passed the next few moments in silence. Jackson could hardly breathe. McKenzie could easily have been in hell right now. *Thank you, Father, for sparing her. Please keep her safe and give her more time to come to you. In Jesus's name, I pray, amen.*

He rubbed her arm. "Do you still want to go tubing?"

"Sure."

He steered the car back onto Route 44. "You know, there are consequences to what we do. For example, that person who ran the red light a few minutes ago could have killed us but didn't seem to care. Many people don't realize or don't care that their lifestyle is offensive to God, so they continue doing whatever they feel like doing without worrying about the consequences in this world or the next. But God will judge each of us one day and require us to give an account of everything we have done or said or thought, whether good or bad. We can choose to love him, shake our fists at him, or ignore him. It's up to us. Whatever we decide, he'll be waiting patiently for us on the other side."

"So, if he's waiting patiently, then I have time to think about all this?"

"God is eternal. He has all the time in the world. Yet, we are finite. We only have a certain number of years to live—ninety or a hundred at most. So, we should seize each day and live it in a way that pleases him, not just ourselves. God will guide us along the way if we ask him. But he's a gentleman. He doesn't force himself on us."

McKenzie nodded slowly. "That was a bit of a long explanation, but not too bad. You always seem to say the right thing in the right way, Jackson."

"Thank you, my dear. I aim to please."

Jackson and McKenzie locked their belongings in the car at the tubing parking lot, then walked to the ticketing area. He bought the passes and left his keys in one of the wooden cubbyholes behind the desk. After picking up their tubes and donning their life jackets, an instructor gave them a safety lecture. Finally, they shuffled down the gravel slope to the river, carrying their inner tubes.

She dipped her toes in the water. "Yikes, it's cold."

"It feels cold even in July, but don't worry. You'll get used to it."

They placed their inner tubes on the water, sat down in the middle of them, and shoved off backward. Jackson took in the lush green foliage lining the river as they floated down. The river's bottom was brown and rocky and a little slippery, but the water was clear.

"The first set of rapids is coming up ahead, just after we go under the Route 44 bridge," he said.

McKenzie squinted in the sunlight. "I see it."

"Do you want to go the safe way or the wild and crazy way?"

"Well, we only live once…"

"Wild and crazy it is, then."

They let the current pull them right through the center of the rapids at the steepest part. Jackson, who was in the lead, looked back and shouted, "Lean back a little and hold tight on the handles!"

His inner tube started through, angling clockwise and then counterclockwise between a small boulder on his left and a large boulder on his right. He spun entirely around, arched backward, and finally splashed down hard at the bottom of the rapids.

Safely through, he twisted around to watch McKenzie.

She followed about five seconds later with the same result, screaming as she went. "That was so cool! Are the other rapids as good as this one?"

"I think the second one is like that, but the third one is a little tamer. We'll find out soon enough."

They drifted through a narrow gorge with hundred-foot rock walls on either side. The water was deep but relatively calm for about a hundred yards. Soon, the second set of rapids appeared. He wiped out at the bottom of the rapids after hitting a rock just beneath the surface, but she sailed through flawlessly.

McKenzie smiled triumphantly. "Need any instructions for getting through the next set of rapids?"

He glared at her. "Oh, you're done!"

McKenzie let out a shriek as he paddled vigorously toward her with both hands. She tried to get away, propelling herself backward and downstream as fast as she could, but to no avail. He caught up to her, grabbed her inner tube, stood up in the river, and flipped her over.

She was laughing as she came out of the water, and he pulled her to him and kissed her.

"Jackson, our tubes!"

They rushed downstream and managed to grab them.

He climbed back onto his. "Good thing we caught these."

"Yeah. We would have been doing a lot of swimming and walking if we hadn't."

He pointed downriver. "Rapids just ahead. The nice thing about this next set of rapids is that there's a trail on the left side, so we can walk back and go over the rapids again if you like."

They went down the third set of rapids, walked back, and then went down them again. After that, they continued lazily down the rest of the river.

Jackson caught a glimpse of someone walking parallel to them along the side of the river. A man was barely visible through the leafy maples. *He must be going tubing too.*

McKenzie trailed a hand through the water. Her movements were graceful but pensive. Without looking up, she asked, "Jackson, do you believe in heaven?"

"Yes, and hell too."

Her gaze lifted to meet his. A frown creased her brow. "Why?"

If he told her he'd seen hell, she'd think he was crazy. "Because Jesus said there's a heaven and a hell."

"Okay. I'm sure I'll come across that in the Bible at some point. Do Christians just believe in the New Testament and not the Old Testament?"

"When I first became a Christian, I didn't think that the Old Testament applied to Christians and didn't believe many of the stories. But, I later learned that Jesus believed in the Old Testament. It prophesied about him. He said that the Scripture—meaning the Old Testament—cannot be broken and that he came not to abolish the law but to fulfill it. He also specifically referred to Jonah and the whale, Abel the son of Adam and Eve, and Noah's ark. So, either those Old Testament stories are true, or Jesus is wrong. You have to decide for yourself."

"You seem to know a lot about the Bible."

"I've studied it for about five years. There's so much to learn, and you can never master all of it. You often learn something new when rereading it. In the end, knowing God, as revealed in the Bible and through his Holy Spirit, is the most important thing you can do in life, along with helping others."

"How do you help others?" she asked.

"After Jesus died and before he went back to heaven, he gave what is called the Great Commission, which is a command to go into all the world and teach others about him. That's what I try to do."

"How?"

"I pour my life into someone and let someone pour their life into me." She wrinkled her brow again, so he explained further. "Reading the Bible allows God to pour into me. I then meet twice a month with Mike, whom you met at church. He's been a Christian a lot longer than I have, and he answers my questions. So, he has been pouring his life into me."

"And who are you pouring your life into right now?"

Jackson paused for a few seconds. "You."

She got a little glassy-eyed.

"You have to figure out what God wants you to do with your life and then go out and do it," he continued. "He'll help you. That's the only way you will ultimately be happy and fulfilled. But it's not just ministry. It's how you treat other people daily. Jesus taught us to treat others the way we'd like them to treat us."

She smirked. "Oh, like flipping poor, helpless girls off inner tubes into the water? Aren't you supposed to turn the other cheek?"

Jackson shoved her inner tube. "I can see you've read through the Sermon on the Mount. I guess I'm going to have to watch what I'm doing from now on."

"I'll be watching you like a hawk, boy."

As they continued to float, he lay back and closed his eyes. His tube suddenly strained, and he opened his eyes to find McKenzie trying to flip him over. He was too heavy for her, so he leaned in the direction she was trying to push him and fell into the water.

She was cheering when he came up out of the water.

"Touché, my dear. And now I can't even exact revenge."

They got back in their tubes and floated for a while again.

"How much farther do we have to go?" she asked.

"The pickup point is just around the bend there." He met her gaze—time for a bit of payback. "You know, you couldn't do this in Florida. There'd be gators and snakes in the water. All we have up here, for the most part, are snapping turtles."

He gave her some time for that thought to sink in. The moment she closed her eyes, he quietly slipped out of his tube, swam underneath hers, and pinched her on the back of her right calf. Her scream was audible even underwater.

He swam back to his tube and resurfaced.

She was glaring at him. "You'll pay for that, Trotman!"

"Bring it on, Baker." He motioned toward himself with both hands. "Bring it on."

The bus pickup point came into view on the left. He sat up straighter in his tube, then jerked around instinctively when something small blasted through the water directly in front of him. A loud clap came from the right side of the river.

"Did you see that?" he asked.

"Yeah. Maybe it was a fish jumping or something?"

A few seconds later, another clap echoed, and Jackson's inner tube exploded beneath him. After surfacing, he looked to the side of the river and saw a small puff of smoke. Another clap, and this time he heard a bullet whiz by his head. "Someone's shooting at us!"

The people floating in inner tubes around him started screaming.

"McKenzie! Get to the bus!" he yelled.

His mind shifted to automatic pilot. *Charge the ambush.* He trudged through the water as fast as he could, whipping his arms and legs to get to the opposite riverbank. As he felt the rocks collect beneath his feet, he sprinted onto the dirt shore, dodging and weaving as he ran. He raced for a large rock a few feet away.

A bullet careened off the far side of it just as he dove behind it. He leaned back against it, catching his breath. But he couldn't stay there forever.

He shed the bulky life preserver and peered around the far side of the rock, looking for the next place to take cover. A tree had fallen about thirty feet away near the base of the hill, and he ran full speed for it, dodging left and right several times. His sneakers squeaked as he ran, and water spurted out the tops and sides. Another bullet whizzed right by his head, then another impacted the ground near his feet, spraying sand all over his shins.

*I can't believe this guy hasn't hit me yet. Either he's a lousy shot, or Mekoddishkem is protecting me.*

The shooter began unloading rounds into the fallen tree, but none of them penetrated all the way through. The guy let out a loud curse.

Jackson peered around the far side of the tree trunk. The shooter slammed his rifle on the ground and rushed toward the dirt road that ran parallel to the river. *His gun must have jammed. He's running to his car.*

Jackson took off after him. The man wasn't a good runner, and Jackson quickly gained on him. Then a police car with its lights flashing appeared on the road ahead of them. Someone must have called 911.

The shooter darted off the road away from the river. Jackson continued his pursuit, caught up to the man in the woods, and tackled him to the ground. Behind them, the police car's door slammed shut and sticks crackled under quick footsteps.

"Which one of you is Jackson Trotman?" the officer asked.

Jackson looked up at him. "Me. This man was shooting at us." He hooked a thumb over his shoulder. "His rifle is back there by the river."

The officer drew his pistol and told Jackson to move away. The man finally flipped over. It was Dexter.

"Officer, this is Dexter Lancaster. I think you'll find there's an outstanding arrest warrant for him on the charge of attempted rape. The incident occurred a few days ago in Hartford."

The officer handcuffed Dexter and led him toward his cruiser.

"I had her first," he called back to Jackson. "She'll always be mine."

Jackson followed them. "Look at yourself, Dexter. You're pathetic… and crazy. You spiked McKenzie's drink in college so you could rape her, and you've been stalking and terrifying her for years. A few days ago, you tried to rape her again, and today you tried to murder her. How can you possibly think she'd ever want you?"

Dexter scowled at him. "I wasn't trying to just kill her, you idiot. I was trying to kill both of you. And what makes you think I spiked her drink in college?"

Jackson blurted out the truth. "An angel showed me the whole thing at Brown University in the Sigma Chi basement. You should be ashamed of yourself. How could you do such a terrible thing to another person? You raped her in the Sigma Chi lounge. I'm the one who was taking her to the infirmary before you attacked me on the street. God will judge you for what you did. You'd better get right with him before it's too late and you end up in hell!"

"An angel showed you? And you think I'm crazy? Ha! I don't need God's forgiveness because he doesn't exist, and I could care less whether you forgive me or not."

The officer plunked Dexter in the back seat of his cruiser and closed the car door. Then he took Jackson's statement. Dexter's muffled laughter came through the glass periodically as Jackson spoke with the officer.

Another police car arrived, and the officer drove Jackson over a nearby bridge to the bus pickup area. McKenzie was there waiting for him. She burst into tears and threw her arms around him as he got out of the car. "Thank God you're okay! Did they catch the guy?"

"Yes. It was Dexter."

She paled. "Dexter?"

"They arrested him. Between the attempted rape and attempted murder, I don't think he'll be bothering us for a long time."

"Good riddance. I'm so sorry."

The police officer rolled down his window. "Would you like a ride back to your car?"

Jackson exchanged glances with McKenzie, then looked back at the officer. "No, we'll take the bus. Thanks anyway."

McKenzie stepped back and stared at Jackson's chest. "What are those holes in your shirt? They weren't there before."

He looked down, then took off his shirt.

"They look like bullet holes. See the darkened rings around them?"

She was right. They looked exactly like bullet holes—but in the center of his shirt. His legs wobbled, and he placed a hand on McKenzie's shoulder to steady himself.

"Thanks, Mekoddishkem," he whispered.

## CHAPTER 33
# TRANSITIONS

THE FOLLOWING MONDAY morning, McKenzie sat on a stool in her kitchen eating a poached egg on gluten-free raisin toast. She picked up the Connecticut section of the newspaper and read that Dexter was arraigned in Hartford Superior Court on attempted rape and attempted murder charges. The judge denied bail and ordered him to be placed in the county lockup to await trial. She slapped the newspaper on the counter and clapped her hands together. "Good. I hope he rots in jail forever."

She brushed her teeth, then was about to walk out the door to go to work when she stopped. She hadn't read the Bible today. *I don't have time. Have to do it later.* But something prompted her to go back. *Okay, one chapter. But that's it.*

She opened the Bible to where her bookmark was, based on her second reading of the New Testament. Reading Matthew, chapter 6, verses 14 and 15, gave her a cold shudder: *For if you forgive other people when they sin against you, your heavenly Father will also forgive you. But if you do not forgive others their sins, your Father will not forgive your sins.*

Dexter popped into her mind. *Ha! Forgive Dexter? I don't think so. He raped me and tried to kill me. He's a horrible person. Surely, God doesn't expect me to forgive him?*

∽

Pam Shuster had traveled to the Aetna offices in Blue Bell, Pennsylvania, for a series of all-day business meetings. Traveling had its advantages—getting away from the everyday routine and seeing old friends—but it had become tiresome after three days. So, after her last appointment, she checked her email for an hour, went back to the hotel, exercised briefly on the elliptical machine, took a shower, and then went out to dinner alone.

Pam returned to the hotel an hour later and got ready for bed. She slipped under the bed covers and flipped through the channels—nothing on.

Perhaps the novel in her suitcase could alleviate her boredom? No such luck—she gave up after two pages. The only other things available were the hotel's room service menu and a local chamber of commerce magazine. Finally, she opened the nightstand drawer. There had to be something else around here. A Gideon Bible sat inside.

Jackson had asked her to read the Bible, but she bristled. After all, her gay friends loved to talk about how the Bible bashed lesbians, so why should she waste her time? Even so, for the sake of intellectual curiosity, she opened it. But where to start? She grabbed her smartphone and googled "anti-gay Bible verses." After clicking through a few sites, she wrote several passages on the hotel notepad—Leviticus 18 and 20, Romans 1, and 1 Corinthians 6.

Pam looked up the passages in the Bible, and fear welled up within her. The fear was familiar. Hadn't Jackson said that she'd cried out in agony from hell while he was reviving her? Other people in her office heard her screams too. Was it true? Had she really gone to hell? If so, why couldn't she remember any of it? How could she be sure what Jackson said actually happened? How could she know anything the Bible said about hell was true?

Pam picked up the Bible, looked at its front and back, then threw it across the room with a grunt. She didn't want some homophobes from several thousand years ago telling her how to live her life.

# CHAPTER 34
## DEADLINE LOOMING

OVER THE NEXT two months, Jackson and McKenzie were insepa-
rable. They talked every night on the phone and often during the day,
ate lunch in the company cafeteria several times a week, and spent
their weekends together. They attended church on Saturday nights
and sometimes Sunday mornings. McKenzie continued reading her
Bible daily and quickly grew in her knowledge of the Lord. Her
questions about God were challenging and insightful. But time wasn't
on her side. Jackson had less than two months to ensure McKenzie
trusted in Jesus as her Savior. He had to wait patiently as she studied
the Bible to be sure it was true.

A knock softly tapped on his cubicle wall. He turned to find Pam
standing there with a blank expression on her face. He tensed but
stood. "Pam. How are you?"

"I just wanted to say that I'm sorry for how I treated you when
you came to my office a while ago. Will you forgive me?"

"Of course. I'm sorry if I made you feel uncomfortable."

"That's okay. Your heart's in the right place. I do have to say,
though, that you've made me curious."

*Whoa! God is working.* "I'm so glad. Would you like to come to the church I attend in Avon sometime?"

She shifted her weight from one foot to the other. "Would I be welcome there?"

"Absolutely."

"You know I'm Jewish, right?"

"Yes."

"And I'm still welcome to attend?"

"Of course."

"Well, to be transparent, I've always hated religion. I was disowned by my family when I came out as a lesbian. Do you think God hates gays?"

"I'm sorry you had to go through that, Pam. It must have been terrible being rejected by your family. I don't think God hates gays, per se. He hates sin. Gays are sinners, just like everyone else. They lie, cheat, steal, curse, lust, and ignore the needs of others, the same as anyone else. Sexual orientation is just one aspect of their personality. They need a Savior, the same as everyone else."

"But doesn't the Bible say homosexuality is a sin?"

"Yes. Several verses state that it's a sin. The twenty-first chapter of Revelation even says it will keep you out of heaven. But, having said that, we're also taught not to judge those outside the church."

Pam shook her head. "You've got a Bible verse for just about everything, don't you? Is your church inclusive?"

"Do you mean do we accept gays as members of our church?"

"Yes."

"Everyone is welcome to attend. To become a member, a person must have received Jesus as their Savior and had a pastor baptize them by immersion. Everyone is at different points in their relationship with God, so the church doesn't expect everyone to be perfect. However, they'd want to know if a prospective member is living in a way that is blatantly contrary to God's Word." He paused to catch his breath. "To take your example, if someone is involved in sexual activity outside of marriage between a man and a woman, whether it be heterosexual or homosexual, they would not be allowed to join the church. If Jesus is their Savior, he will change them on the inside so they'll become more like him on the inside and outside."

"Isn't that homophobic? Isn't that discrimination against gays?"

"It's discrimination against sexual behavior outside of marriage, which the Bible tells us is to be between a man and a woman. If a man is living with his girlfriend, he wouldn't be allowed to join the church either."

She considered that for a few moments. "What if two men or two women have been legally married? Would they be allowed to join the church?"

"They would be welcome to attend. Many people attend our church for years, even decades, without joining. Because gay marriage is contrary to what the Bible teaches, the church would prevent them from becoming members. The US Constitution protects our right to uphold our religious values without interference from the state."

"I see."

"I think it is essential not to get distracted by this issue," he continued. "There are two kinds of people—those who are going to heaven and those who are going to hell. It doesn't matter what a person's particular sins are. Everyone is a sinner. People don't go to hell because they're gay. They go to hell because they're sinners."

"Do you honestly believe that?"

"Yes. Think about it this way. Suppose a person commits three to four sins a day for the eighty years of their life."

She nodded. "Okay."

"That's about a hundred thousand sins in a lifetime. Now let's suppose, for the sake of argument, that ten thousand of those sins are sexual."

"Got it."

"Now, let's say, for the sake of argument, that sex outside of marriage between a man and a woman is not a sin, and we take those ten thousand sins away. That still leaves ninety thousand sins that someone must atone for before a holy God. Jesus died on the cross to pay for each of our hundred thousand sins. He is the only way to heaven."

"I see your point, but I think it's arrogant to state that Jesus is the only way to heaven. What about all the other religions of the world? I don't think we're ever going to see eye-to-eye on that, Jackson." She shook her head. "Just because I'm curious, why don't you think there are other paths to heaven?"

He looked up. "Jesus said in John 14:6 that 'I am the way and the truth and the life. No one comes to the Father except through me.' That isn't me saying something out of arrogance. *Jesus* said he is the only way to heaven."

"How are you able to just rattle off verses like that?"

"I memorized them. The Bible says in Psalm 119:11, 'I have hidden your word in my heart that I might not sin against you.' Memorizing Scripture is an important part of growing as a Christian."

He paused for a moment to let everything sink in. "Pam, I know this has been a very tough conversation for you, but here's the bottom line. It doesn't matter what sins you've committed. What matters is that you repent, or turn away, from your sinful way of living, believe that Jesus is the Son of God, ask him to forgive your sins, and be willing to give up your life to follow him all the days of your life. You first need to count the cost and determine if this is something you want to do. God won't force you to do it.

"And another thing. Even though your family disowned you, Jesus will never disown you. He died on the cross to pay for your sins and my sins, whether we're Jewish or gentile, straight or gay. He loves you."

She eventually nodded. "Maybe I'll give your church a try."

"They have a class starting soon, called Alpha. It's to help people who are searching and have questions about God. It lasts ten weeks. I could go with you every week if you like."

"That sounds interesting. I'll talk to you later about it."

"Sure."

As Pam walked away, Jackson smiled. *Thank you, God!*

༒

That evening, Jackson called Mike. "How are you?"

"Livin' the dream, brother. Just livin' the dream."

"That bad, huh?"

"This new job is a killer. It's a lot more stressful than I thought it would be. I'm getting calls at all hours of the night now. How about you?"

He grinned. "Well, brother, I *am* living my dream. I'm so in love with McKenzie."

"Great. So, when's the wedding?"

"Well, we'll see. I'm just calling to ask you to invite us over for dinner."

"Dinner at our house?" Mike chuckled. "That's rude, even for you, dude."

"I know, but you guys haven't had the chance to spend much time with McKenzie, and I want your opinion of her. I was wondering if you and Sally think she's right for me."

"Well, that decision is really up to you, of course, but we'd be happy to offer our opinion. I'm honored that you'd ask us to help."

"The main thing troubling me is that she's not a Christian yet. As you know, the Bible teaches that a Christian should not marry a non-Christian. On the other hand, I'm totally in love with her. I want to make sure my emotions don't take over my thinking to such a degree that I make the wrong decision—for both of us."

"Yeah, I hear you. When would you like to come over?"

"How about this Saturday night, right after church?"

"Hang on a minute. Let me check with da boss." After a minute or so, Mike returned to the phone. "Saturday night's fine."

"Great. What should we bring?"

"Sally said to have you bring a salad. She's going to make vegetable lasagna."

"Sounds good. Can you ask Sally to make something gluten-free? McKenzie can't eat anything with wheat in it. I know they have gluten-free rice pasta in the stores."

"Sure, I'll tell her."

"I'll bring over some bread for you guys too."

"We're looking forward to it. I can't wait to invite myself over to your place one of these days."

Jackson tapped his foot on the carpet as he hung up the phone. He'd been trying not to push McKenzie, to allow time for God to work in her heart. But as his feelings for her grew, so did his concern for her eternal destiny. What would he do if she never accepted God's offer of forgiveness?

# CHAPTER 35
# DECISION TIME

JACKSON PICKED UP McKenzie at her apartment around two o'clock that Saturday and drove toward West Hartford. "The Tolberts asked me to bring a salad tonight, so I figured we could go to Whole Foods to pick up the salad stuff."

"Do you have a salad bowl?"

"Well, not really."

"We can pick one up at Crate and Barrel. There's one right next to your condo. Do you have salad tongs?"

"No."

"We can get those too." She grinned. "You're in pretty bad shape from a household perspective there, buster."

He placed his hand on hers. "My condo needs a woman's touch."

"I'd be happy to help with that."

They bought what they needed at Whole Foods and placed the groceries in his refrigerator.

"Do you have any friends getting married next year?" she asked as they walked through the front door of Crate and Barrel."

"None that I know of."

"I was just wondering. I bet a lot of people register here."

"I bet you're right." He glanced at her. Was that just an innocent comment on her part, or was she hinting at getting married? He looked from one side of the store to the other. "Any idea where the salad bowls are?"

McKenzie pointed. "I think they're in the next aisle over there on the right."

She quickly found a bowl she liked, and Jackson checked the price tag. "A hundred and twenty-five dollars for a salad bowl?"

"It's acacia wood." She didn't seem surprised. "Beautiful, isn't it?"

"Yes, but I wasn't planning on spending that much for a bowl."

She smiled. "Think of it as an investment for the future, not just for today."

Was that another hint? Less subtle that time. At least it seemed like they were on the same page regarding their future together. "This is getting to be a pretty expensive date, you know."

"You get what you pay for, Jackson. You want something nice for when you have company over, right?"

She had him there. "I guess you're right. I'll get it."

"Good."

Thirty minutes later, they were back in his kitchen pouring ingredients into the bowl and mixing the salad.

"What do you think about this 'wives submitting to their husbands' business?" she asked. "I mean, that's pretty archaic in this day and age, isn't it?"

He shrugged. "When are you going to ask me some easy questions?"

McKenzie shrugged right back.

"Well, we all submit to someone."

"What do you mean?"

"We submitted to parents, teachers, and coaches when we were growing up, didn't we?"

"Yes. Do you have a cutting board and a knife?"

Jackson procured the requested items and handed them to her. "And we submit to bosses and customers at work, right?"

"Yes."

"Have you ever had a great boss at work?"

McKenzie nodded while chopping the romaine lettuce and placing it in the new salad bowl. "My last boss was fantastic."

"What did you like about him or her?"

"He was kind and encouraging. He trusted me. He let me do my job without micromanaging. I think he honestly wanted what was best for me. His goal was for me to grow in my career even if it meant leaving for another department or company."

"And if he called you today and asked you to do something for him, would you do it?"

"Absolutely."

"That's part of the whole submission thing. The Bible doesn't just say for wives to submit to their husbands. It also says for husbands to love their wives as Christ loved the church, meaning that the husband should love and care for his wife so much that he's willing to die for her. Would you submit to someone who's willing to die for you?"

She considered that as she chopped the peppers. "Perhaps."

"So, submission for a wife is only hard if the husband isn't doing his part."

"I see."

"God himself set an example of submission for us in the way that Jesus submitted to the Father while he was here on earth. The Holy Spirit, in turn, submits to the Father and the Son. The church is the bride of Christ. We submit to Jesus because he was not only willing to die for us, he *did* die for us. The Bible also says we shouldn't lord it over others, meaning one person shouldn't dominate another. If you love someone, you won't do that. You always want what's best for the other person."

*Lord, please help me to reflect Jesus to McKenzie. Help her submit to your will before it's too late.*

⤙

When Jackson and McKenzie arrived at the Tolbert's Cape Cod-style house in Simsbury that evening, they went straight to the back-yard because they heard voices there. The kids were jumping on the trampoline while Mike watched them. Sally waved from the kitchen window. After greeting Mike, Jackson and McKenzie carried the bread and salad inside.

"That looks like a great salad," Sally said. "And what a beautiful salad bowl and tongs. Can you help me get dinner ready?"

Since they had the dinner covered, Jackson wandered out to the backyard to be with Mike as the ladies finished the meal preparations. He sat on a lawn chair next to Mike as they watched the kids on the trampoline. "Hey, you guys are pretty good jumpers!"

"I know!" came Joshua's reply.

He grinned at Mike. "No self-esteem problems there, Dad."

"Tell me about it."

"Did you talk to Sally about the plan for today?"

"We've got your back, bro. Got it covered." Mike turned his attention back to the kids. "But so far, I think she's the best thing ever to come your way, and you'd be crazy to let her go."

"Thanks. I don't trust my decision-making in this area. The Bible says a Christian should not marry a non-Christian. I want to make sure I follow that command."

Mike nodded slowly. "Are you behaving yourself with her?"

Jackson looked him in the eye. "So far, but it's been a real struggle sometimes."

"The Bible says if you can't control yourselves, it's better to get married than to burn with passion. In the meantime, I'd advise you to pray, read your Bible, memorize Scripture, exercise like crazy, and lay off the alcohol, caffeine, raisins, Vitamin E, or any other stimulant that will make it tougher for you to control yourself. And remember to walk in the Spirit so you won't fulfill the desires of the flesh. Ask God to fill you with his Holy Spirit each morning."

Jackson crossed his arms. "My theory is that we must have slept together the first time around before she had a chance to become a Christian. Maybe I was partially to blame for her ending up in hell." He sighed. "I don't want to push her. She needs to become a Christian on her own terms, in her own time, and in her own way. Otherwise, it won't stick."

Mike slapped him on the back. "I suggest you stop worrying about what you might have done wrong the first time and focus on doing things right this time."

*Good advice for sure.* "You're right."

"As I said, I've got your back. Have your parents met her yet?"

"No, but I've told them about her. Maybe we'll see them at Thanksgiving or Christmas."

Mike shook his head. "I bet they'll be meeting her sooner than that."

"Maybe so."

McKenzie sliced and buttered the bread in the kitchen. Once she finished, she wrapped it in aluminum foil and stuck it in the oven next to the large and small dishes containing lasagna. How thoughtful of Sally to make a meatless, gluten-free version as well.

"Would you mind helping me set the table?" Sally asked. "The china is in the cabinet in the dining room. Just four plates. The kids have their own."

McKenzie retrieved the plates and set them on the table. Admiring the pure white design with gold trim, she asked, "What kind of china is this? It's beautiful." She held it up to her face. "I can see my reflection in it."

"It's Lenox Eternal. We got eight sets as wedding gifts." Sally appeared in the doorway between the dining room and kitchen.

"I've learned from reading the Bible that people are eternal too."

Sally nodded. "That's true. How's your Bible reading going?"

She tried to align the plates and silverware perfectly on the dining room table. "It's fascinating. I've read through the New Testament twice, and I'm starting on the Old Testament."

"Great. Why do you think it matters what the Bible says?"

That was a tough question. "I don't know. I'll have to think about it for a minute… Only God could perform the miracles that Jesus performed. The words Jesus spoke have a power, clarity, and authority in them that I've never read anyplace else before. I've never been so hungry to read anything in my life. Everything in the world and my life finally makes sense. I feel God speaking directly to me through the Bible. So, to answer your question, the Bible matters because it's the Word of God. It's true and means everything to me."

"That's great, McKenzie! Have you asked Jesus to be your Savior?"

McKenzie tensed. "No, not yet."

"What are you waiting for?"

*She's always pressuring me. When is she going to quit?* "I'm not ready."

"You'll never stop learning about God. You don't have to be a Bible scholar to become a Christian. All you have to do is tell God you're sorry for your sins, be willing to turn away from them, and believe that Jesus died on the cross to forgive them. Are you ready now?"

A sense of panic took hold. "Can we talk about something else?"

"Sure."

❧

McKenzie was relieved Sally acted normally after they changed the subject, but doubts about her standing with God lingered during dinner.

McKenzie stared out the window while Jackson drove her home. *Why haven't I asked Jesus to be my Savior? What's holding me back?*

*Getting raped wasn't my choice or fault, but getting an abortion was. How am I going to explain that to God? Not to commit murder is one of the Ten Commandments, and I've clearly broken it. There's no question I'm guilty. What about all the other sins I've committed? What am I going to do? I don't want to go to hell. Could it be as simple as asking Jesus to forgive me?*

Jackson placed his hand on hers. "You're awfully quiet tonight. What's up?"

"Just thinking."

Fifteen minutes later, they arrived at McKenzie's apartment. Jackson sat on the love seat while McKenzie put hot water on for tea. The pressure of possibly going to hell weighed on her more and more.

The teapot whistled. McKenzie brought over a tray holding two mugs of hot water and an assortment of teas, then set them on the coffee table. "Jackson. I'm scared."

Jackson sat up straight. "Why?"

"I don't want to go to hell."

Jackson held her hands and stared into her eyes. "You're right to be scared. Not everyone will be allowed into heaven. Jesus stated in the seventh chapter of Matthew that only a few would find their way there. God's standard for entry is perfection. Obviously, none of us are good enough to get into heaven on our own. Jesus, the Son of God, died on the cross to pay for our sins so we wouldn't have to pay for them in hell. Do you want to be one of the few?"

Did she? What once seemed restrictive, was now the opportunity of a lifetime. God was offering her the chance to live with him forever in heaven after she died. Eternal joy and happiness would be hers for all eternity. How could she decline such an offer? "Yes."

"Great! You must believe Jesus is the Son of God, repent, which means turn away from your sinful way of living, and give up your life to follow him for the rest of your days. Are you willing to do that?"

The panic from earlier didn't return. Only a deep sense of need. She needed God's forgiveness. "I am."

"Just close your eyes and follow me in this prayer."

"Okay."

McKenzie closed her eyes and repeated quietly but steadily after Jackson. "Dear Lord Jesus, I believe you are the Son of God. I know that I'm a sinner. Thank you for dying on the cross to pay the penalty for my sins. Please forgive my sins and give me the gift of eternal life. I ask you into my heart and my life, and I will serve you forever. In your name, I pray, amen."

Jackson hugged her. "Congratulations, McKenzie. You've just made the most important decision of your life. The Bible says there is much rejoicing in heaven over one sinner who repents."

"Thanks." Tears filled her eyes. She couldn't stop smiling. "I feel like Jesus lifted a tremendous burden off my shoulders. Such joy and peace. It's Jesus's joy, isn't it?"

"Yes, it is. I'm so happy for you, McKenzie."

That evening, Jackson dreamed of a person wearing a lightning-bright robe who stood along the edge of the lake of fire. The figure reached down and pulled a woman out of it.

He awoke with a deep sense of peace. God was so good.

# CHAPTER 36
## INTERRUPTION

THE FOLLOWING AFTERNOON, McKenzie was relaxing on her love seat reading the Sunday paper, and sipping hot tea when Monica called. She answered and hit the speakerphone button. "Hey!"

"Hi, girlfriend. What's up? You and Jackson still together?"

She smiled at just the thought of him. "Monica, I've fallen for him."

"That was fast. You've been going out what, three months?"

"About that. Jackson's such a wonderful guy."

"I'm so happy for you. Listen, I was wondering if I could come up and visit sometime. I haven't seen your new place yet."

"Sure. I'd like you to meet Jackson too. What day would work for you?"

"How about this Saturday, maybe around lunchtime?"

"That works. We can hang out here Saturday afternoon, go to church with Jackson Saturday night, and then go out to dinner afterward."

"Church? On a Saturday night?"

McKenzie shifted to a different position on the love seat. "Our church has Saturday night and Sunday morning services—just like when we were growing up. It doesn't matter when you go."

Monica laughed. "But you don't go to church."

"I do now. My whole life has changed. I became a Christian yesterday."

"A Christian? No way. You got like born again and all that?"

McKenzie paused. *She may think I'm a little weird, but I have to tell her.* "Yes."

"Oh my gosh. It sounds like you've gone off the deep end, babe."

McKenzie smiled. "Not at all. I mean, it is a big change for me, but I just realized that I needed to get right with God. So, I accepted Jesus as my Savior."

"Girl, that's not a big change. That's a huge change."

"Yes, it is. I can't tell you how happy I am."

"Good for you. Do you want me to bring anything this weekend?"

"No, just yourself."

"Got it. Well, I'll be there Saturday, then."

"I can't wait to see you, and I can't wait for you to meet Jackson."

After hanging up, she wanted to tell everyone about her decision to follow Jesus. She'd begin by phoning Sally. "Hi, Sally, it's McKenzie."

"Hey. How are you?"

"I'm great. Thank you for dinner last night. It was great spending time with you and your family."

"Likewise."

"I wanted you to know that I prayed to receive Jesus as my Savior with Jackson last night."

"That's fantastic, McKenzie. I'm so happy for you."

"Thanks. I can't believe how happy I am."

"Write down the date of your decision in your Bible. Satan will try to get you to doubt your salvation later. You were a member of Satan's family, but now you're part of God's family. Satan doesn't like it when people leave his family, so you can expect to come under spiritual attack. You need to get in a discipleship relationship with a mature Christian woman right away."

McKenzie bit her lip. She didn't know any mature Christian women—except Sally. "Would you be willing to disciple me?"

Sally sounded surprised. "Well… sure. I've got a family that keeps me pretty busy, but I'd be honored to help you grow as a Christian."

She smiled. "Great! I'm looking forward to it."

On Sunday afternoon, Jackson got on his knees beside the couch in his condo and prayed for quite a while, asking if it was God's will that he ask McKenzie to marry him. Then, Mekoddishkem's advice came back to him. He said it was up to him whom he married, and that God would not make that decision for him. God's only requirement was that, as a Christian man, he should marry a Christian woman.

So, Jackson prayed for wisdom. He had already received counsel from Mike and Sally, who agreed that McKenzie's prayer of salvation seemed genuine and that she would be a wonderful wife. What else could he do the reach a decision? He could fast. So, he skipped dinner that night.

As he lay in bed, he couldn't sleep. He got a pad of paper and wrote down every question he could think of, along with his answer.

*Are we in agreement regarding our faith in God?*

*Yes.*

*Do I want to be with her all the time?*

*Yes.*

*Am I attracted to her physically?*

*Oh, yes.*

*Do I love her as Christ loved the church, meaning am I willing to die for her?*

*Yes.*

After delving into the practical and logical, he was exhausted. Thankfully, McKenzie would not have to spend all eternity in the lake of fire, but what about the wedding? Had her future changed there too? The clock read one in the morning when he finally went to sleep.

&#8766;

On Monday after work, Jackson went hunting for an engagement ring. There were several jewelry stores in West Hartford Center, including Becker's and Lux Bond & Green, just two blocks over on LaSalle Road. Since Becker's focused chiefly on jewelry, he went there first.

A plump middle-aged woman with light brown hair and gold wire-rimmed glasses approached him when he walked in. "May I help you, sir?"

He noted the name on her tag. "Yes, Nancy. I want to look at rings, please."

"What type of ring?"

"An engagement ring."

"Oh, how exciting." Nancy grinned. "Follow me." As they drew closer to a display case, she asked, "What price range would you like to look at?"

*Three thousand?* "I have no idea how much rings cost."

"Not a problem. Would you like a traditional solitaire or a ring with multiple stones in it?"

"Traditional."

"Silver or gold?"

"Gold."

"White gold or yellow?"

"Yellow."

She then directed him to a jewelry display case in the middle of the store and pointed to the type of ring he had specified. After walking around to the side of the case, she opened it and pulled out the specific panel. "Do you see anything here you like?"

He pointed to a particular ring. "How much is that one?"

"That's a classic round solitaire. It has a round brilliant-cut center diamond that's 1.0 carat, accompanied by round diamond accents that total 0.04 carat. Beautiful, isn't it?"

"How much is it?"

"Six thousand one hundred and ninety-five dollars."

His stomach knotted. "Six thousand? That's not cheap, but it is beautiful. Do you have payment plans?"

"Yes, sir."

"Great. I'm not sure which way I'd pay for it, but I just want to know what the options are. I do like that one, but I'd still like to shop around a bit."

"Of course. Would you like me to put the ring on hold for you?"

"No, thanks. If God wants me to buy it, it'll be here when I get back."

Nancy cleared her throat. "I hope to see you soon, then. Have a good evening, sir."

"You too."

Jackson visited several other jewelry stores, but the prices were higher, or he didn't like the settings.

The next day, he went back to Becker's after work and purchased the ring with his credit card. Hopefully, it would fit, but he could always have it sized later if it didn't.

But where and how to pop the question? He wanted it to be romantic so she'd remember it for the rest of her life. The Riverton Inn would be perfect. He made reservations for Saturday night and then called McKenzie.

"Would you like to go to dinner at the Riverton Inn on Saturday night?" he asked after they greeted each other.

"Sure. My sister Monica is coming in from Boston that day, but the three of us could go together."

His mouth went dry. "Oh."

"Jackson, are you still there?" she asked when he didn't say any more.

"Yes."

"What's wrong?"

"Nothing. I was looking forward to taking you there on Saturday."

"We can still go. Or we could go next weekend."

Jackson was disappointed, but of course, he needed to meet her family too.

"She's coming in at lunchtime on Saturday. Why don't you come over at around twelve thirty? Let's take her out somewhere fun."

"Okay. What does Monica like to do?"

"Well, she works at Starbucks. And she's very artistic."

He already had a plan. If he won over Monica, McKenzie would be more likely to say yes.

# CHAPTER 37
# CREDIT

THE CROWD WAS sparse at Starbucks the following afternoon, so Monica's boss let her leave early. Rather than go straight home, she drove to Ronaldo's office to surprise him.

The quartz gravel on the driveway whooshed beneath the wheels of her car, announcing her arrival. The driver's door thumped as she closed it behind her. She strolled toward the crimson converted barn, opened the massive sliding doors, and walked into the cavernous center section of the building. The wide-planked wood flooring creaked as she strode toward his dimly lit office.

Ruth looked up from the reception desk and smiled. "Hey, Monica. I haven't seen you here in a while. Are you looking for the boss?"

"Yes."

"He went out for a late lunch but should be back soon."

"Thanks. I'll wait in his office."

She surveyed the pictures of kitchens and home additions that he and his crew had completed. His cluttered desk bore the marks of various tools and appliances that had crossed it over the years. His calendar book lay on top of the desk, and the entry for today caught her eye: *Lunch with Clarice, 12–2.*

Monica gritted her teeth and wrote right below it, *Who the hell is Clarice?* Then she stormed out, slamming the door behind her.

She arrived at Ronaldo's sprawling custom home a few hours later after food shopping. She entered through the front door, then strode across the gleaming hardwood floor toward the study. Ronaldo sat at his desk, writing a check.

He looked up. "Sure looks like you had fun last month."

Her eyes narrowed. "What do you mean?"

He held up a bill. "Your share of the credit card bill. It's almost three thousand dollars."

"I put a lot of groceries and gas on there."

Ronaldo huffed. "That's about half of it. The rest is for nails, massages, department stores, restaurants."

She clenched her teeth. "Well, look at all the money you spend on client lunches and that stupid golf."

"We're not talking about me, princess. We're talking about you."

When attacked, she instinctively attacked back, regardless of the consequences. "Who's Clarice?"

He just stared at her, then stood up. "She's a client. I'm planning a new kitchen for her."

"Right. How much did the lunch cost? Were there any other expenses associated with the lunch that day?"

Ronaldo stood up and put his hands on his hips. "That's none of your business. You're the one splurging all the time, not me."

She shrugged. "It's only money."

He walked over and grabbed her by the arms. "I work hard for that money. By the way, it's not our money you're blowing, sweetheart. It's my money. Get that through your thick head."

"If you were a better businessman, you wouldn't be so stressed out about money."

A punch to her face knocked her to the floor. Her left cheekbone throbbed and stung as she got up. She glared at him, then ran up the stairs to the master bedroom.

Monica sat on the bench in front of her vanity set and sighed as she took a close look at her left eye in the mirror. The spot was sore. She'd have a black eye for sure. Then, angrily, she wiped tears from her eyes. *I don't know how, when, or where, but that scumbag is going to pay for what he just did to me.*

Ronaldo's footsteps sounded on the hardwood stairs and upstairs hallway, then became muted as he stepped onto the carpet in the master bedroom. He appeared directly behind her in the mirror's reflection and placed both of his hands on her shoulders. "I'm so sorry, honey. I don't know what came over me. I shouldn't have done that. You know I love you."

"You've got a funny way of showing it," she snapped.

Ronaldo sat down next to her on the bench and hugged her.

Monica sighed. Maybe it was time to move on from Ronaldo.

A few minutes after noon on Saturday, McKenzie buzzed Monica into her apartment building. She waited at the door as her sister rode up the elevator.

"What a great building," Monica said as she stepped off carrying a small suitcase. She hugged McKenzie. "It's beautiful."

"Thanks. Come in. Here, let me take that for you." She took the suitcase and carried it to her bedroom. "I've got a rollaway right here in the closet that you can sleep on tonight."

"Nice," Monica called from the living room. "Wow, what a view."

McKenzie returned to the living room. "Do you want something to drink?"

"I'm good." Monica flopped down on the couch with a sigh. "You've been here for what, four months?"

"About that." McKenzie sat down on the love seat, curling her legs underneath her. "How are you—" She stopped. Beneath Monica's heavy makeup was a barely visible gray half crescent under her left eye. "What happened to your eye?"

Monica blew out her breath. "I slipped in the shower and hit it on the faucet handle."

Her answer sounded rehearsed. "I can always tell when you're lying, Monica. You're an open book to me. Did Ronaldo hit you?"

She scowled. "What do you mean?"

"You know what I mean." McKenzie sat forward. "I knew something like this would happen. That guy is bad news. You've got to get rid of him. Why did he hit you?"

After a few moments, Monica looked away. "We argued about money."

"Oh, honey, I'm so sorry." She moved over next to her and took her hand. "You can't stay with him. Why don't you come live with me? There's a Starbucks right around the corner, and I bet they could find a spot for you there."

"I like where I am now."

"Monica, it's just a job. You can find another one."

"But I don't want to leave."

McKenzie sighed. *Why can't I get her to listen? He's going to kill her someday if she doesn't get out.* "Well, at least call the police and get a restraining order on the guy. You must go back to living in your apartment. Do you understand me?"

She eventually nodded. "Yeah. I can do that."

"Good. You've got to take care of yourself."

"I know." Monica got up and walked to the windows. "So, how do you like living here?"

"It's nice. There are lots of things to do within walking distance, and the exercise room here in the building is great."

"How are things with Jackson?"

"Fantastic."

Monica faced her. "Have you slept with him yet?"

McKenzie stood. "No. The Bible says we should wait until marriage for that."

She grinned. "That never stopped you before."

*Lord, please help me to reach my sister.* "That's the old me. I'm a new person now."

Monica stared at her for a few moments. "You're really into all this God stuff, aren't you?"

"Yes. Jesus has changed my life—for the better."

"So, what are we going to do now, have a prayer meeting?"

Monica chuckled. "No. Jackson should be here any minute to take us to lunch."

"Oh, good. Don't worry. I'll scope Jackson out for you."

Monica stared at Jackson as they walked along the streets of Hartford. She couldn't help it. He was so handsome—much better looking than Ronaldo, and younger too. Whenever he glanced at her, she looked away, knowing she was being a bit too obvious.

Jackson said, "McKenzie tells me you're interested in art. I thought we'd go to the Wadsworth Atheneum. They have a great café. You can give me all the dirt on McKenzie, and then we can look around. They have French and American Impressionist works and a special exhibit featuring the Hudson River School collection. If that doesn't float your boat, we could go to the Science Center instead."

*I'd go anywhere you like, Jackson.* "Oh, I've always wanted to go to the Wadsworth Atheneum. They have a Caravaggio there, don't they?"

"Yeah. I don't remember the name of it, but it has something to do with Saint Francis."

"*Saint Francis of Assisi in Ecstasy.*"

"That's it."

Monica stepped onto a cross street. Someone suddenly grabbed her arm and yanked her backward. A burst of wind blew over her legs. She looked up just as a car whizzed by, nearly clipping her. She squatted down, held the top of her head with both hands, and squealed for a second. "Oh my gosh! That car could have killed me." Then, she stood, looked at Jackson, and hugged him. "Thank you for saving me!"

Jackson sighed deeply. "No problem. I'm just glad you weren't hurt."

After she took several breaths and stopped shaking, they resumed their walk. About ten minutes later, they entered the brownstone Gothic Revival Atheneum building. Monica and McKenzie peeked in the museum shop while Jackson purchased their passes.

"Let's have lunch first and then walk around the museum later," he said when he joined them.

They headed to the Museum Café to eat. After Monica grilled Jackson about his job, childhood, and old girlfriends, they strolled around the museum.

Monica stopped in front of a marble statue of two women overlooking a defeated Roman gladiator. One of them leaned forward and leered angrily with her thumb pointed down, apparently condemning the vanquished man.

"It's called *Pereat*, by Orazio Andreoni," Jackson said, reading its caption. "That sure is a powerful sculpture, isn't it?"

McKenzie raised her eyebrows. "There's no mercy in those eyes, just condemnation."

They moved from there through the Morgan Great Hall, with its majestic fifty-foot-high ceilings and blush-red walls covered with American and European masterpieces, to Caravaggio's *Saint Francis of Assisi in Ecstasy*.

"Wow. I wish I could paint like that," Jackson said.

Monica just stood there in silence, gazing at it. Finally, she murmured, "It's one thing to see a painting in an art history book or projected on a screen. It's quite another to see it in person. Now I know why they say that Caravaggio was one of the greatest Baroque painters in history."

"What does the painting depict?" he asked.

"The moment that St. Francis received the wounds that Christ experienced on the cross—nails pounded in his hands and feet, and the spear stuck in his side."

"It's called the Stigmata." Jackson touched Monica's shoulder. "Do you know why Christ was wounded and died on the cross?"

*How am I supposed to know that?* "Well, sort of."

"Can I tell you what I think?"

She shrugged. "Sure."

"It was to pay the penalty for our sins. Like the statue we just saw of the woman with her thumb pointed down, God will condemn those whose sins he has not forgiven. He will sentence them to hell and then the lake of fire for all eternity. I think this painting depicts the reward experienced by those who accept Jesus's sacrifice for their sins on the cross and who share in his sufferings here on earth."

*This guy is crazy. I have no idea what he's talking about, but I can't offend McKenzie.* "Well, that's an interesting idea, Jackson. I certainly never heard that interpretation in my art history class."

He slipped his hands into the front pockets of his jeans. "I don't think you can understand the art or literature of that period without having an understanding of the Bible. It was so integral to their culture back then, unlike today."

"True." She looked back to the painting. "But why in the world would anyone want to have the Stigmata?"

"I don't know. I certainly wouldn't want it. Perhaps it was because St. Francis wanted to know Jesus better."

*What's the point of that?*

They spent another two hours browsing through the various exhibits, then walked back to McKenzie's apartment via Bushnell Park.

After they had gone to church and dinner, Monica had to watch Jackson kiss McKenzie good night at the front door to the building. *Why does she always get the best? She got the Ivy League education, the plumb corporate job, the glitzy apartment. And now she's got the man of every girl's dreams.* Monica massaged her temples. *I'd love to be alone with him for just an hour.*

Back in the apartment, McKenzie prepared some decaf coffee and brought it out to the living room. She curled up on a love seat and looked at Monica. "So, what do you think of Jackson?"

"You were right. Jackson is wonderful. Kind, caring, generous—and seriously handsome. He's too religious for my tastes, but then, you've changed since I last saw you."

McKenzie sipped her coffee. "In what way?"

"In a lot of ways. You're nicer. And you seem more... I don't know... at peace, I guess you'd say."

"That's because Jesus came into my life and changed me." McKenzie's eyes glimmered.

Monica stared into her mug. "Well, I'm glad you've found peace. I am. I think you guys will be great together."

If only she could find the same happiness.

✍

The following afternoon, someone knocked on Jackson's front door. He looked through the peephole to find Monica standing there alone. Odd. He opened the door. "Hey. What brings you over here?"

She grinned brightly. "I'm on my way back to Boston. Yesterday you joked about wanting the dirt on McKenzie. So, I thought I'd stop by and give it to you. Can I come in?"

"Sure." He closed the door behind her. It was a little uncomfortable being alone with Monica, but she would be family soon, so it shouldn't be a problem. "Would you like something to drink?"

"A glass of ice water would be great." She glanced around. "Nice place you have here, Jackson."

"Thanks." When he returned from the kitchen with her water, she'd removed her light jacket, revealing a tight orange tank top. Her breasts bulged above the low neckline, and he couldn't help staring at them as he handed her the glass.

She took a sip and placed the glass on an end table, then walked to him and wrapped her arms around his neck. Her cleavage brushed against his chest as she looked up at him.

Jackson stared at her mouth for a second, feeling a powerful impulse to kiss her, but he quickly recovered. He brushed aside her arms, walked over to the couch, picked up her jacket, and handed it to her. "I think you need to go."

"Aw, come on, Jackson. We'd have a lot of fun. I'm a great lover. Aren't you attracted to me?"

He took a step back. "I'm in love with your sister."

"But McKenzie doesn't need to know," she whispered.

*Unbelievable.* Jackson pointed to the door. "God would know. You need to go."

Monica didn't move.

He clenched his teeth, walked to the door and opened it, and then stood there, waiting for her to leave. His left hand trembled as it gripped the door handle. "This never happened."

She sniffed. "Your loss." After slinging her jacket over her shoulder, she pranced out the door.

Jackson slammed the door behind her and locked the deadbolt. He slid down to the floor, leaning against the door, and shook his head. "Incredible."

The image of Monica squirming in agony in the lake of fire suddenly popped into his mind. Had he done enough to warn her about that horrible place? Jackson bit his lip. *Oh God, please help Monica to know you before it's too late.*

# Chapter 38
# Riverton

MCKENZIE WAS PUTTING the finishing touches on her makeup when her cell phone pinged. It was Jackson, punctual as always, downstairs and ready to pick her up for their date.

The weather was unseasonably warm that Saturday evening in early October. He smiled and kissed her on the cheek when they met. He grasped her hands. They were trembling.

"Jackson, what's wrong."

Jackson wiped his forehead with his shirtsleeve. "Oh, nothing. It's just a little warm tonight."

On their way to the Riverton Inn, she enjoyed viewing the peaking foliage and clapboard New England homes along the windy roads that ran parallel to the Farmington River. Inside the inn, he led her over the creaking dark wide-board floor, past a full-length gilded mirror, an ancient grandfather clock, and a well-worn Hitchcock bench on their way to the hostess's station. The dining room tables and chairs were all Hitchcock, beautifully stenciled with intricate designs and partially covered with white linen tablecloths. The owners had furnished each table with a candle and a small flower arrangement. The ceiling was exposed, revealing dark, roughly hewn timbers that supported the hotel rooms above. The hostess seated them by a window that looked out over a bridge and the old Hitchcock Chair factory.

They mused about their beautiful drive through the countryside and the fabulous décor of the restaurant as they picked at their appetizer. Then, leaning forward, Jackson asked, "Do you remember how I said there were other things I wanted to tell you about my accident?"

"Yes."

"I'd like to tell you about them now."

This was getting a little weird. *What's wrong with him tonight?*

Jackson hesitated, looking deep into her eyes. "I wanted to wait until I was sure you were a Christian."

What did being a Christian have to do with it? "You're scaring me, Jackson."

"I'm sorry." He paused as the waitress delivered a bottle of Pellegrino and poured a glass for each of them, then he watched her walk away. "This is probably going to sound crazy, but I'll just say it anyway. After the car hit me in the hospital parking garage, I saw my body being carried away on a gurney into the hospital."

"I remember you telling me that."

"Well, it gets crazier. After that, an angel appeared to me. He took me up into the heavenly realms to a place called The Wall."

"You saw a real angel?"

"Yes."

"Wow! The Wall isn't in the Bible, is it?"

"No, it's not. You're right to ask that question. You have to be very cautious about anything anyone ever says about spiritual things that are not in the Bible." Jackson waited as the waitress moved past their table. "The angel, called Mekoddishkem, told me that The Wall was just a representation for my benefit, to help me understand more about God."

"A representation of what? What did it look like?"

"It had a whitish translucent surface that overlaid the universe behind it. It contained billions of small portals, which looked like gold-encircled portholes on the side of a ship. Each represented the past, present, and future of a person."

"You're serious?"

"Yes. Do you believe me?"

It sounded crazy, but he seemed to be telling the truth. "Yes."

He laughed. "You do? I mean, thank you." Jackson placed his hand on top of hers. "That means a lot to me. I wouldn't blame you if you thought I was crazy."

*It's definitely strange, but he hasn't lied yet.*

Jackson resumed his story. "The Wall allowed me to enter the portal of any person I chose. I could specify whether to access their past, present, or future, where I could observe invisibly. The Wall illustrates God's omniscience and omnipresence and that he is not constrained by time and space like we are. The angel and I traveled into the past and the present together. Then we delved into the future, and he showed me you."

She stopped chewing. "Me?" *Where's he going with this?* "Why?"

Jackson gulped. "I asked if I would ever get married, and he showed me you."

Married? Jackson? Tears streamed uncontrollably down her face. *So that's why he's acting so weird.* She placed her hand on his and said, "Jackson, that's so sweet. Where did you see me?"

"On Devereux Beach in Marblehead. It was just before you started your new job at Aetna."

*What? Was he spying on me?* She withdrew her hand and slowly straightened. "Well, that's true. I was there just before starting my job at Aetna. That's pretty amazing, seeing as I hadn't seen you since that summer on Block Island. Who was I with?"

"Monica."

"What was I wearing?"

"A yellow bikini… and you were lying on a red blanket."

I was wearing a yellow bikini that day. How could he know? "I know I said I believed you, Jackson, but this is getting really creepy."

The waitress arrived with their entrees. She cleared away the plates from their first course and placed the steaming hot dinners in front of them. Jackson buttered his baked potato, then began slicing the filet mignon. McKenzie couldn't help staring at him like he was some kind of alien.

"How's the salmon?" he asked.

McKenzie shook her head and took a bite. "It's great. It has an interesting sauce. How's your steak?" Emotion welled within her. Then she slammed her fork on the table. "Jackson! How can you compartmentalize like that? You just told me you'd been spying on me through some bizarre contraption called The Wall, and now you're asking me how my food is?"

He shrugged, staying surprisingly calm. "It's just the way I am."

Something didn't smell right. "And did you orchestrate events to meet me in the cafeteria on your first day back to work after the accident?"

"No." Jackson smiled. "I just prayed that God would let us meet, and he did. You're the one who approached me. Remember?"

She sighed. "That's a wonderful story, Jackson, but now I'm finding it hard to believe you."

Jackson placed his fork on his plate. "I would have a hard time believing me too. But I've decided to tell you everything about that experience. What would it take to convince you?"

"Tell me something that you learned about me that nobody else knows." Her abortion came to mind.

"I can tell you what you were thinking on Devereux Beach."

"That might convince me."

"You were looking at a young girl with long brown hair and wondering if that's what your daughter would have looked like if she had lived."

She stiffened. "I don't have a daughter."

Jackson paused.

McKenzie's gut cringed. He couldn't know about the abortion. That would be impossible. "Tell me what you know."

"You had an abortion when you were nineteen. I saw and heard a demon whisper that thought into your ear. He spoke to you in the first person, trying to make you think those were your thoughts. He was condemning you, but I'm not."

Shame, anger, and amazement alternated inside McKenzie. She'd been found out, but for some reason, it only brought relief. "I remember thinking that on the beach. I never told anyone about it. I don't know how you could have found out what I did, given all the privacy laws we have today. Still, there might be some way, but there is no way you could have known what I was thinking."

"It's true. Every bit of it."

Stunned, McKenzie blinked a few times. Everything he'd been telling her was true. "I believe you."

Jackson took her hand. "Thank you… and just so there is full disclosure here, I've got a similar story."

"Really?"

""I got drunk one night and got a girl pregnant. I couldn't even remember her name. I recently learned that she took a morning-after pill, which killed the baby."

McKenzie withdrew her hand. "I'm so sorry."

He nodded. "I just wanted you to know."

"Thank you for being so honest."

"I have one more thing to tell you." Jackson tilted his head and peered into her eyes. "It's going to be a shock."

"Okay." McKenzie breathed in deeply.

"The angel took me into your portal a second time, but this time it was into the future." He swallowed. "And I saw you on the last day of your life… before you became a Christian."

"Now you're really scaring me, Jackson!"

Jackson sat up straight. "I know, and I'm sorry about that, but I have to tell you the truth." He paused, apparently thinking. "I also saw you killed."

"What? Why are you telling me this?"

"Then I saw you in the lake of fire. Once again, this was before you became a Christian."

Something hardened inside her chest. She stood and leaned over the table at Jackson. "Why didn't you tell me sooner? What if I'd died before accepting Jesus as my Savior? I'd be in hell right now if that kid in the pickup truck had crashed into us a few months ago, or Dexter had killed me, or that bear had gotten me, or who knows what else might have happened to me."

"Please, McKenzie. Keep it down." He got to his feet and reached for her hand. "We're in a restaurant." He glanced around.

How could he worry about what other people thought at a time like this? "I don't care!"

The other restaurant patrons were staring at them, but Jackson refocused his attention on McKenzie. "What was I supposed to do? Go up and tell you that I had a dream and saw you in the lake of fire? I tried that with two other people, and they thought I was a whack job. You would have too. I didn't want to lose you." He exhaled. "God is in control. He gives all of us time to repent. I was trusting in him to draw you to himself. If I tried to scare you into a conversion experience, it never would have stuck. Your destiny is changed forever because you are now a firm believer and follower of Jesus Christ."

McKenzie wiped her eyes with her napkin and collected herself. "Are there any other little surprises you want to tell me about?"

"The night after we left the Tolbert house, I saw a vision of a person, probably Jesus, pulling someone out of the lake of fire. It was right after you received him as your Savior. I hope that makes you feel better."

McKenzie finally sat down and sighed. "Yes, it does. Is it normal for Christians to see visions like that?"

Jackson shook his head. "No, although some Muslims report having seen Jesus in dreams and visions."

"Anything else?"

"Just that Monica was with you."

"In the lake of fire?"

"Yes."

"That's terrible. We've got to help her."

"I know. I tried to be a good witness to her when she came to visit last week."

McKenzie took a deep breath and leaned back in her chair. "You were a good witness, Jackson, but I don't think she's anywhere near becoming a Christian. She could have died walking across the street last week. Thank God that you saved her."

"Agreed."

"So, what you're telling me is that you traveled across the universe and back to rescue me, all because you loved me."

"Yes."

"That's the best line I've ever heard."

Jackson grinned. "Works every time."

McKenzie leaned forward and took his hand, tears welling in her eyes. "Thank you."

"God orchestrated the whole thing, so you should give him the credit. He just used me in the process."

"Amen."

∽

Jackson and McKenzie finished dinner and having herbal tea; then, he paid the bill. Next, he led her upstairs, where they peeked in a few of the bedrooms and looked at the various antiques that graced the colonial hallways. They then headed outside to the parking lot.

"Look at the stars," he said, pointing upward. "There's so many of them."

"You can see so many more without all the streetlights we have in West Hartford and Hartford."

"The background of The Wall was stars, a lot like this, only it was even more beautiful." He looked off to the side. "Look at the river."

Moonlight shimmered off the water in a rippling line toward them. Hundreds of insects still zigzagged over the surface while crickets chirped rhythmically in the woods around them.

Jackson had a knot in his stomach as he guided McKenzie toward a gliding bench located between the parking lot and the river. She was so beautiful, so perfect for him. He loved her smile, her laugh, and her fiery spirit. Now he had to figure out how to ease into "the question."

"Did you have a nice dinner?" he asked as they sat down.

"I did. Thank you."

"This is a beautiful place, isn't it?"

She chuckled. "Every place you've taken me has been beautiful, Jackson."

He shifted to face her. "Anywhere we go is beautiful because you're there with me."

"Oh, that's so sweet."

Getting down on one knee, he retrieved the ring from his pocket and held it up. "McKenzie Baker, I love you, and I want to spend the rest of my life with you. Will you marry me?"

She bounced up and down on the seat and whooped. "Yes! Oh yes, Jackson! I will marry you!"

He took her trembling left hand and placed the engagement ring on her ring finger.

"It's beautiful!" She held out her hand to see it sparkle in the moonlight, as tears streamed down her face.

McKenzie jumped at him, wrapped her arms around him, and kissed him. "I can't believe you had that in your pocket through the entire dinner," she said when they broke apart. "How could you stand it?"

"Tell me about it. I was going to bring you here last weekend, but you made plans with Monica."

"Poor baby." McKenzie kissed him again. "Let's go over by the river."

They walked hand in hand across the street, then over to the center of the bridge. Pure joy infused him. She'd said yes. Everything was working out better than the previous version of their future together, thanks to God's grace. They stopped and leaned over the railing, then looked down into the river as the water bubbled incandescently by.

# CHAPTER 39
# THE PARENTS

MCKENZIE SAID SHE could plan the entire wedding in a month to coincide with her brother being home on leave from Afghanistan, so Jackson left the decisions to her. That seemed kind of fast, but if anyone could do it, she could. Of course, the timeline put the wedding really close to the five-month deadline set by Mekoddishkem, but that shouldn't be a problem. She was now a Christian and had therefore changed her destiny.

The only thing left for him to do was to pass the parent test. Both families agreed to meet at Abigail's Grille and Wine Bar the following Saturday in Simsbury, Connecticut. He picked up his parents that afternoon at the airport while McKenzie's parents drove down from Massachusetts.

The Trotmans arrived at the restaurant promptly at six o'clock as planned. McKenzie's family came in soon after, and Jackson instantly relaxed when he saw Mrs. Baker's smile. They made the rounds of introductions.

Mr. Baker had a rugged face and a firm handshake. His hand felt coarse, and he was a few inches shorter than Jackson. He spoke with a booming baritone voice. "Nice to meet you, son."

Mrs. Baker hugged him. "We're so happy to meet you."

The hostess escorted them past the centrally situated kitchen into a dining room with cherry-paneled ceilings and matching hardwood floors. The cherry dining chairs juxtaposed white linen tablecloths and full-length black-trimmed windows.

After they were seated, the waitress brought the menus and a wine list.

Jackson handed the wine list back to her. "We won't be ordering any drinks tonight."

Mr. Baker straightened and glared at him, but Jackson didn't back down. After an awkward silence, Jackson said, "I hear you're a Red Sox fan, Mr. Baker. Your daughter put me to shame in the trivia department. I think humiliated might be the better word."

He nodded. "McKenzie's been following the Red Sox ever since she was a little girl. She knows more trivia than anyone I know."

The conversation continued throughout the evening as the two families got to know each other. Separate conversations eventually developed, with the men mainly talking about sports while the women focused on the wedding plans. As the evening drew to a close, the couples exchanged phone numbers and other pleasantries and agreed that they'd see each other at McKenzie's baptism the following morning at the church.

McKenzie's baptism brought her such peace. To have her family there was a blessing. And her engagement to Jackson was filled with nothing but excitement and hope. Even so, she was haunted by the possibility, however slight, that Dexter might suddenly appear on the street, in a hallway, at the movies, in the grocery store, or wherever she went. These thoughts plagued her more and more, so she finally called the Office of Victim Services in Wethersfield and scheduled a meeting.

On the day of her appointment, she met with case officer Anita Bassinger. Anita stood up and shook her hand. "Good morning, Miss Baker. Thank you for coming in."

"Thank you for seeing me, Miss Bassinger."

"Call me Anita. How have you been doing since the attack?"

"I've been all right. I just got engaged." McKenzie peeked at her ring and smiled.

"Congratulations."

She returned her attention to Anita. "I want to put this whole Dexter Lancaster thing behind me. He's been stalking me for years, and I don't want to worry about him or even think about him as I start my new life."

"I understand."

"Could you give me a status on the case against him?"

"Let me pull up his file." She typed on her keyboard, then glanced over her monitor screen. "This says Dexter Lancaster has been housed in a high-security Connecticut state penitentiary for several months now, awaiting trial on charges of attempted rape and attempted murder. There's also a federal case pending against him."

"A federal case?"

She skimmed farther down the screen. "Hmm. Something to do with insider trading."

"So, will he be going to trial first in federal or state court?" McKenzie asked.

"It's too soon to tell. But I can let you know as soon as I find out."

"Will I have to testify?"

"That's up to the prosecutors in the case."

McKenzie leaned forward. "Let me be clear. I don't ever want to see him again."

"I understand, but I can't promise you won't be asked to testify. We'll have to see how the cases proceed."

"Well... okay. I guess that's it. Thanks for your time, Anita."

"You're welcome. Have a good day."

McKenzie was about to start a new life with Jackson. Hopefully, she could put the fear of Dexter behind her. *Lord, please help me to press forward, and let Dexter be quietly and easily convicted.*

꙰

When Dexter wasn't sleeping or answering questions, he sat on his bunk, stared at the white concrete walls in his seven-by-twelve-foot cell, and fantasized about McKenzie. She was his constant companion.

She was coming out of the shower in his mind when someone knocked on his cell door.

A corrections officer was peering at him through the window. "Hey, Lancaster, looks like that girlfriend of yours is getting married this weekend."

His heart pounded. He jumped up and went to the cell door. "How do you know?"

"I overheard her talking at the courthouse yesterday. I recognized her from the case file. She had a big rock on her finger."

*No. No, no, no. McKenzie couldn't.*

The officer laughed. "How does that make you feel, lover boy?"

Dexter clenched his teeth and lunged at the door, then slammed it with his fists.

The officer chuckled as he walked away.

# CHAPTER 40
# MOVING ON

MONICA CALLED HER boss at home on Tuesday evening, said she wasn't feeling well, and asked to have someone cover for her the next day. The following morning, she left Ronaldo's home and waited at a Dunkin' Donuts for him to go to work. Then, she returned to his house, packed all her belongings, and moved back into her apartment. She had already contacted the local police and arranged with the courts to have a restraining order served to Ronaldo while he was at work that Wednesday afternoon. In addition, she had the locks for her apartment changed. Since she couldn't predict his reaction, she asked the police to keep a close lookout for his car in her neighborhood and near where she worked.

That night, she called McKenzie to let her know she'd taken her advice. Their conversation soon turned to the wedding. "So, how are the arrangements coming along? I can't believe you're trying to plan an entire wedding in a month. Not much longer before you'll be Mrs. Trotman."

McKenzie laughed. "Everything is set for the most part. I'm just working on some last-minute details with Mom. She wants to add some relatives to the list I've never heard of."

"That's typical of Mom. She never wants to hurt anyone's feelings. Can you give me the address of the wedding and reception again? I must have misplaced the invitation during the move. It's probably in one of the boxes somewhere."

"Sure. But it might be easier for you to google Valley Community Baptist Church in Avon and the Simsbury 1820 House in Simsbury. You can either get directions off their websites or obtain your own directions."

"Give me a minute to write that down." Monica searched around the kitchen, found a notepad and pen, and wrote down the names. "Okay, all set."

"What time are you planning to get here for the rehearsal?" McKenzie asked. "The maid of honor can't be late, you know."

Monica sat on one of the barstools in the kitchen. "I should be there between three and three thirty. That should give me plenty of time before the rehearsal at six. I'm so excited. I can't believe you're finally getting married." She glanced around the apartment. "Well, I'd better go. I still have a lot of unpacking to do."

"Just take care of yourself, okay?"

"I will."

"I can't say enough about how proud I am of you for standing up to Ronaldo. He's such an evil man. Good riddance! I hope we never see him again."

Later that day, Ronaldo spread out the plan for Clarice's massive new kitchen on the oak conference room table in his office. His carpenter, plumber, electrician, and hardwood flooring subcontractors stood around him, looking on.

His secretary, Ruth, entered the meeting with a female police officer. The wide-planked wood flooring creaked as they approached.

"Mr. Ronald Espinosa?"

"Yes."

The policewoman handed him a packet of paper and said, "You've been served."

Ronaldo bolted up. "What? What's this about?"

"You'll have to read the paperwork yourself, sir. Have a good day."

The officer left the room. *What must my men be thinking?* He turned toward them. "I have no idea what this is about, guys. I always pay my bills on time." He set it aside. "I'll look at it after we finish here."

An hour later, Ronaldo ripped open the envelope. He scanned the first page and saw Monica's name listed. She'd filed a restraining order against him. *How dare she do that to me.*

❦

Ronaldo opened the door to his house that evening and hurled his jacket across the room. That ungrateful wretch. After everything he'd done for her, she didn't have the guts to say goodbye. She'd even had the nerve to serve him with a restraining order—at work.

He marched to the liquor cabinet, poured himself a double scotch, and then downed the whole drink in one gulp. "What did I ever do to her to deserve this?" he muttered. "Right in front of my whole staff, no less. It'll be all over town. My reputation, my business, my lifestyle all ruined." He hurled the glass as hard as he could into the fireplace.

Eventually, he went upstairs. Monica's closet, dresser, and vanity were bare now, in sharp contrast to the way she usually left it—messy with hair and eyelash brushes, makeup, nail polish, bras, and panties strewn all over the place. He shook his head. He'd never have someone that beautiful again.

As he plopped down on the bed, he glanced again at the vanity set. The corner of an envelope peeked out from behind it. He walked over, picked it up off the floor, and opened it.

A wedding invitation.

# CHAPTER 41
# GETTING AWAY

A GUARD ESCORTED Dexter Lancaster to an interrogation room at the state prison in Brooklyn, Connecticut. The room had a gray tile ceiling, matching walls, darker gray doors and trim, and an aqua-blue carpet. Two men sat behind a Formica table, dressed in collared shirts, pressed slacks, and navy-blue windbreakers with FBI embossed on them in bold gold letters.

The older one spoke first. "Good morning, Mr. Lancaster. Please sit down."

Dexter sat on the wooden chair directly in front of him. "What's this all about?"

"I'm Agent Morris, and this is Agent Montgomery from the Federal Bureau of Investigation. We've accumulated enough evidence to charge you with insider trading."

His stomach tightened. "That's a bunch of bull. I'm innocent."

"An agreement was made yesterday with state authorities to extradite you to New York City. You'll stand trial there in federal court. We will be leaving in approximately one hour."

Dexter jumped up. "Wait a minute. I want my lawyer."

Agent Morris shuffled the papers he was holding. "This will be a federal trial, not a state trial, Mr. Lancaster. You can retain your current lawyer, get a new lawyer, or we will provide one for you after you arrive."

The corrections officer took Dexter back to his cell and removed his handcuffs and leg irons. He sat on his bunk and stared at the wall. Then he took the plastic bag the guard had provided and placed his toiletries and a few other personal belongings in it.

The guard returned later and refastened him in handcuffs and leg irons. The metal chains grated against the floor as he shuffled down the hallway. The eyes of the other prisoners bore down on him when he passed their cells.

A big burly man called out, "Don't forget to write, sweetie!"

Dexter kept walking, staring at the floor.

A shrill electronic tone reverberated through the hallway. A steel gate opened, and another guard led Dexter into the Inmate Property Storage Room, where an officer handed Dexter his belongings to review. Afterward, they were given to Agent Montgomery. The guard then ordered Dexter to sit on a bench. A moment later, he could see the two FBI agents signing some paperwork through a nearby office window.

The agents soon came out of the office. Each took Dexter by the arm, and they escorted him to the loading dock, where a large black SUV with a government license plate was parked.

Rain splattered off the car onto the cracked pavement below, gradually increasing in intensity. The agent opened the rear passenger's door on the driver's side and pressed Dexter's head down as he scooted onto the seat. The door slammed shut behind him.

He clicked on the seat belt. Both agents sat in the front section of the vehicle. Agent Morris drove.

Dexter cleared his throat and broke the silence. "How long is it going to take us to get there?"

The agents didn't answer.

Rain pummeled the car roof as they left the loading dock area. The windshield wipers struggled to keep up with the heavy flow of rainwater. They stopped at the prison gate, where Agent Morris showed the guard some paperwork. The metal gate creaked open sideways a moment later, and the SUV passed through.

About ten minutes into their trip, as they drove along a back road toward I-395, the SUV swerved sharply to the right. Dexter looked up and saw a deer prancing across the road in front of them. The vehicle's rear slid a full one hundred and eighty degrees forward.

Morris cried out, "Hold on, everyone!"

Montgomery swore.

The SUV continued slipping sideways along the slick pavement and slammed into a dilapidated wire and wooden guardrail. The vehicle broke through the barrier, teetered on the edge of a steep embankment for a few seconds, then careened down it.

He was going to die.

Dexter braced himself as the vehicle flipped on its side and rolled over and over down the hill. His awareness of his surroundings heightened, his body slapping back and forth in slow motion with each tumble. The taut seat belt forced the air from his lungs with each impact. He finally blacked out.

When Dexter regained consciousness, his arms were dangling, touching the SUV's ceiling. How much time had passed? How long had he hung upside down? Blood had rushed to his head. He couldn't breathe through his nose. The seat belt was pressing hard against his chest and waist.

In the front, the driver didn't appear to be moving. He held his breath for a moment and studied Agent Morris carefully. The agent wasn't breathing. Agent Montgomery wasn't in the vehicle, but Dexter heard faint moaning from outside.

*This is my lucky day. If Morris is dead and Montgomery is injured, I could be a free man. Fantastic! The first order of business is to get out of this seat belt. Then I'll take care of the two agents.*

After struggling for a few minutes, Dexter managed to release his seat belt. He fell to the ceiling, cutting his head in the process. Wiping away the blood, he kicked out the partially broken window and exited the vehicle. At least it had stopped raining.

He opened the driver's door, shuffled through Agent Morris's pockets to get the handcuff and leg iron keys, and then removed the chains. He briefly surveyed the wreckage. Somehow, the ceiling hadn't completely collapsed. He was lucky.

The vehicle had come to rest alongside a rocky streambed. Dexter walked around the front of the SUV toward the injured Agent Montgomery and stood over him. The agent was barely conscious and breathing faintly. The force of the impact had crushed the left side of his rib cage. "I'd like to help you, Agent Montgomery. I really would." He smiled. "But you see, I have a wedding to attend, and I need to leave now."

He found a nearby moss-covered boulder, wrapped both arms around it, then shuffled toward the agent.

Agent Montgomery's eyes widened. His arm quivered as it moved toward his gun.

Dexter maneuvered the boulder directly over the agent's head and released it. He paused for a moment, then picked up the boulder and dropped it back into the stream with the bloody side facing down. With any luck, the stream would wash away the evidence.

Dexter relieved both agents of their weapons and cash and then changed out of his orange jumpsuit into his street clothes from his plastic bag. He was also able to retrieve his wallet and phone. He slowly trudged up the hill to the road and buried the jumpsuit under a rock about half a mile away.

At the road, he got his bearings. McKenzie would probably get married at that church he'd seen her going to with Trotman. Not far away, but he had to hurry. First, he needed to call the church. He'd tell them he lost his invitation. If he was too late for the ceremony, he'd go to the reception. Next, he needed a car. He'd pay cash so the cops couldn't track him. "This is so exciting. I can't wait for McKenzie's big day."

# CHAPTER 42
# TAKE TWO

JACKSON AND MCKENZIE became husband and wife at Valley Community Baptist Church. They committed themselves to one another in a fervent service before God. The ceremony, pictures, and transportation to the reception by limousine all went according to plan.

Jackson beamed with joy as he entered the reception room with McKenzie on his arm. They sat at the intimate head table amid cheers and applause.

Glossy white wood trim enveloped the more muted white ceiling, offset by satin lime green walls and shiny hardwood floors. Small tables, each adorned with place settings, a number marker, and a small bouquet of autumn-colored flowers, were cloistered around in various adjoining rooms, yet all the tables had a direct view of the head table. The surroundings looked very different from what Jackson had observed in McKenzie's portal.

As the best man, Mike made a speech in which he mercilessly yet humorously abused Jackson, ending it with heartfelt best wishes for their future. Everyone then began eating their dinner. Throughout the night, the attendees enjoyed the champagne toast, the clanking of glasses to elicit a kiss, and the silly dances that only the young-at-heart ladies seemed to join. Later, Jackson chatted with McKenzie and Mike near the windows. Mike excused himself to go to the restroom, and Jackson lost himself in McKenzie's sparkling eyes.

Suddenly, her eyes widened in horror. She screamed, and Jackson spun around.

Dexter had walked in through the patio doors wearing a gray sweatshirt with the hood pulled over his head. *Charge the ambush.* Jackson instinctively rushed toward him.

Dexter smiled, reached into the front pouch of his sweatshirt, and pulled out a pistol, aiming it at Jackson. He pulled the trigger, but the round failed to leave the chamber. He looked down at the weapon, puzzled.

Jackson knocked the gun out of Dexter's hands and kicked him in his left kneecap, cracking it.

Dexter howled, then punched Jackson in the face, knocking him to the ground with one blow.

Jackson quickly got up and pummeled Dexter's face and torso with punches.

Blood dripping from his mouth, Dexter spit out a tooth. He growled at Jackson, grabbed him by his shirt and threw him through the air onto a nearby table, causing it to collapse.

Dexter then pulled another pistol from his pocket and aimed again at Jackson.

McKenzie screamed.

A shot rang out, and Jackson tensed, waiting for the excruciating pain he'd experienced in Afghanistan. Screams filled the air, and glasses crashed to the floor as guests scrambled out of the room. But the pain never came. He looked down.

Dexter lay in a pool of blood, gasping for air.

Mike trotted over with his .45 at the ready and kicked Dexter's second gun away. Next, he placed his pistol back in his shoulder holster, rolled Dexter onto his stomach, handcuffed him, then called 911 and reported the incident.

McKenzie wailed hysterically. Jackson moved her to the other side of the room, pulled her close, cradling the back of her head with his right hand, then placed her head against his shoulder and gently rocked her back and forth. Their parents flocked around them. As McKenzie slowly collected herself, others cried softly, and at least one person hyperventilated.

The police soon arrived, followed by an ambulance. An EMT knelt, checked Dexter's vital signs, and then shook his head. "He's dead."

McKenzie melted into Jackson's arms, and he held her tight. After a few moments, he released her and moved beside Mike. "The first gun didn't fire. Any idea why?"

Mike crouched down and looked over the weapon without touching it. A smile spread across his face. "Dummy."

"What?"

"The safety was still on."

Jackson sighed, then shook Mike's hand vigorously. "Thanks for saving my life, Mike. I owe you one."

"You're welcome, my friend."

"Thank God he was good with numbers but not so good with guns." *Hmm.* Maybe it was Mekoddishkem who turned on the safety switch. Whatever the cause, Jackson was thankful God had spared his life. It just wasn't his time to go yet.

Ronaldo stood outside the Simsbury 1820 House, peering in through the windows at the reception room. He edged closer to the window casing and caught a glimpse of Monica standing beside her sister. He couldn't wait to pummel that slut's body full of bullets. Suddenly, his heart quickened at seeing police officers standing over a body on the floor. He staggered back from the window, walked briskly to his car, plopped down in the driver's seat, and then pulled the car door shut.

Slamming his hands against the steering wheel, he let out a slew of curse words. Then he took a mask out of the right coat pocket of his dark blue jacket, hurled it against the passenger's side window, and watched it land lifelessly on the seat.

# CHAPTER 43
# THE DAY AFTER

THE NEWLYWEDS SPENT their wedding night upstairs at the Simsbury 1820 House in a room adorned with stenciled red flower wallpaper, matching pinch pleat curtains, a cherry four-poster bed with lace canopy, and a gas fireplace.

Jackson sat on the edge of the bed, waiting patiently for McKenzie to come out of the bathroom. The door finally creaked open, and she appeared in a floor-length white lace nightgown. He glided over to her, mesmerized by her beauty. After kissing her on the lips, he turned off the lights and carried her to their wedding bed.

∽

The following morning, Jackson stood at the front desk with McKenzie, waiting for the clerk to give him a receipt.

Monica appeared in the lobby with her suitcase. She hugged McKenzie, leaned close to her ear, and whispered, "How was last night?"

McKenzie grinned. "Glorious."

Jackson grinned at hearing McKenzie's response.

A moment later, Jackson opened the door for McKenzie and Monica as they left the hotel.

They walked along the slate path toward the parking lot.

Jackson heard a voice coming from the hotel behind him. "Hey, Jackson! Have fun in Bermuda!"

He turned to find Mike peering out the hotel's front door, grinning. Sally frantically shushed him and tried to pull him back inside.

Jackson waved and turned back to the path. Mekoddishkem appeared on the grass next to the parking lot. Jackson startled but then smiled. "Honey, look. The angel Mekoddishkem is here. Can you see him?"

McKenzie scanned the grounds. "No." Concern lined her forehead as she looked up at him. "Jackson, are you okay?"

"Sure." *But why is he here?*

Pebbles crunched under their feet as they crossed the parking lot. Jackson continued to gaze at the guardian. He smiled again, but Mekoddishkem looked grave. *This can't be good.*

A man wearing a dark blue business suit and a Richard Nixon mask jumped out of a nearby car and drew a pistol as he walked toward them.

*Not again.* "Mike!" He shielded McKenzie, placing his hands on her hips and pushing her against a nearby car.

McKenzie screamed.

"Mike! Mike, where are you?" Jackson yelled. He braced himself. Surprisingly, the man walked by them, heading for Monica, who was cowering on the ground beside another car. There, the masked man calmly aimed his gun at her.

Everything slowed down. "No!" Jackson shouted. "If he kills her, she'll go straight to hell!"

He pushed away from McKenzie and ran toward the man. Given the angle, his only option was to leap directly in front of Monica to block the shot. But would he make it in time? He jumped, flying through the air with his gaze focused on the gun—a puff of smoke, then a blast. The bullet struck Jackson with the full force of a sledgehammer on his chest. He landed on the gravel on his side.

A shot rang out, and then another. The gunman slumped over next to him, blood streaming from under the mask.

McKenzie dropped down next to Jackson, lifted him by the shoulders, and placed his head in her lap. Tears streamed down her face as she cradled him.

Mike kicked the pistol away from the gunman, called 911, and then ripped open Jackson's suitcase, took out some shirts, and applied pressure to Jackson's chest wound.

The pain in his chest was excruciating. *I'm really going to die this time.*

He looked up at McKenzie. Gasping for air, he whispered, "I love you, honey. I'll see you in heaven."

His spiritual body departed his physical body, and he hovered over the proceedings, invisible to the others. Sally came running and pushed Mike away, then began giving Jackson's body CPR. Sally prayed loudly for him as she applied the chest compressions.

McKenzie grasped his hand and wept. Mike screamed into his phone, trying to get the ambulance and police to hurry. He soon took over the compressions, and Sally performed the breaths. A few other guests came out of the hotel but just watched.

The paramedics finally arrived. They tried unsuccessfully to revive his body, then continued working on him as they wheeled him to the ambulance with McKenzie by his side.

As the ambulance left the parking lot with its siren blaring, Jackson glided over to Mekoddishkem.

The guardian embraced him. "Greater love has no one than this, that he lay down his life for his friends."

# CHAPTER 44
# RETURNING FOR A MOMENT

JACKSON REMAINED WITH Mekoddishkem on the grass near the hotel parking lot, watching as the local police began the crime scene investigation. "Mekoddishkem?"

"Yes, Jackson?"

"Am I dead now?"

He nodded. "In an earthly sense, yes."

*McKenzie.* Jackson swallowed. "So, I won't be waking up in a hospital this time?"

"No."

Jackson struggled to process this information. Tears filled his eyes. "What's going to happen to McKenzie?"

Tears formed in Mekoddishkem's eyes as well. "She will miss you terribly, Jackson, but she will see you again one day. God will comfort her. The hope of seeing you again will sustain her."

He shook his head. "Why did I have to be taken so soon?"

Mekoddishkem looked down at him. "I told you, you had five months."

"Oh… right." Jackson sighed. "I thought you meant McKenzie had five months to choose a new destiny. I had no idea you were referring to my destiny." He looked around. "To be absent from the body is to be present with the Lord, correct?"

"Yes. You know that."

"And will I be living in a spiritual body until Jesus returns to earth? And then he'll give me a new physical body that will be perfect and will never die?"

"Correct."

"Will you be taking me to see Jesus now?"

"Yes."

Jackson beamed, inhaled deeply, and trembled at the thought of meeting the living God. "On the one hand, I can't wait, but on the other hand, I'm scared."

"Don't be afraid, Jackson. Jesus loves you and accepts you as an adopted member of his family."

"Thank you for saying that. Can we stop by The Wall again before we go there?"

"Why?"

"I want to check on McKenzie. I was only married to her for one day, you know." Jackson choked up and fell to his knees crying.

Mekoddishkem placed his hand on Jackson's shoulder, knelt beside him, and wept with him. A few minutes later, he pulled Jackson to his feet and embraced him. "Jesus will wipe away every tear. Let's go see how McKenzie is doing."

The two were transported from the hotel grounds up through the atmosphere to The Wall. They walked out on the landing, then to the end of the gangplank.

"Mekoddishkem? The Wall. It looks different now."

"Yes."

"The portals aren't translucent anymore. Instead, they all have what look like television screens embedded in them." Jackson leaned forward and scanned several of the portals. One person was playing chess, another was sleeping, another was staring at pornography on a computer screen, and another person was apparently in hell, wailing in agony.

"When you were still attached to your earthly body, you could only see spiritual things dimly," the guardian said. "Now you can see them face-to-face, as they are in the heavenly realms."

At Jackson's request, McKenzie Baker Trotman's portal whirled into position. He shivered as he looked up at the guardian. "Is McKenzie's name written in the Book of Life?"

"Yes."

Jackson inhaled deeply and smiled. "So, we will be in heaven together one day, forever?"

"Correct."

"Is Monica's name written in the Book of Life?"

"No, it is not, but it may yet be. That depends on the choices Monica makes. You have provided her with a great gift, Jackson—more time to choose a new destiny." He paused. "Would you like to know who shot you?"

Jackson shrugged his shoulders. "I guess so."

"It was the man with whom Monica had just severed a relationship, Ronaldo Espinosa. Monica accidentally left her wedding invitation at Ronaldo's house when she moved out."

His mind reeled. "But McKenzie was killed at our wedding the first time I saw it."

"That is true, but was McKenzie not standing in front of Monica when she was shot?"

He stared at the guardian. "So, McKenzie was protecting Monica?"

"Correct."

"And this time, I protected Monica... and McKenzie."

"Yes."

Jackson placed his hands on his hips. He'd been foolish. "I assumed that Dexter was the one who would shoot her. I was wrong."

"Yes. You were trying to protect the one you loved. But you

should not have tried to jump ahead of God's will. If you had asked to see McKenzie's killer, The Wall would have transported you to Ronaldo's portal instead of Dexter's."

"So, the choices I made impacted the length of my life on earth."

"Yes."

He shuddered. That was too much responsibility for one person to bear.

Mekoddishkem continued, "I understand how hard this is for you, Jackson, but your fierce anger in defending McKenzie at the first encounter with Dexter caused him to hate you so much he wanted to kill you. Your foolishness led not only to the loss of your own life but also the life of Dexter. On the other hand, your great bravery and unselfishness led to the life of Monica being spared, for the moment."

"What has to happen to save Monica from her fate?"

"Right now, she is thinking about what you did for her. McKenzie, Sally, and Mike are also praying for her."

He considered that. "How exactly does prayer change things?"

"The prayer of a righteous person is powerful and effective."

"I know that verse. But what does that mean—on a personal level?"

Mekoddishkem spoke in a commanding tone, peering deeply into Jackson's eyes. "Have you learned nothing from your experiences with The Wall? Don't you comprehend the time and effort spent on your one life from before you were born up to now? God not only created you, sustained you, and saved you, but he sent the Holy Spirit to sanctify you so that you will be more like Jesus. He hears your prayers, acting on them in ways you see and in ways you do not see.

"Then, consider all these interactions on behalf of a single individual, and multiply them, factorially, by the billions of people who have died, the billions of people who are alive today, and the billions of people yet to be born, and you will begin to understand the complexity involved in running the universe. Here, let me show you The Wall in a different way."

Thousands of golden bowls flew out of the portals toward heaven, and thousands of angels entered the portals, all in a seemingly random fashion.

"Mekoddishkem, what does this mean?"

"The bowls represent the prayers of the saints who are alive on earth today, while the angels are God's answers to those prayers."

Jackson stared at the bowls and angels. "Why didn't you show me this before?"

"You didn't need to see all the other angels. And besides, you weren't ready. I needed to illustrate one major concept for you at a time so that you could understand it. If I had shown you everything at once, you would have been overwhelmed. There are still many other aspects of God's oversight of the universe that are beyond your ability to comprehend right now. But you will have all eternity to learn about them."

"Mekoddishkem, you seem to know everything about everyone and everything. Do all heavenly beings have as much knowledge as you?"

The guardian gave an enigmatic smile. "Let's leave The Wall now and go meet your Savior."

Jackson smiled. "I can't wait."

They walked down the gangplank toward the landing.

As Mekoddishkem opened the door, lightning-bright light burst through, enveloping both of them.

# CHAPTER 45
# THE AFTERMATH

MCKENZIE HAD JUST finished planning a wedding. Now she would be planning a funeral.

Twelve hours had passed since the parking lot shooting. She should have been spending her honeymoon with her new husband, but instead, she was spending it at St. Francis Hospital. She didn't want to leave Jackson's body. Monica and the Tolberts, who had been with McKenzie the entire time, finally talked her into going home. Jackson's body would be well cared for, and his soul was indeed in a much better place now.

McKenzie was also concerned about her father. He had complained of severe chest pains, so her brother, Duncan, and her mother, took him to the hospital for observation. Her brother agreed to stay with their father that night.

The Tolberts drove McKenzie and Monica to McKenzie's apartment.

Mike asked, "Monica, how are you dealing with all this?"

She swallowed. "I'm wondering what I did to make Ronaldo so angry that he wanted to kill me. I'm wondering why Jackson, on his honeymoon, took a bullet to save my life. I'm wondering why God, if there is a God, allowed all this to happen."

Mike responded, "I can't comment on Ronaldo because I never met him, but Jackson was the most unselfish man I ever met and a true Christian. He made a split-second decision to give his life for you, perhaps to give you another chance to become a Christian. Jackson was a true hero of the faith. Regarding God, it's obvious he exists from observing his creation, particularly his greatest creation—human beings. He does not cause bad things to happen to people but may allow bad things to happen to them because he's given us free will."

Mike parked the car on Trumbull Street, then escorted the three women to McKenzie's apartment. McKenzie collapsed onto one of the love seats in the living room while Monica went into the bedroom.

Sally, who'd agreed to stay the night with them, stepped into the hallway to talk to Mike before he left. "I think the best thing I can do is just wait for McKenzie to speak." Even though Sally whispered, McKenzie could still hear her. "I don't want to force her to talk if she doesn't want to."

Mike squeezed Sally's hand. "I agree. Job's three friends waited for him to speak first."

"Okay, honey. I'll call you when I'm ready to be picked up. Make sure you get the kids from my parents' house in the morning. Mom and Dad will probably be exhausted after having them an extra day."

"Will do."

Sally re-entered the apartment, closed the door, locked it, then sat down on the opposite love seat. McKenzie lay back, sniffling. She still wore the dress she had planned to use for the flight to Bermuda. Jackson's blood covered the front of it.

McKenzie gulped. "The Old Testament says the life is in the blood. Strangely, this blood is all I have left of Jackson. I'm not ready to let it go yet."

"I understand."

Another wave of grief overwhelmed her. "Sally, why did God allow this to happen? What was the reason for it?" Although she'd been crying for hours, more tears came.

Sally walked around the coffee table, sat down, and put her arm around McKenzie. "A sinful, hateful person did this, sweetheart, not God."

"I know." She sobbed. "But he could have intervened if he had wanted to."

"Yes, he could have. But we have to trust God that there was a reason why he didn't."

McKenzie looked up. "Jackson told me he saw an angel near the parking lot just before he died. He said it was the same angel who appeared to him after the hit-and-run driver struck him."

"Really?" She then nodded a few times. "Just like Stephen seeing Jesus standing at the right hand of God in heaven before Stephen's accusers stoned him to death."

"Yes. And just before Jackson left me to protect Monica, he said, 'No! If he kills her, she'll go straight to hell!'"

Monica walked back into the living room. "Jackson said what?"

McKenzie froze, having forgotten that Monica was in the other room.

Sally stood. "That you would have gone straight to hell if Ronaldo had killed you today. Jackson sacrificed his life for you, so you would have another chance to go to heaven."

Monica moved closer, her eyes wide. "Why would he do that?"

"He didn't want you to suffer in hell and the lake of fire, separated from God forever," Sally explained. "He knew that our lives here on earth are just temporary and that our new lives after death are eternal. It was worth it to him to lose his life here on earth so that you would have another chance at life in heaven. It's like the infantryman who falls on the enemy grenade to save the lives of his buddies. They're all a part of the same team, and sometimes the survival needs of one team member outweigh the survival needs of another. In the same way, Jesus died for our sins because he knew our need for salvation was greater than his need to avoid the terrible suffering of the cross."

Monica's chin quivered. "This is all my fault."

"You weren't the cause of Jackson's death," McKenzie whispered. "You were the reason for it, but not the cause. Jackson paid a heavy price so you could choose a different destiny."

Tears filled Monica's eyes.

McKenzie reached out and held Monica's hand, then closed her eyes. "Father in heaven, thank you for giving Monica another chance to place her trust in Jesus. Please help her to make the most of the additional time you've given her. In Jesus's name, I pray, amen."

McKenzie turned to Sally. "Can you help me take off my dress now?"

# CHAPTER 46
# A LIVING LEGACY

THE FOLLOWING AFTERNOON, McKenzie drove over to Jackson's condo. Her brother was waiting for her at the front door to the building. She went inside with him and opened the door. McKenzie gasped. Her parents had stacked all the wedding presents four feet high on the living room floor. Gift envelopes lay across the coffee table.

She zeroed in on a picture of her and Jackson on the beach at Block Island. They had visited there again over the summer. She burst into tears. Duncan raced over to hold her.

Struggling to speak between sobs, she said, "He's only been gone a day, and I miss him so much. I can't believe he's gone. This wasn't supposed to happen. We were going to have kids and grow old together. It may be sixty years before I see him again in heaven. Will he still love me then? Why did God allow this to happen?"

Duncan shook his head. "I have no idea, McKenzie, but he did. You can count on me for the next sixty years to help you through this."

She sniffled and hugged her brother. "Thanks, Duncan."

"Don't forget that Monica would be dead right now if Jackson hadn't given his life for her. He did a courageous thing."

"Yes, he did."

She continued to the bedroom, opened the door to his walk-in closet, and stepped inside. She grasped one of Jackson's pressed shirts and smelled it. It smelled clean and fresh, like he'd just picked it up at the drycleaner. Pressing his shirt into her face, McKenzie burst into tears once again.

Down in the corner of the closet was a shoebox. Something prompted McKenzie to open it. Inside, she found Jackson's medals from the marines. She picked them up and carried them to the living room to show her brother.

Duncan studied them. "I had no idea."

"What do you mean?"

"Didn't he tell you about these?"

"No."

"Jackson was a war hero." He pointed at the medals. "This is a Silver Star, this one is a Bronze Star, and this is a Purple Heart. I'm impressed."

She nodded. "I think Jackson was a hero in God's eyes too."

## CHAPTER 47
# FAREWELL

THE FUNERAL SERVICE was conducted the following Wednesday morning at Valley Community Baptist Church. McKenzie asked Mike to deliver the eulogy. He shared all that Jackson had told him about his experiences with The Wall, including how he saw McKenzie, Monica, and others in the lake of fire and how Jackson had done everything he could to save them. He also shared the last words that Jackson had spoken to McKenzie before he died.

The pastor then continued the funeral sermon by quoting 1 Thessalonians 4:13–18:

*Brothers and sisters, we do not want you to be uninformed about those who sleep in death, so that you do not grieve like the rest of mankind, who have no hope. For we believe that Jesus died and rose again, and so we believe that God will bring with Jesus those who have fallen asleep in him. According to the Lord's word, we tell you that we who are still alive, who are left until the coming of the Lord, will certainly not precede those who have fallen asleep. For the Lord himself will come down from heaven, with a loud command, with the voice of the archangel and with the trumpet call of God, and the dead in Christ will rise first. After that, we who are still alive and are left will be caught up together with them in the clouds to meet the Lord in the air. And so we will be with the Lord forever. Therefore encourage one another with these words.*

He explained that this passage was about the rapture, which would occur when Jesus returned to the earth to gather his followers to himself in the clouds. The pastor encouraged those in attendance to seek God and be sure of their eternal destiny.

Following the service, Carmon Funeral Home staff transported Jackson's coffin to the Riverside Cemetery in Farmington, Connecticut. McKenzie had chosen this location because it was a calm and peaceful place, set on a hill near a bend in the Farmington River, overlooking hundreds of acres of pristine, unspoiled meadows. She had to get special permission to have him buried there because he wasn't a Farmington resident.

A tent was in place beside the burial site, with chairs neatly arranged underneath it. Jackson's coffin was removed from the hearse and carried to the burial site. A Marine honor guard stood by.

McKenzie sat beside Jackson's parents. Her mother stood behind her and placed a hand on her shoulder. It didn't seem real. They were just married. How could she go on without him? The other attendees gathered around. A moment later, the pastor began the internment.

"Dearly beloved, we are here to put to rest a husband, son, brother, and friend—Jackson Trotman. Lord Jesus, we know that he is your adopted son and is with you in heaven. We pray that you will grant him a rich welcome into your kingdom, and with open arms declare, 'Well done good and faithful servant.' And now for a reading from 2 Timothy 4:6–8:"

*For I am already being poured out like a drink offering, and the time for my departure is near. I have fought the good fight, I have finished the race, I have kept the faith. Now there is in store for me the crown of righteousness, which the Lord, the righteous Judge, will award to me on that day—and not only to me, but also to all who have longed for his appearing.*

The pastor turned toward the casket. "Now, dearly beloved, let us lay our brother, Jackson Joel Trotman, to rest."

Tears streamed down McKenzie's face as the marine team leader presented her with the American flag. Jackson had given his life so freely, and he'd taught her how to live. With God's help, she'd have to find a way to live without him. She'd never forget what Jackson did for her and Monica, and she had no doubt that they would meet again in heaven one day.

# BOOK CLUB QUESTIONS

1. What was your first impression of the book?

2. What did you like most about *The Wall*?

3. What did you like least about *The Wall*?

4. What were the major themes of the book?

5. What were the primary motivations of the characters (e.g., Jackson, McKenzie, Mekoddishkem, Dexter, and Monica)? Did they achieve their goals?

6. How did the characters change throughout the story?

7. Did you connect with any of the characters? If so, how?

8. What new things did you learn? How did the book impact you?

9. What unanswered questions do you still have?

10. Were you satisfied with the ending? What do you think will happen next?

You may contact the author at *www.rickstockwell.com* if you have any questions or would like to invite him to your book club.

## AUTHOR'S NOTE

The image of The Wall came to me as I was running on the treadmill and memorizing Ephesians 1. An explanation immediately followed in my mind of what The Wall represented. I wrote this book because I wondered what it would be like to go there. I also wanted to understand what goes on in the heavenly realms.

This book is a work of fiction. I did my best to be faithful to the Scriptures but may have been wrong when speculating about some of the details. My goal was to illustrate biblical truths clearly and understandably for the reader. We can have absolute confidence in the Bible's veracity but cannot assign that same confidence to the writings of fallible human beings like me. *Sola Scriptura!*

I came across a few quotes during my research that I'd like to share regarding the concept of everything in the past, present, and future possibly being accessible to us one day.

Here is an excerpt from a sermon preached by Billy Graham in 1949. Graham said:

> *"Darkness doesn't hide the eyes of God... God takes down your life from the time you were born to the time you die. And when you stand before God on the great judgment day, you're going to say, 'Lord I wasn't such a bad fellow,' and they are going to pull down the screen and they are going to shoot the moving picture of your life from the cradle to the grave, and you are going to hear every thought that was going through your mind every minute of the day, every second of the minute, and you're going to hear the words that you said. And your own words, and your own*

*thoughts, and your own deeds, are going to condemn you as you stand before God on that day. And God is going to say, 'Depart from me.'*[1]

This one is a quote from Randy Alcorn:

*If we will travel to other galaxies, will we also be able to travel in time? Even though I believe we'll live in time, God is certainly capable of bending time and opening doors in time's fabric for us. Perhaps we'll be able to travel back and stand alongside angels in the invisible realm, seeing events as they happened on Earth. Maybe we'll learn the lessons of God's providence through direct observation. Can you imagine being there as Jesus preached the Sermon on the Mount? Perhaps you will be... Our God, after all, is called the one "who is able to do immeasurably more than all we ask or imagine" (Ephesians 3:20).*[2]

---

1    Laura Hillenbrand, *Unbroken* (New York, New York: Random House, 2010), 373. Excerpts taken from "The Only Sermon Jesus Ever Wrote" sermon by Billy Graham, © 1949 Billy Graham Evangelistic Association. Used with permission. All rights reserved. Author's transcription from audio recording.

2    Randy Alcorn, *Heaven* (Carol Stream, IL: Tyndale House Publishers, Inc., 2004), 433, 435.

# ACKNOWLEDGMENTS

No book is ever solely written by a single person. Many people—including family, friends, teachers, pastors, classmates, and coworkers—have written their love, thoughts, desires, prayers, and knowledge into my mind and heart over the years. I am indebted to them. However, many people specifically invested a lot of time and energy in helping me complete this book.

First, I would like to thank God for giving me the inspiration, energy, and insight to write this book. *Soli Deo Gloria!* To God alone be the glory!

Second, I would like to thank my immediate family for their support and encouragement as I spent many hours away from them writing and rewriting this book. To my wife Donna, son John, and daughter Abigail, thanks for the ideas and corrections you provided. To my parents, Bea and Dick Stockwell, thanks for your encouraging words.

Third, I would like to thank my extended family members for their encouragement and suggestions: Jane Arciero, John Arciero, Chris Arciero, Paul Arciero, Phillip Stockwell, Sue Stockwell, Sharon Stockwell, Marilyn Stephani, Tony Scuderi, and Judy Scuderi.

Fourth, I would like to thank my friends who provided suggestions or reviewed drafts of the book: Glenn (GR) Rutland, Les Moretti, Norman Burtness, Cub Culberson, MD, Paul Semanski, Martha Campbell, Jim Mayer, Nate Margolis, Bob Kagels, Marilyn Kagels, Chris Sanford, Captain Glenn Murray USNR, Mike Martino, Tom Kalb, Captain Neil Guinan USN, Bob Sullivan, Eva Lesko Natiello,

Bob Stevens, Jon Neville, Dave Whittmer, and Jim Silk. I'd also like to thank Pastor Carl Abrahamsen for encouraging me to memorize the Sermon on the Mount and Ephesians 1. Thanks also go to my spiritual mentor and friend, Reverend Don Minnich, for graciously and patiently answering my many questions about the Bible.

Fifth, I would like to thank the Jerry Jenkins Christian Writer's Guild staff for providing writing instruction through conferences, correspondence courses, and webinars. I'd especially like to thank my writing mentors, Lissa Halls Johnson, for her careful and insightful critiques of my early coursework, and Kathy Tyers, for helping me begin to learn the craft of writing.

Sixth, I would like to thank the Greater Philadelphia Christian Writer's Conference staff, led by Marlene Bagnull, for their insightful instruction.

Seventh, I would like to thank the three line editors who worked with me during the ten years it took to write the first version of this book: Hanna Lawton, Matthew Brennan, and Christy Distler. Their many corrections and suggestions were invaluable in creating the final product published in 2018.

In 2021, I decided to have *The Wall* become the first installment in the *Heavenly Realms* series, with *The Battle* as the second. Janice Boekhoff did a fabulous job analyzing and integrating the two books, performing developmental and line edits, and transforming them into what they are today.

Any errors or omissions in the text are my own.

# Selected Bibliography

Alcorn, Randy. *Heaven*. Carol Stream, Illinois: Tyndale House Publishers, Inc., 2004.

Barnhouse, Donald Grey. *The Invisible War*. Grand Rapids, Michigan: Zondervan, 1965.

Bell, James Scott. *Write Great Fiction: Plot & Structure*. Cincinnati, Ohio: Writer's Digest Books, 2004.

Burpo, Todd. *Heaven is for Real*. Nashville, Tennessee: Thomas Nelson, Inc., 2010.

Enns, Paul. *Heaven Revealed*. Chicago, Illinois: Moody Publishers, 1989, 2008.

Enns, Paul. The *Moody Handbook of Theology*. Chicago, Illinois: Moody Publishers, 1989, 2008.

Gerke, Jeff. *The Art and Craft of Writing Christian Fiction*. Colorado Springs, Colorado: Marcher Lord Press, 2009.

Goldberg, Natalie. *Writing Down the Bones—Freeing the Writer Within*. Boston, Massachusetts: Shambhala Publications, Inc., 1986, 2005.

Hillenbrand, Laura. *Unbroken*. New York, New York: Random House, 2010.

Kress, Nancy. *Dynamic Characters: How to Create Personalities that Keep Readers Captivated*. Cincinnati, Ohio: Writer's Digest Books, 1998.

Kress, Nancy. *Write Great Fiction: Characters, Emotion & Viewpoint.* Cincinnati, Ohio: Writer's Digest Books, 2005.

Lutzer, Erwin W. *One Minute After You Die.* Chicago, Illinois: Moody Publishers, 1997.

Maass, Donald. *The Emotional Craft of Fiction.* Cincinnati, Ohio: Writer's Digest Books, 2016.

Mac, Toby, and Michael Tait. "Bulletproof"—George Washington (1755). *Under God.* Bloomington, Minnesota: Bethany House Publishers, 2004.

MacArthur, John. *"Commentary on Daniel 9:20–27."* March 27, 1983, Code 1293. *Copyright 1983, Grace to You.*

McDowell, Josh, and Don Stewart. *Answers to Tough Questions Skeptics Ask about the Christian Faith.* Wheaton, Illinois: Living Books, Tyndale House, Inc., 1980.

Piper, Don. *90 Minutes in Heaven.* Grand Rapids, Michigan: Revell, 2004.

Rawlings, Maurice. *Beyond Death's Door.* New York, New York: Thomas Nelson, Inc., 1978.

Swenson, Richard A., MD. *More Than Meets the Eye.* Colorado Springs, Colorado: NavPress, 2000.

Weiland, K. M. *Creating Character Arcs.* PenForASword Publishing, 2016.

Wiersbe, Warren. *The Strategy of Satan.* Carol Stream, Illinois: Tyndale House, Inc., 1979.

Wiese, Bill. *23 Minutes in Hell.* Lake Mary, Florida: Charisma House, 2006.

Zacharias, Naomi. *The Scent of Water.* Grand Rapids, Michigan: Zondervan, 2010.

# PROPHECY PRIMER

*Note: Christians hold various points of view regarding the end times. Plenty of books are available on this topic. The following summarizes the point of view from which I wrote this book.*

A Christian is someone believes Jesus is the Son of God (John 3:16; Romans 10:9), repents of their sinful way of living (Luke 13:3), and gives up their life to follow Jesus (Mark 8:34–38). There is much, much more to the Christian life, but that is where it starts.

When a Christian dies, they go directly to what is known as the "intermediate heaven" (Luke 23:43). They will reside there with God—the Father, Son, and Holy Spirit—plus the holy angels, and all the Christians who died before them and after them until the "rapture."

The rapture occurs when Jesus leaves the intermediate heaven, accompanied by the Christians residing there, and reunites them with perfect/incorruptible versions of their former physical bodies. After that, he causes the Christians who are currently alive on earth to join him in the sky with their new bodies (John 14:1–3; 1 Corinthians

15:51–57; 1 Thessalonians 4:13–18). The rapture could occur at any time, and no one knows when it will happen except God (Matthew 24:36; Mark 13:32).

Following the rapture, Christians will stand before the judgment seat of Christ (bema judgment) to receive rewards for what they did in life (1 Corinthians 3:11–15; 2 Corinthians 5:10; Romans 14:10–12). In parallel, a seven-year tribulation period will begin, during which an agreement will be made between the antichrist and Israel. Halfway through the tribulation, the antichrist will break the agreement and the wrath of God will be poured out on the earth (Daniel 9:24–27; Revelation 6–19). The purpose of these events is to bring about the conversion of Israel and to judge living unbelievers. Raptured Christians will not be on earth at the tribulation's beginning (1 Thessalonians 1:10).

At the tribulation's conclusion, Jesus will physically return to the earth (i.e., the second coming—Revelation 19:11–16) to destroy his enemies at Armageddon, which is Greek for Megiddo, located in Israel (Revelation 16:16; 19:21). Those who became Christians during the tribulation will appear before Christ at the sheep and goats judgment and be rewarded according to what they did in life. Those who did not become Christians during the tribulation, along with the Beast and False Prophet, will be thrown into the lake of fire (Matthew 25:31–46; Revelation 19:20). God will resurrect Old Testament saints during this period (Daniel 12:1–2).

Following these events, the millennium will begin, during which Christ, assisted by select Christians (Luke 19:11–27), will rule over the earth for a thousand years (Revelation 20:4, 6). Satan will be bound and thrown into the Abyss during this period and will be unable to interfere with events on earth (Revelation 20:2). People born during this period will become both believers and nonbelievers.

At the end of the millennium, Satan will be released from the Abyss (Revelation 20:7), gather the non-Christians (of Gog and

Magog) from the four corners of the earth, and they will surround the city of Jerusalem, seeking to destroy God's people there (Revelation 20:8–9). God will destroy Satan and his followers with fire from heaven (Revelation 20:9–10).

The great white throne judgment will then occur. At that time, everyone whose names are not written in the Book of Life—Satan, fallen angels, demons, and unredeemed people—will be judged and thrown into the lake of fire for all eternity (Revelation 20:10–15).

Following the great white throne judgment, God will create a permanent new heaven and a new earth (Isaiah 65:17; 2 Peter 3:13; Revelation 21:1). Jesus Christ will rule with Christians appointed to assist him. Once he establishes his kingdom, he will turn it over to God the Father (1 Corinthians 15:24). The new Jerusalem, the city of God, will descend from heaven to the new earth, and God will dwell there with redeemed humanity for all eternity (Revelation 21).

The unredeemed go immediately to hell when they die (John 3:18). Their punishment will vary according to what they did or did not do during their life on earth (Mark 12:40; Luke 12:47–48; 20:47; Revelation 20:12). Hell is located within the earth (Numbers 16:30, 33; 1 Samuel 28:11–13; Job 7:9; 11:8; 17:16; Psalm 55:15; Proverbs 1:12; 7:27; 9:18; 15:24; Isaiah 7:11; 14:9, 15; Ezekiel 31:15–17; 32:21, 27; Amos 9:2; Matthew 12:40) and is where the unredeemed will suffer in a world characterized by darkness (Matthew 8:12) and fire (Matthew 13:42; Mark 9:43, 48). They will suffer physically and spiritually as they await the great white throne judgment (Luke 16:23). Then they will be cast alive into the lake of fire for all eternity (Matthew 25:31–46; Revelation 20:10–15).

# NOTES

*Note: Having formal endnote references in the body of this novel would do irreparable damage to its readability. The citations below will (a) ensure credit is appropriately attributed, (b) guide those wishing to pursue a particular topic further.*

## Chapter 1: War

1. *The Princess Diaries*, Walt Disney Pictures, 2001.
2. William Ernest Henley, "Invictus," *A Book of Verses*, (London: D. Nutt, 1888).
3. Psalm 138:8 and Jeremiah 29:11 contain a description of the plans God has for each of us.

## Chapter 2: The Other Side

4. Angels carried Lazarus's body to Father Abraham's side in Luke 16:22. The assumption is that demons will carry the unredeemed to hell. See Erwin Lutzer, *One Minute After You Die* (Chicago, Illinois: Moody Press, 1997), page 29, quoted in Bill Wiese, *23 Minutes in Hell* (Lake Mary, Florida: Charisma House, 2006) page 124.
5. The ability of a disembodied soul to pass through physical structures, such as a roof, is mentioned in Wiese et al., page 45. Jesus walked through walls after he was resurrected, as noted in John 20:19, 26.
6. The reference to the Abyss opening comes from Revelation 9:1–3, which refers explicitly to locusts exiting from it during the tribulation period.
7. The reference to a horrible stench in hell is mentioned in Wiese et al., page 7.

8.    The idea that everyone will be naked in hell comes from Wiese et al., pages xv and 37. Biblical references to this include Job 26:6; Revelation 3:18; 16:15.

9.    The notion of demons in hell ripping the flesh of the unredeemed comes from Wiese et al., page 6.

10.   The concept of different punishment levels in hell comes from Mark 12:40 and Luke 20:47. Another reference is Wiese et al., page 26.

11.   A mark on the forehead indicates allegiance to God (Revelation 7:3; 9:4; 14:1; 20:4; 22:4) or the devil (Revelation 13:16; 14:9–10).

12.   The reference to fallen angels kept in dungeons for future judgment comes from 2 Peter 2:4 and Jude 1:6.

13.   The reference to "weeping and gnashing of teeth" in hell comes from Matthew 8:12; 13:42; 13:50; 22:13; 24:51; 25:30; and Luke 13:28. Another reference is Wiese et al., page 8.

14.   The reference to extreme thirst in hell comes from Luke 16:24. Another reference is Wiese et al., page 11.

15.   The reference to feeling extremely weak in hell comes from Psalm 88:4. Another reference is Wiese et al., pages 2 and 4.

16.   The reference to it being tough to breathe in hell comes from Wiese et al., page 11.

17.   The idea of demons in hell looking reptilian comes from Wiese et al., page 3.

18.   Maurice Rawlings, MD, *Beyond Death's Door* (New York, New York: Thomas Nelson, Inc., 1978), pages 17–21, contains an actual description of a patient in cardiac arrest crying out that he is in hell.

## Chapter 3: Stress Reduction

19.   Ephesians 1:3–6 and 1:17–19a describe the sovereignty of God and his desire to reveal himself to those he has chosen.

## Chapter 4: The Office

20.   Pastor Jay Abramson provided the railroad track metaphor.

21.   The reference to anger, rage, and malice comes from Colossians 3:8.

22.   The reference to drunkenness leading to debauchery comes from Ephesians 5:18.

23.  The key to overcoming addiction is asking God to remove our evil desires, as noted in James 1:14. A friend of mine, John Blaine, struggled with alcohol abuse. He pleaded with Jesus to take away his desire for alcohol. Jesus answered John's prayer three hours later.

## *Chapter 7: The Parking Garage*

24.  The description of Elijah going to heaven is from 2 Kings 2:11–12.
25.  The description of the commander of the Lord's Army appearing to Joshua comes from Joshua 5:13–15.
26.  The reference to Jackson falling prostrate before an angel, trembling, is derived from Daniel 8:16–18.
27.  The ability of an angel to take away a person's fear comes from Daniel 8:17-18 and Revelation 1:17. Another reference is Wiese et al., page 32.
28.  Descriptions of angels come from Daniel 10:6 and Revelation 1:20; 2:18; 15:6.
29.  References to guardian angels include Psalm 34:7; 91:11; Matthew 18:10; Acts 12:15; and Hebrews 1:14.
30.  The reference to the guardian's name being beyond understanding comes from Judges 13:18.
31.  The reference to the "spirit of wisdom and revelation" comes from Ephesians 1:17.
32.  The reference to "everything is in full view of the Lord" comes from Proverbs 5:21 and Hebrews 4:13. Related references include Job 24:23; 28:24; 31:4; Jeremiah 16:17; Proverbs 15:3, 11.
33.  The reference to "Satan can imitate an angel of light" comes from 2 Corinthians 11:14.
34.  The warning to add nothing to God's Word comes from Revelation 22:18–19. See also 1 Corinthians 4:6.
35.  The reference to the third heaven comes from 2 Corinthians 12:2.
36.  The reference to God wanting us to be sanctified comes from 1 Thessalonians 4:3.
37.  Isaiah 40:22 is quoted. It refers to the earth being a "circle." *The Message* translates it as a "round ball." See also Psalm 33:13–14. Another related reference is Job 26:7b: "He suspends the world over nothing." The book of Job was likely written 3,000 to 4,000 years ago.

## *Chapter 8: Tough Questions*

38. The reference to our lives being on DVR was mentioned by Sam Moy during a devotional on "God's Sovereignty vs. Man's Responsibility."

39. The reference to Abraham asking God to spare Lot from the destruction of Sodom and Gomorrah comes from Genesis 18:16–33.

40. The reference to the two greatest commandments comes from Matthew 22:34–40 and Mark 12:28–31.

41. The reference to Jackson being "greatly loved" is extrapolated from God's great love for the prophet Daniel in Daniel 9:23; 10:11; 10:19.

42. The reference to people created in God's image comes from Genesis 1:26–27.

43. The Wheat and the Tares Parable comes from Matthew 13:24–30.

44. The concept of "losing your life to find it" occurs in all four gospels. One reference is Luke 9:24.

45. The reference to God not being willing that any should perish but all to come to repentance comes from 2 Peter 3:9. A related reference is Ezekiel 33:11.

46. The reference to people turning away from God comes from James 1:13–15.

47. The reference to no one coming to Jesus unless the Father draws him comes from John 6:44.

## *Chapter 9: Her Special Place*

48. The reference to drawing near to God so he will draw near to us comes from James 4:8.

49. The reference to heaven's streets being paved with gold, and twelve gates in heaven, comes from Revelation 21:21.

50. The reference to Susan wearing a white linen dress is implied from Revelation 19:8.

51. The reference to the new heaven and new earth comes from Isaiah 65:17; 2 Peter 3:13; and Revelation 21:1.

52. The reference to comforting others with the comfort we have received comes from 2 Corinthians 1:4.

## *Chapter 10: 500 AD*

53. The reference to the wife being "lovely in form" comes from Genesis 29:17.
54. The reference to the birth of Moses comes from Exodus 2:1–10.

## *Chapter 11: 1755 AD*

55. The story about George Washington's battle at Fort Duquesne during the French and Indian War comes from an extract called "Bullet-proof" from Toby Mac and Michael Tait, *Under God* (Bloomington, Minnesota: Bethany House Publishers, 2004).
56. The reference to God knowing what the soldier is thinking is inferred from 1 Chronicles 28:9. See also Proverbs 15:11; 16:2; Psalm 44:21; 94:11; Jeremiah 17:10; 23:24; and Matthew 9:4.
57. The reference to momentary suffering outweighing future glory comes from 2 Corinthians 4:17.
58. The reference to a thousand falling at one's side comes from Psalm 91:7.

## *Chapter 12: Semper Fi*

59. The reference that the days of a person's life are preordained comes from Psalm 139:16; Job 14:5; 21:21.
60. The reference to someone dying before their time comes from Ecclesiastes 7:17. A related reference is Job 22:16 (spoken by Eliphaz). See also Proverbs 10:27b; Job 17:1 (spoken by Job); 34:20 (spoken by Elihu).
61. Naomi Zacharias, *The Scent of Water: Grace for Every Kind of Broken* (Grand Rapids, Michigan: Zondervan, 2010), pages 27–40 describe brothels in Amsterdam.
62. The verses 1 Corinthians 6:15–17 contain a warning against uniting with a prostitute.
63. The reference to loathing oneself for sins committed comes from Ezekiel 20:43.
64. The reference to our secret sins being visible to God comes from Psalm 90:8.

65. The fact that all we do is in "full view" of the Lord is found in Proverbs 5:21 and Hebrews 4:13. Also, see Proverbs 15:3 and Jeremiah 16:17.

66. The reference to the prayer of a righteous person being powerful and effective comes from James 5:16.

## Chapter 13: Hidden Motives

67. The reference to the God-ordained authority of the state comes from Romans 13:1–5.

68. The Ten Commandments are found in Exodus 20 and Deuteronomy 5.

## Chapter 14: The Present

69. The Star Trek reference comes from the "Wink of an Eye" episode, which first aired on November 29, 1968.

70. The reference to some things in the heavenly realms remaining secret comes from Deuteronomy 29:29.

## Chapter 15: Consequences

71. The reference to Jesus being the only way to heaven comes from John 14:6.

72. The fact that God is not willing that anyone should perish (i.e., go to hell) is found in Ezekiel 33:11 and 2 Peter 3:9. Similar passages are Ezekiel 18:23, 32.

73. The fact that many will go to hell is found in Matthew 7:22–23.

74. The reference to Jackson not needing to know the location of the entrance to hell comes from Deuteronomy 29:29.

75. Some, but not all, descriptions of the Abyss are taken from Wiese et al., pages 9, 22, 24, and 30.

76. The reference to King David's baby being in heaven comes from 2 Samuel 12:23b.

77. The reference to people having no excuse for not believing in God comes from Romans 1:20.

78. The reference to people who never heard the gospel still being accountable before God comes from Romans 2:12–15.

79. The reference to "weeping and gnashing of teeth" in hell comes from Matthew 8:12; 13:42; 13:50; 22:13; 24:51; 25:30; and Luke 13:28.
80. The reference to fallen angels imprisoned in dungeons comes from 2 Peter 2:4 and Jude 1:6.
81. The reference to the parable of Lazarus and the rich man comes from Luke 16:19–31.
82. The reference to a stream of bodies falling into the Abyss comes from Wiese et al., pages 36, 68, and 69.
83. The idea that there will be no mercy in hell comes from Wiese et al., page 7.
84. The reference to no one being able to fool God comes from 1 Chronicles 28:9.

## Chapter 16: Soul Mate

85. The reference to the Tree of the Knowledge of Good and Evil comes from Genesis 2:9, 17.
86. The reference to the evil done by a person passing down three or four subsequent generations comes from Exodus 20:4–6 and Deuteronomy 5:9–10.
87. The reference to the legacy of the Edwards and Jukes families comes from A. E. Winship, *Jukes-Edwards A Study in Education and Heredity* (Harrisburg, Pennsylvania: R. L. Myers & Co, 1900).
88. The reference to "all have sinned and fall short of the glory of God" comes from Romans 3:23.

## Chapter 17: A Little Surprise

89. Jeremiah 1:5 refers to God knowing us before we're born. Similar references include Psalm 139:16; Isaiah 46:3; 49:1; Luke 2:21; and Galatians 1:15.
90. The reference to God casting away our sins as far as the east is from the west comes from Psalm 103:12.
91. The reference to drunkenness leading to debauchery comes from Ephesians 5:18.
92. The new heaven and new earth reference comes from Isaiah 65:17; 2 Peter 3:13; and Revelation 21:1.

93.    The reference to the sins of some people reaching the place of judgment before them comes from 1 Timothy 5:24.

## Chapter 18: Who's to Blame?

94.    The reference to the Armor of God comes from Ephesians 6:14–17.

95.    The reference to the battle being against powers in the heavenly realms comes from Ephesians 6:12.

96.    The reference to one of the demons looking reptilian and huge comes from Wiese et al., page 3.

97.    The reference to the opening of books and people judged according to what they did in life comes from Revelation 20:12. Other references include Psalm 62:12; Jeremiah 17:10; Romans 2:6; and 1 Peter 1:17.

98.    The reference to torment in the lake of fire lasting for all eternity comes from Revelation 20:10b.

## Chapter 19: One Destination

99.    The reference to casting fallen angels out of heaven comes from Isaiah 14:12 and Ezekiel 28:17 (past) and Revelation 12:9 (future). The past expulsion may refer to the third heaven (where God, the angels, and deceased saints live), and the future expulsion may refer to the second heaven (outer space) or first heaven (earth's atmosphere).

100.   The reference to demonic hatred of humanity comes from Wiese et al., page 30, 35.

101.   The reference "they are not to be touched" is inferred from 1 Chronicles 16:22 and Psalm 105:15.

102.   The concept that the unredeemed will have no hope of escaping the lake of fire comes from Wiese et al., page 37. Biblical references include Job 8:13; Proverbs 11:7; Isaiah 38:18; and Ephesians 2:12.

103.   Anything happening to us must first be filtered through God's will, as illustrated in Job 1.

104.   The reference to the lake of fire comes from Revelation 19:19–21; 20:7–15; 21:6–8.

105.   The reference to the great white throne comes from Revelation 7:9; 20:11–15.

106. The reference to the Abyss opening comes from Revelation 9:1–3, which refers explicitly to locusts released from the Abyss during the tribulation period. It is speculation that the unredeemed will be released from hell to appear before the great white throne in the same manner.

107. The reference that every knee shall bow and every tongue confess that Jesus Christ is Lord comes from Philippians 2:9–11.

## Chapter 20: Stalker

108. Prince, "1999," *1999* Studio Album, Warner Bros. Records, 1982.

## Chapter 21: Back in the Saddle

109. The reference to whom much is given, much will be expected, comes from Luke 12:48.

110. The phrase "The Lord rebuke you" comes from Jude 1:9 and Zechariah 3:2.

111. The reference to "resist the devil and he will flee from you" comes from James 4:7.

112. The fact that God will never forsake us comes from Deuteronomy 31:6, 8; Psalm 9:10; and Hebrews 13:5.

113. The reference to the rich man and Lazarus comes from Luke 16:19–31.

114. The warning against adding anything to what the Bible says comes from Revelation 22:18–19.

115. The warning against being puffed up with idle notions comes from Colossians 2:18–19.

116. The reference to the mystery of God's will comes from Ephesians 1:9.

117. The reference to the wild and cultivated olive branches comes from Romans 11:17.

118. The commentary on Daniel 9:20–27 comes from John McArthur, "*Commentary on Daniel 9:20–27*," in a sermon from March 27, 1983. *Copyright 1983, Grace to You. All rights reserved. Used with permission.*

## Chapter 25: First Date... Round Two

119. Technical descriptions of the human eye come from Richard A. Swenson, MD, *More Than Meets the Eye: Fascinating Glimpses of God's Power and Design* (Colorado Springs, Colorado: NavPress, 2000), pages 32–35. Used with permission.
120. The reference to Darwin's thoughts about the human eye come from Jeremy Rifkin, *Algeny* (New York, New York: Viking, 1983), pages 139–146, cited in Swenson et al., page 32.
121. The technical discussion about evolution comes from Swenson et al., page 67.
122. The statistic that DNA for chimpanzees and humans is 98 percent similar comes from the American Museum of Natural History's website: *www.amnh.org/exhibitions/past-exhibitions/human-origins/understanding-our-past/dna-comparing-humans-and-chimps.*
123. The fossilized miner's helmet reference can be found on the Creation Moments website.
124. The "clickety-clack of the tracks" phrase comes from the Essex Steam engine website, *http://essexsteamtrain.com.*
125. Biblical references to drinking or not drinking wine include Proverbs 20:1; Ecclesiastes 9:7; Jeremiah 35; Matthew 11:19; Luke 1:15; 7:34; 22:18; John 2:1–10; and 1 Timothy 5:23.
126. The key to overcoming addiction is asking God to take away our evil desires, as noted in James 1:14. A friend of mine, Jonathan Blaine, struggled with alcohol abuse. He pleaded with Jesus to take away his desire for alcohol. Jesus answered John's prayer three hours later.
127. The Camelot production description is from the Camelot program on the Goodspeed Opera House website that ran from July 10–September 19, 2009.

## Chapter 26: Anticipation

128. The reference to being unequally yoked comes from 2 Corinthians 6:14.

## Chapter 27: Mandatory Meeting

129. The section on God creating the universe with age comes from a sermon by Pastor Jay Abramson on October 18–19, 2014, at Valley Community Baptist Church in Avon, Connecticut.

## Chapter 28: Revisiting the Stalker

130. The reference to all things working out for the best for the believer comes from Romans 8:28.
131. Daniel 12:2 from the Old Testament, refers to life after death and indicates that some Jews will go to heaven and some to hell.
132. The reference to the benefits of suffering comes from Romans 5:3–5. Other references include Hebrews 5:8 and 1 Peter 1:6–7.

## Chapter 30: Church Together

133. The reference to the prodigal son comes from Luke 15:11–32.
134. Naomi Zacharias, *The Scent of Water: Grace for Every Kind of Broken* (Grand Rapids, Michigan: Zondervan, 2010), pages 27–40 describe brothels in Amsterdam.
135. The reference to liars, thieves, and drunkards not going to heaven comes from Revelation 21:8 and 1 Corinthians 6:10.
136. 1 Corinthians 6:15–17 contains a warning against uniting with a prostitute.

## Chapter 32: Tubing

137. The reference to the world being under the control of Satan comes from 1 John 5:19.
138. The reference to God having created Satan comes from Ezekiel 28:12–19.
139. The reference to Satan having to get permission from God before afflicting Job comes from Job 1:12; 2:6.

140. The reference to being required to give an account of our lives to God comes from Hebrews 9:27. Other references include Job 31:14; Ecclesiastes 11:9; 12:14; Romans 3:19; 14:10–12; 2 Corinthians 5:10; and 1 John 4:17. While not referenced, scriptures indicating there is no reincarnation come from Ecclesiastes 9:5–6, as well as Job 7:9; 10:21; 14:14; 19:26; Ecclesiastes 12:7; and Matthew 25:46. While not referenced, scriptures indicating there is no purgatory come from Matthew 25:46, as well as Hebrews 7:27 and 1 John 2:2.

141. The reference to people continuing to do whatever they feel like doing comes from Revelation 22:11.

142. The reference to whatever we say is subject to judgment comes from Matthew 12:36.

143. The reference to a person shaking their fist at God is derived from Job 15:25.

144. References where Jesus said there is a hell include Matthew 5:22, 29, 30; 10:28; 18:9; 23:15, 33; and Luke 12:5.

145. Jesus said there is a heaven in Luke 10:20. The phrase "down from heaven" is mentioned seven times by Jesus in John 6.

146. Jesus endorsed the full authority of the Old Testament in John 10:35.

147. The reference to Jesus not abolishing the law but fulfilling it comes from Matthew 5:17–18.

148. Jesus referred to Jonah in Matthew 12:40, Abel in Matthew 23:35, and Noah in Matthew 24:37–38.

149. The phrase "Discipleship is pouring your life into someone and letting someone pour their life into you" was stated by Jeff James during a church meeting on discipleship at Valley Community Baptist Church.

150. The Great Commission is located in Matthew 28:16–20.

151. The Golden Rule—treat others the way you want to be treated—is found in Matthew 7:12.

152. The Sermon on the Mount is located in Matthew 5–7.

## *Chapter 34: Deadline Looming*

153. Information about the Alpha Course is available at *http://www. alpharesources.org.*

## *Chapter 35: Decision Time*

154. The discussion about wives submitting to husbands and husbands loving their wives as Christ loves the church comes from Ephesians 5:22–33. Other references include Colossians 3:18–19 and 1 Peter 3:1–7.

155. The directive to not "lord it over" others comes from 1 Peter 5:3.

156. The directive for Christians not to marry non-Christians comes from 2 Corinthians 6:14.

157. The idea that people should get married if they cannot control themselves and are burning with passion comes from 1 Corinthians 7:9.

158. The reference to walking in the Spirit so a person will not fulfill the lusts of the flesh comes from Galatians 5:16.

159. The idea that people are eternal is present throughout the Bible. One reference is Daniel 12:2.

160. The Ten Commandments are found in Exodus 20:1–17 and Deuteronomy 5:6–21.

161. The reference to only a few being allowed into heaven comes from Matthew 7:13–14.

162. The idea that perfection is the standard for entry into heaven comes from Matthew 5:20, 48; and Hebrews 10:14.

163. The concept that none of us are good enough to get into heaven on our own comes from Romans 3:23.

164. The doctrine that Jesus paid for our sins on the cross so that we wouldn't have to pay for them in hell is found throughout the Bible. One specific reference is 1 John 2:2.

165. The salvation requirement of believing Jesus is the Son of God comes from John 3:16 and 1 John 5:12.

166. The salvation requirement to repent, or turn away from our sinful way of living, is mentioned throughout the Bible. One reference is Luke 13:3.

167. The salvation requirement to give up your life to follow Jesus obediently all the days of your life is mentioned in various places in the New Testament. One reference is Mark 8:34–38.

168. Jackson's dream of a woman pulled from the lake of fire is derived from Psalm 40:2. The author had this same dream or vision. Similar references include Psalm 18:16; 30:1, 3; 144:7; and 2 Samuel 22:17.

## *Chapter 36: Interruption*

169. The reference to being "born again" comes from John 3:3, 7 and 1 Peter 1:23.
170. The doctrine that Christians are God's adopted children and part of God's family comes from Galatians 4:7. Also, see Ephesians 2:19.
171. The directive for Christians not to marry non-Christians comes from 2 Corinthians 6:14.
172. The reference to obtaining counsel from others when making big decisions comes from Proverbs 15:22.
173. The reference to fasting comes from Matthew 6:16–18.
174. The reference to God's plan for marriage comes from Matthew 19:5 and Ephesians 5:31.
175. Bible passages that argue against abortion include Job 31:15; Psalm 139:13–16; Isaiah 49:1; Jeremiah 1:5; Luke 2:21; Galatians 1:15; and Ephesians 1:4.

## *Chapter 43: The Day After*

176. The reference to there being no greater love than to give one's life for their friends comes from John 15:13. A related reference is Psalm 116:15.

## *Chapter 44: Returning for a Moment*

177. The reference to being absent from the body is to be present with the Lord comes from 2 Corinthians 5:8.
178. The reference to the redeemed getting a new physical body comes from 1 Corinthians 15:42–54.
179. The doctrine that Christians are God's adopted children comes from Galatians 4:7. Also, see Ephesians 2:19.
180. The reference to Jesus wiping away every tear one day comes from Isaiah 25:8; Revelation 7:17; 21:4.
181. The reference to seeing now in a mirror dimly comes from 1 Corinthians 13:12.
182. The reference to the Book of Life comes from Philippians 4:3; Revelation 3:5; 13:8; 17:8; 20:12; 21:27; 22:19.

183. The reference to the planned length of life being changed comes from Ecclesiastes 7:17. God allows accidental/intentional death in Exodus 21:13. Other references include Psalm 61:6; Proverbs 3:2; 9:11; 10:27; Job 17:1; 22:16; and Psalm 55:23b.
184. The reference to the prayer of a righteous person being powerful and effective comes from James 5:16.
185. The reference to bowls of incense representing the prayers of the saints comes from Revelation 5:8.

## Chapter 45: The Aftermath

186. The reference to Job's friends sitting with him for seven days and nights without speaking comes from Job 2:13.
187. The reference to the life being in the blood comes from Leviticus 17:11.
188. The reference to the stoning of Stephen comes from Acts 7:54–60.

## Chapter 47: Farewell

189. The verses 1 Thessalonians 4:13–18 refer to the rapture. God raises the dead in Christ into the clouds with new bodies, followed by the living.
190. The reference to Jackson being an adopted son of God comes from Galatians 4:7 and Ephesians 2:19.
191. The reference to Jackson receiving a rich welcome in heaven comes from 2 Peter 1:11.
192. The verses 2 Timothy 4:6–8 refers to the Apostle Paul preparing for his death and anticipating his reward in heaven, a crown of righteousness.

Made in United States
North Haven, CT
03 May 2025

68530542R00213